A SHADOW CROWN

MELISSA BLAIR

UNION SQUARE & CO.
NEW YORK

UNION SQUARE & CO.
NEW YORK

UNION SQUARE & CO. and the distinctive Union Square & Co. logo
are trademarks of Hachette Book Group, Inc.

ISBN 978-1-4549-4789-9 (paperback)
ISBN 978-1-4549-4790-5 (e-book)

Library of Congress Cataloging-in-Publication Data

Names: Blair, Melissa, 1995- author.
Title: A shadow crown / by Melissa Blair.
Description: New York : Union Square & Co., 2023. | Series: The halfling saga; book 2 | Summary: "Keera navigates political scheming, backstabbing, and her own grief as she moves against the cruel king that holds her kingdom hostage"—Provided by publisher.
Identifiers: LCCN 2022059436 (print) | LCCN 2022059437 (ebook) | ISBN 9781454947899 (trade paperback) | ISBN 9781454947905 (epub)
Subjects: BISAC: FICTION / Fantasy / Romance | FICTION / Romance / LGBTQ+ / General | LCGFT: Fantasy fiction. | Romance fiction. | Novels.
Classification: LCC PR9199.4.B557 S53 2023 (print) | LCC PR9199.4.B557 (ebook) | DDC 813/.6—dc23/eng/20221213
LC record available at https://lccn.loc.gov/2022059436
LC ebook record available at https://lccn.loc.gov/2022059437

Union Square & Co. books may be purchased in bulk for business, educational, or promotional use. For more information, please contact your local bookseller or the Hachette Book Group's Special Markets department at special.markets@hbgusa.com.

Printed in China

4 6 8 10 9 7 5 3

unionsquareandco.com

Cover art and design by Kim Dingwall
Cover art direction by Gina Bonanno
Map art by Karin Wittig
Interior design by Colleen Sheehan and Jordan Wannemacher

A SHADOW CROWN

For anyone who has ever helped another
achieve their dream.
But especially for Scooby Gang.

Elverath

The Treaty of the Faeland
Aralinth
Caerth
The Dark Wood
The Burning Mountains
The Poison Fields
The Pool of Elvera
Myrelinth
Silstra
The Cliffs of Elandorr
Wolford
The Singing Wood
Belmoor
Volcar
The Barren Lands
The Frostlands

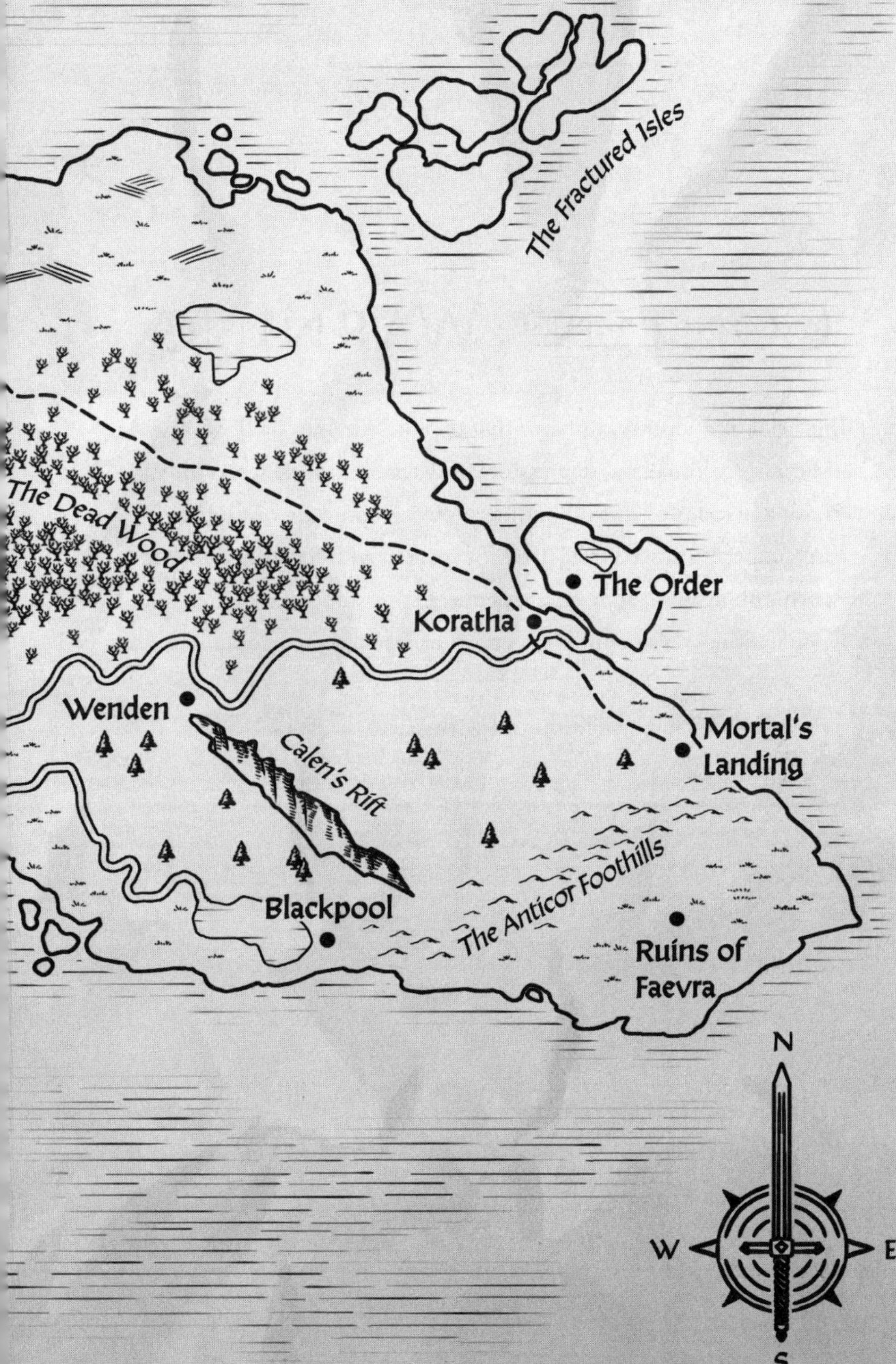
The Fractured Isles
The Dead Wood
The Order
Koratha
Wenden
Mortal's
Landing
Calen's Rift
The Anticor Foothills
Blackpool
Ruins of
Faevra
N
W
E
S

Content Warning

This book is a fantasy romance that explores themes of alcoholism, addiction, colonialism, depression, and systemic violence. While it is not the focus of this book or depicted graphically on the page, some content may be triggering for readers who have experienced self-harm, assault, domestic violence, depression, war, or suicidal ideation. It also contains some consensual sexual content.

Please read with care.

My mind is haunted by shadow,

Memories and regret,

But those shadows don't scare me now

CHAPTER ONE

I PUNCHED THE PRINCE in the face. The blow was hard enough that Killian's gold circlet fell off his head and landed on the ground with a loud clunk. I'd always thought of his brother Damien when I imagined punching a royal, but Killian was a satisfying substitute.

Shock reverberated through the room. None of the spectators moved. Killian had ensured he had an audience for the big reveal. A moment perfectly curated for me to find out the truth: I had allied with an enemy—the king's enemy—to destroy the Crown once and for all only to learn that the Shadow answered to the king's youngest son.

Killian had forced my hand like a fool. I needed to remind him that I was dangerous even if I agreed to play into his scheme.

He spat a mouthful of blood onto the wood-planked floor. I didn't try to cover my grin. His movement, however, had reignited the tension in the room. Suddenly, every one of Killian's most trusted Elverin were staring at me: The calculating violet gaze of the two Fae who stood along the wall, deciding whether or not to use whatever magic they had left. The cautious eyes of the Elves whose immortality had stolen the last of their ability to be shocked. But what made my heart stagger inside my chest was the violent stare of the Halflings in the room. Part Elf, part Mortal, they outnumbered the rest of the Elverin tenfold.

They were my kin. But they didn't see an ally when they looked at me. All they saw was the Blade who had just laid a hand on their prince.

Maybe the punch could have waited until I wasn't surrounded by a hundred rebels who wanted me dead. Killian wiped his mouth with his wrist, a blond curl falling in front of his face as his skin was stained red.

Collin moved first. He swung at me without unsheathing the short blade at his belt, cheeks burning with clumsy rage. I shifted to the side, dodging his blow. He threw out his other fist, and I ducked under that too. By the third, I figured I should put him out of his misery. I caught his wrist and used his momentum to spin him around, pinning his arm against his back. He let out a satisfying yelp.

"Had enough yet?" I whispered in his ear. I had wanted to spar with Collin ever since his antics had cost two Shades their lives. Halfling girls the king had trained from childhood to be his spies and weapons. It had been my job to protect them. I took responsibility for their deaths, but it didn't mean I enjoyed Collin's smug attitude about their loss either. I twisted his wrist just a little more.

Collin thrashed against me but my hold was secure. I looked to Killian. He was patting his bloodied lip with a pristine handkerchief—no doubt provided by Nikolai, who stood beside him, shaking his head and biting his lips so they formed a straight line.

Killian moved his jaw side to side before breaking into a smile. "I'll admit I deserved that." He fixed the black collar of his shirt. The outline of leaves was stitched along its edge, the deep violet dye almost imperceptible from the black.

I shoved Collin back toward a group of Halflings. He stumbled on his feet before taking his place next to Killian. The scowl Collin saved for me melted into a deep frown as he stared at Killian's split lip.

I crossed my arms and shrugged. "You deserve worse."

Syrra coughed behind the prince. I tilted my head to the side, challenging her to say I was wrong, but her lips twitched upward. I took that as all the approval I needed. Killian had kidnapped me, tied me up, drugged me, and shoved me in the back of a carriage for days, to gods knew where.

As there was no longer a threat to my life, I allowed myself a quick glance about the room. The floor was lined with uneven planks of wood, but the walls were black stone. Apart from the faelights hovering above our heads, there was no light. No windows. The only door was the one Nikolai had dragged me through. I'd never been in this room, and there was nothing I recognized. I took a deep breath. No trace of the sea in the air; we were somewhere inland.

My eyes narrowed at the prince. "Where are we?"

"Underground at the moment." Killian gestured for Collin and the rest of the Elverin to exit out the only door. I watched their untrusting faces disappear into the dark hallway until it was just me, Killian, and his two most trusted councillors.

I glanced at Syrra. "Under *what* ground?"

Nikolai answered before she opened her mouth. "We're in the middle of the Singing Wood." He still couldn't meet my gaze and shifted to the right, hiding himself behind Killian.

"How long did you keep me asleep?" They had crossed half the continent since I'd been taken from that cave. That journey would have taken weeks with a group so large.

"A while." Killian gave a noncommittal shrug. "But only for safety reasons."

I raised a brow. "You put me into an elixir-induced sleep for my safety?"

"I meant the safety of the Elverin." Killian tongued his cut lip.

"I would never hurt—"

"You punched me in the face seconds after making an alliance."

I scowled at his smug expression. "I thought we agreed you deserved it?"

"Enough," Syrra said in her usual calm tone. She stepped between me and the prince. "Killian could not reveal himself so close to the capital. There were too many spies, especially after the mess you caused in Silstra."

"I seem to remember us working together to blow up that dam."

Syrra crossed her arms. "He had no reason to trust you with the truth before now."

"Had no reason to trust me?" I ran my hand through the crown of my braid. "I almost died setting off those blasts!"

Nikolai poked his head out from behind Killian's shoulder, holding up a cautious hand.

I rolled my eyes. A single arrow to the leg was not even close to the same. "Nik, your leg is fine."

He opened his mouth and then closed it, tucking himself behind the prince once more.

"We all agree that you proved yourself that night in Silstra," Killian said, trying to hit the same calm demeanor as Syrra but not quite succeeding. "But when would you have liked me to let you in on our secret? Right before you met with the king? The hour before you met with the Arsenal?"

My rebuttal evaporated from my tongue.

"You already had enough lies to step around in that throne room," Killian continued. "I needed—*we* needed—you to convince the king to allow you to keep your title. And if he was going to stumble onto the truth—"

"You didn't want him discovering all of it," I finished for him. I turned away from them and tried to ignore how my chest tightened with understanding. I had walked into the capital that day knowing I might not walk out. Telling me everything beforehand would have been foolish. It could have put hundreds of lives in danger only to satisfy my pride.

There hadn't been a right time for Killian to say anything until now.

I clenched my fists. Hot rage roared through me, setting my blood to boil. "Riven could have told me." I hated the way my voice cracked when I said his name. We'd traveled together for days after the dam blew. Riven had said he trusted me—he'd shown as much—but he hadn't trusted me with this. He hadn't even cared enough to be here when I found out the truth.

My anger settled through my skin, warming my body, but underneath I could feel the cold stings of betrayal. One for every moment that Riven had let the truth hang between us, like a veil I never knew was there, keeping him in the shadows I thought had cleared.

"I thought it best that I be the one to tell you." Killian's voice was softer than before. The same softness settled in his green eyes as they traced my face. "I didn't want anyone accusing you of leveraging your . . . *entanglement* with Riven as a way to get to me."

I blinked. "Why would I—"

"To kill me?" Killian choked on a laugh. "To secure your place as Blade for life? To blackmail my father? What they would have thought doesn't matter, only that the Elverin have very little reason to trust you. I didn't want to make it harder on them." Killian ran a hand through his blond waves. His crown still lay on the ground next to his feet, discarded and forgotten. I stared at it, wondering if I could trust what Killian had said about it being a tool. It might be enough to take back the kingdom from Aemon, but would a prince throw away his chance to rule when his father's crown fell? I didn't know Killian well enough to trust he could.

I tipped the edge of the crown with my boot and lobbed it into the air. Killian caught it with the precision and speed of a seasoned soldier. He let it hang in his fist, never breaking his gaze with me. Whatever Killian had been doing in his time away from the capital, it was not just spending his days surrounded by scrolls and books.

I frowned. "Was publicly outing me as a fool in my best interest too?" I could taste the venom of my sarcasm.

Killian pulled at the sleeve of his jacket. "Yes, it was."

I scoffed.

"I can't make you see things my way Keera, but you being in the dark proves our plan is working. Not even *the Blade* knew about my involvement—you didn't suspect it and neither have the Shades. Forgive me if I let myself take that as a sign we're safe. At least for now." Killian stepped closer to me, his knuckles turning white against the gold in his fist. His body was rigid, perfectly restrained, but I could smell his rage growing; like parchment left too long in the sun, it was beginning to smoke. "The Elverin needed a win. We're on the cusp of war—how many years of heartache am I setting at their feet? How many of them will fight for something they will never see? Today, they felt hopeful, because regardless of what happened in Silstra, most still see you as an enemy, Keera."

Killian took a deep breath and grabbed my hand. It was warm and dry like paper. "Today, I let them see you as a rival we defeated, so tomorrow they could see you as an ally they trust."

I didn't break away from his gaze. There was a sincerity in his eyes that felt unnatural. He shared the same jade irises lined with amber as his brother. Eyes that had spent decades haunting the worst of my nightmares, the worst of my memories. The skin on my back pulled tight, recoiling at the mere idea of trusting one of Damien's kin. But Syrra and Nikolai stood behind the prince and their silence stood behind his words.

I might not trust Killian myself, but I trusted that Syrra and Nikolai would never align themselves with someone like Damien.

I let go of Killian's hand and grabbed the circlet he was still holding. I spun it around my four fingers like a children's toy. "How long did it take you to come up with that speech?"

Killian barked a laugh. "I had some time."

"He made me listen to him practice for three hours this morning," Nikolai quipped, poking out from Killian's shoulder once more.

I caught the crown in my fist mid-spin and handed it back to Killian. "Pretty speech aside, this alliance won't work if you keep me in the dark. I know I have to earn the trust of your people, but I assume I've earned yours?" I glanced at Nikolai and Syrra, holding my breath.

Nikolai nodded, taking a small step out from behind Killian. "Of course. You saved my life and blew up that dam, Keera dear. Besides, how could I not trust a face like that?"

Syrra too took a step forward and nodded. "I have trusted you since Caerth, and I will trust you even after this war is won." My chest tightened in surprise at Syrra's words. The faces of the two Shades I'd laid across that pyre in Caerth flashed in my mind. The guilt burned my throat with the memory of how I'd washed away the pain. Syrra had found me and recognized her pain in mine. I never realized how much that had meant to her. How much it had meant to me. I swallowed the knot forming in my throat and nodded.

Killian tucked his crown under his arm like an old book. "I meant what I said, Keera. I trust you and I want you to help us free Elverath once and for all. When we arrive in Myrelinth, I will brief you on everything we know."

"Myrelinth?" I echoed, tilting my head. "I assumed we would be stationed somewhere in the kingdom, somewhere more connected."

Syrra wrapped my shoulders in her arm and started walking toward the door. I could feel the strength of her muscles pressing into my neck. "My home is more connected than you know, child."

I suppressed the urge to shrug off her touch. I had a tunic and a thick cloak covering my skin, but even Syrra wasn't observant enough to feel the names I'd carved into myself through the layers.

I tilted my head at her. "We're a ten days' ride from there at least."

Killian looked over his shoulder as he spoke. "Are we?"

Then he disappeared into the dark.

We were undeniably in the middle of the Singing Wood. I exited what had begun as a hallway but had quickly transformed into a tunnel. From aboveground, no one would be able to tell that a large encampment existed under the soil. Not that travelers stumbled into the Singing Wood if they could help it.

The forest was dense with twisted pairs of trunks that grew toward the sky in entangled spirals. Their bark was thick and the color of sunlit blue shifting to night. They grew so tall they rivaled the shortest peaks of the Burning Mountains to the west and their trunks were so thick the four of us could not have wrapped our arms around a single one. They were the giants of their wood but what kept the travelers at bay were their leaves.

Bright bulbs of lilac and rose would bloom into twisted tendrils that came in every shade of sunset. Some tendrils hung from the tallest branches and swept the forest floor. The thick vines made it hard to travel on foot or horse and the dense canopy made navigation impossible by day or night. The king would have laid the entire forest to waste if it were not for the singing.

Most hours the wood was as quiet as any other, but when the wind blew through the twisted trunks and spiraled vines, the forest came alive with song. Sometimes the trees sang songs of peace and comfort to guide wayward travelers home, but sometimes their melodies turned vile and travelers were left cutting at their own ears to silence the singing altogether. It wasn't uncommon for the bodies of travelers to be found at the outskirts of the wood. Hanging as if caught mid-stride, they were found suspended from the tendrils like the trees had lured them in only to coil their wicked limbs around their victims' throats to feed their next song.

Fortunately, we were in the middle of a large clearing. The circular meadow was lush with soft grasses and wildflowers sprouting from the greenery. The dense forest formed a wall all around us, scraping the darkening sky above our heads.

I didn't see any sign of a trail or passage through the wood. No clear path that the caravan had used to gather here and no way to get out.

Nikolai appeared at my side. He didn't say anything as he toyed with a yellow bulb by his boot. He still wouldn't meet my gaze; instead his head drooped to the side like a wilted flower.

I sighed loudly—I knew Nikolai would appreciate the added flair. "If you're worried I'm going to punch you in the face, I'm not. At least, not today."

Nikolai's head popped up, his face wearing a cautious smile.

"But I'm still considering lacing your hair oil with an essence of dung."

He grabbed the top of his satchel protectively. "You wouldn't dare."

"Lie to me again and you'll find out." The words didn't come out as playfully as I meant, but I didn't take them back. I let them hang between us like one of the tendrils in the wood, unclear if it had been a threat or a warning. "Why isn't Riven here?" The question had already burnt a hole through my throat; I couldn't keep it in any longer. And Nikolai was the only one who I thought might actually give me an answer.

His smile fell with his shoulders. "If he could have been here, he would've been."

"That's all you'll say?" I hated the desperate way my voice cracked at the end. It was as if a knife had been plunged into my gut when Killian revealed himself, and thinking of Riven's absence pushed the hilt just a little deeper.

The pity on Nikolai's face made it worse. Part of me wished the dagger was real so I could pull it from my belly and stab him too. Before Silstra, I probably would have.

Nikolai's brow lifted like it was issuing a dare. "Would you rather hear it from me or from him?"

I leaned back and sighed toward the treetops that swayed above us. I felt like one of the white geese from the Barren Lands, lost and alone, looking to the sky for its flock that had already returned home. "Him," I admitted.

Nikolai wrapped his arms around me, half in pity and half in comfort. The angry part of me flared with hot rage at his touch, but there was another, larger, part of me that doused the flames with the knowledge that Nikolai had only been following orders. Whatever we had become after weeks of journeying across the continent together, I understood the lies he told to keep Killian's alliance a secret. With his arms wrapped around me, I knew the anger of being fooled would cool quickly, at least toward him.

He leaned back and inspected my neck and arm. "Does it hurt? I told Syrra the dart was too much but she insisted. You took quite the tumble this morning."

I rubbed my fingers across the bump along my arm. "This morning?" I blinked. My body was still sluggish and sore. It didn't feel like I'd only been asleep for a day. "But the Dead Wood is at least a month's journey from here."

A boyish grin sprouted across Nikolai's face. "You woke up in an Elverath that is very different from the one you knew yesterday. I won't spoil your fun discovering it."

CHAPTER TWO

I SPENT THE NEXT HOUR standing in the middle of a field, unmoving like one of the trees of the wood. A tree would have been more useful. The Elverin moved without speaking, readying their horses and carriages in a quick and efficient fashion that made it obvious this was a regular routine. The daily life of a troupe forced to move camp again and again to avoid King Aemon's spies.

And now the best of them stood in their midst.

That truth seemed impossible for any of them to forget. Their stares were like a brisk wind through soaked clothes. I felt every shift of their cold scrutiny but knew there was nothing I could do except keep myself warm and alive. Right now, that meant staying still and quiet, but I couldn't keep Killian's words from echoing through my mind. I would need to melt the icy tension between me and the Elverin.

It was just another mission. But one I'd never trained for.

Syrra walked past me carrying one side of a large wooden crate. The other handle was lifted by a tall Elf with green eyes and a worn leather vest over his traveling robe. It took me a moment to place him.

Tarvelle.

The Elf who had been with Collin the night those two Shades were killed. I let my anger simmer without moving the hands tucked behind my back or even the path of my gaze. I watched them from the sideline of my vision as they stacked the crate onto a large cart filled with six others.

One of the crates was splintered along the side, offering a glimpse of the fruit it held. *Winvra.* Tiny berries the color of Mortal blood and the darkest of nights were piled to the brim and I suspected filled the other crates as well. The red berries had the power to kill the largest man with the briefest taste, while a drupelet of black would bury one alive in acute ecstasy. An entire cartload of *winvra* would cost a fortune most could never pay and one I doubted the Elverin had.

It was stolen, most likely from the northern orchards where the fruit still grew healthy with magic instead of wilted and gray. Lord Curringham, the High Lord of the Harvest, had reported a load of his *winvra* missing to the king a few months earlier. My lips twitched upward, wondering how Syrra and her team had managed the theft without leaving a trace. I'd overseen the Shades' investigative reports myself; the theft had been executed perfectly.

Tarvelle looked up and noticed my smile. I pulled a solemn mask over my face but his eyes narrowed all the same. Syrra sensed the shift in him and tossed me a knowing look over her shoulder. She whispered something in Elvish, too quick for me to parse. Tarvelle nodded, his stare fixed on me like a hawk watching its prey, before walking into the tunnel and not coming out.

Syrra gestured toward the undone straps along the cart and walked away, on to her next task. My shoulders relaxed by the tiniest fraction and I had to keep myself from running to secure the load. I was grateful for something to busy my hands.

I took my time, checking and rechecking each strap, as I watched the Elverin around me form into equal teams. One large cart and two carriages in each, with a sprinkling of horse riders while the rest were on foot.

There were more Elverin here than I had expected. Much more than the small group that had crossed over the Burning Mountains and met us at Caerth. I counted six groups across the meadow, each with eighty or more Elverin. It wasn't enough to storm the kingdom, but more than I'd thought the rebels had to arm their cause. And more people I had to convince to trust me.

I sighed, the tightness in my chest pressing the air from my lungs.

I finished the last strap and saw Killian kneeling beside his horse. An Elf stood beside him, holding two large satchels in her arms while Killian fixed the lace of her boot. I pretended to tighten the strap as I watched them. She wore a well-traveled cloak made of Elvish weft, but there was no embellishment or fancy trim. Her pants and boots were stained with travel and patched in two places. The king would never have let someone so common-looking in his sight, let alone bow at her feet to tie her laces.

Killian tapped her knee to signal she could keep walking. He stayed on the ground for a moment to see if the lace slipped loose before pushing against his knee to stand. Collin rushed to his side, throwing his hand out for the prince, but Killian shook his head.

I coughed a laugh against the crate.

Collin's head snapped toward me, but I had already reset my gaze on the strap. I counted three breaths before Collin trotted off behind Killian to a group of Halflings replacing the wheel of a carriage.

Tarvelle reemerged from the tunnel and marched toward me with a horse in tow. His black hair was braided in two plaits that framed his angular face. He didn't say anything as he thrust the reins into my hand. His head only twitched, like a nod he wouldn't let himself make, and then he was gone again.

My horse sniffed my shoulder before dropping her head to the ground to graze. My saddlebags hung from her side exactly the way I'd left them. The leather flap I had been fixing when the dart pierced my arm was still flipped up along the crest of the saddle.

I tongued my cheek as I moved the rain guard back into place and pulled a small pouch tied along the horn. I traced the outline of the glass vial through the leather and the air emptied from my lungs. I didn't take out the elixir. The familiar ache sat in my throat, as it always did, but the pain was mild. My thoughts weren't consumed by craving, pulling all my attention until my willpower shattered and I was left reaching for my wineskin. It had been weeks since I had felt a craving so strong. I didn't need a drop of elixir on my tongue to manage it, but it brought me comfort to know the elixir was there for the next time the ache rippled through my bones.

I felt the thin tube of my mage pen behind the vial. No one had taken it. The unmarked skin around my ribs tickled in anticipation. I had not carved a new name into myself since I built the pyre for the Shades in Caerth. Alys and Elinar.

I thought of the two other Shades that had died at Silstra—one by my own arrow. The craving in my throat flared knowing that I would never learn the Halfling girls' names, never add them among the list of innocents I wore in defiance of the king who had made me kill them.

My fingers closed around the leather pouch until the sharp edges of the vial left marks in my palm. I pushed their faces into the recess of my mind. Lingering on the pain of their loss did not serve them now. That would only come with vengeance.

The name along my forearm tingled like the scarred skin was tightening. Brenna. She had been the first name I'd carved into myself, the largest and the most important. I had promised that her death would be avenged. That I would tear down Aemon's throne and his crown so no one could rule over the Halflings again. The Shades who had died would share in that vengeance.

I swallowed. My throat ached, but I didn't pull the vial from the pouch. Numbing the pain had only brought on more of it. I wanted to feel the guilt burn through me. To heal myself or punish myself, I didn't know.

It didn't matter anyway. The elixir was just another reminder that I hadn't cared to ask enough questions. It was Elven made, some ancient magic Hildegard had thought would help me, but I had never cared to understand how it would. Perhaps the ebony liquid had made my cravings easier to manage, numbing them enough to let me hope that the pain could really end, or perhaps it had been sharing pieces of my pain with Riven.

Riven.

He was tangled into each one of my thoughts. All of the questions I'd never asked and now wanted answers to more than the air in my lungs.

I leaned my back against my horse. She turned her head to me for a moment before grabbing another mouthful of grass. I stared upward, trying to push those questions away too. The sky was painted with streaks of lilac and apricot, coral clouds with cerulean edges that would soon turn navy with the night.

Darkness and shadow. Like the Shadow who had followed me across the kingdom, somehow always lurking but now was nowhere to be seen.

My stomach churned and suddenly I was grateful that I had my horse to hide behind in the crowd. I knew my anger at Riven's absence was justified, but other emotions swirled inside me, too quick and too fluid to name. I felt like I was lost in a dark body of water with no light to guide me and no way of knowing if the water that held me was a pond, a lake, or the sea. No way of knowing if I should stand, swim, or float. Any choice I made was likely to be the wrong one.

Riven hadn't told me the truth, but did that mean he had lied? We had set the terms of our alliance in Aralinth—*need to know*—and I had jumped at the deal, eager to keep as much of myself undiscovered as possible. Could I be angry that while I had hid pieces of myself, Riven had used those terms to hide his ties to Killian?

I sighed. I didn't know the answer to that question. I doubted Riven knew it either.

Any understanding I had collided with the anger inside me, flaring like a fire burning through the night. I had trusted Riven enough to pull me out of darkness and into the light, but now that trust was scattered like the stars streaking the sky above me.

There had been so many moments since we left Aralinth when he might have confided in me. I understood why he didn't divulge all his secrets the night we struck our alliance or in the weeks of travel afterward. Riven hadn't trusted me; he hadn't even liked me then. But slowly it had changed. Or at least it had changed for me. I had stripped down every part of myself and laid them in front of him, trusting him, but Riven had kept his secrets.

Not every part. The thought echoed through my mind like a mutinous friend. My hand reached for the arm with Brenna's name, holding it tightly as if the truth would drip out like blood from a wound.

The tension in my chest loosened. I still had pieces left unshared. Parts of me Riven didn't know and didn't need to know. I took a deep breath and checked the saddle straps. I didn't need to wade through the depths of my emotions now. That could wait for whenever Riven was brave enough to face me.

My weapon belt and blades were bound in a roll tied to the back of the saddle. I unlaced the Elvish ropes binding the decorative leather. Each blade had been meticulously cleaned and housed in its own sheath within the roll. My belt was folded neatly across them.

"Did I displease you?" Syrra asked. I had not heard her approach, which shocked me. When I turned around, she smirked at my open mouth. "I cleaned your blades. *Ashwirii athra maanthir.*"

"A weapon should always be at its ready," I echoed back in the King's Tongue.

Syrra nodded, her smirk fading into a tight line. "I did not realize Halflings learned Elvish in the Stolen Lands."

My cheeks flushed. "They don't," I replied, sidestepping the question in her statement. I was too exhausted to explain myself further, to call up those memories from the dark. "Those words are inscribed in the courtyard at the Order. All Shades learn it eventually."

Syrra always stood still, her strong legs acting like roots anchoring her to the ground, but now she froze. Her breath stopped and her stare lost its focus. I didn't move but studied the scars that decorated her toned arms and broad shoulders. They had been cut along the curves and edges of her muscles, emphasizing her movements like nature had drawn them on her skin at birth. Each scar was a different branch of magical trees whose names I didn't know and whose leaves I didn't recognize. The scars weren't raised like mine, but fine lines that highlighted the ochre tone warming her dark brown skin. The scars themselves were beautiful, but painted onto Syrra's strong frame, she was a devastating masterpiece.

Syrra's pursed lips gave the slightest twitch. I tore my eyes away from her scars and loaded my belt with my traveling blades. My skin itched, strangely not with the need to cut, but with the urge to pull back my sleeve and show Syrra how my guilt had carved scars of my own.

My fingers tightened around the hilt of my bloodstone dagger. Syrra might have understood my need to drink, but I didn't know what she would think of my need to mark forever the names of those I had killed. Perhaps she would see it as a mockery of a sacred ritual, of what had taken her centuries to earn.

I pulled my sleeve into my palm and swallowed the truth. My scars only served as proof for why the Elverin should not trust me.

"The courtyard still stands on *Niikir'na*?" Syrra's voice was rough, like her tongue was fighting her throat to speak.

I blinked. I forgot that island had been Syrra's training grounds too. Before Aemon had taken Elverath as his own, the Order had been where all the Elvish warriors trained, where they earned their scars. Syrra had spent lifetimes there before Aemon came and turned it into something cruel.

"Parts of it," I answered. "The palace is still there. It is used to house the initiates and some members of the Arsenal. The courtyard is mostly intact, though some stone and statues have been broken over the years."

I'd broken one of the statues myself. Or caused the damage. Gerarda, the Dagger, had a particular knack for annoying me when we were training as initiates. One day I'd had enough and thrown her into a statue of a tall Elf with long locks trailing down her back. The Elf's arm and sword had not survived.

"I assumed it had all been destroyed." Syrra's voice was so quiet I didn't know if her words were meant for me.

I opened my mouth, unsure of what I could say that would give her comfort. Thankfully, I didn't need to say anything because Killian appeared beside us and the warm serenity returned to Syrra's face. "Are you ready to see Myrelinth?" asked the prince.

My brows stitched themselves together. We were ten days away from the city, if not more. I pointed to the night sky that sparkled down on us. "A little late to start such a long journey."

Killian's jade eyes were full of mischief. "Some journeys can only be made in the dark."

CHAPTER THREE

WE LEFT AS THE LAST STRETCH of dusk gave way to a clear, starry night. Nikolai and Syrra led the group to the western edge of the clearing and disappeared into the shadowed spirals and twisted tree trunks. At first, it seemed like everyone who crossed into the Singing Wood simply disappeared, vanishing as soon as their horse or knee hit the threshold between meadow and wood.

I watched in awe as more bodies dissolved into the night. Killian sat on his horse beside me. He rode a tall steed with an ebony coat that glittered in the moonlight. I was grateful he'd sent Collin ahead to help Tarvelle with the carriage transports. I could spot Collin's blond head turning back to watch me again and again before he finally disappeared into the haunted wood himself.

As we rode closer, the dark vines disappeared too, receding into the inky forest to reveal a path now filled with hundreds of Elverin.

A glamour.

I laughed to myself. The same magic had protected a path along the outskirts of Aralinth, shattering like glass as we rode through it. Magic had almost completely faded across the continent, but the Elverin still knew how to use what was left.

I didn't speak to Killian as we rode down the path. It felt like a tunnel with the thick canopy of vines and leaves overhead. Not a single star was visible and the air was damp and stale. No fae-lights hovered above our heads to light our way. The Elverin and the horses walked forward by memory alone. Killian didn't say anything to me either, but I thought he gave me a sideways glance every few minutes. Even with my enhanced eyesight, it was difficult to be sure in the dark. Between glances, he shifted his reins from hand to hand, rubbing the leather raw with his thumb.

A loud crack of splintering wood echoed through the tunnel. My horse stumbled. She didn't fall to the ground but veered to the left to correct her footing. The group of Halflings that had been following behind us crashed into each other in the confusion.

"What was that?" Killian whispered from somewhere in the darkness.

"A wagon wheel," another soft voice replied.

Killian's command was firm. "Leave it."

I reached into my vest to fetch a match. "We should assess how bad the break is before we abandon a cartload of supplies," I whispered, hoping it was in the direction of Killian.

I slipped off the saddle. I couldn't see anyone any longer, not even the vague shapes of a person or horse. I reached out but my fingers touched nothing but shadow.

Something shifted in the darkness. In the thick brush it sounded as if it had come from above instead of somewhere in the tunnel.

Killian's voice rang out, quieter than ever but coated in a desperate worry I didn't understand. "Keera, where are you?"

I scraped the match against the flint. The small stick burst into flames only to illuminate the horrified face of Killian standing right beside me.

"Run!" Killian shouted with no care to be quiet any longer.

A piercing cry rang out through the forest, louder than any person or animal could ever make. It screeched so loudly my bones shook the air from my lungs. Time seemed to slow as I dropped the match and saw Killian clambering back onto his saddle.

A low horn sounded through the tunnel and was met with another piercing cry. A light appeared farther down the path and burned so bright I had to shield my eyes as I mounted my horse.

The light split into tiny pieces of faelight that shot down the tunnel in all directions and bathed the forest in silver. Now illuminated, I could see the long slashing claws digging through the thick canopy of vines and tendrils above our heads. The entire ceiling shook as the Elverin ran farther into the Singing Wood below.

The riders dispersed into the crowd of Elverin, pulling two or three of those running on foot onto their saddles as they charged toward a destination I still could not see.

I glanced back at the abandoned wagon and noticed the wheel had not broken but fallen off its axel entirely. The pin that held the wheel in place was nowhere to be found.

"Keera!" Killian shouted from across the tunnel as he pulled a Halfling behind him. He threw a glass vial, and I plucked it from the air with one hand. Five *winvra* berries were locked inside the glass. I looked up to ask what they were for but Killian was already cantering down the path, reaching for an Elf who was struggling to run.

I tapped the side of my horse and charged toward the crowd. A large claw pierced through the vines above my head. I swung off the edge of my saddle, hooking my foot through the stirrup that was now resting on the seat to keep me as secure as possible.

My heart hammered in my chest and something hot pooled at my shoulder. I was still wearing Riven's tunic and now the sleeve was stained with amber blood from where the creature had cut me.

I groaned through clenched teeth as I pulled myself back onto the seat and kept charging onward. A loud crash bellowed from behind me, and I knew one of the creatures had broken through the canopy and plummeted onto the path below. I glanced over my shoulder and saw one Elf fleeing on foot behind me the riders had missed.

Behind him was a tall beast. It had the face of a stag with long antlers that scraped the canopy above, leaving a cascade of fallen vines in its wake. It walked on two hoofed legs while its long arms galloped along the ground with claws longer than any dagger I owned. Spindles of drool fell from its lips as it gnashed the air with sharp teeth made to devour flesh.

The Elf would be dead on foot.

I pulled back on the reins without a second thought and charged toward the beast. I leaned down and unsheathed one of the straight swords from my weapons belt and launched it at the creature. The blade embedded itself in the shoulder of the beast, who howled in pain as it fell backward onto the ground. Thick, black blood bubbled from the wound as it tried to pull the sword free with its mouth.

I released the breath that had caught in my chest and circled my horse around the Elf. He was missing one shoe and his feet were already coated with blood. I lowered my hand, but he shook his head and refused to grab it.

Another crash sounded from the tunnel. A second deadly creature fell from the thick canopy of trees above. Half of this one's face was missing, so we could see the bones of its jaw and the pale socket that no longer held an eye.

"Ride with me or die!" I shouted. The Elf's gaze darted between my outstretched hand and the creature. It had steadied itself from the drop and was running toward its fallen brethren. I flexed my hand at the Elf once more. "Decide. But know none will mourn such a foolish death."

His black eyes narrowed, but he reached for my hand and pulled himself onto the horse.

"What are those creatures?" I shouted over the beat of the mare's hooves on the well-packed earth.

"The Unnamed Ones," the Elf shouted back. He reached down and grabbed the white bone hilt of my bloodstone dagger.

I veered to the right, just out of reach of the creature's swipe. "Too small—grab the brown handle and ready yourself."

The Elf pulled out a long, thick sword that glinted under the silver glow of the faelights shining above us. The sword was too heavy to throw at the beast, but the creature was too close anyhow. It swiped and its claws cut through the split ends of my horse's tail.

"Wait for the next swipe. Then aim for the back of the neck," I shouted. I didn't have time to look back before the creature launched itself at us once more.

The Elf screamed as he plunged the sharp edge into the creature's neck. An earsplitting shriek shook through the tunnel, so loud my eardrums ached as loose vines fell from the canopy above. I veered out of the way of a tendril hanging loose from the others and sighed in relief when I didn't hear the pounding footsteps of the creature behind us.

But as I rounded the sharp turn of the tunnel, I saw three more sets of claws digging through the canopy between us and what appeared to be a shimmering pool of water framed by gray stone.

"What's your name?" I called over my shoulder to the Elf.

"Pirmiith," he shouted back.

"Pirmiith, if we survive this, remind me to thank you for saving my life."

I could hear the smile in his reply. "And I shall thank you for saving mine."

I steered our ride around another abandoned cart as a third creature fell through the canopy just behind us. I lifted the glass vial that still rested in my hand, urging my horse to run just a little faster.

"Open it and throw the berries into the portal before we pass," Pirmiith shouted as he pulled another blade free.

We had made it to a large cave, wide enough to fit thirty men across with ease. The mouth of the cave was cast in silver ore that shimmered like a gemstone in sunlight. But the light did not come from the suns; instead it came from the wall of water that rippled just inside the cavern's entrance. Or at least I thought it was water.

I didn't have time to ask. The Unnamed One slashed with its long claw and our horse whinnied as a deep cut was left on her hip. I unstoppered the vial and poured the tiny berries into my hand. Just before we hit the wall, I tossed the *winvra* into the standing lake and dropped my jaw in amazement as the water swirled around us in golden light that sent the creature reeling backward, covering its eyes as it whimpered.

I expected to be hit with the thickness of water, like diving into a lake, but instead it was like passing through a veil of cool mist. The same auric light swirled around my body and the bodies of Pirmiith and Killian, who was waiting at the threshold of the veil. The veins in his neck were thick and pumped like he had been struggling to breathe. The touch of warmth that his pale skin usually held was gone and he was white as snow.

I jumped down from the saddle. Killian must've sent his horse onward with the Elverin he'd saved. I glanced up at Pirmiith, who nodded once. "I will make sure her wound is taken care of," he said in lieu of goodbye. I watched as he and the horse continued down the path and realized we were at the bottom of a lake.

Ribbons of golden light shone around them like a shield keeping the water from wetting their skin or their lungs from breathing the liquid in, yet as I watched them disappear into the inky darkness of the lake, I could see the thick walls of seaweed that lined the path. A school of swimmers darted between the blades and there was another overhead without care that we were in their home.

"How is it possible?" I whispered, turning back to Killian with a laugh blooming in my throat. All thought of the deadly creatures we had narrowly escaped vanished from my mind.

Killian's jade eyes were locked on my bloody shoulder. He closed the distance between us in two strides and ripped the sleeve clean off my arm before I had time to react.

I turned away from him and tried to cover the names that I had cut into my arms or the ends of the thick ridged scars Damien had carved into me that curved over my shoulder. "I'm fine," I snapped, wishing I had not sent Pirmiith away with my horse and clothing.

Killian's brow furrowed. "If an Unnamed One made that cut, I need to check it. Their claws are toxic, Keera."

I gritted my teeth. There was no way I could make it to wherever we were going without Killian seeing the truth written on my skin. I took a deep breath and slowly turned toward him. At first Killian didn't even notice the scars—his focus was anchored on the red line that cut lengthwise down my shoulder. The wound was tender, but my healing magic had already stitched the skin together.

Killian traced a gentle finger down the line of it. "No signs of necrotic tissue at all," he whispered to himself more than to me. "Incredible."

His finger reached the end of the slash and traced over the first name. Killian's eyes widened as he truly saw my arm for the first time. His cheeks flushed and he shook his head before turning away.

"I should have asked before I removed your sleeve." He bowed his head. "My greatest apologies if I have made you uncomfortable."

His neck flexed as he stared at a patch of billowing seaweed.

"I'd be comfortable if we don't talk about them." I swallowed. A sudden fatigue plagued my body. My leg shook as I looked down the path where Pirmiith had disappeared with my cloak.

Killian nodded and pulled off his black jacket. He wrapped it around my shoulders, letting me feed my arms through the sleeves. It was warm and smelled of smoke and parchment. I pulled my braid loose from the collar and caught Killian's stare lingering on my neck.

He cleared his throat and pointed down the path with an arm coated in golden light. "Myrelinth is this way."

Thick logs and tall rocks covered in marine life marked our path along the bottom of the lake. A large fish swam above my head, its fat belly and short tail gliding beside my long braid that floated upward in the water. I brushed the white scales along its bottom with my finger, surprised that I could touch it. The fish paused mid-glide before scurrying away and disappearing into the inky black once more.

"What kind of magic is this?" I asked, turning to Killian who was walking with his hands folded behind his back and picking at his elbow.

He smiled proudly. "Portal magic. If you know where they are, and when they open, you can enter in one spot on the continent and emerge in another."

I raised a brow. "How does the portal know where to send you? Does a Fae have to make the decision?" My stomach tightened as I wondered if Riven had been waiting at the entrance of the portal to open it for the Elverin arriving home.

Waiting for me.

Killian shook his head and my hopes were dragged away in the undertow of the lake. "It's not the kind of magic that can be wielded, but a natural part of Elverath that has always existed. This portal contains two paths—one can be accessed under the light of the suns and the other under the light of the stars. After dusk, this portal leads to Myrelinth and then at dawn it will change again."

"Is there only one portal that leads to Myrelinth?"

"There are a few." Killian kicked a pebble along the sandy bottom of the lake. It rolled lazily along the ground and scared a group of minnows into a frenzied scurry.

"Then why choose such a dangerous path to journey through?" I gestured behind us where we had left the Unnamed Ones in the Singing Wood.

Killian sighed. "It was the quickest route. And the Unnamed Ones are usually harmless. If travelers respect their nature, a journey through the Singing Wood poses little risk."

"And what of their nature?" I shivered against the memory of that cold claw slicing through my skin.

"They detest loud noises, and when the suns have set, they will search out any light that dares shine in their wood."

I blinked. "The match."

Killian nodded slowly. "I should have warned you. After so many years being the least knowledgeable among the Elverin, it is too easy to forget there are many things you do not know that I do."

"Like how to hunt the Unnamed Ones?"

Killian shot me a quizzical look. "The Elverin do not hunt them. They pass on the knowledge to live *with* the creatures of this wood. Before my father claimed these lands for the kingdom, one of the most prosperous cities in all of Elverath called the Singing Wood its home."

"The Mortals know of no city hiding in this wood." Most travelers did everything they could to avoid the Singing Wood entirely. Those who ventured in often did not venture out. I'd once traveled along the road around the Singing Wood and found a Halfling hanging from the vines on the outskirts of the forest. His middle was cut to the spine, leaving a pool of amber blood on the brush below.

Killian waved his arms out in front of him with a warm smile on his lips. "Haven't you learned that there are many things the Mortals do not know?"

My thoughts lingered on that unknown Halfling. Had he been on the run or working for one of the nearby Mortals when he'd found himself traveling the Singing Wood? Either way, the somber truth struck me deep in my core, like one of the Unnamed had cut me in two. The Halfling should have known the secrets of this wood—he should have learned it from his people. That knowledge was something else that Aemon had stolen from our kin. It had cost that Halfling his life. How many more had fallen to the same fate as he?

We came to the top of a small hill and at the bottom was the entrance of an identical cave to the one we had passed through in the Singing Wood. I could see the refracted image of people and lights on the other side, swaying in the ebb and flow of the undercurrent.

Killian kicked another rock. He picked at the skin around his thumbnail absentmindedly. After almost perishing in a race with the wicked creatures of the dark, I didn't know what could make him so nervous.

"Unlucky for that wagon wheel to break," Killian said with a shrug, seemingly to fill the silence.

I pulled his jacket tighter around my neck to make sure no signs of my scars were showing. "It wasn't broken. The pin was missing. It must've fallen out along the way."

Killian stopped and spun on the same spot. "The pin was missing?"

"Do you want me to repeat myself or are you talking to yourself again?"

Killian ignored me and shook his head. "Did you see a pin? Did you see any damage at all?"

I shrugged. "None that I saw, but I did have a demon deer trying to make me its dinner."

Killian grabbed both my arms. My back straightened at his touch; he was so informal in the way he acted with me it was almost jarring. But then again, while I'd only been his ally for a few hours, Killian had been allied with me for *weeks*.

"Keera, whatever happens when we cross into Myrelinth, I need you to stay calm."

My eyes narrowed. "Why do you expect me to act otherwise?"

Killian took a deep breath before answering. "Allying with you was not a popular decision. Revealing myself and inviting you into the heart of the *Faelinth* was even less so. Those most opposed may test your loyalty in any way they can."

I swallowed. "You mean Collin and Tarvelle."

Killian didn't confirm my guess, but he didn't deny it either. "With enough time, all the Elverin will come to see that your loyalties lie with *us* and always will. Even your detractors."

"But until then you want me to *play nice*?" I crossed my arms.

Killian craned his neck toward the moonlight that filtered through the tens of feet of water between us and the surface. His cheeks puffed out as he let a slow breath bubble up to the surface. "Yes, I do.

If you come with your weapons drawn, the Elverin will only ever see you as the Blade."

I ran my tongue along my teeth as I studied Killian. I had very little reason to trust him apart from Nikolai and Syrra's willingness to accept him as one of their own, to help lead their rebellion. His curls swayed above his head with the flow of the water, but he did not drop his gaze. It was earnest and unyielding.

I sighed with closed eyes. "I will not be the first to swing, but if they attack me without reason, I *will* defend myself."

I raised my chin as I waited for Killian's reply.

He blinked once before straightening his stance. "I would expect nothing less." He squeezed my hand gently. "And I think it's important that I recognize this moment, that it was *you* who first compromised for this alliance, and so soon after it was struck. I will remember that, Keera. It is no small feat for anyone who carries the responsibility you do."

I was grateful for the coolness of the lake as heat flooded my cheeks. I was not accustomed to others realizing the responsibility I felt for the Shades, let alone have a prince of two realms recognize it so directly. A tiny crack splintered the base of the stone wall I placed between me and others. Somehow Killian had known exactly which brick to tap.

I cleared my throat and started down the hill to the cave entrance. Killian followed and we reached the mouth of the sister cave. He did not pull out any *winvra* before he stepped through the wall of water. I stepped through after him, feeling the same veil of mist as the cool night air filled my lungs.

We were in a wood of a different kind. My neck craned upward to take in the view. Ancient giants stood before us. Their weathered trunks, wider than a city block, towered above our heads, swirling against the stars in the night sky. Thick blankets of needled moss hung from their strong branches, illuminated by thousands of orbs of faelight as large as the suns and as small as a grain of sand.

Each of the giant trees were connected above by layers of twisted branches and vines that formed walkways across the sky. Along the trunks were large burls and splits that served as dwellings for those that lived there. I could see the shadows of children and their parents cast along the warmly lit walls inside the trees. There were hundreds of them, some occupied and others empty.

It was a city of branches and leaves. The Elverin living within the limbs and hearts of trees like birds in their nests. I turned slowly to look in every direction. The trees kept going, trunk after trunk, homestead after homestead.

It was the most beautiful thing I'd ever beheld.

Killian stepped beside me, his gaze also fixed on the treetops that seemed to shimmer with stars. "Keera," he said with a wide, enchanting smile. "Welcome to Myrelinth."

CHAPTER FOUR

As we walked through Myrelinth, the city began to take shape around me. Placed between a lake that stretched into the night on all sides and the towering peaks of the Burning Mountains, the city was alive. Circular groves of trees created neighborhoods, dwellings in close proximity that were easily connected from above. Those groves formed a large circle of their own. Inside was a clearing lined with orbs of fire that contained the flames and smoke within a thin veil of magic. The fires were ever-burning in shades of crimson and sapphire that alternated around the curved edge of the grove.

In the middle stood a tree larger than any of the others. It reminded me of the Elder birch of Aralinth in its great size, but this tree was not dressed in gold leaves. Instead, five large branches cascaded from its towering height, creating spirals that curved around the trunk until the branches buried themselves into the ground, becoming the tree's roots as well. No leaves marked the tree, no needles hung from the smaller branches to soak in the sun. Instead a thick layer of moss the color of faded turquoise dressed the trunk and the bottom of its thick branches.

Nikolai and Syrra stood in front of it. Nikolai's face was lit by the flickering shades of lapis and cerulean. It cooled the warmth of his brown skin, his wide grin haunting like he was a ghost tied to the life of the ancient tree beside him. Syrra stood next to a flame of amber, the molten hues radiating off her high cheeks and scars. I was taken by how the firelight showcased the two sides of Syrra I had met, a devastating beauty with a fiery humor she rarely shared and an experienced warrior cloaked in shadow and mystery.

Killian embraced them both as if we had not just seen them a couple of hours earlier. Syrra's dark gaze immediately fell on Killian's jacket on my shoulders. "None of the Elverin were tainted though it seems you were not as lucky."

Nikolai ran toward me, his eyes wide in panic. He slapped his hand against my forehead. "No fever yet, there could still be time to fetch the ointment." He snapped his fingers at a Halfling standing cautiously at the end of the clearing. The Halfling scurried behind one of the thick branches and seemed to disappear inside. My eyes glanced around the rest of the clearing. A crowd had formed, with each member watching me, some in fear, some in anger, and some in bored curiosity.

"Where did it cut you?" Nikolai moved to pull the jacket free but Killian stopped him.

"I already inspected the wound. Keera's healing gift seems to work on more than just cuts and scrapes."

Syrra's brows shot up in a singular moment of surprise. "Immunity to the Unnamed Ones is a rare gift indeed. I have never heard of a such a powerful gift among the *Valitherian*."

My breath caught in my throat at that word. I was still unsure about Rheih's theory of my lineage. I owed her my life; she had healed me after the explosion in Silstra that left me on the cusp of death, but I was not sure I trusted the Mage enough to believe her theory. That would mean that one of my parents was a Halfling, but the other had to have been a Light Fae. And they had not been seen since the first days of Aemon's conquest, nearly a thousand years ago.

But despite my doubts, I couldn't deny that I healed quicker and more easily than I should. And based on the lack of tenderness along my shoulder, that healing power was only growing.

Tarvelle and Collin broke from the crowd to the west and walked toward us. A murmur of whispers sounded from the groves above and from the large crowd that now surrounded us in all directions. The two of them looked at me like hungry predators circling their prey.

I wanted nothing more than to show them who the real predator among us was, but I'd given Killian my word. Unless they pounced, I would not attack them. I glanced at Killian, and he gave me a sympathetic nod before stepping in front of me.

"Is this so urgent that it could not wait until our meeting on the morrow?" Killian asked in a calm tone but his hands had turned to hard fists beside him.

Tarvelle glared at me as he spoke, his loud voice ringing with anger. "She lit that match on purpose to set the Unnamed Ones after all of us!"

The crowd gave one united gasp. I saw some parents gripping their children as they stared at me with wide, horrified eyes.

Killian grit his teeth. "What reason would Keera have to do such a thing?"

"She's the Blade," Collin scoffed, crossing his arms. "Whatever vows she'd made cannot be trusted. How do you know she doesn't serve Aemon still?"

My vision blurred with rage. "I didn't know about those beasts! If I had, I never would have lit that match."

"And we are meant to trust the words of a Halfling who earns her keep killing her own kin?" Tarvelle seethed. I flinched and saw his eyes glitter in the night. He knew he had hit his mark.

I wanted nothing more than to grab the dagger that hung from Killian's belt and show Collin what the Blade could do with a little purpose, but I couldn't. Killian was right. The entirety of the Elverin was watching. I would not win them over by playing into the terrifying reputation they knew of me.

"I will not deny the lives I have taken," I said, loudly enough for everyone to hear. Collin stepped back, as if he had not been expecting such an honest reply. "I have done unspeakable things serving Aemon and his stolen throne, enough that even here, in the Faeland, you know I do not send others to do my bidding. Not the Shades, nor those creatures lurking in the woods."

Tarvelle stepped toward me with his fangs barred. Syrra unsheathed her circular blade but I held up my hand to stop her. I would not cower at the disdain of an Elf who didn't know me. I held Tarvelle's hard gaze for a long moment before glancing over his shoulder at Collin. "Did you learn of the Unnamed Ones before or after you escaped the kingdom and found yourself a home among the Elverin?"

Collin hissed with his hand on the hilt of his sword. "You have no right to ask me of my life in the kingdom, *Blade*." He said the last word like a viper dripping venom.

Killian crossed his arm over his body and rested both hands on the hilt of his dagger. "Answer the question." It was more than a command; it was a threat.

I raised my brow and turned back to Collin.

"After," Collin mumbled. He bowed his head as his cheeks turned crimson.

Syrra raised her chin, amber flames reflecting in her dark eyes. "You issued your accusation loud enough for all to hear. You must answer the question so all can listen."

Collin gulped down his breath and nodded like a little boy being chastised by his mother. "I learned of the Unnamed Ones *after* I came to Myrelinth," he said, barely loud enough to be heard by the front row of Elverin.

Killian nodded once and addressed the crowd as he spoke. "I too did not know the creatures existed until I made the journey across the Burning Mountains searching for my people." He glanced back down at Collin who could no longer meet the prince's gaze. "Such knowledge is not known to those of the kingdom. It would be difficult for Keera to attack the Elverin with information she did not possess."

Collin gritted his teeth. "This is not her first time in the Faeland. Perhaps the Blade heard stories of the Unnamed when she came to kill the Shadow and his allies."

Another murmur passed through the crowd like a cold breeze. It pierced through my throat with such sharpness that I could gather no words to defend myself against his claims. Collin had lived with the Elverin for decades; he knew them better than I did, but more than that, he had their *trust*. He knew exactly where to strike for a swift and brutal victory.

"She saved me," a voice shouted from the back of the crowd. The Elverin split in two and Pirmiith walked into the clearing. His skin was as black as the night sky with streaks of red across his round cheeks from the flames. "In the chaos the other riders had not realized I was left behind. One of the Unnamed had almost bested me before the Blade made her choice to ride *toward* it, even though the odds favored both of us perishing in that wood."

Killian's shoulders relaxed as he gave the faintest sigh. "Were there any witnesses to this act?"

Pirmiith shook his head. "None besides the Unnamed who were in pursuit of us. There was no one left to witness a performance. Her bravery was an act of truth, not an act of deception."

My chest swelled with relief as I gave Pirmiith a grateful smile. Killian glanced between Tarvelle and Collin. "Do you wish to refute the testimony of your fellow Elverin?"

They looked at each other with fallen shoulders and hard jaws. Both shook their heads and stepped back from the tree and disappeared into the crowd. I couldn't help but grin.

Nikolai clapped his hands together. "Now that all that nonsense is out of the way, I think it's time I take Keera to her room."

Killian lifted his hand like he was going to grab mine but changed his mind at the last moment. His neck flexed and he nodded goodbye before disappearing into one of the large branches without a word. Nikolai waved his hand over my shoulder and two young Halflings, no older than fifteen, appeared with my bags hoisted onto their backs.

Nikolai wrapped a lazy arm around my shoulders. "Keera, it's a pleasure to welcome you to our home." He stretched out his other arm, pointing at the tall tree at the heart of the city. He gestured for me to take his hand, guiding me to one of the five branches shooting from the ground.

Syrra took the first step, followed by the Halflings carrying my bags. They walked easily along the rough bark of the branch; like a spiral staircase up a tower, we climbed the tree until the balls of flame that had reached my shoulders below looked like pebbles on a black sand beach.

At the top of the tree the air was thin but fresh. Tiny balls of faelight lined the various bridges, one for each of the inner groves that circled the middle tree. I realized all of the trees were connected; some bridges were wide and sturdy, made for frequent travel, while others were like back alleys, hidden and used only by local dwellers. I wanted to run along the branches and vines, discover every pathway and every shortcut until I knew the tree city as well as any in the kingdom.

Syrra took a small bridge to the groves closest to the lake. I took a step on the same bridge to follow, but Nikolai grabbed my arm. "Syrra prefers to sleep in an empty nest."

I glanced over my shoulder and watched the trail of Syrra's thick waves cross another bridge, bringing her closer to the lake and into a grove of trees left empty by Elf or faelight. It felt wrong to have her sleep alone after weeks protecting each other at every campfire, but the Crown posed no danger to us in the Faeland.

I turned back to Nikolai. "Where do you stay?"

His eyes flicked downward. "I prefer to spend my nights belowground. Fewer people around to disturb my activities." He raised a brow and a grin quivered along his lip, like it was all he could do to keep himself from winking.

I followed him around a small bend and onto a thin bridge too wide for both feet. "I'll want to sleep far away from you, then."

Nikolai crossed the bridge without a moment's hesitation, his straight torso perfectly still as his long legs glided across the thin branch, feet turned out like a dancer.

"You have no idea, darling." Nikolai's voice was coated in mischief as he watched me slowly maneuver across the bridge. The branch was thin but sturdy. My core flexed, keeping me upright as I made thirty-four cautious steps across.

Nikolai brought me to the smallest grove of trees. Some burls were lit by faelight, but most were dark and vacant. The two Halflings carrying my bags were ahead of us, climbing a thin, twisting branch to the very top of one tree. I followed Nikolai slowly, overcome by just how high we had climbed. The tree seemed to sway beneath me yet I could not feel a breeze, just a whisper of cold mountain air rolling down the peaks that stood to the east.

We stopped at the topmost burl. It curved away from the trunk on one side. A split in the bark served as a doorway to the hollow cavern. The Halflings left my bags on the large bed across the room. There was a hole along the side of the bed that acted as a window to the marvelous view of the gold-capped mountains covered in Elder birch trees. From this height, the tiny orbs of faelight gave way to the stars so it looked like the room was wrapped in the night sky itself.

"It's impressive, I know." Nikolai tugged me through the door and twirled at the center of the open room. Luxurious fabrics and pillows covered furniture that seemed to grow from the tree itself. A long couch lined one wall, accompanied by small stumps with pillows for the stools and bejeweled trays for the tables.

"That"—Nikolai pointed to one of two convex curves along the south side of the room—"is your closet. I had it filled with some of the best designers in the *Faelinth* and this fabulous Mortal shop in Cereliath that I adore. I grabbed your measurements from the tailor you charmed in Aralinth."

I raised a brow. I doubted I had charmed her at all, but the heavy sack of gold I'd given her would have been enough to convince most to do work for the Blade. "You're a fan of Wilden?" I asked. There could only be one shop in Cereliath lavish enough to catch Nikolai's attention.

Nikolai's jaw dropped and he tilted his head toward his shoulder. "You know of him? By how dirty you let your clothes get I would have thought artists like Wilden were beneath your notice."

I laughed. "Did you think I made my Harvest gown myself?"

Nikolai sighed and looked longingly at the closet. "You'll find more than one gown in there to rival that masterpiece."

I cocked my jaw to the side. I doubted there would be much time for pretty outfits in the days to come.

"Don't worry," Nikolai mumbled as he rolled his eyes. "There's room for your fighting clothes too."

I gave his arm a gentle squeeze and glanced at the other curve. "Please tell me that's not a second closet."

"Unfortunately, no. Space in the trees is limited."

I turned my head around the gigantic room that was at least three times as large as my chambers in the capital, but Nikolai didn't seem to notice.

"That is your bathroom. And since you like my hair oils so much, I made sure to stock it with some of my favorites."

I flashed him a wicked grin. I knew he had noticed I'd used them the night of the ball in Cereliath. Nikolai was as observant as Syrra when it suited him. I untied my belt and let my weapons fall to the floor. Nikolai watched in horror as I leaped onto the beautiful olive-colored mattress.

"Keera, dear, that's Elvish spun silk. It's over a thousand years old." He rubbed his brow and looked away.

I hastily unlaced my boots and kicked them to the floor. "I'm exhausted, Nik. That's the best I can do."

Nikolai shook his head but didn't argue.

I could see the other trees in the grove through the doorway without a door. I pulled myself up onto my elbows and jutted at them with my chin. "Do I know the neighbors?" My stomach dropped at the idea of having to live beside someone who hated me.

Nikolai shrugged. "Not at the moment. The rooms on the shorter tree are mine, but I rarely use them. Though my guests will stay there from time to time when they aren't sharing a bed with me."

"How gallant of you." My usual sarcasm had melted away into a laugh. It had become a pattern between me and Nik.

"That one there"—he pointed to the tree to the right—"is Syrra's but you'll find she never stays there. She avoids this grove entirely if she can." I cocked my head, waiting for Nikolai to explain, but he didn't.

I pointed to the tree directly across from mine to change the subject. "Who lives there?"

Nikolai suddenly could not meet my eyes. He shuffled his pristine boots along the floor and pulled at his hair.

I leaned back onto the bed, my body feeling heavy with understanding. The empty burl with its dark windows was Riven's.

A rush of words tumbled out of Nikolai's mouth, almost too fast to hear them. "I can find somewhere else if that makes you uncomfortable. Riven won't be arriving tonight so we can move everything in the morning if you like, but it just felt right having you here with the rest of the family."

That final word rammed into my chest with enough force to push the air from my lungs. My cheeks flushed and I kept myself from blinking so Nikolai wouldn't see the tears pooling at the corners of my eyes.

Family.

The word felt foreign—like it belonged to a language I didn't speak. I knew logically that somewhere in my past I had parents who made me, if not raised me, but their faces were nothing more than figments of my imagination. Nikolai was real. His flirtatious humor and loyal nature were more than I could've dreamed of, especially in the dark pit of loneliness he had found me in.

I blinked. One tear on the far side of my face fell onto the silk. The realization shook me to my core. I hadn't felt lonely in weeks. Even in that room where Killian had revealed the truth, Syrra's and Nikolai's presence had given me a comfort I couldn't recognize until now. I was angry at them for keeping it from me, and I would be for a while, but I also knew that the anger would fade. It wouldn't swirl around us forever, separating me from them. I was angry, but I wasn't alone.

If that was what it felt like to have a family, then I would welcome them just as Nikolai had welcomed me.

"Thank you, Nik." My voice was a hoarse whisper.

Nikolai perched on the bed next to me, toying with the end of my braid. "It was the least I could do."

"Killian does not stay in the grove?" I asked, hoping I sounded casual.

Nikolai stilled with his mouth hanging open. He looked down at the ground before shaking his head. "No, Killian prefers to stay in the lower city. It's closer to the library."

"I see." His love of books and history was not part of the facade then. My stomach churned with uncertainty. Everything I knew about the prince had been an illusion, a perfectly executed act. From where I stood, everything I knew about Killian was a lie.

"Do you trust him?" I turned to Nikolai, who was still frozen in his spot.

He nodded immediately. "With my life and our people."

I leaned back. I'd only seen that level of loyalty from Nikolai when it came to Syrra and Riven. But Killian was his family too; just because I hadn't known that didn't make it less true.

"*Why* do you trust him?" I pushed. "Why should *I* trust him?"

Nikolai gave me a heavy look. "You shouldn't."

I could not hide my shock at that answer.

Nikolai chuckled. "I'm not trying to dissuade you, but when we first found Killian stumbling around the border, we didn't trust him either. It took time for our suspicions to fade. He had to *earn* our trust, and he did. But it would be unfair to you if I said anything that would keep him from earning yours."

"Do you think he will?"

Nikolai broke into a comfortable smile. "Yes. As long as you give him the chance to do so." I watched his throat tense and he looked away from me again. I waited, looking up at his strong jaw and round cheeks, knowing he had something more to say.

He took a deep breath. "I don't like lying to those I care about." The truth of his words pierced me with his gaze. His lips pinched to one side, revealing a deep dimple in his cheek.

"I don't like it either, but I've done it." I stared at the grain of the ceiling. I could see small bubbles of liquid moving through the wood like blood through veins. I turned my head toward Nikolai, taking a deep breath of my own. "I am angry that I didn't know . . . but I understand why you couldn't tell me about your alliance with Killian. In Aralinth and after."

Nikolai's shoulders released with my words. He gave my braid a gentle tug. "Even so, it felt wrong."

I lifted my chin to meet his eyes. "We're headed to war, Nik. I reckon our days of doing things that feel wrong are only just beginning." The truth of the words settled into my bones with a familiar coolness. My entire life had been choosing between options that felt wrong and cruel. Balancing my service to Aemon without raising suspicion, while undercutting his control and torture of my kin. Those choices still haunted my dreams, marked me in so many ways apart from my scars. I wondered how this war would mark me still.

I sat up, feeling like my words were too important to say lying on a bed. "No matter the choices you're forced to make, Nik, I believe you will do the best for the Halflings—for the Elverin—and for that, you have my trust. I won't hold your decisions against you, if you don't hold mine against me."

Nikolai froze. His brow was creased and his lips hung in a serious line across his face. They twitched twice like he was deciding on what to say but couldn't find the words. I held my breath until he did. "I would never do that, Keera." I noticed the melancholic edge to his words but didn't press him. War was a heavy burden for anyone to carry.

My gaze found its way back to the dwelling across the grove. My heartbeat quickened for a moment seeing a glow emanating from the doorway, but the stray faelight floated past the burl and into the tangled branches below. My chest dropped and somehow I felt as empty as that room.

"Will you extend him the same understanding?" Nikolai's words were barely audible. He leaned back slightly, preparing for an outburst of rage.

I shook my head. "I understand why *you* didn't tell me. I don't know if I can say the same for Riven." My stomach churned. My skin yearned for Riven's touch, to have his scent wrapped around me, but it also flushed with rage. As an ally, I understood Riven's reservations with the truth. Even as a friend. But we had been more than that. I didn't know if I could separate the secrets I'd told him from the ones he'd kept from me.

Nikolai was quiet for a long time. He tugged on the stretched strand of hair as he stared at Riven's empty room too. "I don't know if he made the right choice." Nikolai scoffed. "I don't think he knows either . . . But I know Riven cares about you, Keera. He was wrecked at the thought of losing you in Silstra. He made his choice thinking it was the best one. For him and for you."

It was my turn to scoff. "Yet you're the one here to defend that choice. Not him."

Nikolai's face turned hard like a waterfall frozen mid-stream. "*That* I have no answer for." His words were ice, but he didn't elaborate. He stood from the bed and walked to the doorway. "Do you want the lights out so you can sleep?"

I nodded, suddenly aware of the fatigue tugging at my eyelids.

Nikolai said good night and walked out the door. He pulled something over the doorway, a thick piece of bark I hadn't noticed before. The faelights hovering in the room swirled together into one shuffling ball before floating out the window, leaving me to rest in the darkness.

CHAPTER FIVE

I woke as the first rays of sunlight warmed the Burning Mountains. My bones had turned to lead through the night, sinking into the mattress and begging me to fall back asleep. The drowsy effects of the sleeping draught still pulsed through my veins from the darts, but I rose from the bed anyway, forcing myself to shake off the fatigue. I wanted to explore the city while most of the Elverin were still in their beds. I dreaded the idea of spending the day being watched by untrusting Halflings and doubtful Elves. I had yet to see any Fae in the city, but I was sure someone with purple eyes and the ability to curse me with their magic lurked among the trees.

I stumbled into the bath to find no tub or basin to wash in. Instead, in one corner of the room hung a skinny branch over a collection of tiny holes in the wood floor. This part of the room was darker than the rest, like damp wood that had not completely dried out.

The holes in the floor were a drain. I walked under the branch, looking for a water source, and a rush of warm, fresh water poured from the tiny twigs along the branch. I stepped back and the water stopped. Somehow the tree was pumping hot water from its roots up its trunk to this spout.

I chuckled as I stripped out of my clothes, which were now soaking wet. I was still wearing Riven's tunic, stained with days of travel and my blood. I flung it to the ground, content to never wear it again. I peered out of the room to ensure the bark door was still clasped around the entrance. I didn't want any glaring eyes to catch a glimpse of my scars.

A large mirror hung on the other side of the room. It was the first time I'd seen myself since Rheih, the Mage, had healed me after the explosion. I let my eyes linger on my scars. The urge to turn away never came, though a surge of heat warmed my throat. I twisted an arm behind my back to caress the middle of the large scar Damien had carved into me and was happy to find it did not hurt. I took a breath and the craving settled, still there, still waiting as it always did, but no longer scratching at my skull.

I stepped beneath the shower and relaxed under the warmth of the water. A bottle of essence of birchwood sat along a flat branch acting as a shelf; it was the same as the one Riven had bought me in the kingdom. I didn't open it. It reminded me too much of him, his scent. I didn't want that lingering on my skin all day. I used a different bottle to wash myself that smelled of flowers and sea breeze. I used the same scent for the oil in my hair, letting it dry into loose waves before braiding it down my back like a long tail.

Usually I brushed my hair over my ears, pinning the long points against my skull so no one could see the mark of my Elvish lineage through the dark strands. I huffed and the breath was caught on the mirror, leaving a circle of fog that slowly faded away. I didn't need to hide my ears here. Here they were normal. They weren't a danger to me or those I tried to protect. I pulled the side strands upward and tucked them behind both points.

I searched through the closet for something to wear. Rich silks and heavy fabrics lined the hanging clothes. Nothing practical enough to spend the day climbing in and out of trees. I opened one of the drawers and gave a sigh of relief. They were filled with traveling clothes and training outfits. Trousers and tunics, leather boots and wool socks. Some of the clothing I couldn't wear—the sleeves were too short to cover my arms or the front too loose to cover the scars along my chest.

Eventually, I found a pair of black trousers lined with pockets and thin slits to hide my favorite weapons. The tunic I wore was loose and could shift enough to display my scars, but I covered it with a leather vest that I laced in the front. It too had pockets to store blades and vials. I found my leather wraps from my satchel bag and looped them around my wrist, tucking in the sleeve of my tunic as I continued to wrap the leather up my forearm.

I doubted it was the stylish appearance Nikolai had been hoping for, but I couldn't deny that these clothes were the most comfortable I'd ever worn. I strapped my belt along the waist, leaving some blades behind. I didn't want to give anyone more reason to fear me than they already had. I kept the curved blade, a small knife, and my bloodstone dagger along my thigh. I usually armed myself with three times that amount in Koratha, but something told me the Elverin were not as fond of weapons as the king.

I stepped to the doorway, pulling at a small groove along the bark door. It slid back against the tree, blending in with the trunk so well I forgave myself for not realizing it had been there the night before. I stepped outside into the fresh morning air, the taste of snow and smoke on my tongue. The tree swayed slowly underfoot as I looked down to the empty grove below.

It was a long walk across the bridge and down the spiraled branches of the main tree. My shins burned at the mere thought of it. A thick vine dangled beside the thin bridge, blowing gently in the morning breeze. I reached for it. My hands barely wrapped around the plant; it was thicker than any rope I'd used. I tugged on the vine, excited to feel the resistance against my pull. I checked the grove below to make sure it was still empty before jumping from the branch.

Cool air swept under me, rippling through my clothes and carrying my braid back toward the burl shrinking behind me. The trees faded into a green blur. I was moving too fast to focus my vision but I could see the damp ground getting closer. I laughed, letting my body stay in freefall for a moment longer before gripping the vine spooling through my hands.

I expected it to burn my palms, but the bottom of the vine was smooth and slick with dew. My feet hit the ground and I rebounded into a quick roll. The vine swayed beside me only a few feet off the forest floor. The last third of the vine was so worn it looked like it had been sanded down and brushed with an olive glaze. I smirked. If this was how the Elverin of Myrelinth traveled, I could get used to it.

I stared up at the burl I'd spent the night in. It looked tiny from the ground, like a stray acorn pressed to the trunk of a normal-sized tree. My stomach fluttered with the excitement of jumping from that height again.

Myrelinth looked different by day but just as beautiful. The first signs of sunrise had crested over the mountains, turning their snowy tips pink. Some Elves and older Halflings were beginning to stir. The sound of doors opening and birdsong filled the city as I walked through each grove, trying to capture every inch of the city in my mind, laying it flat like a map.

I came to the edge of the lake. The shore curved around the northern side of Myrelinth before turning southeast toward the mountains. A path cut downward from the white sand of the beach, sinking lower until it came to the mouth of a silver cave. It stood like a looking glass peering into the lake, holding back the water with an invisible wall of magic. The water stirred with hints of gold and silver dancing in the morning sun. I could see the rocky bottom and fish swimming past without concern.

I walked north along the beach until I came to a small clearing. Targets lined the far side, a stray arrow piercing the middle of one, forgotten. The grass was worn in twisted circles. I recognized the footwork of swordplay—the grounds of the Order were marked in the same way.

My pulse quickened and my palms dampened with sweat. It had been so long since I let myself get lost in a training field, and here one stood completely empty. I cut through the meadow, walking uphill, and saw a large hole carved into the next one. Its edge was marked by thick wood, cresting unevenly overhead. It reminded me of an exposed root creating a divot in the ground.

I paused and realized that was exactly what it was: a giant root from one of the monstrous trees lining the far side of the clearing. Underneath the root was a room filled with weapons and training equipment. Further in was a tunnel in the black earth that disappeared into the ground where the sunlight could not follow.

Seven spears hung along the wall. Each one hand-carved with a different design along its shaft and leather handles. I pulled the plainest off the wooden hook and marched outside. A tall stump stood to the edge of the clearing, just a little taller than me. It was chipped and slashed so deeply in some places the resulting groove had turned black.

I twirled the spear in my hand, feeling the even weight distributed along its shaft. I threw it into the air and caught it with my other hand, slashing it toward the ground. My lungs filled with fresh air and the thoughts cleared from my mind. My shoulders relaxed as my muscles pumped with anticipation.

I struck the stump once. The sharp end of the spear chipped a piece of wood away. I struck again and then again, beating the wood like a drum. It set the beat while my feet danced around the tree creating a harmonious rhythm. I let myself get lost in the music of my movements, striking and twirling until my breathing was heavy and my skin lined with sweat.

I thought of Riven's absence and felt the rage stored in my body. It clung to the muscles along my back, crept up my neck like a shadow. It warmed my blood and fueled each swing. I imagined him watching me sleep in that cave, staring down at me, knowing that he was leaving me to be taken by the prince.

I rolled along the ground and swiped the bottom of the stump like I was swinging for his legs. With each strike, I let myself feel my anger, dwell in the heat of it while it slowly released through the spear.

When I finished, the stump had transformed into a brittle stick threatening to collapse in the middle. I inspected the sharp blade of the spear and was surprised to find it just as sharp and pristine as before.

"It will take more than that to dull an Elvish blade." I turned toward the voice. Syrra stood underneath the thick root assessing my work.

I grabbed the water sack she tossed me. "How long have you been there?"

"Long enough." Syrra's arms were folded against her chest. She wore no tunic under her leather vest. I swelled with envy; it was not even midday and the air was already thick with damp heat. "If that is how you handle your anger, child"—she pointed at the tree I'd whittled to nothing—"then you must practice regularly. Rage will cloud your judgment." She eyed the waterskin I was pouring down my throat. Her pursed lips made it clear she was picturing that night in Caerth.

I swallowed the last gulp of water and wiped the wetness from my lips. My body was tired but loose. My anger had faded and so had the familiar burning in my throat. I handed the sack back to Syrra. "I'll make sure I train."

She walked to a cabinet along the wall and pulled out a pair of sparring gloves. Syrra slipped them on her fingers and wrapped the thick laces around her wrist three times as she walked over to me. She lifted them up and nodded. I threw a punch, but Syrra ducked under it and knocked my head with the padded glove before I had the chance to react. Her smirk was almost imperceptible, but it was there.

I threw another punch and smirked back as my fist collided with her glove.

The suns had risen to the middle of the sky by the time Nikolai found us. He emerged from the tunnel in the equipment area to see Syrra locking my head with her leg and throwing me to the ground.

Nikolai stood over us, crossing his arms. "You missed breakfast." He sniffed the air. "And you need a shower."

"You have to teach me how to do that," I told Syrra, ignoring Nikolai entirely.

She grinned and nodded. Her chest heaved as she unwrapped her wrists. "You know how to use your opponent's movement against them but you forget that your momentum can be just as powerful."

I rubbed the back of my thigh. I now had firsthand experience in just how powerful Syrra could be. I stood up with a wince.

Nikolai rushed to grab my elbow. "Maybe we should pause the sparring for a few days."

"No." I slapped his arm away from me.

Syrra gave a single chuckle. "You worry too much, *niikor.* Keera has a warrior's spirit; the sparring never ends. And with her healing gift, the bruise will be gone by dinner."

Nikolai didn't seem convinced, but he changed the subject anyway. "Killian has requested your presence. Both of you." His gaze shifted from me to Syrra.

"Has Riven arrived?" Syrra asked, her dark brown eyes suddenly preoccupied with a large ant crawling across the grounds.

Nikolai glanced at me and cleared his throat. "No. Killian is expecting him later on."

My stomach fluttered. I hated knowing that some of it was from excitement at possibly seeing Riven.

"He's expecting a report from Mortal's Landing. He wants the council there when he receives it." Nikolai continued not to meet my gaze.

I raised a brow. "Council?"

"Don't picture anything too fancy, Keera dear." Nikolai leaned against a sparring bag and inspected his fingernails. "Most of the rebellion leaders are here, so Killian wants to make the necessary introductions and catch you up on the status of our plans before you take your place on the council."

"Killian wants me on his council?"

"Did you expect anything less, child?" Syrra asked before taking a drink from the waterskin. It shook slightly in her hand.

I bit my lip. Killian had said he wanted me to help lead the fight, put my strategic mind to work against his father. I shouldn't have been surprised he was holding up his end of things, but I'd learned long ago not to trust a royal.

"Take me there." I stepped toward the lake, prepared to march back around to the outskirts of the city.

"It's not that urgent, Keera." Nikolai leaned backward and rested his finger under his nose. "You have time to shower."

I collapsed onto a stool made out of a stump. "Do you know how long it takes to walk up that tree?"

Nikolai grinned. "I promise I'll get you to a shower quicker than you can imagine."

I folded my arms across my chest. "If you think I'm showering in your room, Nik, you will be sorely disappointed. And I should emphasize the *sore*."

Syrra let out a soft laugh.

"I promise I'll get you into *your* shower quicker than you can imagine." Nikolai held out his hand for me to take. "Happy?"

I shrugged and grabbed it.

Syrra waved goodbye as Nikolai guided me into the tunnel. It smelled of damp earth and mulch. The cool breeze whispering against my cheek was a welcome surprise. A small faelight floated at Nikolai's ear, bathing the tunnel in so much light it was like one of the suns had fallen out of the sky and into the ground with us. I could see the faint scar along the back of his ear, slightly paler than the rest of his skin. Whoever had stitched Nikolai's ears in that Mortal orphanage had been highly skilled. The lines of sewn tissue were barely noticeable even to my Halfling eyes.

"I haven't seen Syrra train with anyone in a long time." Nikolai batted a faelight forward.

"She's good at it." I hadn't had a workout like that in years.

Nikolai gave a solemn nod. "One of the best. She doesn't train with just anyone, Keera. You should know that."

I nodded, not sure what to say.

"It's a pity, really. Vrail has been begging her for years."

I paused. "Vrail?"

Nikolai's face melted into a warm smile at her name. "She's in Volcar but you'll meet her soon. She's what I believe the Mortals call a 'librarian.' She wants to learn how to fight almost as much as she loves old books."

I held back my laugh. "Tending to pages is a very unpredictable and dangerous endeavor."

Nik grinned. "You laugh now, but I doubt she'll be here a day before she moves her sights from Syrra to you."

I shrugged. I would deal with that if the time came.

We passed two forks in the path that were smaller than the wide tunnel we followed. I suspected they led to different groves of dwellings from underneath. The farther we walked, the more offshoots to the main tunnel we passed. Nikolai never turned.

"Nik." I nudge him with my elbow. "Where are we going?"

"The Myram tree." Nikolai spun his finger in a large spiral like the five spooling branches of the tree at the center of the city. "It is the heart of Myrelinth." I could hear the love Nikolai had for his home in his voice.

When we reached the Myram, I understood what Nikolai meant. The tree continued underground, carving an expansive space completely lit by faelight.

Large roots twisted together to form a curved ceiling larger than any ballroom in the kingdom. Smaller roots formed each floor, stacks of rooms thirteen stories high. The entire hall was lit with faelights as if the suns could shine through rock and earth. If I had not just walked through a tunnel of black soil, I wouldn't have believed we were truly underground.

Children with long ears and braids that fell to their knees ran about the room, chasing one of the faelights. Their laughter rebounded up the walls where the smiling Elverin were looking down from their balconies. On the far side of the room, water gushed down the roots in waves of laurel and lapis. It collected in a small pool filled with violet blooms and lined by older Halflings wetting their calves in the fresh water. Some had long ears and Elvish features with the gray hair of Mortals. The others' wrinkled skin and folded posture hid any Elvish lineage apart from the slight length of their ears. Some Elves sat between them, marked by their ageless beauty, laughing like old friends.

Nikolai walked us toward the pool. I could feel the stares of curious Elverin following us—following *me*—as we entered another tunnel. Less than a hundred feet later, we reached a small opening. A strong breeze blew through my hair, causing my braid to sway against my back.

I looked up and saw the hollow inside of the Myram tree. Thick bark towered above our heads like we were at the bottom of a giant well with only a tiny circle of blue at the top to mark the sky.

Large balls of faelight hovered along the ground at our feet. Some were the size of a children's toy while others were wide enough to sleep on. Nikolai opened a small cabinet I didn't notice before and pulled out two dark green rolls. The fabric was like nothing I had ever seen. When Nikolai untied the first roll and it tumbled to my feet, I realized it wasn't a piece of material at all.

A large green leaf lay between us. It was thick and the same mossy color as the vine that hung from the burls swaying overhead. Nikolai passed me a leaf and I grabbed it with soft hands, unsure how much pressure would rip the lamina from the veins. My shoulders sagged under the weight of it.

Nikolai unfurled the second with a dramatic whip of his wrists. He flared it over a large faelight. The leaf did not sink through the orb or extinguish it as I expected. Instead, it clung to the edges of the orb, forming a solid green ball.

"It's much easier to travel this way"—Nik waved my leaf over my faelight—"trust me." I froze. Nikolai couldn't mean to float our way to the top? He climbed onto his orb, his body weight folding into the sphere like he was being carried on a cloud. He patted the empty leaf between us.

I bit my lip as I climbed on. My body sunk into the faelight deep enough that I felt secure on crossed legs. The orbs, as if sensing our readiness, floated toward the sky. At first, it was slow and gradual, mimicking the way faelights floated around a room. When we reached the hollow trunk, a strong breeze swept under each orb and shot us toward the sky. We flew in spirals around each other. I stood on my knees, needing to see the ground shrinking below us and the sky growing closer all at once.

Nikolai laughed, loud and free. The sound was so intoxicating that my own laughter burst from my belly and our joy echoed down the Myram tree and reverberated back up in an explosion of harmonies.

We sprung from the top of the tree and regained our gentle pace as the faelights descended to the highest bridge. I disembarked my faelight, and it spun around and disappeared into the hollow trunk where it would wait for its next climb.

I couldn't catch my breath from the laughter and altitude. "That was incredible," I said between huffs for air.

Nikolai hopped off his orb with a surprising grace. "Not the first time I've heard that."

I rolled my eyes and headed for my burl. I would die before admitting it, but Nikolai was right: I was in desperate need of soap and water.

Nikolai sat on the lavish couch as far from the bathroom as possible. I made sure to grab my change of clothes before I closed the door to the bath. Even without my scars, I wouldn't give Nikolai the satisfaction of seeing me in a towel.

Clean and dressed, I rejoined Nikolai, who was stretched out on the couch sketching some plans in his notebook. I braided my hair as I watched him. His eyes narrowed at the charcoal scratching the paper, but the shape was nothing I recognized.

"Another invention of yours?" I asked, tying off my hair with a green ribbon I'd found in the closet.

Nikolai nodded, plopping the charcoal holder into his mouth. It flicked from side to side between his teeth as he studied his plans.

"Do I get to know what it is?" I gripped the notebook between my thumb and fingers, but Nikolai snapped it shut.

"Stop stalling, Keera dear." Nikolai tucked his notebook into his jacket with a wicked grin. "We have a meeting to go to."

I picked up my weapons belt and started to tie it around my waist.

"It would probably be best if you left the blades. Or anything pointy, really."

I paused mid-lace. "Let me guess, Collin is on the council?"

"And Tarvelle." At least Nikolai had the decency to look apologetic. I dropped the belt onto the bed with an exaggerated sigh. Nikolai eyed my boot. "No knives either."

I crossed my arms, refusing to remove the knife I'd stashed between my calf and the leather. "I can be deadly with or without a weapon."

Nikolai ran his tongue along his teeth. "Fine. But I will remind you that this jacket would be ruined if you got blood on it."

I tucked my arm into his and walked out of the burl. "I'll keep that in mind."

CHAPTER SIX

The meeting was in an underground room on the western side of the city. Five giant roots pierced through the black earth of the floor, circling each other like the branches of the Myram tree. A large stone circle sat atop and was surrounded by eight chairs made of smaller roots that also shot from the ground.

Nikolai plopped himself into one. I started to sit in the one beside him, but he clucked his tongue. "I wouldn't sit there. It's Syrra's chair."

I cocked a brow. "I doubt Syrra has ever been upset by a *chair*."

"She hasn't." Nikolai shrugged, and I sat. "But it may be that no one has dared sit in her spot."

His face was deadpan, no hint of warning or trickery. I sighed and moved to the chair on the other side of him. Thankfully, the door opened so I could ignore Nikolai's smug grin.

Tarvelle entered, his gaze instantly falling on me. I stared him down, unwilling to look away first. After several long moments, his green eyes cut to the far side of the table and the Elf took a seat as far from me as possible.

Killian walked in next. His black cloak grazed Collin's knees, the Halfling was following the prince so closely. Killian gave me a small smile as he unfastened the clasp at his neck and folded the cloak over his ebony sleeve. Collin scurried away with it, hanging it across the room and returning with a glass of water. He placed it in front of Killian before taking a seat for himself.

When he finally looked away from his prince, it was to glare at me. I stitched a sarcastic smile onto my face and waved, wishing it was with a blade rather than my hand. Nikolai coughed beside me, but not loud enough to cover his laugh. Collin glared at him next.

A shadow fell across my face and I sat up straight against the back of my chair. Syrra—somehow she'd entered the room without anyone's notice—stood in front of me. She folded her arms and didn't say a word. I tilted my head at her and her brow raised like a sword preparing to strike.

I closed my eyes. "This is your chair, isn't it?"

Nikolai burst out laughing. Syrra nodded coldly.

I stood, letting Syrra sit, while I took my original chair.

"Are we ready to begin?" Killian asked, his jade eyes darting among the three of us.

I smiled sweetly as I punched Nikolai in the arm—hard enough to illicit a gasp. "We're ready, Kil," he wheezed, clutching his bicep. I smiled wider.

"Good." Killian nodded at me. "I trust I don't need to make any introductions."

Collin scoffed. I shot him an icy glare before answering. "Not if this is everyone." I eyed the two empty chairs, one beside Killian and the other between Tarvelle and Syrra.

"Riven and Vrail won't be joining us tonight." My heart twisted at Killian's words. "Though I hope they will both be in Myrelinth soon."

I nodded. "Then we should discuss how we're going to kill the king. Or do you just call him *Father*?" I locked Killian in my gaze, but he didn't rise to the bait. He only laughed.

"Fair enough. Though I think we should get you caught up on where we're at first." Killian looked at a loose piece of parchment in front of him. "Tarvelle, any updates on the refugees?"

Tarvelle stood in one swift motion. "We were able to move eighteen out of Silstra before the blast. They were brought to a safe house and will stay there until we bring them into Aralinth."

My brows raised. "Eighteen Halflings at one time?"

"We have completed rescues with far higher numbers before," Tarvelle said through tight lips.

I leaned forward and placed my elbows on the table. "Where is this safe house?"

Tarvelle didn't answer, making it clear he didn't want me to know. He looked to Killian, who gave a diplomatic response. "Just outside of Silstra."

I whistled a low note. "Isn't it a little dangerous to transfer them now considering we blew the city to bits?"

Tarvelle folded his arms. "My team and I know how to dance around a few Mortal guards. When we need to *kill* Halflings instead of save them, I will ask for the Blade's assistance."

"Careful," Syrra whispered in Elvish. Her calm stare pierced through Tarvelle hard enough he sat down.

"I know you'll bring them home," Killian cut in to extinguish the heat building within the room. He nodded to Syrra next. "Any news from your eyes?"

Syrra did not stand but placed her hands gently on the stone tabletop. "All Shades along the eastern shores have been called back to *Niikir'na.* The Dagger has been spotted running drills with them across the capital and more arrive each hour."

"That was the last order I gave Gerarda," I said. "We called in all Shades within a fortnight's ride to the capital. Gerarda is meant to devise a plan to catch the Shadow once and for all." I forced myself not to look at the empty seat beside Killian. I turned to Syrra instead. "You should also notice the Shades to the west positioning themselves along the border."

Syrra nodded.

"They've been ordered to stay back and keep watch for anyone passing between the kingdom and the Faeland," I continued. "Though I doubt they'll be much of an obstacle since you travel by magic."

Syrra grinned, flashing her fangs. "I do not foresee any issues with the Shades. Though I received word from the Fractured Isles this afternoon about unmarked ships docking at port with no crew to sail them."

"No insignia or name on any of them?" Killian leaned forward.

Syrra shook her head. "And they are foreign made."

I turned to Killian, the muscles in my back tightening. "If the king ordered ships for his navy, the Arsenal was never told about it."

"Nor I," whispered the prince. He nodded to Syrra. "Have your spies keep watch. If anyone comes to collect those ships, I want to know immediately."

Syrra nodded and leaned back in her seat.

"Collin, have you selected the targets for the next phase of our attack?" Killian turned slightly in his chair to face the Halfling beside him.

Collin's jaw pulsed. "Yes." He stared at the table instead of saying anything else.

"Care to elaborate?" Killian pressed.

Collin's gaze flicked to me, and I saw his jaw hardened even more. "No."

I took a deep breath through clenched teeth. Nikolai had been right when he said not to bring any weapons.

Killian leaned over his armrest and had the decency to whisper even though everyone in the room could hear him all the same. "I meant what I told you. If you cannot accept that Keera is here to help, then it will be *you* who is excused, not her."

My chest flushed with heat at Killian's words. Collin had been a part of the rebellion since the beginning yet he would choose me over him. My stomach churned, unsure of what that meant or how I felt about it. I waited for Collin to make his choice.

He stared at me and I could see the way he wanted to slice me in two right there and be done with it. I raised my chin and glanced at the hilt of his sword peeking over the tabletop. He would have to strike first, but it would be his only chance.

Collin slumped back into his chair and pulled a map from his vest. Killian plucked it from his hand and laid the parchment along the stone. The entire continent of Elverath sat before us with twelve locations marked in red ink.

"These are the vulnerabilities in the kingdom's trade routes." Collin stood and made a point of not looking at me. "Bridges. Narrow passages that can easily be obstructed by rockfall or flooding."

I stood to lean over the map. There was at least one mark along every major road in the entire kingdom. I brushed my hand over the edge and gasped softly. "This would cut off the trade networks entirely."

Collin's cheeks flushed red, but from the way his knuckles laid white along the table, I knew I wasn't making him nervous. "That would be the point."

I looked to Killian, who was already watching me. "If we play this right, we could completely isolate the king from his guard while we recruit for the rebellion."

Killian nodded, but the way his eyes lingered on me felt like an assessment. "Yes. We plan to attack the southern routes first. They're the largest networks for food transport and the first snows will hit there soon. While my father is busy readying his guard, we will supply Volcar and the southern villages with the food they need. Liberate as many Halflings as we can, and bring them to the *Faelinth*."

My stomach twisted. "You intend to liberate them by laying a war at their feet?"

Killian's face froze into hard lines. "No one we free will be forced to fight, Keera, but how many do you truly believe will refuse the chance?"

That cold truth ran down my spine causing the hairs along my neck and arms to raise. Had I not been given the same choice again and again and always chosen to fight? The promise Brenna and I had made, the deal Riven had offered me, and now Killian's alliance. Each had been a choice to fight, and each would only bring violence and pain, but I had chosen the same each time. Because for a Halfling, it was really only a choice of how to die: under the king's reign or overthrowing it. There'd be violence either way.

"The king has twenty thousand men in his guard." I pointed to Koratha, the capital city, on the map. "It would take a miracle to recruit that many Halflings."

Killian nodded solemnly. "That's why trapping the guard will be necessary. The king will have to send troops to feed and defend the cities—and when they come, we'll be waiting."

I could feel the weight of everyone's stare pressing down on my shoulders. The tactics were sound, but it would take a meticulous effort. One mistake and we would leave the Halflings in a worse position than before.

"Aemon will send the Shades to fight us." The coolness of my words did nothing to soothe the rawness at my throat.

Killian glanced to Syrra before speaking. "We will try to spare as many as we can, Keera—"

"But this is war," I finished for him.

The time of words and allegiances had passed. I looked around the room, knowing that regardless of whether the others saw me as a friend or foe, the choices we made would be cast in bloodshed. Now it was only a matter of controlling the spillage.

"What about the Light Fae?" I asked the room.

Tarvelle scoffed. "You want to waste time chasing ghosts? The Light Fae have not been seen in near a thousand years, Blade."

I pocketed my tongue in my cheek. "I'm well aware the Light Fae have gone." I glanced at Killian. "Did Riven or the others tells you what Rheih believes of my lineage?"

Killian swiped an ink-stained hand through his hair and nodded gruffly. "Feron believes the same."

I crossed my arms. "If I have at least one Light Fae parent, there must be more to their disappearance than we know." I was not even seventy. All Light Fae could not have disappeared centuries before if at least one had been alive decades ago to sire me.

"Any additions to our forces would be an asset," Syrra interjected. "And if the Light Fae gifts are somehow untouched, only a few may be enough to turn the tides of the war to come. Dozens would secure our victory with certainty."

Killian drummed his fingers across the stone table.

My knee bounced wildly until I was forced to stand. "If the Light Fae can be found, their healing magic would save countless lives. The Elverin cannot sustain heavy losses and we cannot yet ensure a swift war. If we had access to gifted healers, the bloodshed would be minimized for *all* sides. Fae, Elf, and Halfling." I leaned on the tabletop with my fists, silently urging Killian to agree to at least consider the possibility.

Without it, countless Shades would die in the conflict. I wouldn't be able to save them.

After several antagonizing moments, Killian nodded. I slammed my fist into the tabletop in excitement. "When do we start?"

Killian opened his mouth to answer when a knock rang through the room. Our gazes locked themselves on the doorway.

"Enter," Killian called, folding the map in half so the red marks were covered.

A short Halfling with long black hair opened the stone door and peered inside. She carried a folded piece of parchment in her hands, a wax seal peeking from between her thin fingers. "A letter from Mortal's Landing."

The prince nodded his head and she scurried over, placed the letter on the table directly in front of him, and scurried out once more. Killian's deft hand pulled the wax from the parchment and unfolded the letter. His jade eyes slid across the paper six times before they closed for the briefest moment. When they opened, he issued an order to Collin and Tarvelle.

"Prepare our horses. We need to leave for Mortal's Landing tonight."

Collin stood without question, already stepping toward the door, but Tarvelle held the prince's gaze. "What news comes from the coast?"

Killian flung the paper onto the table. The scrawl was small and blotted, like the message had been written in haste. "Our storehouses have been plundered."

Collin froze midstep. "Who sent word? Your brother?" I didn't miss the sharpness of Collin's words, but I didn't understand his meaning. Prince Damien was our enemy as much as the king was. Why would he send word to Killian at all?

The silence in the room was palpable. I looked at Nikolai but his gaze was cast along the floor. Syrra met my eyes but her jaw was clenched. Even Tarvelle and Collin stared at me. The heat drained from my body. I felt like I was being plunged underwater without the will to swim to the surface. Without wanting to, I turned toward Killian knowing the answer would make me wish that I had drowned.

"Brother?" I choked.

Killian took a deep breath as if he was preparing himself for battle. "Yes," he breathed out slowly. "I thought you had realized the truth yesterday, but I see that was an unfair assumption. You were at the brink of death when he told you who his mother was."

I swallowed. Killian's words pulled me from the depths of my fear and left me cold and shivering. Damien had never rescued me from the brink of death.

"I never would have intentionally kept it from you." Killian shot a severe look at Collin, who took the opportunity to flee the room. Tarvelle followed behind him.

I closed my eyes, and suddenly it was the night of the bombing. My body shrieked in pain from the places where my skin had been torn and melted. Riven had held onto me, held me to consciousness as he revealed one of the only truths about himself that I knew.

"Laethellia Numenthira," I whispered. Killian swallowed and pressed his hands onto the stone table. I didn't need to see his nod to know the truth; it had already settled into my bones. "She was Riven's mother . . . and yours."

Killian reached out his hand for me. "If I had known you didn't remember, I would have told you imme—"

I pulled the small knife from my boot with such swiftness even Syrra didn't react in time. I grabbed Killian's wrist and forced his palm upward before carving a slice into it. Red blood streamed between his fingers and dripped onto the floor like a leaky plume. Killian hissed and his hand recoiled into the safety of his chest.

Syrra grabbed the short blade stored along her belt and I dropped my knife onto the stone. I held up my hands in the picture of innocence. "I just wanted to make sure I understood."

"That knives cut people?" Nikolai's deadpan statement did not match his wide eyes.

I scoffed. "That the blood of kings and the blood of Fae do not a Halfling make, just the lying brother of a Shadow." I coated the last words in venom and launched them at Killian like they were poisoned arrows.

His eyes narrowed and he took a step toward me. He was close enough that our breaths melded the distance between us. He grabbed the knife from the table and held it at my belly. My breath caught, and for a moment, I thought I'd pushed him too far. Had humiliated the royal rebel too much.

Killian pierced my shirt with the knife and ripped through it in a straight line, freeing the bottom few inches from my vest. He wrapped the ribbon of linen around his hand without breaking my gaze. "You didn't need to cut me to know my blood runs red and not amber."

I crossed my arms and raised a brow. "Not for you to determine."

Killian tied a knot in his palm with his teeth. My gaze flicked to his mouth for a moment before returning to his unbreaking stare.

He leaned forward ever so slightly. "My bloodied lip ran red, not amber, if you remember."

"Did it?" I smirked. "I didn't notice."

Killian sighed. "Keera, you can't argue that I kept this a secret. It's been less than a day and everyone in the city knows about my lineage."

I couldn't keep my brow from raising. I was too focused on the questions flooding my mind, deciding which ones to ask first.

Killian ran a hand through his curls and stepped back. "How did you think the Elverin accepted Aemon's son as one of their own? Trusted me enough to lead them to war? I crossed the border to find answers from my mother's kin. When I found those answers, I swore I would do everything I could to protect the Elverin of the Faeland and liberate the ones outside of it."

I cocked my jaw to the side. My chest heated knowing one of those kin was Riven. I didn't want to think of him, so I didn't think of why Killian was allowed into the heart of the Faeland unchecked and unrestricted.

Killian's face softened. He brushed his fingers along my arm like he was comforting a friend. "Ask me anything you want when I return, but I must make haste, sunset is only minutes away. Syr and Nik, can I count on you to check on the others while I'm in Mortal's Landing?"

Syrra nodded once, and Killian grabbed his cloak from the hook and threw it around his neck. He dashed to the door, pausing to turn back like he had something else to say. I had no words to say to him, no offers of peace or luck. His jade eyes stared at me, mouth open, before he turned and left. Apparently, he had no words for me either.

"Why must he leave before sunset?" I asked Syrra. It was easier to level my voice now that Killian and his secrets had run through the door.

Syrra nodded at the map still folded in half along the table. Nikolai reached out and straightened it, so once more the entire continent was looking up at us. Syrra pointed to the large lake and the cluster of trees that marked Myrelinth. She held her hand out and a ball of faelight, warm like the summer sun, floated into her palm. She lifted it to the map and golden circles appeared across the parchment, one nestled next to Myrelinth.

It was a similar magic as the map Riven had given to me. The moment sunlight hit the parchment, hidden markings appeared. Syrra lifted her other palm and another faelight drifted to her, this time an orb glowing silver like the moon. She cast the moonlight across the parchment and silver markings flooded Elverath too. A small circle melded with the gold one over Myrelinth.

"These are the portals that exist in this realm." Syrra flicked the two faelights so they floated above the map in lazy spirals around each other. "Those marked in gold open from dawn til dusk. Those marked in silver open from dusk til dawn. Ones marked with both"—she pointed to the two circles over Myrelinth—"have portals that shift between two paths."

My fingers traced over the parchment searching for the two markings I already knew would be there. A gold circle was inked along the coast outside of Mortal's Landing, and a silver circle was etched into a clearing within the Singing Wood. I marked both spots with each of my hands and the taut line across Syrra's mouth twitched upward.

"If Killian wishes to make it to the eastern coast, he must pass through the portal before the second sun sets or he will have to wait for dawn."

I scanned the rest of the map. There were countless pairs of symbols across it, an entire network of portals that covered every mile of Elverath. I looked up to Syrra. "Can I keep this?"

Syrra and Nikolai exchanged soft smiles. "Yes. Though I expect you will have it memorized before Nikolai and I return."

My stomach plummeted onto the floor. "I can help you secure the storehouses," I pushed, not wanting to be left behind.

Nikolai gave me a pitying smile as he carefully folded up the map and handed it to me. "You need to stay here, Keera. You won't gain the trust of the Elverin if you're gallivanting through the kingdom with us."

I crossed my arms. "Leaving me here alone, seemingly unsupervised, isn't going to do much to gain their favor either."

Nikolai's grin was full of mischief once more. "Keera dear, whatever gave you the impression that you would be left alone?"

CHAPTER SEVEN

THE BRIGHTEST STARS STILL hung in the sky when Nikolai came bounding through the door of my burl. "Rise and shine, Keera dear," he said as he whipped the coverlet from my body.

I froze, panic-stricken on the mattress, too dazed to realize that I had fallen asleep in a long tunic and my scars were still covered. Several moments passed before I relaxed into the mattress and threw a pillow at Nikolai. "Go away." I hurled the blanket back over me, grateful it had not completely lost its warmth. "It's not even dawn."

"War doesn't sleep, Keera." Nikolai disappeared into my closet and reemerged with a handful of trousers and tunics. "And neither does kitchen duty."

I pulled myself up on my elbows and stretched my neck. "Kitchen duty?"

"Yes. Everyone in the *Faelinth* plays their part." Nikolai laid out the options on the bed and started mixing and matching pieces. "Most of us cycle through duties, but the kitchen was excited to have you."

I rolled myself out of bed and tossed my braid over my shoulder. Nikolai handed me his selection of clothes. "You mean the kitchen was the only place willing to take me." It wasn't a question.

Nikolai bit his cheek and fetched my weapons belt from the chair. He stood facing the far wall while I pulled on my clothes. "When you win over the city, I'm sure you'll have your choice of chores."

"And which chores do you choose?" I eyed his pristine teal robe and coral vest, each finished with elaborate stitching along the hem. I couldn't picture Nikolai peeling potatoes in the kitchen.

A devilish grin grew along his lip. "I work *very* hard to *please* the people of this city."

I rolled my eyes and chucked another pillow at him.

Nikolai laughed and caught the cushion with soft hands. "I'm not as picky as some, but usually I help the older Elverin gather medicines from the woods. I collect samples along the way."

I pulled my boot on with a swift tug of the leather. "Samples?"

Nikolai tossed me my belt and nodded. "I've been keeping a record of the potency of magic in various parts of the *Faelinth* and the Stolen Lands. Hopefully one day I will figure out why the magic is receding and how we can get it back."

I peered out the door where the faelights hung along the trees like stars of their own. "It doesn't seem like magic is dying here."

Nikolai swallowed and looked over his shoulder. "Not to eyes as young as yours, but for the immortals, the changes are staggering. Soon the *Faelinth* will be as barren as the lands Aemon took for himself."

I laced my boots in silence. Something about what he said tugged at my mind. It was too annoying to let go, like a fly buzzing through the dark while I slept. "Yet the magic here is fading much slower than in the Faeland. Have the Elverin done something to slow it?"

Nikolai walked us through the door and onto the bridge of twisted branches. "Feron believes the magic has faded more quickly under Aemon's rule because the Mortals take more than they need. Acres of *winvra* are harvested each year and shipped across the seas. Those berries never make their way back to the land and neither does their magic."

Nikolai launched himself off the bridge, a thick vine skimming between his hands. I followed behind him, the last of my drowsiness blowing through my body as the ground appeared underneath my feet. I landed a second after Nikolai but not as softly.

"But you believe Feron is wrong?"

Nikolai led us to an entrance at the base of one of the five branches of the Myram tree that curved into the ground. The branch was submerged in black earth but created a hollow burrow through the soil. Inside was a staircase that spiraled to the undercity below.

"Not entirely," Nikolai said once we were both inside the staircase. "But I've done the calculations and the extraction does not fully account for the loss in magic. It's not even close. Not to mention that some of the areas that have been impacted the most are areas that the king has never cultivated."

Nikolai bit his lip, and in the dim light I could see the shadows under his eyes and the permanent line etched between his brows. Scars of his own, ones I knew marked the questions that kept him up well into the night.

I followed him through the main hall. It was empty apart from the soft rumble of the waterfall flowing into the wade pool. Nikolai took the tunnel at the middle of the west wall and followed it for a few hundred steps. Then he turned left and we stepped into a wide room centered around five large hearths. Flames danced playfully inside two of them, their smoke rising through the communal chimney made of stone.

A tall Fae with two black braids framing his face stood in front of the flames. His tanned arms were thick with muscle and crossed over his chest. In the firelight, I could see the array of faint scars along his hands, the cuts and burns of a cook. His nose was sharp and hooked between his brows under which sat bright purple eyes. As I assessed him, each of the muscles in his forearm flexed, daring me to make my move.

There seemed to be only enough room for one of us to be sullen and he had claimed the role. I smiled, hoping it was friendly and not condescending. "Thank you for letting me work in your kitchen." I dipped my head in a bow.

The Fae didn't say anything.

Nikolai shot an uneasy smile between the two of us. "Keera, this is Lash'raelth. Though most just call him Lash." Nikolai turned to him, as if asking for approval for me to call him Lash too. The Fae hadn't moved; I wasn't convinced he was even breathing. After a long moment, he nodded and Nikolai let out an audible sigh.

His gaze caught on the root-packed ceiling as if Nikolai could see the sky through the soil. "I'm already late and Syrra's going to have my head if we don't make it through the portal before it switches. You two have fun!" he called over his shoulder while hurrying down the tunnel.

I turned back to Lash and a large knife pointed at my nose. I froze and my breath left a line of fog along the blade. Lash flipped the knife through the air, and I caught the handle without breaking our gaze. He pointed to a table at the back of the room. On top of it was a pile of root vegetables so mountainous I was convinced it would feed the entire kingdom.

Lash only spoke one word to me the entire morning. "Peel."

CHAPTER EIGHT

I DIDN'T SPEAK TO ANYONE for the next three days. Without Nikolai, Syrra, or Killian by my side, the cautious glances had turned to hushed whispers whenever I was in sight.

Lash didn't speak to me once. Each morning he would point at the pile of vegetables he wanted me to slice or peel, the knife already sticking out of the mountain. When the other kitchen workers arrived they didn't speak at all. By the third day, I considered it progress that they joked and laughed like I wasn't in the room.

By the time I finished kitchen duty, I would already be sweating from the heat of the fires. I took my breakfast to the training fields and ate by myself. After, I would train until my legs shook and I had to nap before making the journey up the Myram tree.

At night, I studied the map. I memorized the paths until I knew exactly where each of the dozens of portals were and where each one connected. A few were marked in black ink instead of gold or silver and others were marked in red. There was no legend along the bottom, and I was too stubborn to ask Lash what they meant.

With only the silver and gold portals, there were enough that, with the right strategy, you could travel to any part of the continent within a day. Organized strikes could happen simultaneously across the kingdom and the teams could scurry away without a trace. Having each route memorized would be lifesaving in the war to come. We could ferry Halflings to safety, the wounded to healers. And if we found the Light Fae? Their healers could be stationed at nearby portals, close enough that even those on the brink of death could be saved without having to risk the lives of the healers too.

Tarvelle and Collin may have thought it was a childish hope, but it was one that I wanted to explore. I needed to. I carried enough proof on my skin that too many Halflings had died under Aemon's rule. I would do everything I could to keep their deaths to a minimum in the war to come.

I laid awake, trying to remember anything from my past. A shadow of a face—the faintest hint of a memory—but nothing came. Whomever my parents had been, their faces were lost in the darkness of my childhood. Part of me was glad I would have to find some other way to search for the Light Fae. Barely eight years old and I had been lost only to be plucked up into the king's clutches. I wasn't sure I wanted the answers to how I had ended up in the Rift.

A chorus of cheers erupted from the grove below. I darted from my bed and peered over the edge of the bridge just outside my burl. I could hear Killian's warm laugh as he and someone I didn't recognize were swarmed by a group of children.

I launched myself off the bridge, realizing too late there was no place to land with so many children circling below. With a hundred feet left in my drop, I clamped onto the vine with all my strength and stuttered to a stop. The force of the arrest was too strong and my body flung forward so I hovered above everyone's heads, upside down, with my braid swaying just above the ground.

Killian blinked, unable to move.

I was about to say something about his fatal lack of awareness, when a laugh bubbled up from underneath me. A Halfling, no more than three, was jumping, trying to catch my braid, and pointing at where I still hung upside down. The rest of the young ones joined him while some of the older children jumped onto nearby vines to hang the same way.

There was no fear on the children's faces, just joyous smiles and laughter. To them I wasn't the Blade but a funny Halfling wanting to play. I laughed with them, letting my body spin around as I hung from the vine. I spotted Tarvelle at the edge of the clearing while I laughed. He was standing beside an Elf, whispering something in her ear. When Tarvelle pulled back her jaw dropped open and she scurried across the grove to fetch her son from the crowd of children.

"You must not disturb Killian and his guests," she told them in Elvish.

"They're not disturbing us," I called back in the same tongue. The Elf's eyes widened in shock before narrowing into a glare. She had never cared about disturbing the prince; she only wanted the children away from *the Blade*. I glanced at Tarvelle, who gave me a smug nod before disappearing into a neighboring grove. My heart sank and I dropped a bit lower to the ground with it.

Killian cleared his throat and looked up at me as if hanging from a vine was normal behavior. Perhaps in Myrelinth it was.

"Keera," he said, pointing at the Halfling beside him. "May I introduce Vrail." She was shorter than most Halflings, with stout limbs that matched her rounded belly. The skin along her wide nose was freckled. Long black hair was braided down her back and wrapped in a scarlet ribbon that matched the long robe she wore.

Vrail nodded her head five times in quick succession and spoke just as quickly. "It's a pleasure to meet you, Keera. Killian and the others have told me so many wonderful things about their new friend. Though I've also heard some troubling things from others." Her tawny cheeks flushed as she eyed the dagger along my belt. "Though I doubt any of that is true. You didn't choose to become a Shade, or Blade for that matter, and people need to consider such things before they make a judgment—"

Her rapid speech came to a halt as Killian placed a hand on her shoulder. "She's a little nervous," he whispered in apology.

"Very true," Vrail agreed, blushing more fiercely.

I chuckled and finally flipped down onto the ground. Vrail's eyes went wide in amazement and I could see her retracing my movements through the air.

Killian gave me a smug smile. "I'm glad you found your way down."

I straightened the leather wraps around my wrist and ignored the raw skin along my palm. "Want me to bloody your lip again, princeling?"

Vrail gasped and threw her body in front of Killian's.

I peered down at her. Her frame was round but solid, though her stance was amateur at best. Killian would have a better chance of defending himself than she did. I bit my cheek to keep from laughing.

Killian leaned down to Vrail's shoulder, keeping his eyes locked on me with a carefree smile on his lips. "She's kidding, Vrail."

Her arms dropped and the tension in her stance gave way to the softness of her features. She looked up at me with a full smile and even fuller cheeks that crinkled her eyes. "I knew that."

I cocked my head but didn't push the Halfling any further. "Why do you wish to speak to me?"

Killian glanced around the grove to make sure none of the children were still lurking overhead. "There have been some . . .

developments." He leaned in closer for the last word, so close his breath sent a tingle across my cheek.

I darted back. I tried to cover the abruptness with a cough but Killian and Vrail only stared at me with identical furrowed brows.

"Meeting room?" I gestured to the nearest Myram branch and tried to ignore the scent of parchment and fire smoke washing over me.

We walked to the same room with the circular table and chairs made from earth-packed roots. Nikolai was already there, slumped back in his seat and eating a steaming bun and dried meat. He nodded lazily to Killian but rushed to his feet as Vrail and I walked in. He gulped down his food and started his report. "Nothing has been taken from the other storehouses. Though Syrra and I moved the best stores just to be safe." He took a large bite of his bun. "Now they're—"

"Don't tell me." Killian took the seat at the back of the room. "I don't need to know, and it's safest for everyone if the new locations stay as secret as they can." There was a rough edge to Killian's voice. Like he had spent much of the last three days yelling.

"The glamours had not failed, then?" Syrra cut in, suddenly appearing in front of the hearth. She pressed her hands together like she was preparing for a fight. In the firelight, I could see the branches that carved around her wrist and up her forearm.

I took the chair next to Nikolai and perched on the armrest. "The storehouses were glamoured?"

Nikolai gulped back the rest of his food. "All the safe houses are. It's the only way to ensure that Mortals or Shades don't accidentally stumble onto something they shouldn't."

Killian's expression was harder than I'd ever seen it. He picked at his thumb while he stared at the stone tabletop, completely lost in thought.

I glanced at Syrra. Killian's concern could only mean one thing. "If the glamours are still intact that means whoever stole the supplies knew where they were."

Killian gave me a grave nod. "We have a mole somewhere within our ranks."

Those words washed over me like a blizzard after a long winter. I slumped back into the chair. "I should leave this room before Tarvelle and Collin storm in with any more accusations."

"Why are you volunteering to leave?" Syrra asked, turning away from the hearth. "You are one of the only people we can say *for certain* did not know where those safe houses were. No one can think you are the mole."

I rubbed my brow in disbelief at Syrra's naivete. "The facts don't matter. Do you believe any of the rebels will accuse one of their own before they point their finger at me?"

Her mouth snapped shut. I slapped my hands on either armrest and stood. We didn't have time to convince the rebels to accept me; there was too much at stake and too little time to waste. I didn't need to be on the council to fight for the Shades. I didn't like it but I could bear it.

"Sit down, Keera." Killian's command was heavy and brooding. He strummed his fingers against the stone until I sank back into my seat. "Syrra is right. The facts will absolve you of any accusations that *may* arise, but this transition is proving difficult. Until we find out who the mole is, only essential information will be shared at this table. The specifics of your assignments remain with you. I trust you all and it will be the quickest way to discover *who* is leaking information."

"And to whom they leak it," Syrra added.

Killian nodded glumly. "And more importantly, *why*."

I shook my head. "You told me when I arrived that I needed to earn the trust of the Elverin. The whispers that I set the Unnamed

Ones on the convoy still breeze through this city. If the Elverin find out you suspect one among your ranks is leaking information to some unknown threat, that breeze will turn to a gale none of us will be able to control. We should save ourselves the trouble until the mole is found." My chest was hot and my stomach churned with uncertainty. There was nothing I liked less than relinquishing the little control I'd carved out for myself, but if that was what was needed to be done to ensure the focus stayed on liberating the Halflings and ending the Crown, the fight was not worth my pride.

Killian stood and pressed his hands into the table until his knuckles turned white against the gray stone. "There is something else. Witnesses of the theft in Mortal's Landing all report the same thing. Four small figures, dressed in black hoods and black clothes, were spotted transporting crates of food onto an unmarked foreign ship."

I stood, filled with the instinct to put myself between Killian's accusation and the Shades. "The Shades had nothing to do with this!"

Killian held up his hand to calm my rage. "I know that, Keera. I am not accusing the Shades of the theft."

Syrra took a step toward the table, her dark eyes danced between me and Killian. "The ship is of the same description as the ones spotted in the Fractured Isles?"

Killian nodded. Nikolai exhaled a low breath before pulling out a leaf full of nuts and nervously stuffing some into his mouth.

"So the ship owner is conspiring with someone from the Faeland?" I knocked my knuckles against the edge of the table. "To what possible end?"

"That I cannot say." Killian shrugged. "But I don't think the thieves dressing as the Shades was an accident. What other motivations the mole and this unknown entity have, they seem invested in tainting your relations with the rebellion. For that reason alone,

I will not allow you to remove yourself from this council. That is exactly what they want."

My body turned to ice. Was it possible that while we had been focused on the king, another enemy had appeared and infiltrated our midst without any of us realizing? A chilling anxiety crept up my spine, making me feel like I was being watched. "How many people knew the location of those storehouses?"

Syrra shrugged. "We have used them for decades. Dozens know, if not more."

I sighed. That was a longer list than I was hoping for.

Vrail's gaze flicked so quickly from one person to the next it looked like her head was shaking. "So we compile a list of names and start gathering the evidence to remove them one by one."

Nikolai let out a defeated sigh. To me, the list was tedious, but to him and the others the list was full of their friends and comrades.

I gritted my teeth. "No. It will take too long and it would certainly alert the mole."

"What do you suggest we do, Keera?" Killian asked. There was no disdain or sarcasm in his voice; he was just a man looking for answers anywhere he could find them.

I took a deep breath and looked away. The trust in his gaze was unsettling. "Nothing."

"You want us to wait for something else to happen?" Nikolai raised a brow. "That's dangerous, even for you, Keera dear. Their next attack could hurt someone or *worse*."

"Not likely." Four pairs of wide eyes stared at me. I stood and placed both my hands along the stone table top. "They didn't attack the rebels; they attacked our food stores and that wasn't without reason. The food is feeding someone and we need to find out who. Find the food and we find the mole." I glanced at Syrra and her sharp

Elvish blades. "After that, I'm sure we can convince them to tell us who they've been leaking information to."

Syrra nodded, a cold smile on her lips.

Vrail bounced out of her chair. "So the question becomes: Why would someone need ships and enough food to keep hundreds well-fed?"

Nikolai was the one to say what we were all thinking. "Perhaps we have not been the only ones making moves against the Crown."

"An army?" Vrail gasped.

I cocked my head to the side, considering the implications of that possibility. "If the stores are for an army preparing to attack Aemon, better their men die than ours."

Killian sat down in his chair and brought a knuckle to his lip. "If it was an army, the ships would be full, not empty." He lifted his chin at Syrra. "What kinds of vessels were docked along the Fractured Isles?"

"Cargo," Syrra answered immediately. "Almost all carracks and none heavily armed."

Nikolai plopped a nut into his mouth. "So the ships are waiting to ferry something across the sea? Why would merchant trade be clouded in so much secrecy?"

"There is no reason, unless the merchant stood to make a fortune from selling the goods under the king's nose." Vrail nodded excitedly at her own words. "Aemon imposes a heavy tax on any *winvra* sold across the kingdom or overseas. Evading the taxes is motivation enough."

At least the list of lords with enough *winvra* to require an armada was a short one.

"Curringham," I said, clapping my hand on Vrail's shoulder.

Vrail blushed and nodded.

I turned to Killian. "His orchards are beginning to fail and he just married the daughter of a foreign merchant. Perhaps he's planning for this harvest to be his last. Taking his entire stock would buy him a life of luxury in his wife's country and it would bankrupt the kingdom in one safe passage."

"Maybe we should just let him do it," Nikolai mumbled.

Killian picked at the skin of his thumb absentmindedly. "But why would one of our own help Curringham flee the Crown to a foreign land? What does the mole have to gain?"

"Money. Power. The chance of a new, free life across the seas?" I shrugged. "Do you expect an honorable reason from a traitor?"

The room went silent. No one even dared to breathe. None of them liked the idea of having a traitor in their midst. My heart ached for them. The cut of betrayal always stung most.

Killian's nostrils flared as he exhaled. "I agree with Keera. We will not launch any attacks against the kingdom until we can learn more about the mole and whether it is Curringham they're whispering our secrets to."

Syrra cocked her jaw to the side. "I do not think it wise for us to be cowering in the dark while the hunters storm the woods."

Killian stood tall against the heavy weight of the Elf's stare. "We are not cowering but defending our post. I will not send the rebels into war when we know we're missing critical information."

I thought Syrra would push back, but she only held the prince's gaze for a long moment before nodding and stepping away from the table.

"In the meantime," Vrail said with a shaky voice, "I have something that might occupy our time while we wait to see what the mole and his master have in store."

I raised my brow. "You have many interesting things to say for a librarian."

Vrail pushed out her small chest with pride. "My family has been the keepers of a single truth since before the Age of Wielding. *Niikenth daasowin quil apiithir.*"

"Knowledge is the most important of it all," I echoed back.

Vrail nodded excitedly. "Feron asked me to research anything having to do with the *Valitherian*"—she gave me a pointed look—"as he thought that Keera being one meant there might be something left undiscovered about the Light Fae and their disappearance."

Vrail pulled something from a hidden pocket. "I found this letter while I was locating records of the first Mortals. It was tucked between the scrolls. Parts of it have been burned but you can still make out the beginning of the message. I think a Mage sent it sometime during the firsts Blood Purges."

She passed the letter to Syrra. I peered over her shoulder to glimpse the message. The script was flourished and the text was Elvish. Syrra translated the three lines that had survived the fire.

Our Cousins have gone.
Like their mother kin before them, their power will reawaken
by the fruit of an Elder birch.

I took the letter from Syrra's hand to read the script for myself. Some of the words were different from the Elvish I knew, older versions from a world long passed. "Cousins?" I asked to the group. I didn't understand the phrase.

Vrail's hand shot through the air enthusiastically. "That's why I think the letter was authored by a Mage. The Mages were gifted their magic from Kieran'thara from whom descend all Light Fae. They called the Light Fae 'cousins' out of respect for their shared magical lineage."

I blinked. Never had so many words I didn't understand been spoken so quickly.

Vrail's jaw dropped. "You've never heard of Kieran'thara?"

I shook my head.

"She was one of the *niinokwenar.* The Faemothers." Vrail held up her three middle fingers as if that explained what she'd just said.

I shook my head. "Haven't heard of them either."

Vrail was about to launch into an hours-long history lesson, but Killian placed his hand on her shoulder. "You can explain the history of magic tomorrow, Vrail."

Her shoulders fell and she nodded her head. Nikolai stepped around me and offered Vrail half of the sponge cake he had pulled from his satchel to curb her disappointment.

"One charred piece of one letter and you believe the Light Fae have been hiding somewhere all this time?" Syrra asked Killian. Her jaw was hard and the muscles in her arm flexed like she was holding a shield.

"I don't know where they've been or what happened before, but I think they've reemerged. The Mages seemed to think it would happen eventually," Killian replied, standing taller under Syrra's doubt. "At the time they disappeared, they had some of the most gifted seers in their midst. Maybe they knew something the rest of the Elverin didn't and they did something before my father came for their power too."

Syrra did not seem convinced. "What possibly could have kept them hidden for so long?"

Vrail rocked back and forth on her toes as she spoke. "They could have left knowing they would return at some point. Though after rereading the letter a hundred times, I would think Elvish sleep to be a strong possibility."

I raised a brow. "Elvish sleep?"

Vrail nodded enthusiastically. "It's a protective magical state that can happen to Elverin when they are in grave danger. It's rare, but can last for more than a century."

Syrra crossed her arms. "There is *one* record of Elvish sleep lasting that long."

"One means it's possible," Vrail mumbled as she poked the ground with the toe of her boot.

"It's not only this letter." Killian waved his hand at the letter and looked at me. "But Keera too."

I leaned back with wide eyes but Killian continued. "She is not yet seventy. What is more likely: That she is truly centuries old, or that the Light Fae have reemerged and are waiting for us to find them?"

"Creating a choice between two unlikely options is not the foundation of a sound decision," Syrra said solemnly.

Killian turned to Nikolai. "What do you make of this?"

Nikolai glanced among Killian, Vrail, and me before shrugging. "If anyone would have been forewarned of what was to come, it would have been the Light Fae." Killian raised his hand in victory. "And they would be an invaluable ally in the fight to come. I think pursuing this is worth the effort." Nikolai sheepishly looked away from Syrra.

I rubbed my brow and met Killian's gaze. "So you believe that the Light Fae were *forewarned* of Aemon's attacks and did something to keep themselves hidden all this time? That they've been alive and well in secret?"

Killian nodded with excitement.

"You think they left their people to be slaughtered and captured? To spend their lives chained to a crown?" The thought stoked a fire in my belly that made each word burn hotter than the one before. "You think the Light Fae *knew* that would happen and they *let* it." My throat went dry.

Killian nodded slowly. "Yes."

I slammed my fist on the table so hard the stone groaned against the roots holding it up. I turned to Syrra. "Are these the people you remember? The ones the Elverin seem to hold in such esteem? Fae gifted with silver eyes and a coward's spirit?"

Syrra took a step toward me and reached out like she was grabbing for my hand. I stepped out of reach. My mind flooded with hateful questions I had long put to rest. It was dizzying.

Killian was baffled as he looked at me. "You knew that we would be looking into this. Encouraged it, even."

I clenched my jaw. "When I thought that something had happened *to* them. But if what you believe is true, they have already abandoned their people once. Why would they support our cause now?"

Killian rubbed his brow. "If we find them, you can pose that question directly."

"I will not speak to them at all." I snarled and stepped backward toward the door.

Killian threw up his arms in exasperation. Nikolai tried to calm him, but he stepped out of his reach toward me. "You know the odds are stacked against us, yet you cannot put a leash on your pride to win the war?"

His words landed like arrows in my chest. "Did I not just surrender my position on this council for the *betterment* of rebellion yet you take issue with my pride?"

Vrail blinked nervously between us. Nikolai and Syrra did not react, only watched Killian swell in his frustration. I turned away from them all. The pressure building inside me pushed against my ribs and chest, threatening to burst. I didn't want them to see me.

"You are not the Blade here. You cannot win this war on your own." Killian's voice was hard and resolute as he took a step toward me. "Seeking out the Light Fae is not weakness."

I snapped and turned around. "I have not been the Blade since I made that alliance in Aralinth." I took a step forward so that Killian and I were close enough I could feel the heat radiating from his chest. "An alliance I reaffirmed, at your behest, in the Singing Wood. If there is someone in this room who believes seeking out help is a weakness, it is not me."

Killian swallowed but did not back away from me. "Then why do you hesitate to find the Light Fae now?"

My jaw snapped shut and hot tears burned at the edges of my eyes. "Perhaps I need some time to digest that I may have been left willingly." My voice cracked. "If the Light Fae have truly been hiding all this time, then that young girl who was found in the Rift was not lost. She was not an orphan. She was *abandoned*." I wiped the tear from my cheek and took a deep breath. "I will help you find them, but I do not owe you pleasantries while I do so."

Killian's hard eyes softened as I stared at him, unwilling to look away first. His hand twitched at his side, like he wanted to reach out and say something to me, but he remained where he was. I turned on my heel and left the room. The heaviness in my gut magnified when no one moved to follow me.

CHAPTER NINE

THE NIGHT AIR WAS WARM and full of laughter from the groves below, yet the moment I walked into my burl, all I felt was cold loneliness. As a child in the Order, I'd grown grateful that I couldn't remember my life *before.* Even the eldest initiates would cry into the long hours of the night. Sometimes they woke themselves screaming the names of their family members, haunted by the memories of being taken or, even worse, being left behind.

Whatever fears had haunted me seemed inconsequential in comparison at the time.

But the unanswered questions followed me like an old injury, often forgotten. Except when the weather shifted and the pain would flare with vengeance. It had hurt, learning to live with that pain. Still, I'd survived it. But perhaps all that time I had more in common with the other girls than I'd realized. Perhaps, I'd been spared by the ghost of that loss.

"Keera?" There was a knock at my burl. The scent of parchment and ink fluttered through the room.

I crossed my arms, readying for a fight. "Did my storming out give the impression I want to discuss this further?"

Killian gave me a halfhearted smile as he stepped into the burl. "No. I came to apologize." He waved his black cloak over the chair across from my bed and sat down.

I narrowed my eyes at him. He slumped over his knees, leaning toward me, waiting for me to make the next move.

"I didn't realize princes were capable of apologies."

Killian's half smile dropped to a straight line. "I do not see myself as a prince, Keera. Of anyone, least of all you."

I raised my chin and waited him out. I'd learned as Blade that truth was often spilled to fill uncomfortable silence. I'd already bared enough of myself in that room; it was Killian's turn to expose his belly.

"I let my exhaustion of the past few days get the better of me. I shouldn't have assumed you were being needlessly cross. You've never done anything without good reason before now. I should've known to ask what was upsetting you instead of starting a row."

I crossed my arms. "I've never given you reason to grow wary of my pride either."

Killian sighed and ran an ink-stained hand through his unkempt curls. "No, you haven't," he admitted in a breath. "I was painting you with the brush of my own fears, and for that I apologize too. You were right when you said that I didn't want to find the Light Fae."

I couldn't help but raise my brow. "You do not wish to seek the Light Fae?"

Killian had seemed to be a voice of logic of the group. He couldn't deny that the benefits of finding the Light Fae outweighed the possibility of chasing a dead end.

Killian shook his head and leaned back in the chair. His throat bobbed as he searched for the right words. "It's not that I don't wish to find them; it's that I wish I didn't *need* to find them." Killian looked at me and I recognized the pain behind his eyes.

"Most days I feel like I'm failing at this," he continued, holding his head in his hands. "It's *my* father who caused this destruction, *my* father who built a throne on the backs of my kin. It's my responsibility to end it—end my legacy—but most days it feels like I'm chasing a future that can never be."

My chest tightened at his words. Hadn't I felt the same way trying to balance my plot to end the Crown and my need to protect the Halflings? Looking at Killian, crumpled in my chair, I couldn't help but grab his hand. It was a small gesture, but I knew it was a comfort I had yearned for so many nights keeping the same storm of defeat at bay. "It is not your sole responsibility, Killian. We're in this rebellion together."

He squeezed my hand. His jaw flexed as he looked at me with misty eyes and a trembling lip. He knew the truth of my words, but he also knew that no one else in Myrelinth could understand the position he was in. The mask he had to wear to protect the rebellion, the atrocities he had to ignore to keep his crown—all to protect his people. He was a prince and I was an assassin; he had his crown and I had my cloak. They both tore at our skin until we bled, but we wore them still.

Killian finally looked away and rubbed his palms across his thighs. "The war has not yet begun and I already tire of fighting. I will do anything I can to free our people. I will search every realm for the Light Fae if need be, but I must admit that part of me wishes the fights we've already fought had been enough. That *I* had been enough." He touched my knee and my chest twinged at the warmth. Suddenly the room was no longer cold and I no longer lonely.

"You are enough." I barely knew Killian at all yet it didn't taste like a lie on my tongue.

He scoffed. "I can't even trust my own rebels. A good leader would not have a mole in his midst."

I shook my head. For some reason Hildegard flashed across my mind. "A good leader is not born from a lack of conflict, but his response when it arises."

Killian blinked as he looked at me, like he was staring directly into the suns. "You are much wiser than you give yourself credit for."

My breath hitched in surprise. "Thank you."

Killian gave me a teasing smile I'd never seen before. "I didn't realize Blades were capable of gratitudes."

My body stiffened against the mattress. For a moment, I could see Aemon's features along his son's face. The same heavy brow and rosy cheeks, the same green eyes that struck me with uneasiness as if my mind were being watched as well as my body. I spoke to him as much as I did to Killian. "I have not considered myself the Blade in a long time," I said, dampening the fiery edge of my words. "A blade is a weapon that must be wielded. The king no longer wields me."

"And he never will again." Killian's words rang with a conviction neither of us had earned. I would never let Aemon control me again, but my future was most likely a short one. When the king realized his sheath was empty, I would become his sole target. We may win the war to come, set fire to all the king had built, but Aemon would do everything in his power to make sure I died in the flames alongside him.

Killian leaned back in the chair, picking at the nail of his thumb. His gaze was still on me, but there was no weight to it, like he was seeing through me or perhaps seeing nothing at all. "You know he erased every trace of her from the kingdom?" His voice was a soft rasp, almost like it wasn't meant for me to hear.

I pushed myself further onto the mattress and crossed my legs. "Your mother?"

Killian nodded. "He never said her name. He forbade anyone at court to speak it and I know he cut out more than one servant's tongue."

I swallowed, remembering the older scullery maids who had always worked in silence.

"Have you ever been in my father's rooms?" Killian asked and I could feel the presence of his gaze once more.

My jaw pulsed as I shook my head.

"Of course you haven't." Killian raised a hand in apology, realizing the implication too late. "There's a beautiful mural of a tree painted in his chambers. I think it's meant to be an Elder birch. He commissioned it the year before Damien was born. He said he wanted a way to track his lineage, since his blood would reign for ages to come." Killian scoffed and rubbed his neck. The skin along his forearm was stained with indigo ink. "My mother's portrait was painted alongside his, opposite his first wife. When I was eight, my portrait was added beneath theirs. I remember being so excited when he showed it to me; my father had never let me enter his chambers before that day. He'd wanted me to look at my portrait, but all I saw was the scorch mark where he had ordered the servants to burn the paint from the wall."

"He burned her portrait?" My chest tightened for the young boy who had come into the world as his mother left it.

Killian pressed his face against his fist. "He did much more than that. I should have realized you may not have known her name when you heard it. My father had it inked from every record in the kingdom, burned every portrait commissioned—he tried to erase their marriage and her existence from everything but my mind."

"You remember her?" I hoped Killian didn't take the question as a challenge.

Killian shook his head. "No, I don't remember her. But my nursemaid saved a few of her things. She was too scared to ever tell me my mother's name, but she made sure I knew I'd had a mother." Killian exhaled and stared forlorn out the window. The moonlight had turned the gold peaks of the Burning Mountains silver.

"That must have been a difficult thing to carry as a child," I said, turning back to him. "It must be a difficult thing to carry as a man."

Killian cleared his throat, the tendon in his neck flexed. "Yes, it was. It still is." His eyes settled on me, sharp and focused. "Which is why I should've known it is hard for you."

My throat tightened. I crossed my arms over my body, as if that would make Killian see less of me. "I put those questions to rest long ago."

"That may be. But I've found the loneliness is much harder to bury." Killian didn't turn away from me, even when my breath stopped and my body hardened. I became a boulder on that soft mattress, the rock I needed to seal the tomb I'd buried my loneliness in.

Killian pulled the chair to the edge of the bed. His hand hovered over my knee, asking for permission before he placed it there this time. I didn't move to stop him, but I didn't know if that meant I wanted to feel the gentleness of his touch. It was difficult to be hard and rigid while being held by softness.

Killian stroked my knee with a swipe of his thumb. "You can be lonely here, Keera. We won't let it bury you if you decide to put down your shovel."

Something in me cracked, not completely in two, but enough that the hollow ache in my chest didn't fill my lungs with worry until I could no longer breathe. *We.* The friends I had found to replace the family that had left me behind.

"What if they didn't want me?" I whispered so quietly I could pretend the words weren't my own. "What if that's the reason they left me there and never came back for me."

Killian shook his head, his eyes swimming with determination. "It's not."

I sucked in a breath and ignored the stinging along my eyes. "You don't know that. No one does."

"Yes, I do." Killian cupped my hands in his. "I know *you*, Keera. That's enough to know your parents didn't leave you willingly." Killian looked down at where our hands lay entangled on my lap. He lurched back and dropped his hold of me. My skin missed the warmth of his touch.

"Is it wrong that part of me wishes they're truly dead?" The question clanged through the room like a coin at the bottom of an empty well. The truth of my words reverberated around us, pulling the prince and me into a chasm of our own. Not that it mattered—an empty well granted no wishes, nothing could. But I would have to live with the truth that some part of me would prefer the Light Fae gone, would prefer the Elverin—the Halflings—to take on the crown without the help of their magic or their numbers so I did not have to face the truth of how they could leave me behind.

"No." Killian stood, his black cloak trailing along the grain of the floor. "We are not the sum of our desires and hopes, Keera, even the selfish ones. We are defined by what we do about them, or in spite of them. And you have always made the choice that you felt was *right*, not the one you wished for."

His words sat heavy in my gut, hard truths I would carry with me into sleep. But I could leave that choice until we knew where the Light Fae were. Killian nodded goodbye and walked toward the door. My chest tightened as I realized I would spend the night alone.

"Killian," I called, stopping him in the doorway.

He turned with a soft smile on his face, half covered in shadow. "Yes?"

I asked the question before I had time to think myself out of it. "Where is Riven?" My words were too rushed to be filled with anger.

Killian's smile fell and his body hardened slowly, like magic was creeping up his legs, along his spine, and down his arms, turning his bones to marble. He was a statue of himself without any of the warmth he'd just shown me. "I will ask him to return."

And then he was gone.

CHAPTER TEN

THE SUNS HAD NOT RISEN when I jumped from the Myram tree. Thankfully, no one else in Myrelinth had either. I landed with a soft bounce and headed north. The map of Elverath was tucked into the pocket of my vest, but I didn't need it. I'd memorized every portal and knew that the one I needed was just north of the city.

My quiver was stowed along my back with my bow. I walked silently through the northern groves of the city, gathered a few fae-lights to follow me, and stepped into the Dark Wood. It was like one of the underground tunnels of Myrelinth. The forest was so thick, only the next few steps of the path were visible in the dim lights that followed me. But the path did not smell of wet earth or wood; instead the air was packed with the scent of blooms I could not see. Sweet nectar enveloped my senses, growing stronger with each step until I felt like a bee searching for its next drink of honey.

The tunnel of brush opened wide. The faelights hovered along the canopy of branches that bent in unnatural places, their large leaves of burnt sapphire and amethyst fluttered in a stale breeze. I motioned a faelight to the trees first, looking for a hint of deception in their roots, but I found none.

I wouldn't find the glamour by examination alone.

I unlatched my bow from its holster and nocked an arrow. I let it fly north, hoping it would disappear through the glamour, like our horses had in the Singing Wood. It embedded itself in a concave branch. I walked over to retrieve it and something scuffled against the forest floor behind me.

I whipped the arrow out of the wood and spun around on my knee.

"Don't shoot!" Nikolai yelled, holding up his hands. They held two leaves folded around something that smelled warm and buttery. I put down my weapon and Nikolai tossed me a leaf. Inside was a fresh pastry, still warm from the oven.

I swallowed hungrily.

Nikolai took a bite of his breakfast and nodded to the bow. "What exactly were you trying to do with that?"

I picked a piece of crust from my pastry, too embarrassed by my failed plan to meet his gaze. "Shatter the glamour."

Nikolai shook his head. "And if you accidentally shot someone on the other side of it?"

"It's barely dawn. I didn't think anyone would be up at this hour. Least of all you."

He lifted his arms to stretch and yawned loud enough that something moved overhead. Nikolai gave me a wicked grin. "I never went to bed, Keera dear."

The rumpled state of his clothes became apparent then. The same cream tunic and velvet green trousers he'd been wearing the day before. I rolled my eyes. "Who had the displeasure of your company?"

"I didn't hear any complaints from Lash, though I can't say it'll be the same for you." Nikolai gave me a pointed look. I'd skipped out on kitchen duty.

I mimed vomiting onto the ground. "That's all I'll be able to think about peeling those potatoes."

"I didn't realize you were so keen to think of me in bed." Nikolai tugged playfully on my braid.

I shoved him with my hip. "Show me the portal."

Nikolai yawned again and walked to the west side of the clearing. His hand hovered over a thick tree trunk for a moment, but when he reached further, nothing touched his skin. The glamour erupted, like a ball of snow making impact, the pieces of the broken illusion fell to the ground to reveal two trees. They sprouted from the same spot in the ground, their trunks curving away from each other until their branches came together at the top forming a perfect circle.

The forest was thick and dark, yet between their trunks was the garden of Aralinth. Held in an eternal spring, thousands of flowers were just beginning to bloom under the morning light of the first sun. The view of the vibrant garden was faded through the trees, like a thin veil hung between where we stood and the city we could see.

Nikolai opened his satchel and plucked two tiny flowers from his bag. They were dry and flattened, but too pristine for it to have been on accident. "This portal likes blooms the most," Nikolai explained as he placed the two flowers in a small pool of water at the base of one of the trees. The moment they touched the surface, the flowers opened into marvelous layers of azure. The petals swirled in the pool, surrounded by streaks of gold.

The sound of flowing water filled the clearing and each of the unnatural bends now held a small pool of water carrying its own bloom. The scent in the air changed, still floral, but with the added fruity aroma of Nikolai's offering.

He held out his arm and bowed his head like one of the gentlemen from court. "It's enough for us both to pass."

I stepped through the portal, my body caught for a moment in sun and shadow, existing in two places at once. Nikolai chuckled beside me. "Don't stay like that too long; you'll get lightheaded."

I snapped my other leg out of the portal and followed Nikolai down the well-worn path into the ancient city of spring. The giant Elder birch of Aralinth towered over us, its gold leaves casting auric beams onto the city below. Stone walls marked off the garden, not laid by a stonemason, but solid sheets of rock pulled from the ground by the Fae from long ago. Dew roses every shade of blue covered the walls with their blooms and thorns.

More Elder birch stood watch along the edges of the garden, though they were tiny in comparison to the ancient tree in the center of the city. Nikolai waved to someone in the distance. My head snapped forward. A pair of Elverin sat at a bench admiring the blooms. I recognized them both immediately.

My eyes fell on Dynara first. Her long brown hair streamed down her back in rolling waves. Her features were sharp, all but her long ears that curved at the end. She was the Halfling who helped me fool Riven's scouts when I was hunting the Shadow. The escaped courtesan who believed that I could bring the salvation she'd found to all the Halflings still left in the king's clutches.

The taller was Feron, the most ancient of the Fae, having lived near ten thousand years, though his face was of a man in his prime. His black skin glowed with the reflected light from the Elder birch above. His coarse hair hung in long twists, tied back at the nape of his neck. He wore a peach robe that was so long it sat in a pile covering his feet. No weapon hung from his hip; he didn't need one. Fae magic had faded considerably, but even dimmed, Feron's powers were a force to be reckoned with.

That was exactly what I was counting on.

Feron's smile was wide, deep dimples appearing beside his lips. "Keera, welcome back." His words were kind and slow, a trait common among the older Elverin. They had never been without the luxury of time.

"Pleasure to see you again," Dynara said with a light laugh. It fluttered across the garden like one of the songbirds nearby.

I pulled her into my arms. She squeezed me back, understanding the thank-you hidden within the embrace. "What brings you to Aralinth?" she asked, raising a brow at me and then Nikolai.

"You know I want to kill the king." There was a dangerous edge to my words. "I am here to further that mission." I looked to Feron, his smile turned to a soft line across his face.

"How can I be of service?" he asked, knowing my purpose. I wondered if he had used his magic to pluck that thought from my mind. I didn't sense any touch of his power, but my experience with Fae magic was limited. Riven's felt like an electric current pulsing through my skin, filling my body with a warmth and vitality that was beyond anything natural.

Perhaps Feron's felt different.

My chest tightened at the memories of Riven. I pushed them from my mind. I had made my decision. Now it was time I saw it through.

"Killian and Vrail have reason to suspect the Light Fae are still alive." Dynara's brows stitched themselves together. She turned to Feron, but he was an unmoving statue waiting for me to present my request. "If the Light Fae still walk among us then we must try to find them. Each Fae is worth fifty non-wielders on the battlefield and their healers could save hundreds of Elverin in the battles to come."

Feron's chest stopped mid-breath. I rooted my feet to the ground, preparing for him to refuse to help us. I wouldn't leave until I got what I needed from him.

"I know nothing that would help in your search," Feron said, his voice perfectly even like he was weighing the cost of every word. "I believed the Light Fae to be dead."

"But not anymore?" I asked.

Feron shook his head, his face turned dark like a cloud drifting over the sun. "I will admit the night you dined at Sil'abar was the first night I allowed myself to hope that the Light Fae may not be lost forever."

"My eyes?" Feron had remarked on them over dinner that night.

He nodded. "Riven told me of the Blade with eyes of silver, but when I saw them myself it was as if centuries of time melted away. I was able to see the faces of friends I had not seen in a very long time." Feron's brow creased. "I doubt any of those memories will help you find them."

If the Light Fae had truly been hiding from Aemon all this time, then I might be the only one who could find them. I steeled myself by taking a deep breath. "I didn't come here for your memories. I came here to retrieve mine."

Feron assessed me. I didn't know what he was looking for, but I felt like I was back in the Order standing for a test I didn't know how to take, let alone pass. Feron's gaze trailed over me once more before he nodded. Whatever Feron had seen, he seemed satisfied.

"There is no guarantee my gift will uncover your lost memories. And if it can, the process will be painful and extremely uncomfortable for you." He eyed the small pouch that hung underneath my vest. I froze. Did Feron know what I kept inside it? "You will have to face your past. All of it."

I stood tall. "I can handle it."

"I will be privy to every part we uncover." It was a statement of fact. There was no avoiding Feron's entry into my mind. I swallowed, wondering what he would see as we journeyed through the last six decades together.

I nodded. Feron had lived a hundred lifetimes. Whatever I thought of my past, I knew he had faced crueler monsters than me.

"Then we will start tomorrow." Feron nodded to Nikolai. "Make sure she eats well today. You will also need a long night's rest, Keera. The process is always more taxing than one thinks."

Feron nodded and returned his attention to the blooms. He stayed seated on the bench while Dynara walked us down the path. She pulled a dew rose from the drape of her sleeve and tucked it into my braid. I tilted my head so I could see the flower better. "A thank-you for Silstra," Dynara said in her deep voice, "and for the justice I know you'll serve."

Our eyes locked, both full of understanding. After years of service to the king as a courtesan, she wanted him dead just as much as I did. The last time I saw her, she had asked for it to be a painful one. I caressed the damp petals with my thumb.

Aemon's death would be long and bloody.

"I am told that the Halflings will be arriving soon. You can expect word from Tarvelle any day now," Nikolai said. There was something odd about the way he spoke. His tone was unusually formal and his back was straighter than I'd ever seen it.

"I'll make the necessary preparations." Dynara noticed my confusion. "I help run the refuge here for Halflings returning home."

Warm waves of gratitude pulsed through me. The Halflings would need someone who understood them to help with the transition; I couldn't think of anyone better than Dynara. "I have told my connections to start sending their refugees north to Cereliath and Caerth."

Dynara nodded. "We heard whispers of a change of direction along the Rose Road. We connected with a woman in Silstra to help us move them out of the kingdom for good."

I blinked. "Victoria?" My stomach knotted with guilt. Her safe houses had surely been impacted by the release of the dam. I hoped that little Halfling babe she had the last time I saw her was able to cross before the war came to a head. The kingdom was already so harsh to Halfling children, and the chaos of rebellion would not help.

Nikolai pointed to the first sun emerging over the lowest peaks of the mountains "The others will be wondering where we are." He turned to Dynara. "We will take our leave," he said with a small bow.

I raised a brow but held my tongue until we had reached the portal. On this side, it was twin Elder birches twisted together.

"So you and Dynara . . ." It was the only explanation for his odd behavior.

Nikolai looked stricken. "Absolutely not."

I raised my hands. "You just seemed so *cordial*. You didn't wink at her once."

Nikolai dropped two dew roses into the pond at the base of the trees. They swirled in golden light across the surface and we stepped through, back in the Dark Wood once more. "Did Dynara tell you how she escaped?" Nikolai's voice lacked any of its usual levity.

"She stole the purse of a sleeping lord she was meant to entertain while stationed at Lord Curringham's and used it to buy passage to Caerth. From there, she journeyed to Aralinth on foot." My chest ached at the bravery that must have taken. The Burning Wood was full of creatures that did not roam within the kingdom, and some were not friendly to Halflings, no matter how desperate the Halfling was.

Nikolai's brow furrowed. "That's all she said?"

"More or less." I flicked a faelight down the path ahead of us. "I am well aware of what the king makes his courtesans endure. To survive that and get herself here, Dynara is stronger than most."

"She almost didn't." Nikolai stopped along the path, ignoring the faelight that bounced against his ear. "I was part of the group that found her. Half dead, only a few hundred feet from the end of the wood." Nikolai took a deep breath; his eyes looked sunken, haunted. "She'd been beaten, Keera. To the edge of her life, the night she left Cereliath. How she made it to Aralinth is a gift from the Elder tree herself. Both her arms were broken and her wrist. The only reason no one came searching for her was because they believed her to be dead."

My chest cracked. Dynara had mentioned that Damien had been there that night. My hands turned to fists at the realization. He had done that to her, just like he had to so many others before her. My heart fluttered in a familiar panic for Gwyn, my chambermaid who lives in the king's palace. Damien's proclivities had never turned as extreme with her, but each day she spent tethered to that palace, the risk on her life grew.

I squeezed Nikolai's hand. "I didn't know."

Nik wiped his eye with the palm of his hand. "I know I am a flirt. I enjoy it. But that day . . ." Nikolai took a deep breath. "I had never seen such unnecessary violence. *Ikwenira* are meant to be revered . . . treating her like that is a heinous act beyond all measure." His words were coated in something beyond disgust.

"It was a long time before Dynara could be in the presence of anyone. She hides it well but there are days she still finds it difficult to share space with anyone who reminds her of the men she fled from. She is strong, but I make sure I give her no reason to fear me or my intentions. My only wish for her is that she's never uncomfortable again, and certainly not around me." Nikolai started back down the path.

I took his arm in mine. "You're a great friend, Nik. To me and to Dynara."

"Exceptional, really."

I jabbed his side with my elbow. "Don't push it."

Nikolai spent the rest of our walk back to Myrelinth showing me hidden paths along the trail. Tunnels of branches cast in pitch-black that the Elverin used to gather medicines and food from the land. We took one, following it around the perimeter of the city toward the lake. It was well past the time I usually trained, but I suspected Syrra would be there waiting.

She was standing in the field, arms tucked behind her back in her usual relaxed stance. Beside her was Killian, wearing a cream tunic and garnet leather vest that looked too elegant to fight in. I would have said as much if it weren't for the tall Fae standing next to him.

Nikolai was too preoccupied waving at the group to notice what my rage had set into motion. I pulled my bow free in one smooth movement, my arm already reaching back for an arrow. Killian turned to face us, his jaw falling as he watched me load my weapon.

Nikolai turned, reaching out to grab me, but I'd already stepped out of his reach. I nocked an arrow and aimed it at Riven's head. His violet gaze locked on me with magnetic focus. I took a deep breath, ignoring the scent of birchwood and dew that filled the air, and let my arrow fly.

CHAPTER ELEVEN

Riven snatched the arrow out of the air. His arm moved so fast I could barely see it until it froze just beside his head, clutching the bolt. Nikolai and Syrra chuckled; hers was amused while his was nervous. Killian only blinked at Riven and then at me.

"Leave," I told the others.

Riven didn't move. His arm still hovered in the air as he tracked me across the equipment room like a predator. I dropped my weapons belt and quiver on the ground. When I turned around, no one had moved an inch.

"I'm not sure you should be alone together," Nikolai mumbled, tucking his body behind Syrra. She just shrugged and walked into the tunnel without a word.

I grabbed two fighting spears that hung on the wall and threw the shorter one at Riven. Killian ducked as Riven grabbed the pole with a straight arm protruding from his chest. His grip was tight enough I could see his knuckles bulge along the wood.

Killian stood tall beside Nikolai, now leaning against a pile of mats, tugging on his hair. I gritted my teeth and turned to Riven. "Tell them to leave. Unless you want me to hurt your best friend and your *brother.*" I made sure to coat that last word with all the rage that had festered in the past week. Killian scratched his head but didn't dare say anything.

Riven's jaw pulsed. He lowered his spear to stand beside him before addressing the others. "Leave us."

Nikolai leaned forward, whispering to Riven. "Maybe you should wait until you've both had a chance to calm down." He glanced at Riven's feet where dark shadows were beginning to swirl around his legs.

Nikolai was lucky Riven didn't use his weapon on him with the look he shot the Elf. Killian placed his hand on Nikolai's shoulder and walked him toward the tunnel. He met my gaze for a long moment before disappearing into the earth below.

"Keera." Riven's hand gripped the spear so tightly the wood groaned under his touch. "I won't fight you." The shadows at his feet flared and then receded back toward his legs. He kept them in a tight circle around his body as he stepped closer to me.

I whipped my spear at Riven's face. He blocked it easily with his own. "You will," I said, this time jabbing the pointed end at him.

Riven blocked that too. "We need to talk."

I pulled my lip over my fangs. "I'm aware of that, Riven. Just as I'm aware that if you try to explain yourself while I'm sitting still, one of us is going to end up with a blade in their gut. Maybe both."

I swung again. Another block from Riven.

He widened the space between him and me, pulling us both into the field. The grass was still damp with dew under my feet. Riven finally held up his spear, though we were too far apart for either of us to land a blow.

Riven stepped sideways to the left. "Start."

I mimicked his movement. We were circling each other like wild cats waiting to attack. "Where have you been for the past week?"

"Many places."

I lunged toward him but he stepped out of the path of my spear. "If you didn't come with answers, I have no interest in talking." My chest heaved; the rage had built up so much my entire body felt tight. Sparring with him only released enough that I didn't implode and take us both down in the rubble.

"I've mostly been in the kingdom," Riven answered. The tendons in his neck were as hard as his stare. "Checking safe houses and supply levels."

I scoffed. "Do you always task yourself with something any of your rebels could do?"

Riven shifted the pole to his other hand. I took the opportunity to slap mine against his back. He hissed from the sting but didn't lunge at me.

Coward.

"I needed to keep myself busy while I—"

I turned on the ball of my foot, lowering myself to the ground as I grazed Riven's boot with the blunt edge of my spear. He stumbled forward, his jaw completely stiff. "Stayed away?" I finished for him.

Riven pivoted. I prepared myself to block but no strike came, he only changed directions.

"What do you want me to say, Keera?" Riven's words were liquid flame. "That I stayed away for a reason that would please you? We both know there isn't one that will satisfy you."

I grazed the tip of my fangs with my tongue. "Then tell me the reason that was good enough to please *you*?"

Riven changed direction again. This time a wave of shadow blew through the grass and toward the lake. A flock of birds scattered into the sky as Riven flexed the hand that had shot the magic. "I needed to stay away for a while. I needed time to think, and you needed time to adjust."

I twirled through the air, slashing my spear in one rapid strike. I caught the tail of Riven's cloak, slicing it clean. "Am I supposed to thank you for making decisions on my behalf rather than consulting me?"

Riven closed his eyes and took a deep breath. The shadows crawled further up his leg. "It wasn't like that."

I lunged again, this time landing a hit with the back end of my spear against Riven's chest. Hard enough that most men would be on the ground, but Riven barely flinched against the impact. "It is *exactly* like that." My breaths were ragged between each word as I circled him again. "You just can't see it. You've grown used to it, haven't you?"

Riven paused midstep. "Used to what?"

I whipped the spear around my head and down to the ground where he stood. Riven rolled out of the way and widened the distance between us once again. "To that crown upon your head."

A cold disdain covered Riven's face. It was violent and dangerous, just like the words he spat at me. "I wear no crown."

I smirked. "Don't you, though?" Riven bared his fangs, but that didn't stop me. "Killian is your half brother, born with his crown upon his head. He wears it well, masquerading as a good and loyal second son. How long did it take for you to realize you could use his crown to your advantage?" I held out my arm and pointed the sharp end of my spear at Riven. He breathed deeply enough to cast a fog along the blade. "You use it just as he does—his crown of gold and your crown of shadow."

Riven closed the distance between us in two strides. He was so close I could feel the heat radiating from him with each rise of his chest. "If you take issue with my connection to Killian or my connection to the crown, I can assure you I didn't choose either."

I stepped even closer. The electric current that always pulsed between us filled the air until I was sure something was going to catch fire. "I take issue with you not telling me that you had allied with the prince. That you are his *brother*."

"You knew there were secrets I did not share with you. Ones that I *couldn't*."

I jabbed his toe with the end of my spear. "You're going to justify this with *need to know*? Are you a child?"

Riven narrowed his eyes. "If I recall, *need to know* was your idea."

I lifted my arm to strike once more, but Riven caught my wrist and kept it suspended above my head. "To tell you was to risk our most vital alliance. I won't apologize for keeping it from you, Keera, when my people would be the ones to carry the risk. No matter what I feel for you, they *must* come first."

I hated the way my heart pulled at his words. Riven's feelings for me were not of consequence, only his actions.

"What risk did I pose to your people in that cave?" I yelled even though I could see the glean on his lips, almost taste the sweat on his skin. "You could have told me then, but instead you abandoned me and let me face the Elverin alone."

Riven's mouth twitched and his grip on my arm loosened. "I thought it would be better if you met the Elverin without my shadow hanging over you."

I clenched my jaw. "And you thought it best to make that choice *for* me."

Riven bowed his head. His mouth hovered just above mine; that current pulled at my chest, urging me closer to him. Riven's jaw pulsed like he could feel it too. "There were so many times I wanted to tell you." His voice was only a hoarse whisper. "So many nights I wished you would discover the truth so it didn't cover us in its shadow." Riven still held my arm but lowered it to our sides. "But that shadow was cast by a shield, Keera. Who knows if you would've been safe if I'd told you sooner. Or if the Elverin would have been."

I thrust myself out of his hold and stepped back. "The truth was not a shield; it was a wall between us. One only you could see yet refused to tear down."

Riven's shoulders fell in defeat. "The wall has been torn either way."

"And with it any trust I had in you."

Riven's shadows exploded behind him, lashing out in every direction except where I stood. He pinched the bridge of his nose and took a deep breath. They receded once more, though the black circle around him had grown.

"I am so sorry, Keera. The last thing I wanted was to hurt you." Riven dropped his spear and grabbed my shoulders. "I never expected *you*. You were a complete and utter surprise that I'd never thought to hope for and had no idea how to handle. Even now, seeing you, touching you"—his fingers grazed my cheek so softly it could have been the wind—"you're unfathomable to me still."

I let go of my weapon and wrapped my arms around myself. To keep from reaching out for him, but also to shield me from the sting of how his words pained me, yet were somehow what I wanted to hear.

Riven looked down where his shadows were swirling around both our feet. "I'm sorry that I can't change the decisions I made, but I swear I will build your faith in me again."

"You made a fool of me." I took a ragged breath. "I understand why you didn't tell me before that last night. I don't hold it against you—just as I wouldn't have held it against you had you told me the truth in that cave. But you kept me in the dark, while the entirety of the Elverin, everyone I was supposedly allied with, knew the truth. While you *commanded* them to keep it from me."

Riven bit his lip and nodded. "I did."

It bothered me how easily two words could make my lip tremble. "You didn't trust me."

Riven shook his head. "I didn't trust *myself*." I scoffed but let Riven continue. "I thought you'd be angry, much angrier than you are. I already knew what the Elverin were whispering about—that your interest in me was a ruse to gain access to the *Faelinth* to secure Aemon's favor. That our union would be the curse that lost us the war."

All the heat drained from my face. I knew accusations had spread after the incident in the Singing Wood, but I didn't realize they had begun well before we'd arrived.

Riven's neck flexed as he gripped my shoulders once more. "Leading does not come easy to me. I often doubt every decision I make, but after what happened in Caerth . . ." Riven's brows knitted together as he sucked in a breath through clenched teeth, remembering how his lack of leadership had cost two Shades their lives, one of which he had taken. "Everything after that felt like one misstep after another, I couldn't find my footing. Everything except you, and then I failed in that too. I thought you would fare better winning over the Elverin without me by your side and I truly believed Killian revealing himself publicly would help ease the rumors. I thought it would help you gain favor here more quickly."

I tilted my head to the side. "You were trying to protect me from whispers and lies?"

Riven nodded, his violet eyes were desperate, but I could see the earnestness in them too.

My rage bubbled up my throat and released as a fit of laughter. "That is the most ridiculous thing I've ever heard."

"I would do anything to take that choice back." Riven's shoulders fell.

I dropped to the ground and picked up my spear. "But you can't. A wound can't be undone, Riven, only healed."

He dropped to his knee to grab his own weapon but stayed there looking up at me. "How do I heal this?" His words were rough, like a plea that had fought through his chest to be spoken.

Part of me wanted to turn away. That wasn't a question I needed to answer. I wasn't sure I even could answer it. But as I looked down at Riven, pleading on the ground, I couldn't deny there was part of me that wanted to heal this too.

"Are there any more secrets you need to tell me?"

Riven flinched at my question. His brows creased as his shoulders fell and he shook his head. "Everything our people know, you know too."

I stamped the blunt end of the spear into the ground. "And what of the things your people don't know?"

Riven's eyes flashed, the storm behind them raging once more. Or perhaps it had never stopped. "There are things I can't tell them. Secrets I keep to ensure my people are safe or at least as safe as they can be while I bring war to their groves. You kept secrets to protect the Shades; I assume you keep them still." He raised a brow at me.

I drummed the pads of my fingers against the spear. He was right. There were things that I wouldn't share, especially with a mole in our midst. My loose tongue would not be the reason another Shade died. I fought the urge to feel the ridges of Brenna's name on my forearm. There were still parts of me I was keeping to myself. It was not fair for me to keep those a secret while demanding complete transparency from Riven.

I turned back toward the storage racks. "I will not begrudge the choices you make leading the Elverin, past or present. But if a decision must be made in regards to *me* and no one else, then I expect to be the one making it."

I heard Riven stand. I saw his shadows on the ground, reaching for my ankles like the stretched arms of shadowed figures, before he stepped in front of me. "I will not undermine you again."

"Good." I nodded. "There is still one more justice that needs to be corrected."

Riven's brow raised. "Say the word and I will do it."

I punched him square in the jaw. Riven reeled back three paces, rubbing his face in surprise. His focus snapped back to me, filled with shock and hunger.

I shrugged, causally placing the spear back on its rest. "Fair is fair. I punched Killian in the face for his lie. Some could argue you've gotten off easy." I smiled at him over my shoulder as I disappeared into the tunnel and left him in the training room. "Wouldn't want the Elverin to think I'm performing some kind of *ruse*."

CHAPTER TWELVE

THE NEXT MORNING I was cutting vegetables for a stew when Riven appeared in the kitchens. The other Elverin on kitchen duty swarmed him like wasps, stinging him with their kisses and buzzing with laughter. Unfortunately his popularity with the Elverin had not rubbed off on me. I made a point to ignore them until Riven came to stand beside me. I sighed and looked up at him, but Riven was watching the knife in my hand.

"Feron has arrived." His voice was hoarse and blunt. His hand rested on the hilt of a small blade that peered out from under his cloak, but I knew it was out of habit rather than warning. Even though my faith in Riven had been shaken, I trusted he would never hurt me. At least not with a blade.

I nodded and stood.

"You have three more bowls to cut," Lash shouted in Elvish, eyeing the chunks of dew root by my seat. Some still had slivers of the thick turquoise rind left on them. I slumped back into my chair and cut the vegetables. Riven slipped a paring knife from his boot and started at the pile himself. Lash shook his head but didn't say anything else.

Twenty minutes later, I plopped the last bowl on the counter in front of Lash and plucked a pastry from the sheet he had just pulled from the hearth. He swatted at my hand with his spoon but I retracted it too fast for him to land a hit. I made a show of taking a big bite. Lash rolled his eyes and set another tray to bake in the hearth, though some of the others chuckled.

"You've been making friends," Riven said with an amused smile.

I folded the light dough in half, encasing the rose cream inside, and took a bite. "More accurate to say I haven't made any enemies."

"Yet," Riven mumbled. I ignored his joke and let him lead the way to Feron.

We walked through the northwest tunnels until we came upon a pair of large stone doors. Each were circles placed on a groove along the ground. Riven pulled one open and its sister moved back too. I stepped inside and blinked at the rows and rows of books that filled the giant room. Each aisle was marked by a ball of flame just like the ones that surrounded the Myram tree. The air held no dampness here, and with so many faelights hovering along the ceiling, it felt like we were outside instead of seven stories underground.

Feron was seated at a small desk next to a long chaise. He wore a short robe the color of the sea at dawn that complemented the soft purple of his eyes. He stood, nodding to me, and took a slow uneven step toward us.

I paused. The Feron I'd met in Aralinth was an ancient Fae unmarked by time. He had toured me around his ballroom while he greeted guests, unaided, for hours. Now, he stood in front of me the same but different. He used an elegant cane carved from birchwood to hold his weight as he walked. Both of his legs were wrapped in leather bands around the calf, the back of them made of stained wood to support his stance. He favored his left leg to carry his weight; his right calf was much thinner and stepped in tune with his cane.

"How?" I asked. There was a casualness between him and Riven, making it obvious that this was not some new predicament for the Fae. Yet it was impossible I hadn't noticed before.

Feron's eyes narrowed slightly but his smile remained. "I wondered if you would see more clearly now." He pulled a large ring from his hand and placed it in my palm.

"A glamour?" I looked to Riven and back to Feron. "But Riven didn't say anything. No one did. How did it break?"

Feron studied the ring in my hand. It was thick and cast in gold with a large green gemstone in the center. He had worn it the night I'd met him at the ball.

"It is not like the other glamours you have seen and as such cannot be broken in the same way." Feron slipped the ring onto his finger. "This ring was a gift from a Fae who has long since passed. She gave it to me when the first Mortals started roaming our shores. She knew an enemy was coming and we needed to protect as much truth from him as we could. The glamour is made to mask anything another would use against the wearer. I apologize for the ruse, Keera, but I could not risk Aemon knowing. I have heard too much of the way Aemon values some bodies over others—I did not want to tempt him to attack the *Faelinth* out of hubris and his perceived weakness of me."

My mouth hung open. What did that say about me, to know that I had not seen through the magic that first night we met? "But I would never—"

Feron gripped my hand and squeezed it. "Do not worry, child. Aemon only values those who help him produce *winvra* and retain his power and wealth. Almost everyone who is raised under his rule does not see the truth at first. It takes time to leech a poison so strong." He patted my arm and pointed to the chaise. "Enough about me. We should begin."

I shivered in my seat at those words. I had steeled myself to do what was needed to help win this war but that did not mean I liked the idea of Feron toying with my mind. I leaned back on the chaise. I didn't know what he would find, what he would see.

Feron sat on a chair beside me, holding the ball of his cane in one hand. "It is best if we start slowly. For the first session I only hope to—"

"Read my mind," I finished in a nervous breath.

Feron chuckled softly. "In a sense, every mind is different. Thoughts and memory are like water in a stream—they can be hard to catch, hard to understand. Sometimes the water veers off into stagnant pools or freezes into ice. Such memories can be painful to explore. For you, it will feel like you are back in that very moment. You may even forget what is truly happening, that you are here in this room and not lost in the past."

My fingers tightened around the edge of the sofa. "Will you see the memories too?" I swallowed the fear rising from my chest.

Feron tilted his head back and forth. "Sometimes I see images; they are often blurry like the moment is covered in a haze." He placed his other hand on top of the one holding his cane. "But I will *feel* the memory with you. However your body responds, I will feel it too. Your pain, your joy, your fear."

"Are you sure you want to do that?" There had been several days where I had yearned for death rather than feel the pain anymore. To burden someone else with that, even for a moment, was almost too much to ask. "I don't remember anything from before I was brought to the Order. There might be nothing but pain to find."

Feron bowed his head. "If you are willing to relive it, then I will share whatever pain may come."

Feron glanced at Riven pacing along the back wall. He stopped, feeling our gazes on him. Riven looked only at me. "You don't need to do this."

My heart twinged. Riven's worry was painted onto his face, layers of protective caution and apprehension were cast under the hard set of his jaw and dark brow. I didn't have any more space for worry. I laid back on the chaise and let Riven carry his along with mine.

I looked up at Feron and nodded. "I'm ready."

Feron stood and placed his chair directly behind me. "I do not want you to focus on anything in particular," Feron said in a low, soft drawl. "Familiarize yourself with the sensation. Let your body relax into itself until all you can see is blackness."

My mouth turned dry. I closed my eyes and felt Feron's gentle fingers touch my forehead. He rubbed small circles across my brow and hairline and I felt the warmth of his magic trickle down my body like rain running down the branch of a tree. My leg twitched.

"Focus on your breathing," Feron directed in a whisper.

Something warm crept up my legs, spiraling around them like the golden light that surrounded me as I crossed through the portal in the lake. My eyes were closed, yet I knew similar ribbons of light were swirling around my legs and now my arms. Each hair on my body reacted to the touch of Feron's magic, raising in its warmth and leaving my skin raw and sensitive.

Slowly, the warmth inched up my neck. My breath hitched. The magic was warm like a blanket of summer sun wrapping itself around me. I grabbed the fabric of the chaise in my hand and fought for the strength not to open my eyes.

"The more you fight it, the more uncomfortable the magic will feel." Feron's gentle voice sounded farther away than it had before.

"You are safe, Keera. The magic cannot take you anywhere you cannot return from."

I took a deep breath and imagined myself sinking into the chaise like a warm bath. The magic still circled around my throat, but I managed to keep calm. Under Feron's spell it was too hard to keep time, but eventually the warmth of his magic gave way to utter darkness.

I was surrounded by night. No, nothingness. The only sounds that existed were the sound of my breaths and racing heart. Panic flooded my body. I reached out, desperate to feel something around me, but there was nothing.

No shape took form in the blackness. No memory came forward.

I was completely alone in the dark.

I screamed for help, but I could no longer hear Feron or sense the library in Myrelinth where my body lay. I was trapped in unending blackness. Tears streamed down my face, old fear reawakening inside me as I ran forward toward nothing at all.

As a child I had been afraid of the dark. It took years before I was able to sleep unaccompanied by a lantern or candle. That old panic ripped at my chest, more powerful than any memory, until it hurt to breathe. Until my screams were so ragged, no noise left my throat any longer.

I scratched at my traitorous neck. I could see my hands and arms in front of me. They were uncovered and unmarked by scars. My fingers were small, as were my hands. I was a scared child once more, brought back into all I had known those first years of my life.

Brought back into the darkness.

I fell to my knees. I was not truly a child. I was grown and lying underground in a Fae city. I took one final deep breath, sucking in so much air I thought my lungs would burst, and then I screamed for the one person I thought could find me in shadow so thick.

Riven.

CHAPTER THIRTEEN

I CALLED OUT TO Riven again and heard something shifting in the darkness. A soft sound, like a breeze moving through linen, but in that expansive nothingness the sound was thunderous. Something I could search for, something outside of myself.

I followed the noise and it grew louder with each step, the whisper of wind shifting to a gust. Something touched my hand. The touch was warm yet different than Feron's magic. Feron's gift felt like sunlight falling on the skin; the new sensation burned from within me.

I looked down at my palm and saw strands of shadow flickering across the skin like black flame. It curved upward, licking my wrist and my arm. The shadows did not scare me. Somehow, I knew they were a different breed of darkness, one I need not fear.

I closed my hand around the shadow and felt them grasp me back.

"Keera!"

I heard Riven shout as I was pulled from the darkness and back into the library with him and Feron. I sprung up from the chaise, desperate to catch my breath, as Riven's shadows detangled themselves from my limbs and receded into the earth like creatures going to rest.

Riven kneeled beside me. A faint line of sweat marked his brow and his breathing was almost as heavy as mine. I tried to fill my lungs, but the taste of earth and stale air was poison on my tongue. Being underground felt too much like the chasm of darkness I had just fought my way from.

"Fresh air," I said in way of explanation before bolting from the room. I took short breaths, just enough to scent the fresh air in the tunnels to guide myself out of the underground city. I gripped the wall to keep me upright as I moved as fast as I could.

I could see a light at the end of the tunnel, blue sky marking the outdoors just ahead of me. I came aboveground along a beach, the lake rippling only a few feet from where I collapsed on the sand. I took a breath, thankful for the way my chest relaxed as it filled with fresh air.

I lay back on the sand, relaxing into it until I was fully anchored to the present instead of the past. My stomach churned with nausea. I didn't know if that was an effect of the fear or the magic, but I felt like I'd been thrown ashore by a raging gale.

The spinning began to slow and I sat up, hugging my knees. I spat on the ground next to me. "I know you're there."

Riven stepped out from the tunnel and onto the beach. He hovered beside me until I patted the sand and he sat too. "This will make you feel better." He handed me a goblet of what looked like water but smelled like honey and mint.

I slammed it back in one gulp, eager to have my stomach settle. A few moments later and I no longer felt like I was swaying on the ground. "What is that?" I asked, passing the goblet back to him.

"Cold tea made with dew root and a flower the Elverin call *miski-ithirin.*" Riven refilled the goblet with a small waterskin tucked under his cloak. He gave me another cupful. "It helps calm the body after an overexposure to magic."

I huffed a laugh. "Is that what this is?"

"Yes." Riven's jaw pulsed. "It's not usually this bad; you should have only been under the influence of Feron's magic."

"Your shadows." I remembered the way they had sunk into the ground when I broke free from the trance.

Riven nodded. "I'm sorry. That never should have happened." His face was hard with guilt as he twisted the waterskin between his knees.

I turned to look at him. "What do you mean? Your shadows are what pulled me out of there."

Riven's eyes widened. There was a storm raging behind them, a fight to stay afloat while the winds raged inside him. I wondered if Riven felt just as unstable as I did.

"My shadows *helped* you?" he asked in barely a whisper.

I nodded. "I felt Feron's magic lull me into the trance. At first everything was fine, but then the blackness came. The nothingness. I didn't realize what it would feel like, how I would react. I started to panic and I couldn't feel the tug of Feron's magic anymore so I called out for yours."

Riven was completely still beside me. He didn't even dare to breathe.

"I grabbed onto them and felt them tug. They pulled me out of there. *You* pulled me out of there."

Riven swallowed once. "They didn't hurt you?"

"Why would they hurt me?" I pushed my shoulder against Riven and a rough gasp came from his chest. It sounded like a wounded beast. I turned to see tears streaming down Riven's cheeks. He wiped them away with his hand, his jaw pulsing as he tried to steady his breath.

"I thought your screams . . ." Riven coughed and took another minute to compose himself once more. "Only two Fae have been born since the Light Fae vanished. I am the second. Our magic is not weakened like the others but *tainted.* Feron believes an imbalance in the magic caused my gift to fracture somehow, to end up taking more than it gives."

I placed my hand on Riven's knee. "What do you mean 'tainted'?"

Riven looked at me. I could see that same storm in his gaze, deciding whether or not to tell me the truth. "Only Nikolai, Syrra, and Feron know."

I swallowed and waited for Riven to decide if he trusted me enough to add my name to that list.

He leaned into me and took a deep breath before he spoke. "My magic is painful. No—my magic *is* pain. Sometimes it's manageable, but sometimes it grows too wild for me to tame and lashes out. When I'm in that state, I have no control. I have no control over who I hurt."

Riven tilted his head to inspect my face, ensuring that he had not missed a stray wound or scrape. "I didn't mean to call those shadows forward. It's gotten worse, I can't control them much anymore. And then they started circling around you and then you started screaming"—Riven's voice broke—"I thought . . . *I* was doing that to you."

My chest cracked open and I grabbed his hand. "I *promise* you, they did not hurt me."

Riven froze. He knew the meaning I put on that word, that I would never use it unless it was the truth. He squeezed my hand and exhaled in one deep breath.

I leaned into him and listened as his heartbeat settled. "Who is the other Fae? The other with wild magic."

Riven tossed the waterskin on the sand. "He died before I was born."

I didn't like the haunting edge to Riven's words. "How did he die?"

"His magic killed him."

My stomach recoiled like I had been pierced in the gut. Dozens of questions swirled in my mind, pressing on my tongue to be asked, but I didn't let them loose. I could see in the defeated way Riven sat beside me, he had no answers. Asking them wouldn't settle my curiosity or bring him any relief.

"I was not brought to the Order when they found me in the Rift." I wrapped my arms around my knees and tucked them under my chin. "Not at first."

Riven rested his forearms on his bent legs and turned to me. His jaw was hard but there was a longing in his face. I didn't know if it was for distraction from the pain or to have a conversation where I didn't hold a weapon to his throat. Either way, I would give him what he wanted.

"Mistress Carston was the head of the Order then. She held me in the cells under Koratha. Pits so far underground I forgot that the suns existed, with only enough food and water to survive."

Riven gritted his teeth. "How long did they see fit to imprison a girl of eight?"

"Five years." I twisted the toe of my boot into the sand. "Every few months they would take me out and run tests on me."

Riven looked like he wanted to vomit. "What kind of tests?"

"Sometimes they took my blood." I shrugged. "But mostly they were tests of endurance and strength. Mistress Carston was not convinced I was a Halfling when she found me. She spent years trying to prove herself right." I didn't swallow the venom in my throat. It was a happy day when Carston's arrogance cost her her life.

"There was someone else held down there with me." I turned to Riven. I had never told anyone this story. Whispering about it would have gotten me killed in the Order, and by the time I left, the habit had set. "I never saw her face. I could only hear her through the walls of our cells. I believe she was an Elf who had been there for a long time before I arrived. She didn't speak a word of the King's Tongue, and I barely spoke anything at all. She was the one who taught me Elvish."

"What happened to her?" Riven's fingers were squeezed together.

I looked up at the clouds covering the suns in large bands of white. "I believe she died in there. One day when Hildegard and Carston had taken me for their tests, a cave-in happened in the lower section of those cells. I don't see how she could have survived it, and I never learned of an Elf in custody when I became Blade."

"Did you know her name?" Riven asked. The Elverin lived a long time; in all likelihood one of her kin would know her still.

I shook my head. "That's part of why I think she had been down there a long time. When her stories made sense, they were more like riddles. Sometimes I would ask a question and she would answer it, but most times my queries were ignored or sparked a tangent I couldn't follow. By the time I was placed in those cells, she didn't remember her name at all."

We sat in silence for a long moment. A family of diving birds floated across the lake, completely unperturbed by the story I had just told. How long did it take for someone to forget their own name? I shivered at the thought of that.

Riven blinked and I watched the understanding settle on his face. "You're afraid of the dark?"

I leaned back on my elbows, suddenly too restless to stay in one position for too long. "I was for a long time, years in fact. I had nightmares of those cells for more than a decade when I was at the Order. Though after twenty-five years of training on that island, the fear had all but faded. Yet when Feron plunged me into that trance, all those fears came rushing back. I was a child again, lost in a nightmare I couldn't escape from. I was completely helpless."

A deep crease appeared between Riven's brows. "You do not need to try again."

I smiled through my sigh. "But I do." Riven opened his mouth to argue and I held up my hand. "This war is bigger than either of us. Can you honestly say you would let the pain of your magic keep you from doing everything you could to help free your people?"

Riven's jaw flexed. He shook his head.

"Then don't ask it of me." I turned my body to face Riven directly. "Finding the Light Fae wouldn't just help us win the war. Their healers could save countless lives. The Shades will be forced to fight against us, many will fall, but with the Light Fae healers, we could save some of them." I swallowed a thick gulp of air. "My fears do not outweigh the needs of the war, Riven. Nor your pain. We will be asked to endure both in the days to come."

I stood and reached my hand down to him. Riven's lips curved into a grin and he grabbed hold. I steered us down the beach. I was still too dazed to feel comfortable underground. Riven understood. "I can be at each session," he said, kicking a pebble into the water. "If you'll have me. It might make the process easier if you know you can call out to my shadows again."

My heart swelled in my chest. "I would like that."

Riven squeezed my hand, and for a moment I thought he was going to lace his fingers through mine as we walked, but after a second gentle squeeze, he dropped it. My stomach dropped a little too.

Riven halted a few hundred feet from the portal. The last place we could expect to not be overheard. "I told you it was my job to rebuild your trust." He reached into the pocket of his trousers.

"Riven you don't need to—"

He brushed his thumb along my lip to silence me. My pulse skipped at the shock of his touch, that familiar electric current pulsating from the tiniest place where our skin met. Riven looked down at me with a hunger in his eyes, the same hunger I felt in the pit of my stomach, waiting for him to move his hand to my neck.

He swiped his thumb once more. "Keera, let me do this." It wasn't a command or a question. His voice was suddenly hoarse, pleading that I let him speak before whatever resolve he had crumbled.

I nodded and his thumb grazed my neck. I stopped breathing.

He pulled out a piece of parchment. It was too small to be a letter. Moreso a scrap piece of paper with two words written in black ink.

Ashrynn
&
Paevral

I took the parchment. It shook in my hands as I reread the words. Not words, *names*.

I knew what they were as soon as my gaze touched the ink. My chest tightened as I closed my eyes to stave off the stinging. "They're in order?" I asked, barely capable of a whisper.

Riven nodded.

My heart cracked. I'd had never thought it worth the time to go searching for their names. It would've drawn too much attention for the Blade with a reputation of disinterest to suddenly ask for the names of the Shades who had died in Silstra. But Riven had thought them important enough.

He had found them for me. Given those girls their names back, at least in my memory. Ashrynn, the Shade who had come to rescue her partner, not realizing I was doing everything I could to save her. We had been given a choice between our mission and death, and fate had chosen me as victor.

I traced my fingers over Paevral's name, remembering the ghost of a smile left on her face after the explosion. They had both been too young to die, but the king had asked them for their lives anyway.

I leaned my forehead against Riven's shoulder. "Thank you."

He grasped my neck, pulling my face toward him. "Their deaths will be avenged. By your blade or mine."

He let go of me and I was grateful for it. Riven's touch warmed my body in too pleasing a way for what I was about to do. I pulled the small satchel from under my vest, and Riven left me on the beach to etch their names onto my list.

Each one a promise inked in blood. Aemon's reign would fall, and the Crown would tumble after him.

CHAPTER FOURTEEN

I WOKE EARLIER THAN usual and left for the training grounds while the moon was still bright and high over the grove. When I arrived, someone was already training in the field. Punching and kicking a stuffed target. I thought it was Syrra, but as I walked out of the tunnel, I realized the shadow figure was too short to be her.

Vrail launched a heavy kick to the side of the target. Her leg ricocheted off and she landed with a heavy thud in the grass.

I grabbed the pair of training gloves Syrra usually wore and walked out into the field. "You need to turn your body sideways. You'll make more impact and have better control that way."

Vrail's head snapped to me. Heat flushed across the tawny beige of her cheeks. "I didn't realize you were there. I thought you and Syrra trained after dawn."

I shrugged. "Nikolai said you want to learn how to fight."

Vrail bit her lip, but it wasn't enough to keep the rapid-fire words from falling out. "He shouldn't have said anything. I am well aware of how foolish it sounds."

"Why would you say that?" I tilted my head.

Vrail's leg shook before exploding into a frenzied explanation. "I spend the majority of my day surrounded by books and texts. Therefore, beyond the most basic defensive maneuvers, learning how to fight is not an effective allocation of my time or my ability. Besides, Syrra has made it clear that she has no interest in training me, most likely because I do not possess a suitable combination of physical traits for combat—"

I held up my hand to stop her. "Vrail, do you *want* to learn how to fight?"

She bit her lip and nodded vigorously. Her dark eyes stared up at me like a pup waiting to be fed.

"Then that is reason enough." I pulled her shoulders straight and assessed the proportion of her limbs to her frame. She was short for a Halfling, but I'd trained with shorter girls at the Order. Her thick legs were built for power, as were her strong arms. I guessed they had only grown stronger in her decades of ferrying piles of books. "You don't need certain physical traits to fight. The trick is to find a style that works *for* you and develop your skills from there."

I grabbed the padded gloves and began to wrap my wrists.

Her arms fell to her side. "You'll teach me?" Her eyes were wide with disbelief and a little fear.

"I'll make you a deal."

Vrail had to physically bite her knuckle to keep herself from spiraling into a barrage of questions.

I smirked. "I'll train you, and in exchange, you teach me Elvish history."

Vrail flung her fist toward the ground. "There's so much to learn. How far back do you want to start? Elvish history predates Fae and Mortal histories by thousands of years—that alone would take weeks to even scratch the surface, not to mention—"

I slapped my padded hands on her shoulders. "How about we go about it the same way as training. Start with the basics, and you can fill in the gaps as needed from there."

Vrail exhaled a deep breath and nodded. I could see her already mapping out lesson plans in her head. After a moment she halted mid-thought. "You're sure you want to do this?"

I nodded. "I'll need the exercise either way." I took a step forward. "Now, show me what you've been working on."

Her face fell into a mask of pure concentration. She turned her body sideways and readied herself. One deep breath and then she swung.

We sparred until dawn. Our chests heaved in unison as Vrail landed hit after hit. I showed her how to integrate her footwork into each swing. Vrail studied my movements like they were words on the page, devouring the knowledge quickly and asking for clarification when she needed to see something again. By the time the first rays of light streaked the sky, we were orbiting each other over heavily trodden circles in the grass.

I grabbed a drink of water for us both as Syrra walked into the equipment room. Her gaze anchored on Vrail without a word. She stared at the sweat soaking the neck of her shirt and the beaten pads wrapped around my hands. She met my gaze for a moment before grabbing a fighting pole and walking across the grounds in silence.

Vrail bit her lip and pulled at her fingers. "Should I leave?" she whispered, glancing at Syrra, who seemed intent on ignoring us.

I shook my head and walked back to the grassy meadow. I lifted my hands and nodded at Vrail. "Let's go again."

I needed a shower by the time we'd finished training. My burl was too far to walk in the heat so I let Vrail and Syrra return to their rooms while I went to the lake. I walked into the water with my trousers and tunic still on, in part to cover my scars but also to wash the stench of training out of them as best I could.

Once I'd scrubbed them enough, I left them to dry on a large boulder that sat half in the water and half in sand along the beach—just as I'd seen other Elverin do. With only my head peeking through the surface, I made sure I was alone. There wasn't even a crab along the beach that I could see. I sighed in relief. Everyone was eating lunch in the banquet hall just as they always did at midday. I let myself float on my back and enjoy the sun. A light breeze blew through the forest and carried the scent of pine and mint across the calm water.

It was a lovely day, almost *too* lovely. The serenity put me on edge, and I couldn't help the way my ears strained to hear every sound as if the King's Army was about to spill over the peaks of the Burning Mountains and sack the city. Sixty years in the kingdom had taught me that the worst moments of my life always came with a prelude of peace. Like the calm that taunted sailors before the storm.

I swam to the far side of the boulder and double-checked that no one was near to see the scars lined along my back or the names down my torso and arms. I shivered as I stepped out of the water, partly from the chill, but mostly from the idea of someone spotting my scars. Killian knowing about the names was already too much. I did not want to be in that position again.

I reached for my clothes and chuckled to myself. They were perfectly dry. I lay my palm flat against the white stone. It was warm to the touch, like the top of an iron hearth, and it had dried my clothes all through. I pulled the trousers up to cover the scar along my hip and threw the tunic on to cover the rest.

I flung my leather vest across my shoulders with my weapons belt and wrist guards and took the tunnel connected to the training room but turned left instead of my usual right. No part of me wanted to cross through the main hall while the entire city feasted for lunch. I preferred to eat alone in my burl, and while the leftward path was longer, it would lead me there without the need to walk through a room of angry and terrified faces.

The tunnel wound around the north of the city. I passed a large room filled to the brim with broken inventions and prototypes of others that Nikolai had made over the centuries. Even without him tinkering inside, the room seemed to hum. My lips twitched at the scattering of drawings and designs across the floor before continuing down the path with a small faelight hovering over my shoulder to light the way.

Heavy footsteps rang from one of the adjoining tunnels. A body rammed into me, and only when my faelight lit the side of his face did I realize it was Collin. His face transformed from apologetic shock to the vile sneer he saved only for me.

"What are you doing in these tunnels alone, Blade?" He seethed, making a point to show his fangs. "*Spying?*"

I flashed him my own, knowing they were longer and sharper. "I should ask the same of you, walking down here with no light. Why are *you* lurking in the shadows?"

I wanted to scratch the smug grin off Collin's face. "Because this is my *home*. I need no light to guide my way." He made a point of eyeing the faelight hovering between us.

I hated the way my shoulders fell. As miserable as Collin was, the Elverin had accepted him. He had every right to call Myrelinth home. I ignored the way my stomach tightened into knots just as I ignored the thought that the Elverin would never truly accept me.

I had no home.

Collin grinned, knowing his words had found their mark. "Go warm Riven's bed. You're not needed here, Blade."

Collin pushed into me as he passed me.

"Does the jealousy eat at you?" I spat. "To see Riven care for me while you pine for his brother's affections?"

Collin paused midstep but did not turn around. "I have no idea what you mean."

I smirked, knowing my words had found their mark too. "Yes. You do."

Seeing Collin's hands harden at his sides gave me more pleasure than it should have. He left without saying anything else to me, lost in the darkness once again.

The coolness from my swim had melted away with the anger now stoking in my chest. I turned up the same tunnel Collin had come out of and headed in the direction of Nikolai's room. Out of everyone, he would entertain my distaste for Collin most.

I had just rounded the last curve before the downhill slope toward Nikolai's chambers when I heard them whispering.

"Just tell her if it's bothering you so." Vrail's voice was unmistakable.

My chest sank into the wall behind me. I could tell by the defensiveness in Vrail's tone that they were talking about me.

"And the mole?"

Killian.

I sunk further into the black earth and roots. What did Killian have to tell me about the mole? He had seemed just as disheartened by the idea of one of his own betraying him as Nikolai or Syrra.

"Tell her the truth and she'll see reason." Vrail again. "You did it to protect our people."

"Or out of a foolish abundance of caution." I'd recognize Nikolai's sarcasm anywhere.

"Someone has to be the cautious one." Killian again.

My breath stilled. Whatever they were discussing, it wasn't something Killian wanted me to know. And about the *mole*? After he'd gathered the four of us in a room and claimed to trust us all. Apparently that applied to everyone but me.

My mouth went dry. Killian could keep his secrets, but I was done telling him mine. Nikolai had told me to wait to see if Killian would earn my trust, but I didn't think Killian wanted to do that. Perhaps he'd grown too used to the crown upon his head and how little the world expected of those who wore them.

Nikolai's drawn-out sigh echoed down the tunnel. "We cannot keep having the same conversation. We can accept your decision even though we don't agree with it."

Vrail's voice was quiet. "I wouldn't go *that* far."

There was a sound like someone slapping their legs and standing up. I knew it was Nikolai before he spoke. "I need to go prepare the rooms for the Halflings. Collin said they're leaving the farmhouse in the morning and their closets still aren't full."

The soft groan of stone being pulled against the ground echoed down the tunnel. My breath caught in my chest as I slowly stepped backward and extinguished my faelight. The last thing I saw was Nikolai's furrowed face before turning back down the tunnel and running as silently as I could.

CHAPTER FIFTEEN

There was nowhere in Myrelinth I could find peace. I went to fetch food from the kitchens only to find Collin packing supplies for his journey to Silstra. The stables were always empty so late in the afternoon, but Tarvelle and his team were in there preparing the horses. I walked out only to see Killian speaking to Riven across the center grove. He gave me a cautious wave over Riven's shoulder.

I clenched my teeth and stared at the prince until his hand dropped. Thankfully, Riven didn't notice the way his shadows stretched in my direction along the ground, always reaching for me like a needle finding due north.

Even that set a scorching heat through me. I felt like a fire in a stone hearth with all the fuel and rage to burn a city to the ground, but I was stuck between the stones and ashes. My flames could never melt a throne, let alone a crown.

I pulled at the collar of my tunic. The sneers and secrets were closing in on me, trapping me in place when all I wanted to do was keep moving forward, keep moving toward *something*.

I marched along the edge of the city to the north path in the Dark Wood, careful not to be seen. As I passed through one of the gardens, I bent down and snapped a bloom from a bright bush of turquoise flowers. I twirled it under my nose until I reached the twin trees of the portal and placed it in the tiny pool of water, letting the spicy floral scent fill the clearing.

Gold swirls appeared in the veil of mist that hung between the curved trees. I took a breath and stepped into Aralinth.

The giant Elder birch towered over the middle of the city, warm light reflecting off its leaves from the setting suns. I looked over my shoulder at the identical twinned trees that stood in the middle of the garden I was now in. Once the second sun had set, I wouldn't be able to return to Myrelinth until morning and no one would be able to find me.

I stood there, becoming one of the garden's statues until the lilac streaks in the sky deepened to indigo and the first stars appeared. The mist in the portal exploded with light, like the final flash of a sunset, and my entire body loosened.

"I thought you would have left by day three," a velvety voice sounded behind me. "I'm impressed."

My lips twitched to the side as I turned and saw Dynara standing there. "Have you been haunting the portal every sunset just to see me again?" I batted my eyelashes dramatically.

Dynara looked at me like someone reading a story they already knew the ending to. Her eyes lingered on my arms at the scars she'd seen the day we switched places in the bathing room. "You have enough ghosts haunting you."

The words slammed into me, but Dynara's deep eyes were flooded with the empathy of someone who knew what it was to be haunted. I shrugged my shoulders. "The ghosts I can handle; it's the living I needed to run from."

Dynara's returning smile was conspiratorial. "You want distraction?"

"*Yes.*" I was too tired to care about how desperate it sounded.

"Then follow me. We need you out of those clothes into something a bit more *distracting*." Dynara's tongue flicked her lip as she spoke and she looped her arm through mine to lead us out of the garden.

An hour later, we were in her lavish chambers in one of the white stone dwellings that overlooked the base of Sil'abar. No expense had been spared in furnishing the room or filling Dynara's closets.

"You may have more luxurious taste than Nikolai," I said, feeling a layered silk skirt between my fingers. It was made of deep greens and shimmering jade. Together it looked like a swirling pool of emerald.

"Hardly," Dynara said, hanging a long necklace down her back. She nodded at the skirt I was holding. "That will look lovely on you."

I swallowed. There wasn't a top in Dynara's closet that could cover my scars. Dynara noticed my hesitation and disappeared into her third closet. She came out with a malachite ring set in a golden band. She dropped it into my palm. "As long as you wear this, no one will see your scars."

There was a warmth to the ring that was becoming familiar. "A glamour?"

Dynara nodded as she pointed to the holder on a shelf behind me. It held a garment made of Elvish gold chain that hung from a single layered pauldron cast in gold. The mesh would barely cover the top of my rib cage, but the armor silhouette gave it a strength that only added to its beauty.

Dynara smirked at the way my mouth hung open. "Wear this with the green skirt and you won't even need the glamour. No one will be looking at your face long enough to realize you're the Blade."

My head whipped around. That was what Dynara was offering me. A night of anonymity. A feral smile split across my face and sent shivers of anticipation through my body. I lifted the gold garment off its holder and slipped the ring onto my finger.

Aralinth was a city of blooms by day, but at night the city shimmered. The canopy of flowers that hung between each of the buildings was coated in magical dust that shimmered every color as the Elverin walked beneath it.

My heart pounded against my chest as we took our first steps out of Dynara's apartment and into the lively street. I didn't hear any shocks of horror as we passed Elverin, the deep ridges along my back completely bare. By the time we reached the garden, my pulse had settled and I believed that the magic of the glamour had hidden the truth written along my skin.

Booming drums sounded through the city, shaking the blooms overhead until rose petals drifted down onto the dancing Elverin below. Five large drums sat in a circle at the middle of the garden. Each had ten Elverin standing around it, half with padded sticks to beat the hide and the other half chanting an ancient song. I was certain I'd never heard such music in the kingdom before, but there was something familiar about the way the chorus was able to blend their voices to mimic the sound of wind whistling through the Burning Mountains.

The drumbeats quickened and Dynara pulled me into the crowd.

"I don't know the dance," I shouted over the music.

Dynara shook her head and laughed. "There are no steps, Keera. Just close your eyes and let your body move with the sound."

I glanced around the crowd. No one was looking at us. Most of the crowd had their eyes closed too. I swallowed my fear and did the same. The music crashed over me and pulled me into the undertow of its melody. My feet moved without thought, matching the beat of the drums as my arms twisted and spun like branches in the wind.

The music quickened and so did I. Dynara clapped her hands as I spun four, five, six times before coming to a dizzying stop. Dynara gripped my hand and spun with me until we tumbled to the ground. We laughed until the tiny sliver of the moon slipped behind the tallest trees of the Dark Wood.

When the crowd dispersed, Dynara looped her arm through mine and led me down an alley until we reached a short wall in the middle of the city. There were no faelights glowing nearby. Most of the Elverin lived closer to Sil'abar, and the ones who lived nearby had long since gone to bed.

Dynara jumped onto the top of the white stone wall and used it to boost herself onto the thick canopy. I held my breath, waiting for the vines to give way to her weight, but it held strong. I climbed up and lay next to her.

It was more comfortable than I thought.

"I hope the distraction met your expectations," Dynara said through her steadying breaths.

I nodded, staring up at the mass of stars that hung above us. "It was perfect."

"I missed the kingdom for years after I made it here," Dynara said after a long moment.

I turned my head to face her. "Why?" The kingdom had been nothing but cruel to Dynara.

She sighed. "I may have hated my place in the kingdom, but I understood it. This city, these people . . . it was a whole new world. It took time to catch my breath."

"It would be easier if the Elverin didn't see me as a monster." I plucked the head of a flower from the bed beneath us and tossed it at our feet.

"It's easier for those of us who lived in the kingdom to see the difference between the true monsters and those who must wear the mask of one." Dynara reached out in the dark and squeezed my hand. "The Elverin will see it eventually, but you could help them see it quicker if you took off the mask."

I lifted my hand and looked at the glamoured ring on my finger.

"Not your scars," Dynara whispered. She trailed her fingers over her wrist where the courtesan crest was burned into her flesh. "You are *not* your pain, Keera, and you do not owe anyone that story to be welcomed here."

I puffed my cheeks and blew my breath to the sky. "Pain is all I have."

The entire canopy shook with Dynara's head. "You can't be made only of pain and laugh as endlessly as you did tonight. Feeling that pain can be overwhelming, *consuming*, I know, but you can feel more than pain. If you allow yourself."

The weight of that choice fell heavy on my chest, pinning my body in place. I could feel every curve and edge of the names along my skin. Ignoring the pain—or worse, feeling something other than pain—felt like I was ignoring my debt to them. That I was dishonoring their deaths, my vow to end the king, if I allowed myself even a moment of happiness.

But that pain had drained me of everything I had. Before I struck that deal with Riven, before I came to this city, I hadn't brought any of my names justice. Decades of guilt and sorrow had accomplished nothing. Perhaps Dynara was right, and making room for something more than anguish would bring me what I needed. I squeezed her hand back. "You were right. I should've come here on day three."

Dynara's laugh filled the air like the timbre of a cello. "You're welcome anytime, and you can keep that ring in case you need a break again."

I smiled my thanks. "How did you really know I was coming?"

Dynara smirked and fished something out of her bodice. It was a tiny red bead held by three gold prongs along the thinnest chain I'd ever seen. "Riven gave this to me. He thought you would come here eventually. When he lights his, this one glows."

I grazed the bead with the tip of my finger. It felt like cold glass. "He saw me leave, then." My chest twinged. Somehow without even looking at me, Riven had known I'd needed space.

"I suspect Riven would never let you out of his sight if he thought you'd allow it." Dynara gave me a knowing smile. "That will be half your battle winning over the trust of the Elverin, you know—you've managed to charm Riven where all others have failed." She jabbed me lightly with her elbow. "And I do mean *all*."

"Did he lie to them all too?" I hated myself as soon as the words left my mouth. Regardless of how my anger lingered, it was something between me and him.

Dynara turned on her side to face me. "I remember how it felt when I first arrived. Only strangers, no friends. It must be even more isolating knowing everyone's allegiance lies with Riven first."

My throat tightened. "I had no friends in the kingdom. I never expected to have them here. I've grown fond of Nikolai and Syrra, even Vrail. I don't mind that they knew Riven first."

Dynara's eyes narrowed. "Still, you need someone to cool your flames when Riven does something stupid again."

I raised a single brow.

Dynara rolled her eyes. "If we survive this war, there will be centuries sitting at our feet. He is bound to do something ridiculous at least once a decade."

"And me?"

"Once a month."

I feigned an insulted gasp.

Dynara laced her fingers through mine and laid them on the canopy between us. "We survived the kingdom in a way they can never understand. It's only right that we stick together."

The urge to push Dynara away didn't come. I was too tired of feeling alone. If Dynara was willing to extend a hand to me, I would take it. I pointed to the bead along her neck. "Do you have any more of those?"

CHAPTER SIXTEEN

DYNARA BURST THROUGH THE DOORS to her room the next morning. I rubbed my eyes and saw that the suns had barely begun to rise. "We need to go," she said, tossing me my training clothes.

I slipped out of bed and pulled off the sleeping dress Dynara had lent me for the night. "What's happened?" I asked through a yawn. I doubted we'd had more than a couple hours' sleep.

Dynara ran a hand through her immaculate dark waves as she paced the length of the room. "The Halfling rescue never showed. They should have been here as soon as the portal switched. I waited for an hour, but they're not here. Something is wrong."

I made the decision before I had stood. I could not sit idly by while there was a chance those Halflings were being captured or worse.

I strapped my weapons belt over my trousers and accounted for each of the blades I'd brought. Fewer than I would have liked, but I'd won fights with less. "How many were you expecting?"

"Eighteen." Dynara pulled at her hair, panic-stricken. "Plus the party leading the rescue."

I tied up my boots. "When did you last have contact?"

Dynara swallowed. "Tarvelle confirmed they made it to Silstra when we returned from the garden party. They were supposed to head to the safe house and ready the Halflings for the journey. We didn't have any checks planned after that."

I nodded at the door. "Go tell everyone you need to."

Dynara opened it but then stopped. "Aren't you coming?"

"No." I shook my head and slipped the malachite ring into the pouch on my belt. "Tell the others I have a head start. I'm going to the stables."

I reached Silstra just after midday. Without my cloak or silver blade, I didn't venture into the city itself, but I could still see the pouring spout of the river over what had been the dam I'd blown to bits. A chain of laborers stood on both sides of the river, passing pieces of debris through the chain to a mountain of rubble.

It would take years to clear the mess by hand. A satisfied smile tugged at my lips as I rode past on my way north of the city. Nikolai had mentioned a farmhouse when I eavesdropped on his conversation with Killian the day before. There was only one farmhouse that aligned with the rebels' choice of safe house. A grayed, derelict building on the road to Cereliath. Though what it looked like beneath the glamour I didn't know.

The city disappeared behind me, and I rode my horse over a long hill. The scent of ash and burning wood filled the air but I saw no smoke in the sky. My horse jerked her head and I knew she smelled it too. As we reached the other side of the hill, the decrepit walls of the farmhouse came into view. It was just as old and ruined as it always had been. Too decayed to tempt thieves, and without a roof it didn't serve as a shelter for travelers either. I veered off the main road onto the grass, and suddenly the image of the farmhouse shattered to reveal the truth.

A large building that was alight with purple flames. The fire burned so high and bright, I had to hold my arm to shield my eyes from the heat. No smoke filled the sky, even as the rafters of the building fell and were consumed by violet flames.

I'd seen colored fire in the Faeland, but this was something different. Something unnatural. I rode in a wide circle around the flames and saw a thick line of burnt grass on the edge closest to the forest. I dismounted my horse and ran my fingers over the scorched earth. It was still hot, almost too hot to touch, but a thin wire was left behind, curving through the grass toward the burning building like a snake.

I turned back to the farmhouse. It didn't make any sense. A fire that burned bright violet and didn't smoke could only be one set by magic, but yet the arsonist had used a detonator? I was not an expert on the Fae, but I didn't think any of them needed help to wield their magic. And from how high and strong the flames burned, this was more than all the fire wielders in the Faeland could manage if they had combined their powers.

I followed the burnt earth to where the detonator had been lit. There was a pile of violet dust. I poked it with my finger and rubbed it in with my hand. I snarled at the sting of it.

It was not dust, but finely milled glass. Amber blood pooled along my finger and thumb. I wiped it on my trousers, not bothering to bandage it with how quickly my body healed now. There was something sticking out of the pile of dust. I nudged it with my boot before pinching it with my unbloodied hand.

It was a pin. Two crossed sheaths of wheat were cast in bronze and coated in the milled glass. It was the crest of the House of Harvest. The pins were only worn by the assistants to the Lords of Harvest.

Like Curringham.

Something moved in the sideline of my vision, and I saw Killian and others crossing through the field. I slipped the pin into the pouch along my weapons belt. If Killian didn't see reason to share his knowledge with me, then I would be more selective in revealing mine.

"There she is!" Collin shouted, pointing his arm at me. "How can you deny it now?"

My back tensed. I'd fled Aralinth with no thought in my mind other than saving the Halflings. Violet flames reflected in Collin's eyes as I considered how this appeared: my tall frame silhouetted against the raging fire, set at a safe house whose location I wasn't meant to know.

I turned to Riven as he jumped off his horse. "I didn't do this," I whispered as he grabbed my cheeks and checked my face.

He noticed my bloody hand and his jaw pulsed twice. "I know," he whispered back.

"She left Myrelinth before we did, she's had more than enough time."

Nikolai dismounted his horse. "Dynara already told us Keera spent the night with her and didn't leave Aralinth until a few hours ago. She only had a head start of a half hour at most." Nikolai spoke disjointedly, studying the ground and the pile of violet dust with complete concentration.

"Was the fire set when you arrived?" Nikolai asked, not looking up from the ground.

I nodded. "Yes, already as high as this."

Nikolai cut himself on the dust just as I had. His brows shot up beneath his curls before scribbling something in his notebook.

A creaky sound burst from the flames and we watched the remainder of the roof crumble to the ground. Syrra jutted her chin toward the collapse. "Whoever this was, they waited to set this. They wanted us to see it."

"We will have to wait for the flames to settle before we can begin our search," Tarvelle said in a hard voice.

I froze. "Search?"

Riven gripped my shoulder and bent down to whisper. "For the Halflings."

Despair shot through me like one of the fallen rafters had crushed me into the ground. "They can't be dead," I choked. I refused to believe it.

Collin scoffed. "As if you care about some dead Halflings."

I marched across the grass to Collin until I was close enough to wrap my hands around his neck. "I would never hurt the Halflings." My hands shook with rage at my sides. "I would never hurt my kin."

Collin huffed a laugh. "We both know that is not true."

Killian stepped beside Collin and placed a gentle hand on his shoulder. His jade eyes were hard with a warning. "Collin, not here."

"The Blade need not pay for her crimes?" Collin's voice was raw. "Past or present?"

"I did not do this!" I yelled at the Halfling. "And what crimes have I ever committed against you?"

Collin stepped away from me with the speed of a viper. In that instant, I knew he'd been laying a trap, waiting for the perfect moment to unleash whatever was waiting on his tongue.

"You killed my family."

The noise of the fire evaporated like water on a hot grill. One moment, I could hear the crackle of flame behind me, the breaths and heartbeats of everyone standing near, and the next it was silent. My heart hammered in my chest yet I couldn't hear it. I could only feel the pressure building up inside of me.

I knew the day would come where I would have to face the surviving kin of one of the names on my list. I'd never expected it to be Collin.

I closed my eyes and searched my memories for a face that looked like Collin's. There were too many. Too many lives where I'd been the villain of their stories. Just as I was the villain of Collin's.

His eyes narrowed at me. "You don't remember."

I swallowed the guilt. Collin had not given me enough information. The king had sent me after entire families many times. "I was the Blade for a long time," I said, knowing it was a pitiful excuse.

"Cereliath." Collin spat. "Toman Franshire."

The memory of his face cut through me like a blade of ice. I could picture him and recall his death in every detail, but there was nothing in that memory that would bring Collin comfort. Tears stung my eyes as I shook my head.

Collin's words were sharpened darts, each one landing in my chest. "You kill so many even their names mean nothing to you."

I wiped my eyes but said nothing. Shadows swirled around my legs protectively. My shoulders fell as I took a step back, unable to look anyone in the eye. "I'm sorry." The words scraped my throat, slicing like the dull blade they were—useless and unneeded.

Collin's sneer was one of disgust. He crossed his arms and stepped behind Killian.

"If you did not light the fire or ambush our team"—Tarvelle stepped away from his horse—"then how did you find the safe house with its glamour still intact?"

I twisted my boot into the earth. "I overheard Killian and Nikolai talking about the retrieval."

Tarvelle snarled. "*Miinishki raavranthir.*"

I stomped my boot into the ground. "I am no traitor."

"So you *were* spying," Collin said with too much glee in his voice. He turned to Killian. "I caught her in the tunnels outside your chambers yesterday. She had no answer when I questioned her."

I shook my head. "It wasn't like that. I was looking for Nikolai."

"*Raavranthir*," Tarvelle repeated, flinging his arms in my direction.

Syrra gripped her blade and rooted herself behind me. She stared at Tarvelle with an expression that would send most running. "I would not say that a third time."

Collin turned to Killian. "How can you trust her after everything that's happened? First, she sends the Unnamed Ones after the entire rebellion. Then, she's found alone at a burning safe house she only knew the location of by listening in on your private conversations. If you cannot see that her allegiance still lies with the kingdom, then *please* see that this alliance will be the ruin of us all."

Killian's leg bounced as he glanced between me and Riven. He bit his lip as he tried to find the words, but they didn't come.

Nikolai finished filling his glass vial with the dust and stood in one graceful motion. "Keera didn't do this, Collin. It took an entire team to sedate and apprehend your team. Even Keera cannot be multiple people. Besides, Tarvelle told us the attack happened before dawn while Keera was asleep in Aralinth."

"You do not know—"

"Are you questioning Dynara's loyalty as well?" Nikolai crossed his arms. I'd never thought of him as scary, but in that moment, Nikolai even gave me pause. Collin reluctantly shook his head. "Good." Nikolai clapped his hands. "Anything else?"

Collin's resignation melted into vile hatred as he stared at Nikolai. "Good to know you're fucking the Blade too."

The air exploded. Light no longer existed. Where there had been towering violet flames the moment before, now was only the deepest, darkest shadow. I reached my arm out, but my fingers did not brush against anything.

I focused on the six heartbeats near me and heard a strange wheezing like someone struggling to breathe. My body turned cold as I stepped backward, somehow knowing exactly where Riven was. I grabbed his hand. "Enough. You'll regret it if you hurt him."

A gasp broke through the darkness. Another moment later, the shadows had mostly faded, and everyone could see Collin rubbing his bright red throat. Tiny dribbles of amber blood coated his neck.

Riven curled his lip back, exposing his fangs as his chest heaved with anger. "Consider that your only warning."

Killian raised his hands. "Enough. We cannot expect to win a war if we're too busy quarrelling among ourselves. And we can no longer deny that we have a second enemy in our midst. This is no longer about stolen food; we have almost twenty Elverin missing. We need to get to the bottom of this and fast."

Syrra mounted her horse. "I will search the city and see what I can find."

The harvest pin had turned to lead in my pouch, tugging at me to show the others, but I couldn't. Collin and Tarvelle did not need any more reason to call me a traitor. I glanced at Killian. He was the only one who had not defended me. When the wolves had been circling, he'd chosen to hide in the bushes rather than put himself between me and their teeth. I didn't blame him for it, but I would not shield him from sharp bites either. I swallowed the dryness in my throat and let the pin stay where it was.

Riven unfastened his cloak and wrapped it around my shoulders. "I'll bring Keera back to Myrelinth and we can plan our next move from there."

Collin's lip raised but one look at the thick shadows streaming from Riven and swirling around me was enough to keep his mouth shut.

CHAPTER SEVENTEEN

I WAS GRATEFUL Riven didn't speak to me as we left Silstra behind. He rode beside me with our horses in matching rhythm until we came to the first portal of three. Riven steered his horse through a narrow trail on the edge of the Dead Wood until we reached two burnt trees. The unnatural bends in their spines reminded me of a blade of grass after someone had stepped on it.

Riven pulled two *winvra* berries from his pocket and placed them in the small pool of water along their black roots. The sulphuric scent that plagued the Dead Wood was overpowered by an aroma of sweet juice as the scorched vines hanging from the trees shimmered with gold and we crossed through the portal into the woods along the eastern side of the Burning Mountains.

"I wasn't spying on Killian," I said, cutting through the silence. "I truly was looking for Nikolai." My chest burned with the urge to tell

Riven everything I'd overheard, but Killian was his brother. Asking him the meaning behind the prince's words would be issuing a test of loyalties, and I didn't know if I could handle failing at that too.

"I know." Riven's words were solid and unwavering. "I trust you, Keera. And I know you didn't have anything to do with that fire or the Halflings."

The relief of his words eased the sting that Collin's had left behind. I was glad to know that Riven's omissions and disappearance had not ruined his ability to calm me. Even though my anger at him had not entirely faded, I couldn't deny Riven had been a comfort to me since he had returned to Myrelinth. First with the names he'd taken the time to find, then each session with Feron, and now with his unwavering support.

Perhaps the part of my anger that lingered for Riven was the anger I had for myself. Anger for moving as quickly as I did in trusting him and not asking questions. I'd been so swept up in the feeling of being *seen*, of having someone beside me in the midst of my loneliness, that I'd never taken the time to realize I didn't know Riven very well at all. I knew the Shadow, the scorned enemy of the king who fought his people, but the Fae riding beside me was still a mystery. We had moved from enemies to bedmates so quickly we never got to know one another as friends.

"What's your favorite time of day?"

Riven's brows were stitched together as he turned sideways to look at me. "My favorite time of day?"

"Do you like daytime?" I pushed. "Does sunlight help control your magic or do you prefer the night?"

Riven clamped his jaw shut. We'd reached a fork in the path, but Riven halted his horse instead of veering left.

"Moonset," he said after a long moment. "It doesn't happen every night, but when it does, there are few things as beautiful as that."

I nodded and rode past him. "I need to go to Koratha."

Riven set his horse to a trot to catch up to me. "I'm not sure that is the best idea. We have not confirmed who is tampering with our warehouses and tensions are high."

I swallowed. "I know the timing is not the best. But word of that fire will reach the capital soon now that you took down the glamour. My title wields no power if the king believes I've abandoned my post."

Riven rubbed his leather reins as he chewed his lip. "Collin and Tarvelle will not like it."

"I did not realize I needed their permission to go."

Riven sighed. "You know that is not what I meant."

A twinge of guilt pulled at my chest. "Tarvelle and Collin won't be able to make their accusations once the mole, and whoever they're helping, are unmasked. If there are whispers of this new enemy being spread in the capital, I need to be there to hear them."

Riven's shadows wrapped themselves tighter around my legs. A wave of warmth spread over my body at their touch. "Best to leave once Tarvelle and Collin are asleep. I'll manage their anger when they wake."

I woke well before dawn in a pool of sweat, with the fresh scrape of a scream in my throat. Adrenaline coursed through my veins from the same nightmare of the dark. I pulled myself out of bed, knowing any chance of sleep had disappeared the moment my eyes had opened.

I still had hours to wait until I could portal into Aralinth and then from there to a lake just outside of the capital. My bags were already packed and the Halflings working the stables promised to have my horse ready by first light.

I showered and dressed in the dark. I wrapped my leather guards around the sleeves of my tunic and my black cloak around my neck. It pulled my shoulders back like a weighted chain dragging behind me as I walked. It no longer felt like a uniform I had to wear, a tool I could use to masquerade as the Blade. It felt like a choker clasped around my throat, getting tighter with each breath. I ripped it off and threw it on top of my bag. I could stow it until I entered the palace. That cloak was a curse I no longer wanted to wear.

I opened the door for some fresh air and saw the burl across the grove was still lit. Riven was awake too.

My feet moved without permission, stalking across the bridge in light steps and jumping onto a net of vines that connected the branches of my tree to the one that held Riven's burl. I stepped inside and heard the water running in the shower. I could smell nothing but birchwood and dew in the air. Riven's scent invaded the entire room and wrapped me in it. I couldn't ignore the way my back released and my heart rate slowed walking through his space. Somehow the stresses of the day dwindled here.

Riven's burl was smaller than mine. Only enough room for the bath, closet, and bed. There was no table or sitting area to entertain guests. Not that I'd seen anyone in his burl since he'd arrived. He was barely in it. I took a seat on the bed, ignoring the way my breath hitched when I heard the water stop.

Riven came out of the shower wearing nothing but a towel wrapped around his waist. His long hair hung behind him in thick strands; they stuck to the muscles on his back, moving with him as he stepped toward me. If he was surprised to find me on his bed, he didn't show it, though his shadows moved toward me, instantly swirling at my feet. His jaw pulsed as he looked down at me. "What's wrong?"

I shrugged, unable to admit to the nightmares. "I couldn't sleep. And then I saw the light and wondered if you couldn't either."

Riven grabbed a tunic from his closet and pulled it over his head. My chest twinged watching his toned body disappear under the linen. The memory of that body pressed against mine was still fresh. I squeezed the mattress between my hands. Riven grabbed a pair of trousers and I laid back on the bed to avert my gaze.

"I just got in. I needed to release some of my magic where no one could get hurt." Riven cleared his throat. "That outburst with Collin should never have happened."

I toyed with the end of my braid. "You regret it, then?" I asked, instead of the question I really wanted the answer to—*do you regret defending me?*

Riven took three steps and stood between my knees. His face was stern as he gazed down at me, holding me to that spot on his bed. "No," he finally answered. "But I never should have lost control."

I swallowed and could feel Riven's gaze shift to my throat. He bit his lip but didn't move from where he stood. "Why did you ask me about my favorite time of day?" Riven's hand grazed the top of my knee. I ignored the wave of goosebumps it sent up my thigh.

"Because I'm still mad at you."

A deep line appeared between his brows. "I don't understand the connection."

"I'm also mad at myself," I sighed. I pulled myself up on the mattress. Riven lowered himself to one knee so we faced each other eye to eye. "I realized that part of the reason I'm upset with you was that I felt toyed with. It wasn't just the secret you kept from me, it was realizing how much of myself I'd shown you without noticing how little you'd given me in return."

Riven's hands gripped my thighs, anchoring himself after the blow of that truth. I could see the hurt in his eyes before he bowed his head and pressed it against my knee. "Keera, I never meant to toy with you." His lips brushed my leg as he spoke. "There has been so little time, and after Silstra I just wanted to know you in as many ways as I could. Sharing myself in that way doesn't come naturally to me."

I clucked my tongue. "You think it comes naturally to me?"

Riven chuckled and I felt the heat of his breath on my belly. "No, but you're braver than I am and much more practiced at *this*." He waved his hand back and forth between us.

"Neither of those things is true."

A soft smile played on Riven's lips. "Yes, *diizra*, they are." I started to ask what *diizra* meant but Riven continued. "I've never been with anyone, Keera. Not in a way that's ever mattered. There's only *you*. Before, now, and for however long you'll have me."

I blinked. "But the maidens in Volcar . . ." Nikolai had teased Riven about them during our travels.

Riven grinned. "Nothing but a few quick kisses here and there. Nothing more, Keera. Not until you."

I couldn't help trailing my eyes down the full length of him. "Why?"

Riven laughed and his chest pressed into the side of my leg. I liked the feel of it so I pulled him closer with my calf. "Nikolai has been asking me that question for decades."

The heat from Riven's body called me to it. It would be so easy to pull him into my arms and claim his lips with mine. I nudged my face closer to his until I could taste his breath and feel his exhale on my neck. I shivered and watched his eyes track it all the way down my chest. So, so easy, but wouldn't that be moving just as quickly as before? Riven had said many nice words, pleasing things that I hoped he meant.

I needed to give him time to show me he did.

I pulled back from him, my skin missing his touch already. "I need to pack before first light."

Riven nodded and loosened his grip on my calf, but it took a few moments before he stood. He held out a hand and helped me up from the bed. "I'll leave you to it, then." His hands found my waist and he leaned into me. The decision I'd just made evaporated under the heat of his touch and I knew I'd let him kiss me.

But his lips pressed softly against my forehead. "The trip will not make it easier for the Elverin to trust you." His hand settled on my neck while the other played with my braid.

"I know, but I have time to earn their trust. For now I only need yours." I looked up at him, hoping he understood. I was going whether he agreed with it or not.

Riven tucked a loose strand behind my ear. "Always."

My shoulders relaxed at his words and I headed to the door. As long as Riven and the others believed that I would never help the mole, that would be enough. With them, I could take the brunt of the Elverin's doubt and prove them wrong.

"Keera," Riven called as I stepped out into the night. The moon was a large crescent in the sky, beginning to set. I turned back to Riven. He ran his hand through the wet strands and stretched his neck. "I was scared of heights until the day Syrra made me jump off the top of the Myram tree."

"She pushed a child off the top?" It sounded scandalous even for Syrra's rigorous training.

Riven smiled widely then, a brighter smile than I'd ever seen him share with anyone else. "I landed on a bed of faelight. And I was thirty-one."

CHAPTER EIGHTEEN

It was midmorning when I rode into the capital. Three bodies hung from the outer wall of the city. From the stench, they'd been there for days. I flashed the silver blade at my neck to the guards standing watch and waited for the large wooden doors to open.

Inside the walls was a city that was dying. Everywhere I looked, I saw signs of violence and poverty. Even in the third ring of the city, where most people were rich enough for hot suppers each night, the crowds were bare and the market tables empty. Wooden planks had been nailed across windows as reinforcement to keep thieving parties out.

Soldiers marched along each of the rings, interrogating anyone who looked the least bit suspect. I didn't see many criminals lurking in the alleys, but I saw more hungry beggars than I had ever seen in the capital.

I pulled down my hood and addressed one of the guards walking by. "Has the king not started doling out the rations?"

The guard was young, I doubted he was more than twenty. He eyed the fastener at my neck and swallowed. "His Majesty stopped the order before it had begun. There will be no rations until the first snows of winter."

My jaw hardened as I continued on to the next ring of the city. The first snows were likely months away. Half of the city could starve by then while Aemon sat in his palace, comfortable and well-fed. We would need to find a way to get a steady supply of food in, especially for the Halflings who couldn't flee.

I finally made it to the last gate. Four guards stood outside the iron doors and pushed them open without a word when they saw me approach. "Tell the king I've arrived." I told the shortest of the four. "I will take my leave on the morrow, but until then I can make my report at his convenience."

The guard nodded and jogged down the path, his armor clanking with each step. I stalked up the front lawns to find a figure dressed just like me only several inches shorter. "Good day, Gerarda," I said, pulling back my hood enough to show my face.

Gerarda let hers fall to her shoulders, the silver dagger at her neck glinting in the sun. "You didn't send word you were arriving." She flipped a throwing star through her fingers. "I was under the impression I would meet you in Mortal's Landing at month's end."

That had been the last assignment I'd given her. To be my eyes and ears in the capital while she prepared the Shades for an attack against the Shadow and I gathered information in Mortal's Landing. That was before Nikolai shot me in the arm with a sleeping dart and Killian dragged me to Myrelinth. Plans changed.

"I'm not here to assess you, if that's what you're worried about." I tapped my bags. "I needed to resupply and the stores in Mortal's

Landing are worse than here." I took Gerarda's silence as acceptance of my excuse. "I caught wind of another fire being set in Silstra on my journey."

Gerarda's eyes narrowed. "How quickly whispers fly. That fire still burns."

"They fly as fast as a bird can carry them," I said, looking up at the white doves that were perched along the garden wall. "What has the Arsenal heard?"

Gerarda straightened her back, the picture of formality even though there was no one else to hear her report. "We believe it was done by the Shadow. It appears a number of Halflings have also been reported missing from the area and we suspect the two are connected. The fire was likely a diversion, like the one that was set when the dam blew."

My stomach tightened. It was best that the Arsenal thought the Shadow was behind the fires. It gave me time to confirm my suspicions about Curringham. I would have to do some searching while I was here.

"It still burns because it cannot be doused, not even by the rain that fell through the night." Gerarda gave me a hard look.

"Magic," I replied as if I hadn't seen the flames myself.

"Do you think fire is a signature of his?" Gerarda asked, jumping up on the garden wall and balancing the throwing star on the tip of her finger.

I raised a brow.

"The Shadow." Gerarda took a graceful step along the stone. Her short black hair grazed her jaw as she spoke. "This is the third fire he's set in two months."

I blinked. There had only been two fires in Silstra and only one set by the Shadow, though Gerarda didn't know that. There hadn't been a third fire . . .

But there had. The letter the Shades had given me that day in Caerth with orders to move to Volcar. There had been a fire and Halflings had gone missing there as well. My stomach turned to rock. I wouldn't know until I asked Riven, but I didn't think his Elverin had anything to do with that fire either.

Meaning whoever this third party was, they'd been using the Shadow as a cover for much longer than we knew.

I cleared my throat. "I need every report on the Shadow brought to my chambers."

Gerarda nodded. "I'll have a Shade bring them over from the Order immediately."

"Thank you." I looked at the direction of the Order. The island where we both had spent our childhoods being forged into weapons for the crown. "How goes your training with the Shades? Will they be ready to draw arms against the Shadow?"

Gerarda hopped off the garden wall so gently it looked like she was floating. Her sharp eyes narrowed at the twin palace across the sea. "They will be," she said coolly. "They have no other choice."

In that moment, Gerarda wasn't the adversary I had grown up with. The second-in-command lurking in the shadows for an opportunity to move up in rank. She was a Shade, just as I was, resigned to her fate that her life was forfeit to the king's whims.

If I played my cards right Gerarda might get a chance at freedom. She could spend her life throwing knives if she wanted. If she managed to survive.

The guard I'd sent to the king with my message stepped onto the grass of the garden. His head was bowed, but when he glanced at the Dagger, his legs started shaking. I grit my teeth. There was no possibility that Gerarda was more terrifying than I was.

"Mistresses," he said with a voice just as shaky. I nodded for him to relay his message. "The king asks that you send your report in writing."

I cocked my head to the side. Aemon had never requested such a thing before. The guard's gaze darted between me and his boots. "Anything else?" I asked, sensing he was not finished.

The guard nodded, his cheeks flushing red.

"If you don't spit it out, I'll cut out your tongue and feed it to one of my dogs." Gerarda emphasized her threat by whipping out her dagger and holding it up to the guard's nose. I leaned back—maybe she was scarier than I was.

"His Majesty also said"—the guard took a deep breath—"that if he does not have the Shadow's head by the full moon than he will take a head for himself."

I scoffed. The king had used this threat once before, but he couldn't afford to lose his best sword when war beckoned at his doorstep. "It will be hard for me to fetch the Shadow if the king beheads me, won't it?" I mumbled to Gerarda.

"He won't take your head," the guard said, stepping away from me. I stilled and felt all the blood drain from my face. "He said: for every day after the full moon without word of the Shadow's death, he will put a Shade's head on a spike and leave it waiting for you at the Order."

Bile rose up my throat but I swallowed it down. I couldn't let the guard or Gerarda see how hard that hit had landed. If the king was making such extreme threats, any trace of resistance could be met with death. And likely, it seemed, not my own.

I dismissed the guard and he scurried back to his post at the gate.

Gerarda grasped my elbow and moved us farther into the garden, out of sight of the guards or the high walls of the inner ring. "The king refuses to leave his chambers at all," she whispered. "If he must, he travels surrounded by a guard and all his meals are tested by two servants before he eats or drinks."

I glanced around the courtyard. "Did something happen?" I barely moved my lips as we pretended to be enjoying the summer blooms.

"At first his servants said he'd fallen ill." Gerarda picked a pink lily from a small garden patch and twirled it under her nose. "But he has not sent for a nurse or healer. No special order from the apothecary either."

I bent down and swiftly undid the lace of my boot to tie it again. "Strange."

"Stranger still. His moods are changing swiftly. There have been many days where he passed the entire afternoon talking to himself as if he couldn't see or hear the servants in his chambers. They said he would look right through them, almost wild with worry. Yesterday, he was muttering to one of his servants that he can die."

I stopped tying my boot. "The king is dying?" I hoped I didn't sound too excited.

Gerarda shrugged. "He only said he *can*. A curious way to phrase it if he's truly fallen ill."

I nodded. Very curious indeed. I stood and tugged my tunic down where the sleeves had ridden up. "If I'm not being called before His Majesty, then I will be on my way." I nodded to Gerarda. "I will expect a full report at month's end, same as before."

Gerarda grabbed my arm as I stepped past her. Even though I could see the top of her head, her glare still managed to be menacing. "I don't begrudge the Blade her secrets. But if the king makes good on his threat, I will not stop searching for you until *your* head is on a spike. I hope your secrets are worth the risk."

I swallowed my hot remark and nodded. There was less than three weeks until the next full moon.

I walked down to the beach from the palace without going to my rooms. The quicker I spoke to Hildegard, the quicker I could get out of the city. The glass bridge that led to the Order sparkled in the sunlight, reflecting bright colors onto the swirling sea below. I reached the abrupt end at what should have been the middle of the bridge and ran the last three strides before soaring through the air.

I landed on the first post shooting from the water and then the next. I'd crossed this way so many times I could do it blindfolded; my muscles knew the jumps without thought. With a final push, I launched myself off the last post and landed in the soft sand of the island that used to be my home.

The white towers of the Order loomed overhead, casting me in their shadow. I knew that the palace of Koratha was ten times the size of the Order, but somehow the miniature always felt bigger to me. Maybe because I was free to roam all of it as head of the Arsenal, but even as a child the Order had felt big. That was why it took me so long to realize it was a prison too.

The grounds were full of Shades and initiates training together. There was little size difference between most of them, but the Shades had covered shoulders from their hoods while the initiates wore the same plain sleeveless garb. All of them were much too young to throw their lives away for a king.

Or for me, if the king made good on his threat.

I found Hildegard in her office. I watched from the open doorway as she stood at the window observing the training below. I'd watched her stand there so many times over the years, always in the same tucked position with her hands behind her back and her chin tilted upward. As an initiate, she'd always seemed tall with her brown bun pulled toward the sky. Now her back curved with the weight of decades and her hair had grayed completely apart from the ends.

"You look well," Hildegard said, still turned toward the window.

I huffed a laugh. "Don't you have to lay your eyes on me to make that assessment?"

"I can't smell you from across the room, so I would say it's a marked improvement." Hildegard smiled over her shoulder.

I shrugged. I was too familiar with her to be embarrassed. Especially when she was right.

"I want to see the records of the royal accounts," I said, looking at my fingernails. "And the tax reports from every *winvra* supplier in the kingdom."

Hildegard's brow shot up. "You want to look at the books?"

"The king threatened to kill a Shade a day unless I catch this Shadow menace by the full moon. I figured I should pursue all my options." Hildegard paled. It was a cruel truth to burden her with; now she would spend the three weeks worrying that an execution order would arrive for one of her girls. But I needed to keep our conversation short and her suspicions low.

"I will have them sent to your chambers." Hildegard took a seat at her desk and began inking a message onto a piece of parchment. "How long are you here?"

"I leave on the morrow," I answered as Hildegard rang a bell. At once, an initiate stepped through the door.

She handed the parchment to the young girl. "Give this to Myrrah. She'll know what to do from there."

"I didn't realize Myrrah was here." The Shield usually spent her time at the palace when in the capital. It made it easier for her to meet with the king and his guard instead of traveling back and forth between the Order and the city in her wheelchair.

Hildegard gave a solemn nod. "The king refuses to see even his Shield, so Myrrah has been taking residence here."

My lip twitched upward. "She's lucky you're so accommodating as to share a room with her."

Hildegard ignored my comment. She and Myrrah had been lovers since I was an initiate, but they were both quiet about it, especially in front of the king. Coupling between two men or two women wasn't explicitly outlawed, but most of the lords or ladies kept their proclivities a secret at court. I teased her in private because it amused me, but I knew outside of these walls it was dangerous. There were few things that the king hated more than a happy Halfling.

"I might send her back regardless." Hildegard laughed. "She's been reorganizing the archives for days and it may be the death of me."

I could only imagine the state of the records downstairs, splayed over every table and the floor. Myrrah liked to work in chaos, shifting interests at any moment. Even though she shared a bed with Hildegard, her fastidious organization had yet to rub off on Myrrah.

I rubbed the inner side of my forearm, the place where Brenna's name was marked on me. "Does it make it easier being the Bow when you have someone to warm your bed? Or do all the nights you spend apart only add to the burden?"

I wasn't sure where the question had come from or why I was asking it now, but out of everyone in Elverath, I knew Hildegard was the only one who could give me an answer I might believe.

She leaned back in her chair and tucked her spectacles into her hair. "Before I became the Bow, I only had to worry about myself. My sole concern was fulfilling my duty as a Shade and making sure me and my partner lived to see another day. Then I was given my title and I had to worry about *every* Shade. I worried about the ones I trained, knowing I would lose so many of them and it couldn't be helped. I worried for the ones I *had* trained, knowing they would go out to serve the king's whims and I would lose even more."

Hildegard pursed her lips and stared out the window. "When I carried Myrrah out of that collapsed roof, we weren't even friends. I thought she was annoying—fresh to her post as Shield with all these new ideas, flitting from one hypothetical to the next." Hildegard chuckled under her breath. "It was exhausting. But Myrrah had broken protocol and climbed onto that roof to rescue a squadron of Shades. She got all six of them out before the house fell in. From then on, I knew that she worried about her duty to them as much as I did. And from that mutual respect grew something more. So yes, now when Myrrie is off sailing across the kingdom doing gods-know-what, you could say it is merely another worry that I have to carry. But I don't worry on my own any longer. The burden is shared."

I leaned against the edge of her desk. I could still see the faint mark from where I'd spilled ink across it. "But if one of you dies, how does the other not end up crushed by the weight of all that worry *and* their grief."

Hildegard raised her chin, her keen eyes lingering on my face. "You already know the answer to that better than Myrrah or I could ever say."

I pulled at the sleeve of my right arm. "Sometimes I wonder if the Shades would have been better off if I'd been the one who died."

Hildegard stood and placed her hands on my arms. "You do yourself a disservice judging Brenna by decisions she never had to make."

My breath hitched when Hildegard said her name. Three decades I'd gone without hearing anyone say that name in these halls. I thought it would be haunting and painful, but it sounded *right*. Brenna was as much a part of this place as I was, as Hildegard was, or any other initiate who had trained on this island.

As long as her name was remembered here, her fight continued.

As Hildegard looked at me, it was clear I was one of the things she worried about. I wished there was something I could say to appease that worry, but it was not without merits. Hildegard might not know the specifics, but she could sense the change in the tides better than anyone on this island. She knew war was coming, and she worried for all those who might not survive it. Just as I worried for her.

"What happened that day was the cruelest thing I have ever witnessed." Hildegard whispered so quietly I could barely hear her. "No person should be forced with a choice like that and especially not for the entertainment of a spoiled, vile prince." I flinched in surprise. I'd never heard Hildegard be so forthright with her distain for Damien before. She was usually more careful than that.

She pressed her palm against my cheek. My heart twinged at her touch; the gesture was almost motherly. "I'm glad to see you have survived through the worst of it and joined the living again. I'm proud to say I trained you and even prouder to say I serve under you now."

My throat was too raw to speak. I nodded my head against her palm and squeezed her other hand with my own. I made a silent vow to myself that I would make Hildegard prouder still by freeing the Halflings and bringing forth a world where she could love her Shades in peace.

I left her at her desk and headed down to the records storage in the basement. The large room looked exactly as I thought it would. Long shelves of scrolls and leather-bound books stood empty while their contents were spread across the entire space in a chaos only Myrrah could understand.

"Just getting the last of your order together," Myrrah called from her spot on the floor. In the dim light, her pale skin looked almost orange as she sat on a soft pillow with all her weight on her hip and her chair locked in position behind her. In front of her were numerous scrolls and records she was organizing into seven different piles.

"Actually, I came to ask about those Halflings that went missing in Silstra." I moved a scroll out of the way so I could kneel on the floor beside her. "Is there any chance they were taken in by the king's guard and we were not informed? That's a lot of Halflings to go missing without a trace."

"You always have such stupendous timing." Myrrah glanced about the room, the stray curls she hadn't captured in the bun at her neck fanned out from her head. "Do you see a book with a throwing dagger on the cover? Green hilt."

I spotted an emerald hilt poking out from underneath her boot. "That one?"

Myrrah looked down. "That's the one." She lifted her feet off the thick book with her hand and wrenched it free. Its cover was made of leather and marked with the seal of the king's guard. "I just received their latest report this morning." She pulled out a folded piece of parchment tucked inside the book and passed it to me.

I scanned the report. The number of prisoners had decreased in Silstra and the capital since the fire. I pointed to those numbers on the record for Myrrah to see. She held up a small piece of glass at arm's length to read them. "Yes, that's to be expected now that the king has refused to feed the prisoners any longer. Those who don't starve in their cells will be hung soon enough."

I noticed one line at the bottom of the page that didn't make sense to me. "I didn't realize the black cells were still being used after the cave-in."

Myrrah looked at my finger hovering over the list of prisoners by cell location. The words *black cells* were inked at the bottom though the rest of the information had been left blank. "They're not. I've made note of that error several times, but the captain of the guard never bothers to tell his scribe to fix it. I don't push the issue; we're lucky enough to receive reports."

"You're certain those cells are empty?" I asked. My palms were sweaty. As far as I knew, Myrrah had no idea I'd spent the first few years of my life in those cells, but I also had no idea what secrets she and Hildegard had whispered to each other over the years.

Myrrah shot me a deadpan stare. "You know, I'd go down that tunnel to check myself but"—she smacked the cushion of her chair—"also, it's not my job."

I smiled and bumped her shoulder with mine. "Fair enough."

Myrrah smiled back but it did not reach her eyes the way it normally did. "No one has serviced those cells in decades, Keera. The entire cell block would've been taken off the report years ago if it weren't for the inability of men to take direction from Halflings or women."

My lips twitched. Myrrah had never been one to shy away from her perceptions of the world. A dangerous trait for a Halfling, but one she bore well. "I'll keep chasing other leads, then," I said, standing up to my full height. "Send the records over once you're done finding everything." I swirled my hands over the documents strewn about the room.

"Mock my methods all you like, but I know exactly where each record is."

I hid my smirk behind a bow. "I have no doubt."

Myrrah pointed the daggered book at me. "Careful, Keera. You may be Blade, but I only tolerate such gall from my wife."

CHAPTER NINETEEN

WHEN I GOT TO MY CHAMBERS, Gerarda's reports had already arrived. An hour later, the ones from the Order came. My desk was surrounded by stacks of books and piles of scrolls so tall I couldn't see over them when I stood. I'd only made my way through a quarter of them by nightfall, and I already knew more about the taxation of *winvra* than I ever thought possible.

I leaned back in my chair and draped a cold cloth across my face. After days of fitful sleep, the thought of staying up all night was not a welcome one. My throat already burned with the craving for something that would help keep me up. I ignored it and wiped a damp cloth down my neck.

The door opened, followed by an excited shriek. Gwyn wrapped her arms around my neck. "Why did I have to find out you returned from the gossip in the kitchens?" She sat herself down on the one clear spot on my desk and crossed her arms. "You usually call for me."

I sighed and dropped my plume back into its holster. "It was a last-minute decision."

"Clearly." Gwyn waved her hand at the mountain of books I still had to get through. Her bottom lip protruded ever so slightly.

I laughed. "I was going to see you before I left. How else would I give you your gift?"

Gwyn sat straighter on the desk at the mention of a present. "How long are you here for this time?"

My chest tightened. "I leave in the morning."

Gwyn's shoulders fell. She filled her cheeks with air and let the breath out slowly so it buzzed through her lips. "It's so boring when you're gone."

"Boring?" I felt my own shoulders fall and my next breath was an easy one. Gwyn might not like it, but I would love for every day she had to share the same home as Damien to be a boring one.

Gwyn read the true question in my reply with ease. "Damien hasn't called on me in weeks. He just laments to all the lords at court about how the king won't let him leave. He says a lack of freedoms is deadly to those of royal blood." Gwyn rolled her eyes and twisted her ankle where her tether was marked into her skin.

As long as the king lived, Gwyn could not leave this palace. She was a true prisoner here, just like her foremothers from whom she inherited the debt.

"Good." One less problem for me to worry about. I grabbed a small package wrapped in a thick gold leaf and tossed it onto Gwyn's lap.

She opened it with delicate hands and picked up the small ball inside. Gwyn held it up to the window. Tiny rays of gold light scattered across her freckled cheeks. "It's a marble?"

"Of sorts." I leaned in closer so we could talk as quietly as possible. "If you ever need me, if you ever feel that tether beginning to fade"—I pointed to her ankle—"all you need to do is throw this ball into a flame and I will come for you."

Gwyn's brow furrowed as she studied the ball even closer. "A candle is enough or does it need to be a hearth?"

"Either will do." I closed her fingers around the bead so it was safe in her palm. I tugged on the matching sphere wrapped in a leather strap around my neck that Dynara had given me. "Keep this on you at all times."

Gwyn's eyes turned soft. She pressed her forehead against mine as she spoke. "The king is not sick, Keera, even Damien says so." She said it like she was comforting a child who'd lost their toy, like she had no reason to wish for the king to die.

I tapped her hand. "Keep it on you either way. It will make it easier to leave you knowing you can reach me no matter where I am. And if yours ever lights, come here immediately. I do not care what you are doing or who you are with, you need to wait for me here."

Gwyn placed the hard ball inside the bust of her dress. "A swift bird can reach Mortal's Landing within a day."

I swallowed guiltily. I wished I could tell Gwyn of where I had really been, describe all the wonders of the Faeland to her as we sat on the beach. Even better, I wished I could take her there with me and leave the capital behind. But that would have to wait until I struck my dagger through the king's heart.

I tucked a scarlet curl behind her ear. "This is much quicker than a bird."

Gwyn hopped off the desk and clapped her hands. "Where should I start?"

I shook my head. "Gwyn, you have to work in the morning, you need your rest."

She jutted her hip to one side and hit me with an icy stare. "As I said, where do I start?"

"You're the only maid in the entire castle with enough daring to talk back to me." I held out a book for her.

Gwyn's smirk was full of mischief. "They must confuse you with Gerarda."

I pulled the book back and slapped it on the desk.

"I'm kidding!" Gwyn laughed.

I passed the book back. "Mark any page that mentions the Shadow."

Gwyn stretched her arms above her head and took the book. She laid down on my bed on her belly and placed the book in front of her. "I never realized being a spy required so much reading."

Gwyn was still sleeping on my bed when I left. I took the layers of books she'd gone through off the mattress and laid the covers over her. She still had a few hours before she'd be expected in the kitchens.

I closed the door as gently as I could and made my way through the east wing. I was just about to cross through the garden toward the stables when someone stepped in front of me. "Leaving so soon, Keera?" Damien asked, trailing a gloved finger under my throat. "You only just arrived."

I stepped back out of his reach. "A Blade must cut quickly, Your Highness." I gave the smallest bow I could manage.

Damien sloshed the goblet he was holding. "Especially a Blade with a deadline." He chuckled as he finished the rest of the wine. "The full moon, is it?"

The rich scent of Elven wine filled the air. I held my breath and swallowed the burning that had started to tickle my throat. "Yes, sire."

"My father can be an unnecessarily cruel man. Threatening all those Shades for one Shadow." Damien wiped his mouth on the sleeve of his embroidered tunic. "I would never be as wasteful as that."

Sharp words armed themselves on my tongue. I bit my lip to keep myself from launching them at the prince. "Of course you wouldn't, Your Highness." It took everything in me to nod my head.

Damien ran his hand through his short blond waves. His jade eyes trailed down my body before locking on the patch of skin along my neck. The faintest line of a scar curved over my shoulder there, lit by the red light of the torch that had not quite burned to ash. Only someone who knew the scar was there would ever spot it. Thirty years later, Damien still remembered every slice he had cut into me.

He took a step toward me and touched the spot with the end of his goblet. I clamped my jaw shut and turned my hands to fists to keep from punching him. "I will make a much *wiser* threat," Damien whispered. His breath warmed my ear like a fire poker threatening to scar me again. "Bring me the Shadow's head by full moon or it will be that annoying chambermaid you adore so much who will pay the price." Damien leaned back and pulled his hand across his throat in a slow, straight line.

It took every ounce of will I had to keep myself rooted into the ground. My heart beat so hard against my chest I thought I might explode. The edges of my vision went blurry until all I could see was Damien's smug grin. He looked like the bull's-eye of a target, teasing me from across the field, urging me to shoot.

I didn't. But my hand gripped the white hilt at my hip.

Damien's gaze dropped to the bloodred dagger and he let out a breathy laugh. "I've been locked in this house for much too long, Keera. Hurry up, before I get bored."

He dropped his empty goblet at my feet and sauntered back into the palace.

I picked up the cup. The opening was a crown, cast with deep red jewels that matched the ones on Aemon's throne. I chucked it with all my might at the pillar Damien had disappeared behind and left to fetch my horse.

CHAPTER
TWENTY

I DIDN'T TRAVEL THROUGH the same portals on my way back to Myrelinth. I needed to make a stop before I faced the rest of the Elverin again. A stop I didn't want Killian or any of the others knowing about.

I couldn't risk the mole finding out. Not with the lives of the Shades and Gwyn on the line. I passed through the fourth and final portal, appearing in the Dark Wood. A wall of water had risen from the lake, shimmering in the same auric light as all the other passages. I rode my horse through it, feeling the misty veil on my skin for the briefest moment before we stepped onto the pebbled beach.

Aralinth was only a few short hours south. I hoped that the person I needed to see was waiting there.

I pulled my traveling hood over my face as I came into the city of eternal spring. The cloak was brown like many of the others who lived there and hid my face well enough. I returned the horse to its stable, grateful that no one was there to bother me about taking her in the first place. I tossed the horse a piece of fruit out of an abandoned bucket and cut across the city to Dynara's apartments.

I knocked once before sliding between the grand white doors of her rooms. Dynara lifted her head from where she lay across a chaise holding a book along her stomach.

"I'm not in the mood for distraction unfortunately." She sighed, not bothering to sit up as I took the chair beside her. She tossed the book onto the table next to a teapot that still steamed through its elegant spout.

There was no glint in Dynara's eye as she laid there, no witty quip on her tongue. She was not dressed in one of her Elvish gowns, but a plain robe the color of an overcast sky. Her full lips were turned down in a way that felt unnatural for her just like the messy state of her hair.

"What news of the Halflings, then?" I asked, knowing that was the cause of her low mood.

She tilted her chin to the ceiling, pinching the crown of her hair between her head and the armrest. "No bodies were recovered at the safe house."

My shoulders relaxed. That was good news—for the Halflings—but also for what I was about to do. "That means they could still be alive, Dynara."

She snapped her head at me. "And depending who has them, that is worse." Her lips curled against her teeth in disgust. She had seen too much of the kingdom's cruelty. I understood why it might be more comforting to know those Halflings had been lost to the flames instead.

"That's why I've come." I glanced about the lavish room. "Are we alone?" My last question was barely more than a whisper, but it piqued Dynara's interest enough that she pulled herself to a sitting position as she nodded.

"This is not the first attack on our safe houses," I whispered.

Dynara's eyelashes fluttered. "More Halflings have been taken?"

"I think so. When did you receive the last group of rescues from Tarvelle?" Halflings had gone missing from that fire in Volcar. With everything I learned rummaging through those books in the capital, I had a feeling that first fire had nothing to do with the Shadow at all.

Dynara pursed her lips in thought. "About a month before you first came to the *Faelinth*. Tarvelle rescued a group of four from Mortal's Landing. After you struck your deal with Riven, the rescues were sent to Silstra to wait until Tarvelle could arrange transport."

I nodded. I'd suspected as much. The mole had been leaking information to Curringham for much longer than anyone had realized. But I couldn't tell Killian and the others without risking the mole finding out what I knew. My throat tightened. For all I knew, the mole could be one of them.

I grabbed Dynara's hand. She was the only one in the entire Faeland who I was certain would *never* work with Curringham or do anything to risk the lives of Halflings. "There's more," I said in the same quiet tone. "There's a mole in our midst. That's how these attacks are happening."

Dynara leaned against the back of the chaise. Her hands were shaking like she was going to hurt someone or be sick. I couldn't tell which. "Those Halflings were taken because someone is spilling secrets?" She crossed her legs and arms. "To whom? For what reason?"

I ran my fingers through my hair and took a deep breath. "Yes, that's why they were taken. For what reason or to where—I do not know. But I think I know who did it."

Dynara straightened in her seat. Her already angular features seemed to sharpen like freshly honed steel. Her next words sliced the air as she spoke. "Tell me."

I held her gaze, refusing to look away as I answered her. "Curringham."

If the name cut open old wounds, Dynara didn't let it show. She sat firm in her seat, her only movement coming from the way her dark eyes narrowed at his name. "That can't be right."

I raised my brows in shock. "You don't think Curringham capable of such a ploy?"

Dynara ran her tongue along her teeth before she spoke. "Curringham is a man who likes his comforts and his pleasures. He has both. I don't see why he would risk his livelihood to . . . What does he have to gain by attacking our storehouses?"

"A life of infinitely more comfort and pleasure across the sea." I leaned back and pulled my ankle onto my knee. "He has procured over a dozen ships to ferry his fortune and leave Elverath for good."

Dynara propped one elbow onto the back of her chaise and held her hands together. "So his attacks are meant to confuse the crown? Clever." There was an edge to her final word.

I tilted my head and waited for her to explain.

She leaned forward and grabbed the cup of tea from the table beside us. She took a sip, never breaking her stare. "Curringham is a man in love with wealth and power but little mind for either."

I spread my arm along the back of the seat and drummed my fingers along its edge. I'd had the same thought when I found that harvest pin at the safe house. The man I'd tailed for weeks in Cereliath was not a master of plots or wit. He was an oaf of a man. One with too much love for wine and hands that liked to travel where they shouldn't. Still, I couldn't deny where the facts lead me. Curringham had been falsifying his tax reports for years; I just needed the last piece of evidence that would prove his treachery to the king.

I took a breath and studied Dynara. "And what do you have a mind for?"

Dynara ran a finger around the brim of her cup. "Do you mean to flatter me or proposition me, Keera?"

"Both."

I plucked the malachite ring from my pocket and placed it on the table.

Dynara's eyes locked on the gold. Her finger froze as the recognition washed over her and understanding with it. She didn't look up from the ring as she spoke. "You're asking me to go back there?"

I'd expected rage or hurt. I'd prepared myself for wild screaming and outright refusal. That was how most would act when asked to return to the place where all their fears had been born. But Dynara was calm, perfectly reserved as she finally looked up from the ring and met my gaze.

"It's unfair of me to ask," I said, jutting my jaw to the side. "But I cannot trust anyone else and I cannot abandon my work with Feron to be the spy myself." I swallowed and picked a loose thread from the chair. "The king has set a deadline. If I do not return to the palace with the Shadow's head by full moon then he will start killing Shades one by one. We both know he won't stop."

Dynara took another small sip of tea. "You're looking for proof, then? To offer Aemon something in place of the Shadow's head?"

I nodded.

"And you want me to find it for you? In that house . . ." She trailed off, turning away from me for the first time. Dynara had been almost flippant about the night she'd escaped when I first met her in Aralinth. Seeing the way her pulse raced and the rash that had appeared along her chest, I knew it had only been how she coped. The House of Harvest was the place of her nightmares, and I was asking her to return to it.

I walked around the table and grabbed her hand as I sat next to her. "I know what I ask of you. I know what happened the last time you were in that house."

Dynara's bottom lip quivered. "That was not Nikolai's story to tell."

"No, it wasn't." I squeezed her hand. "But I want you to know that if you say no, I completely understand."

Dynara leaned her head against my shoulder. "What do you think he's going to do with those Halflings?"

I wrapped my arm around her and tried to keep my own hands from shaking. "He will need help to ferry that much *winvra*."

Dynara scoffed. "Those Halflings will either end up dead or forced to spend their lives in servitude cut off from their lands and kin. Even if you defeat Aemon, they will be lost."

I nodded solemnly. She took a large inhale of air and sighed. "I will not let that happen."

"You will go, then?" I stilled against her.

She nodded and stood. I watched in disbelief as she crossed into her bedroom and came back with two sleek books bound in leather. She dropped one on my lap. "When you need to reach me, write a message on the parchment from that book and then set the page alight." She held up the twin journal. "I will have it the instant the paper turns to ash."

I opened the front cover to find the inside was filled with blank sheets though the parchment felt softer and smelled earthier than a journal should. I snapped it shut and stood myself. "I will send you with a letter asking the Lords of Harvest to host the lady cousin of the king's late wife. That should be enough to gain you entry."

Dynara nodded. There was only a hint of her fear left in her eyes; most had been replaced by cold resolve. "I will need gold. Lots of it."

"Do you plan to buy out the city merchants while you spy?" I chuckled.

Dynara's grin was the feline smirk of a wild cat trapping her prey. She lifted her sleeve to reveal the brand of the king's crown on her wrist. "I will buy every courtesan in the city and bring them back when I return."

From the dangerous edge of Dynara's words, I knew she planned to do more than that. I pulled her into a tight embrace. There weren't enough words in either tongue I knew to tell her how grateful I was so I offered her the only thing I could.

"I will send word to the bank and tell them to empty to my account for you."

CHAPTER TWENTY-ONE

FOUR HOURS LATER, Dynara and I had said our goodbyes. She was packed with my sealed letter and her journal. Thankfully, her closet was already lavish enough to masquerade as a lady of court. She slipped the malachite ring on her finger and stepped through a portal to the west of Aralinth under the guise of a Mortal beauty.

My stomach churned, but I knew she would reach Cereliath safely. Dynara couldn't have survived her past without being quick-witted. She would find Wilden soon enough, and once he read my letter, he would outfit Dynara with the finest carriage in the city to drive her to the House of Harvest.

I swallowed the dryness in my throat. The guilt was scorching. I had kept secrets and information from Riven and the others before. Mostly information about myself and the Shades, but now I would be keeping a secret from them about their friend. A friend we might never see again if she was discovered.

I dropped my bloom into the small pool of the twin Elder birches and took a deep breath of the floral mist as I walked through the portal. The city was buzzing as I walked along the edge of the Dark Wood. Everyone was preparing for dinner.

I spotted Nikolai walking up a well-worn trail in the grass headed toward the empty clearing by the lake. He carried a bouquet of flowers in his hand that was slightly wilted. "You should put those in water," I said by way of greeting.

Nikolai looked down at his hand as if he forgot he was carrying the blooms. "I think I will." He looped his arm through mine. "Feron was looking for you earlier. I think he's in the library now."

I squeezed his arm. "I'll go meet him, then. What is everyone doing?" I pointed to where a group of Elverin were hanging long strands of fabric from the Myram tree. Whatever they were preparing, it was more than dinner.

That boyish grin appeared on Nikolai's lip. "I'm not going to ruin the surprise, Keera dear."

I rolled my eyes and gave his arm one last squeeze before disappearing into one of the tunnels of the nearby groves. Nikolai waved at me with his bent blooms as I disappeared into the earth.

When I walked into the library, Feron was seated in the same chair as always. I sat on the chaise next to him, sticking to our routine. We'd already had three sessions, but I had yet to pull any memories forward from the blackness.

My neck tensed. I couldn't let the fourth time be a failure. There was too much at stake with the lives of the Shades and Gwyn on the line. If I couldn't figure out a way to appease the king before the full moon, I'd have no other choice. With the Light Fae or not,

I would try to kill the king before Damien ever got the chance to hurt Gwyn.

Still, if my memories could help us find them, I would exhaust myself completely trying to recover them. I barely had a fortnight to do just that.

Feron noticed the tension in my body as he settled into his seat. He tucked his long lilac robe under the chair and stuck his cane through a loop on his mulberry sash. He stared down at me with cautious eyes. "I want to try something different today."

I swallowed nervously.

"Focusing on memories you cannot remember has yielded few results."

I sighed. "*No* results."

Feron smirked and placed both hands at the sides of my head. "I think we need to focus on something you *do* remember. Let your body become familiar with the sensation of sharing a memory just as it became familiar with the darkness."

I stilled against the fabric of the chaise. "*Any* memory?"

Feron nodded. "Whatever blows into your mind. If my gift can realize the memory then I will call today's session a success."

I took a deep breath and nodded. I glanced at the back of the room where Riven usually stood but he wasn't there. I'd come to the library so quickly there hadn't been time to find him.

Feron turned to the empty wall and then back at me. "We can wait."

I shook my head. We didn't have the luxury of time and my heart rate had barely twitched the last time. I shifted along the chaise, getting comfortable as Feron lifted his hands to begin.

I closed my eyes.

Someone crashed through the door.

"I was helping Collin." Riven knelt over, wheezing in long breaths. "Just heard." He met my gaze, his face soft and apologetic. My heart melted into the chaise as my body relaxed.

"Don't let Syrra know running down one set of stairs tired you so thoroughly." I shot him an assessing look. "She'd have you training from dawn till dusk."

Riven smirked. He took another deep breath and claimed his place at the back of the room. I looked up and Feron nodded before I finally closed my eyes.

The warmth of Feron's magic fell over me like a veil of sunlight. I counted three breaths before I was coaxed into a place between sleep and life. An opaque blackness swept over me, consumed me fully, until I couldn't picture the library in Myrelinth or hear Riven pacing along the floor. I was weightless, suspended in the nothingness. The chaise beneath me didn't exist and neither did my body.

The blackness didn't scare me anymore, but I was glad Riven had left Collin and come to me. I liked knowing his shadows were only a call away.

The darkness shifted and swirled with lines of gray. They formed blurry edges along a newfound horizon, suddenly blooming into full color. I recognized the city immediately. The sandstone manor set high in the distance looked burnt in the light of the setting suns.

Cereliath.

I was riding at top speed down an alleyway, the taste of wine fresh on my lips. Peasants and merchants jumped out of the way as my steed galloped by.

I blinked. My vision was blurry.

I stopped outside a small dwelling in the merchant corridor, jumping off my horse before it came to a full stop. I felt the hard impact of the cobblestone under my feet as if everything was happening in that very moment and not twenty-five years earlier.

The stone walls of the house were decorated with dusty tapestries that matched the brass sign hanging from the door. My heart raced, hoping I was not too late. I'd ridden for two days straight once I'd heard what the king had ordered. I only hoped the Shades had not carried out the sentence yet.

My stomach sunk to the floor as I stepped through the entrance and saw the discarded toys of a child left in the hall. I took a deep breath and secured the hood of my cloak across my face.

Two Shades stood in the main room. Next to them were three bodies with sacks over their heads. I spotted the smallest one right away. She was trembling, holding on to a stuffed doll made of patchwork linen. The two black hoods bowed as I stood in front of the family on their knees. I took a swig of my wineskin and nodded to the Shades.

They pulled the bags free from the parents first. I knew immediately by the frenzied look in the mother's eye and the way she lashed against the gag in her mouth that she was the Halfling. The husband kneeled in silence, his wide eyes unfocused and still, as if he were already dead. Their daughter leaned against her mother, who bent unnaturally, trying to console her even though her arms were bound behind her.

I held out my hand. One of the Shades placed the order in my hand. The one the king had given them on purpose. To spite me or test them, I didn't know. All I knew was these Shades were not even seventeen. I would not allow them to execute an entire family just so Aemon could prove a point.

I read the order slowly because the words were dancing on the page. The king had demanded that the execution take place in the city circle, but I would at least spare them that. I undid the scroll and cleared my throat.

"Toman William Franshire, you have been accused of knowingly harboring a Halfling in violation of the Halfling Decree. You are also accused of unlawfully procreating with said Halfling in violation of the Halfling Decree. Furthermore, you stand accused of harboring the half-breed child of said union also in violation of the Halfling Decree. How do you plead, sir?" My throat ached at the unfairness of that question. The verdict had been decided a week ago when the king learned that the man who decorated his chambers had a Halfling wife. I was only filling out a formality.

Toman did not respond. He continued to stare, unseeing, into some abyss. Lifeless, even in his last moments. His wife shrieked behind her gag. Her eyes flooded with tears, begging me to let her speak. I nodded to the Shade closest to her, who removed her gag.

"He didn't know, he didn't know!" she wailed. "I tricked him. He didn't know. He didn't break any laws. He thought I was a good wife who bore him a good child. Please, hurt *me*. Not them. Not her. *Please*." She collapsed to the ground in front of me, her words indecipherable from her sobs.

"Is this true?" I asked her husband. I knew it wasn't. I had seen the reports. Toman was a doting spouse who adored his wife and child. No man that involved would have missed the amber blood of his wife, let alone his daughter. Still, I had let parents free on less.

Toman's eyes focused for just a moment. He looked at me and I recognized the pain of someone who had no plans to live past his love. He shook his head and his wife wailed harder next to him.

I swallowed. I didn't want my voice to crack while I read the sentence out. "Toman, you have been found guilty of all charges by order of His Majesty, King Aemon, the first of his name. For your blatant violation of the king's law, you will be put to death. Your wife, the fugitive Halfling, who aided your attempt to embarrass the king, will also be put to death. Your child, being a female, would have been taken into the king's service and tested at the Order. However, due to your blatant disregard of your king, you shall be punished before His mercy is carried out. Your daughter is to be put to death and her father is hereby ordered to observe."

For the first time, his face crumpled but he did not sob. My chest ripped open and I was unable to breathe. I rolled the parchment up and tucked the scroll into my pocket. I was glad for the hood covering my face. Aemon had been cruel in his design to ruin this family. It was why I had raced for days on horseback so no one else would have to carry out that burden.

Now I had to carry it out for the second time. My arms felt like lead as the young girl stared up at me. I knew Aemon would follow up with this report, take glee in his revenge, and I would need to carry it out as instructed. But I would not make a spectacle of this family's death. The cost of the lives I had to take already weighed too much.

I dropped to my knee and freed the little girl of her gag. "I'm going to untie you now and then you can give your mother a hug." She trembled silently as I untied the binding around her ankles and arms.

I moved to her mother who had sat up and watched with wide eyes. "Do not run," I ordered before I sliced through her bindings with my knife. Her daughter crawled into her lap and cried in her mother's arms. I pulled a vial of sleeping draught from my belt. It was almost empty, but I only needed a few drops.

I turned to Toman. "Kiss your daughter," I whispered. His lips quivered as he bent forward and pressed a kiss against his daughter's soft curls. Then I grabbed the girl's chin as she cried and let three drops hit her tongue. She fell asleep immediately, peaceful and serene in her mother's arms.

I shook the vial and clenched my teeth. "I only have enough for one of you."

"Give it to her," Toman said without hesitation. "I don't want her to see this."

His wife cried as the draught splashed into her mouth and then she was silent too.

Toman stared down at his family lying on the carpet. His wife's arms were wrapped around their daughter as they lay heart to heart. He bent over and pressed a kiss to his wife's cheek and then looked at me. His eyes were no longer cloudy, but resolute. I struck my blade through the two in one quick blow and then I used it on Toman.

He fell on top of them, his arms wrapped around his loves even in death. I stood, unmoving above them all, watching the pool of amber blood mixing with the trail of red. My throat seared with pain. One of the Shades sniffled under her hood.

I turned to her. "Make sure to cry all your tears here. You *cannot* cry when you present your report to the king. He *must* believe you did this." Her hand disappeared under the shadow of her hood and she nodded. I turned and exited the door.

I fell to the ground and it disappeared. I was surrounded by darkness again as the memory faded away. I screamed into the abyss and ripped at my chest. The skin on my upper rib burned where their names were carved into my flesh. I slammed my hand into the ground, expecting to feel a hard surface but instead it was soft.

"Keera," a strained voice was calling me. "Keera, come out of it."

It was Riven. I could feel his hands on me, the weight of them bringing me back into the present. I opened my eyes and Riven's face was inches from mine, his breath racing as he stared down at me. "You're safe. I'm here." His shadows swirled around our limbs, tying them together.

Feron was leaning back in his chair. His chest heaved and I saw the tears in his eyes. I hid my face in Riven's chest. I did not want to face the pain a third time by telling him what Feron had seen. By telling him what I had done.

"Riven, you are no longer needed here," Feron said in too even a voice for what we had just experienced.

I heard Riven's teeth clamp shut. "I'm not leaving."

Feron glanced at me and I knew that he wanted to discuss the memory. He was giving me the chance to keep Riven from the horror of it.

I cleared my throat. "It's okay," I whispered. "I'm fine now."

Riven's jaw pulsed. He held my gaze for a long moment, giving me the chance to change my mind, but he didn't protest.

"I'll be in my room if you need me," he said, and then he was gone.

I pressed my hands into the chaise; all the energy had drained from my body and I needed the support to keep myself upright. I glanced at Feron. "I didn't mean to pick that memory." I swallowed back my tears. "It just happened."

Feron nodded slowly. "I suspect you were thinking about Collin after Riven mentioned him."

I blinked. "Yes, just before the memory came to life."

"The magic grabbed onto that thought. You were thinking about this night recently." It wasn't a question, but a statement. He leaned back in his chair. His shoulders and lips drooped toward the floor, and for the first time Feron looked old.

"I've been dreaming about it," I admitted. "Collin confronted me a few days ago."

Feron was quiet for several moments before he spoke again. "Did you tell Collin how you spared his family?"

I recoiled back into the chaise. "*Spared?* They died because Toman dared to serve the king and take a Halfling as his wife."

Feron nodded so calmly it set my blood to boil. "Their deaths were meant to be much crueler than the ones you gave them. You spared each of them the pain of that cruelty."

I held my head in my hands, crumpling where I sat. "I spared them nothing." My voice cracked as a tear rolled down my cheek.

Feron stood, holding out a hand for me to grasp. "I think Collin would find you spared them in every way that mattered. He still believes his family was hung and beaten in the square. You cannot spare him the pain of that falsehood, but you can free him from it."

My throat was raw; it hurt to speak. "Collin hates me."

How Feron managed to chuckle, I didn't know. "Then you have nothing to lose in telling him."

CHAPTER TWENTY-TWO

Riven was waiting for me when I stepped out of the shower. His eyes trailed down my slick arms, pausing at the hem of my towel, before he turned around to let me dress. I pulled on a long tunic and sat on the bed.

He stepped between my legs and traced the line of my jaw with his finger. "Are you okay?" His long black hair framed the worry in his face. "You were crying through the memory."

I let my head rest against Riven's chest. He ran his hand down my hair again and again while I mustered the strength to tell him, but no words came.

Riven pressed his lips to the top of my head, understanding that I couldn't speak of it yet.

"Most days, Myrelinth is my favorite city on the entire continent, but nothing compares to Volcar when it snows. No matter how many times I visit, I'm always amazed." Riven's voice was soft and comforting, caressing me with his words as his hand stroked my hair.

I nudged him with my head. "More."

He laughed softly, but it rumbled deep in his belly. "I can mimic any bird I've come across and sometimes I use my talents to scare Syrra."

I scoffed. "Syrra is afraid of birds?"

"Owls." I could hear the grin in Riven's voice. "I like to swim but never let myself do it because the water makes it hard to control my magic. I secretly think Nikolai is the wisest person I know, but I'll never tell him."

A laugh bubbled out of my chest. "He would never let you forget it."

"Exactly." Riven twirled a strand of my hair between his fingers. "I've always wanted to take up painting but I think I'd be terrible at it. I would never admit it to Syrra, but I could go my entire life without eating rabbit ever again. And my favorite soup is stew."

I looked up at him with a raised brow. "There's not enough broth in stew for it to be considered a soup."

Riven smirked down at me and I couldn't deny the thrill it sent through my body. "And you're an expert on soup?"

"No, but I spend every day peeling potatoes for one. I can ask Lash right now." I stood and stepped toward the door. Riven grabbed me by the waist and spun me around.

I laughed so loudly my stomach ached. Only when I promised not to go running after a five-thousand-year-old Fae to ask him about the necessary ratio of broth to potatoes did Riven put me down. My body slowly slid along his chest until my feet were on the ground.

His hands settled on my waist. I wrapped my arms around him and pulled him tight against me. "Thank you," I whispered in his ear. "I feel much better now."

Riven stroked my cheek with his thumb. "I'm always here for you, Keera. Whatever you need."

I smirked into his chest. "Unless it's rabbit."

He lifted my chin with his finger and parted my lips with his thumb. My skin burned at the touch. "I would eat rabbit for every meal if that's what you wanted, *diizra.*" He let go of my mouth and I regained the ability to breathe. His gaze caught along the doorway to where the suns had completely set and he turned to me with an excited grin.

"It's time."

The Myram tree was covered in silks and tulle. Long strands wrapped around the trunk and hung from every branch and vine. Tiny silver faebeads were stitched into the fabric, making it look like the night sky was pouring into the grove like black ink glittering with stars.

There was no moon hanging in the sky tonight, making each star and bead shine all the brighter. Riven held my hand as we walked down one of the twisting branches of the Myram. I held out my hand and scraped the tulle like I was touching a cloud.

If I hadn't seen why Myrelinth was Riven's favorite city before, I did now.

We joined Nikolai and Syrra at a table right next to a large fire that danced with flames of blue and crimson. Syrra passed me a plate of food she'd gathered for us and went back to eating her own meal. I picked up a cube of fresh cheese and a sliced bit of root I didn't know the name of but now could recognize on sight.

They were warm and delicious, packed with a spicy aftertaste that I'd never been served in the kingdom. Nikolai pointed to a piece of flaky, black cheese. "Try that one next."

We had just finished our meal when a chorus of drums filled the grove. Lash stepped forward, and everyone stood in unison like a wave at sea. I followed as everyone else stepped back from their tables and watched as Lash moved his arms in every direction, turning the roots into a stadium facing the fire and the Myram tree.

When he was done, Lash wiped his brow. That tiny exercise of magic already taking its toll.

The children flooded in first, sitting on the ground at the front while the adults took the seats. Nikolai claimed the first row. "Newcomers always get the front row," he said loudly, as if justifying his choice to the cautious Elverin seated next to us.

Behind us was Pirmiith, the Elf I had saved from the Unnamed Ones. He smiled widely as I sat down and bowed his head. I returned the gesture and sat.

Feron and Lash stood behind the flames. Feron waved his hand over the ground and a root shot up, creating a seat for him to perch on. I leaned over to Riven. "I didn't know Lash shared Feron's gifts."

"Lash is only touched by the gift of earth and he doesn't have Feron's ability to mindwalk. His true specialty is flame." Riven pointed to the long fire with his chin.

Lash spun and slashed his hand across the flame. It split in two, creating a path between the fires that an ancient Elf walked through. Her skin was a deep shade of brown etched with wrinkles and worn lines that marked the decades like the rings of a tree. Her hair was a thick mane of silver coils that spun tightly down her hunched back.

She stepped forward, leaning on a wooden contraption with four legs to keep herself steady. She turned it around and flipped down the front to form a seat. Nikolai glanced at me. "One of my inventions."

The woman moved her hands in quick intricate motions, and the entire grove fell into anticipatory silence. She lowered her hands as she sat and the flames burned low in deep shades of cobalt beside her.

Nikolai squeezed tighter beside me. "I'll interpret for you. Though I think you'll find most of it is self-explanatory."

"Interpret?" I asked, but the drumming had started. All around the tree, loud clashes of hide boomed against the Myram, echoing back like cracks of thunder. The old Elf waved her hand above her head, and Lash made the flames flare high enough to tickle the upper vines of the Myram tree.

"My name is Darythir," Nikolai whispered in my ear, interpreting what the Elf was saying with her hands. "I was gifted this story long ago from an Elf as old as I. It is the story of our people. A story that can only be told on nights where the moon has turned to shadow."

The flames burned high once more, but then they flattened completely into shades of the deepest blue, creating a map of Elverath with their embers. Darythir fluttered her hands over the hearth, her fingers moved, too quick for me to catch the intricate movements. Nikolai leaned in once more.

"Before the time of Elves, a magic rain fell across this land. Everywhere the rain touched, new magic sprouted. New creatures ran across the lands, new swimmers appeared in the lakes and seas, even the plants and trees were magical after that rain."

Figures of flame danced across the hearth. Large beasts that roared and swiped at other figures that jumped from a sea of fire. Tall trees swayed in the flames, their leaves flickering to the ground as Lash waved his arms behind them.

I turned back to Darythir, forgetting Nikolai was speaking and not her. "But that magic needed someone to tend to it. So when the clouds rained over Elverath once more, the first Elves sprouted from the earth themselves. Some the color of wet sand, others formed from damp clay, and some were born from earth as black as the soil that feeds the Myram tree."

The children gasped as Elven figures emerged from the flames, standing so tall their heads reached the upper branches.

"For thousands of years, the Elves were the caretakers of this land. But something evil had sprouted from that rain too, growing stronger as the Elves nurtured the magic of Elverath. Dark creatures made of ash and shadow, too strong for the Elves to defeat on their own."

The children screamed as a large-winged beast rose up from the flames, its body cast in smoke. A young boy, too brave to scream, raised his hand and Darythir nodded her head at him. "What happened next?" He knew how to ask his question by both tongue and hand.

Darythir laughed and patted the boy on his head. She moved her hands and the shadowy beast blew away and a small tree made of flame took its place.

"The Elves knew that they could not care for these lands as long as such creatures roamed across Elverath. So they planted a sapling in the middle of a large field and danced around it for three days and three nights calling for magic rain."

The children shook with anticipation as their eyes locked on Darythir to continue the story.

"On the fourth day the sapling grew taller than any tree in the forest. It sprouted gold leaves the size of ponds and cracked open right down the middle."

The logs of the fire crackled as if on cue and the flames depicted the great Elder birch of Aralinth opening its door for the very first time.

"This is my favorite part," a little boy squealed in Elvish.

Nikolai continued to interpret the story in my ear. "Faelin, the first Faemother, was born from Sil'abar with eyes of molten gold as bright as the sun that shone above the Elder birch. She was gifted with magic so powerful she defeated the first of the shadow creatures with ease."

Lash created the image of a fiery Fae with a thick mane of hair using her gifts to defeat the shadowed creatures. The crowd cheered and gasped until all the creatures had disappeared and the Fae was standing victorious.

"But Faelin knew that one Fae was not enough to keep the creatures from returning. She danced for rain but it didn't come. She danced for a week, and there was no cloud in sight. On the third try, she danced so long she fell asleep on a long beach and turned to stone. A hundred years she laid there, in a deep Elvish sleep, as the white stone grew tall and thick. On the first day of summer on that hundred and first year, the stone cracked along the top, and Faelin emerged carrying two babes in her arms."

Lash swirled his hands and the large stone of flame transformed into the palace of Koratha. My throat swelled. I had spent so much of my life in that city, feeling disconnected from my kin in so many ways. To see their history performed in front of me, to finally hear the stories I had longed for as a child, healed some of the pain I carried in my chest.

"Faelin named her babe with golden eyes lined in violet *Ara'linthir* and her babe with golden eyes lined with silver was called *Kieran'thara*. Together they became the three Faemothers who banished the dark ones for good."

A little girl stood up holding her doll in one hand. "The second sun! The second sun!" she yelled as she danced in a circle. The Elverin behind her chuckled.

Darythir nodded and glanced at Lash. Suddenly the flames receded and three small creatures made of smoke slithered forth from the ashes. "The Faemothers knew that the dark ones feared the power of the sun. Its magic stung their bodies and made them too weak to hunt or set the world aflame. Faelin gathered all her power and used her magic to set a spell upon the sun. As long as the Elverin walk these lands, the sun will be followed by a shining shadow to keep the dark ones at bay. Faelin said that sun would be the last babe she ever bore, and she was right. A millennia later, when Faelin faded from this land, Elverath was lush with Fae of violet and Fae of silver, each descended from Faelin's daughters."

Everyone shifted in their seats to glance at me. I swallowed and tried not to focus on how the flames made my silver eyes glow.

"The Elves and Fae are both born of these lands and its magic, and for that we are one people. *Elverin.*"

Darythir dropped her hands and so did Lash. The flames sputtered out as another thunderous chorus of drums rang through the grove. The crowd stood and bowed to their storyteller. A line of Elverin appeared at the front of the stadium carrying trays of pink nectar.

I turned to Nikolai as he took one. "It's a tea infused with the magic of the *winvra*. Drinking it ends the ceremony. It connects the Elverin as one."

Beside me, Riven and Syrra took their own cups. I lifted my hand for one but caught Darythir's gaze just before my fingers brushed the wood. Her expression was hard and cautious. I dropped my hand without taking a tea and she nodded.

I had not earned my place with the Elverin yet.

CHAPTER
TWENTY-THREE

"THAT'S ENOUGH FOR TODAY." I rubbed my back where Vrail had managed to land a kick not once but twice. She was improving faster than any initiate I had ever taught. Syrra trained across the field, cutting slow and refined slices through the air with her blades as if she were fighting in slow motion.

Vrail collapsed to the ground with her limbs spread out in all directions. In her yellow pants and long tunic she looked like a large leaf resting on the forest floor. I tossed a waterskin onto her chest and sat down beside her. "You're a quick learner. I'll need to think of something to better challenge you," I said between ragged breaths. "I've sparred with Shades who have never managed to land a blow on me."

Vrail nodded in the direction of Syrra. "I've spent a lot of time watching Syrra train over the years. Once I grasp the basics, the rest just happens." Vrail took a big swig of her drink. I wasn't sure if it was from fatigue, but she didn't race through her words with me anymore.

"Do you think she'll ever train me?" Vrail whispered, turning her head to me on the grass.

I shrugged. Only Syrra knew the answer to that. "I think you'd only want to learn from a warrior willing to teach."

Vrail exhaled. "Fair enough." She grabbed her waterskin and swallowed it all in three quick gulps. She grabbed a folded leaf from her bag and unwrapped the sandwiches we'd stolen from the kitchen before coming to the field to train. She tossed me one and took a large bite out of the bread and then another. Soon her cheeks were stuffed with the entire sandwich.

"Must you do everything so fast?" I laughed, taking a second bite of my own sandwich.

Vrail spotted Collin walking along the beach with a group of Halflings and blushed feverishly as he disappeared from view once more. Vrail swallowed and then swallowed again. "Everyone asks me that and I promise I don't do it on purpose. I just can't help it. I feel jittery all the time. And when I'm jittery, I talk fast and say more than I should or more than others want to hear." She took a deep breath and started again. "I just want to finish everything as quickly as I can so I can get back to my books."

"You don't feel jittery when you're with your books?"

Vrail shook her head five times. "Never." Her mouth snapped shut and she bit the inside of her cheek.

"So you don't feel jittery when you're alone."

She shook her head.

"Or when you're training." I'd noticed the way Vrail's entire body relaxed during our session and how her words started to flow like a speedy river rather than a crashing waterfall.

Vrail's gaze didn't leave her boots but the tops of her cheeks flushed. She wrung her fingers back and forth in her hands as we sat on the grass.

I took another bite. Sometimes I wanted to throw my paring knife at his head, but I couldn't deny the Fae could cook. "I used to have a hard time being around people too."

Vrail's head shot up. "Really? But you always look so relaxed around other people. Never nervous at all. And people listen to you whenever you have something to say and you never seem to have to overexplain anything." She took a huge gulp of air. "How did you do it?"

I laughed and took a swig of the waterskin Vrail had dropped on the pile of mats. "I made sure whenever I stepped into a room people were more nervous to be around me than I ever could be around them."

Vrail's shoulders slumped toward the ground. "You make it sound so easy."

I watched as she pulled a long blade of grass from the ground. I didn't know if it was because of my sessions with Feron or that I'd spent so much of my time thinking about the past, but in that moment sitting in front of Vrail, I remembered how scared I'd been as an initiate. The threat of *something* always lurking behind me but never showing its head. "It's not. But it gets easier quicker than you think."

Vrail lifted up her arms. "I want to be scary."

My chest heaved with the force of my laugh. "Vrail, I can make you absolutely *terrifying*."

A childish glint flashed across Vrail's eyes. She flopped back on the soft ground. "How did you like the ceremony last night?"

I sighed, picturing the dancing flames in my mind. "I've never seen anything so beautiful."

"I thought you'd enjoy yourself." Vrail grinned. "I hope you don't mind, but I suggested that story to Feron and Darythir. My history lessons can only teach you so much."

I shot her a soft smile. "It was lovely, thank you."

"Now we just need to wait until the next new moon to cover the fall of Faevra. We skipped over so much last night." Vrail flexed her hand like she was imagining a pile of history books in front of her and didn't know where to start.

"Have you found any more clues to what happened to the Light Fae?"

Vrail shook her head defeatedly. She bent one knee so it stood taller than the rest of her. "Have you had any luck uncovering your memories?"

I mimicked her stretched position on the grass. "No," I sighed. "And I thought training you was going to be the hardest part of this war."

Vrail chucked my waterskin at me.

I pulled the cork free with my mouth and squirted her with the rest of its contents. Vrail shrieked a laugh and ran toward the equipment room. She glanced back at me to make sure I wasn't chasing her with more water and ran straight into Syrra.

Vrail's eyes went as wide as they could. She bowed her head. "Forgive me, I did not realize you were there," she said so quickly I could barely parse the Elvish. Then she curtsied like a lady at court.

I choked on my laughter, and Vrail threw me a vicious look.

Syrra stared down at the Halfling with a stern lip and discerning eyes. I could see Vrail gulp from where I still sat in the field. "Your left arm is stronger than your right," Syrra said in a slow, even tone. "You need to arrive thirty minutes early each day and work on strengthening it. Your blows will land harder."

Vrail nodded her head so many times, so quickly, I thought it might detach and roll to the ground.

It took a full minute before Vrail was able to breathe again. "Did Syrra just give me direction?"

I grinned and nodded.

Vrail jumped into the air, bucking her legs back as she laughed.

I folded my arms and feigned a sour mood. "You weren't this excited to be trained by me."

Vrail kept laughing as she headed for the tunnel. "Yes, I was," she shouted over her shoulder. "I just waited until you'd left to start screaming."

Feron was late meeting me in the library. Riven wasn't there either. I busied myself by perusing the shelves and shelves of books that were kept in the warm, dry room. Each one was meticulously organized, no doubt by Vrail, with tiny tags encoded by some kind of numeral system.

I smirked. Hildegard would adore this room and Myrrah would absolutely destroy it.

Someone opened the door, and I turned around expecting to see Feron, but it was Killian carrying a load of books with his garnet jacket thrown on top of them.

"Thank you," he said, blowing a curl out of his face when I took half the stack. "These have been sitting in my room for ages."

I scanned through the spines and saw that most were Elvish histories. I raised a brow at a particularly dusty volume.

"Apothecary records," Killian answered with a tight nod. "I've been scouring anything I could find that may hint at where the Light Fae have gone. But . . ." He trailed off. I shrugged. I'd accepted that the best chance at finding the Light Fae was locked away in my memories. I turned to the door. Still no Feron.

Killian began stacking books. "Any news from the kingdom?"

My jaw tightened. I couldn't reveal anything about Curringham to Killian. I didn't think he was the mole, but next to Nikolai, Syrra, and Riven, he was the only one I could see entertaining a deal with the lord. I already knew there was something he wasn't being completely honest with me about.

"Your father has taken to holing himself up in his chambers," I replied to sidestep what I'd learned about Curringham. "He believes the Shadow means to kill him."

Killian's brow furrowed, creating a deep line across his forehead. "He's always known the Shadow means to kill him."

I shrugged. "It seems now he believes the Shadow *can*."

"Strange." Killian's bottom lip protruded as he shelved another book. He didn't even need to look at the tag to find its place. "I may need to return to the capital, then. My father is not one to act without cause."

"Your father has ordered Damien to not leave the palace, let alone the city. How do you manage spending so many days here without drawing attention?"

Killian's hand hung in the air, holding the book he was about to squeeze between two large tomes. After a long moment, he chuckled, but it did not warm his eyes the way it usually did. "I am nothing but a disappointment to my father. I'm not his heir and my demise poses no threat to him, or his throne, so I am free to travel as I like."

There was a finality in his tone that told me I shouldn't ask the questions biting at the tip of my tongue.

Fortunately for the prince, the door slid open behind us.

"Apologies, Keera," Feron said as he walked slowly through the door. "I was helping make an elixir for Lash. It will be a few days before he is able to walk again."

My breath hitched with worry. "Is he ill?" Lash hadn't been in the kitchens that morning, but I'd assumed he had taken a day off. None of the others worked every day.

Feron's smile was tight but warm as he lowered himself into his chair and stowed his cane. "He is fine. The new moon ceremony is very taxing on his gifts. As Elverath's magic lessens, it takes longer and longer for a Fae to recuperate from using their power, but he *will* recuperate."

My shoulders fell back down and I nodded. Black ribbons of shadow appeared along the door, reaching for me and circling around my ankles. I noticed Feron's curious looks as Riven walked through the door.

"Sorry," he grunted. "I was getting Tarvelle's and Collin's reports." Riven's jaw was hard and his face dark. I swallowed guiltily. He had to hear everyone's reports separately now because Tarvelle and Collin refused to meet with me.

"I'll leave you to it," Killian called from the back of the library. He adjusted his collar as he walked up to the door. He stopped just before the threshold and turned to Feron. "Have you seen Dynara?" he asked the Fae. "I was expecting her last night but she never came."

Feron shook his head and it took everything ounce of will I had to keep my body from reacting to Killian's question. I pretended to be looking at the book on the table beside Feron and focused on breathing normally.

Killian shrugged. "I'll send a letter to Aralinth, then." He waved goodbye and disappeared out the door.

I eased back onto the chaise to keep from sighing.

Feron's gaze lingered on me. I could feel my pulse skip under his assessment. "How did you like the ceremony?"

My shoulders fell in relief. "It was extraordinary," I answered. "Though . . ."

Feron ducked his head, waiting for my question.

I bit my lip. Asking a question about history to Vrail was one thing, but asking someone who had *been* there was another.

"You will not insult me, child," Feron said, as if reading my mind.

My lip twitched upward. "Faelin and her kin were so powerful and by the time the Mortals came there were so many of them . . . How did Aemon possibly defeat you?"

Feron bowed his head, deep in thought. Riven stilled beside me, his shadows curling higher along my legs.

"I think it is best if I show you," Feron said after a long silence. He stood and took small steps to the side so he was standing directly between Riven's knees and mine. He sat back on the table and grabbed each of our hands.

I glanced at Riven. His face was still hard and sour, but it softened when he looked at me. He nodded and closed his eyes. I did too.

The warmth of Feron's magic washed over us, but this time it was not darkness that covered my senses but pure white light. It washed over everything, erasing where we were sitting until Riven, Feron, and I were standing in an expanse of white nothingness.

"The history Aemon tells in the Stolen Lands is a partial one. One he has amended over the years to fit the legacy he created." Feron lifted his hands and swirled them through the air. At the same moment, the whiteness stirred and colors began to seep into the light and morph into Feron's memory.

We were standing in a familiar landscape. It was the fields south of Silstra with one of the rivers flowing nearby. It had not yet been dammed and canalled. In the distance should have been the Dead Wood, but the trees were lush with life and color, not blackened and scorched with twisted trunks that bent toward the ground.

Whenever we were, it was before Aemon had built his throne and cut his King's Road through the magic wood.

"The Fae were plentiful when the first Mortals came. Their numbers did not rival the Elves, but I had many kin." Feron walked without a cane through the forest, staring forlorn at a time of peace and prosperity for his people. "Some of us were even more powerful than the stories told over the Burning Mountains, but most of us never trained our gifts for combat. The darks ones of Faelin's time were long since gone and we had no enemies to fight. Our magic was used to help the Elverin, to build communities that lasted through the millennia."

Feron waved his hand and the landscape shifted. In the north stood Koratha, its white palace shining with the light of the gold, silver, and purple stones that crowned the top of it. To the south was Volcar with its snowy mountain that smoked with the threat of fire hail. To the west, a view of a city I did not recognize. It was placed in a thick wood with a large orb of water suspended in the air by some kind of net. I turned to the east and saw Sil'abar and its large gold leaves shadowing Aralinth below them.

"Aemon landed on the eastern shores of Elverath," Feron said, shifting his hands once more so the landscape changed to the sandy beach with the Order standing in the distance. "How long he stayed with the Light Fae, I do not know. It is hard to explain to those so young who have lived among the Mortals for so long, but in those days, years would pass between friends without notice. We could travel quickly, but we lived long, slow lives."

Feron took a deep breath. I could see in the limp way he held his arms that this was tiring to him. And not only from the use of his magic. I squeezed his hand, and he smiled wistfully at me before continuing.

"Aemon learned enough from our eastern kin. He tells his kingdom he gained his immortality from slaying the Elves one by one, their blood became his life." The look on Feron's face was one of pure disgust. "That is true in a sense, but Aemon gained more than just immortality. Whatever magic he had used to do it, he was able to steal the magic force from any being he slayed. Soon he grew as powerful as the strongest Fae, and by the time I signed the treaty, he was more powerful than all of us combined."

My mind was dizzy with all the questions swirling in my head. "You signed the treaty after the Light Fae had gone?"

Feron nodded. "After the last of the Blood Purges." He moved his hands once more and the fiery scene of a village aflame was brought to reality. Elverin screamed in torment as their homes were set on fire and their kin were slain by Mortal soldiers wearing metal helmets painted with a golden arrow on the helm.

Behind the horror was a figure towering over the scene on a large rock he had risen from the ground. An Elven war cry broke out behind the village and a Dark Fae, taller than I had ever seen, launched herself into the air and cast a bolt of lightning at the figure.

The man on the rock held up his hand and the lightning forked, burying itself in the ground on either side of him. His laugh was unmistakeable as he raised his hands and shot boulders larger than any of the dwellings in Koratha at the Fae. She dodged the first but was crushed by the second. All I saw in Feron's memory was her hand behind the stone going limp.

Feron waved and returned us to the memory of a peaceful landscape. "That was the day after we learned of the Light Fae's disappearance. Every attack we threw at Aemon was thwarted. He did not need his army. Anything that touched him healed instantly. He was not only immortal, but he had become invincible."

Feron's voice was a raw rasp. "Until I met you, I was convinced that Aemon had managed to kill the Light Fae entirely. That he had stolen their magic and made himself a monster we had no hope of defeating. Even now, I am not sure where your questions will take you."

Feron lowered his hands and the landscape faded entirely, returning to the white abyss once more. I felt the warmth of Feron's magic retreat and the scent and sounds of the library came back into focus.

My eyes fluttered open. Feron was still sat on the table and Riven on the chaise next to me as if we had not just witnessed the atrocities Aemon had committed. "But Aemon has no magic now," I whispered, still caught in my disbelief at what I'd seen. "If he had that kind of power, he wouldn't be a man who could hide it."

Feron's lip twitched and turned into a small smile. "No, he is not. And he did not for a long time. He ruled for many centuries using his power to build his kingdom and to seal his dominance over the Elverin. It is how he dammed the Silstra and rerouted the Three Sisters to make the canals. But over time, I suspect his powers weakened like the Fae's. He has not spoken of them in over two hundred years and those stories are now lost to time. An easy feat when his people live decades and not millennia."

What Gerarda had said echoed through my mind. *The king can die.* Had Aemon's power depleted enough that even his immortality was at risk now too? My chest swelled with hope. Perhaps I wouldn't need the Light Fae to free the Shades and Gwyn after all.

"Do you still believe the Light Fae to be dead?" I asked Feron. Riven shifted in the chaise beside me.

Feron tilted his head to the side, considering the question. "For almost a thousand years, I have lived believing my kin to be dead. But your existence comes with many questions I do not have the answers to. You may not remember your parents, Keera, but I cannot ignore the healing gift you have or the silver of your eyes. The facts lay with you—you inherited those traits from someone and they may very well still be alive."

My stomach twisted into knots, tugging my insides so tightly my throat closed too. I wasn't sure if I wanted the answers to some of the questions my parentage came with. Especially if it meant confronting the parent who had left me in the Rift.

Feron reached for his cane and stood. His steps were stiff and slower after expending all that magic. "I am afraid I will need to rest before we have another session." I nodded as Feron took a seat in the soft chair once more. He tapped something inside the inner pocket of his clementine robe.

"Thank you," I said. I leaned back into the chaise and let Riven's shadows crawl into my lap, blanketing me in their warmth.

Feron's gaze fell to the swirling tendrils of darkness. "Have the elixirs been helping?" he asked, looking up at Riven.

My brow furrowed. Riven grabbed my hand. "Feron makes elixirs for me to help control my magic for when I travel the kingdom. I don't usually use them here but . . ." Riven gestured to the shadows that had wrapped around my legs completely.

I frowned. I didn't like the idea of Riven needing to dampen his magic because of me. Feron tapped his cane against the table, still waiting for his answer. Riven sighed. "Nothing helps."

Feron raised a single brow. I knew he was asking Riven a question he did not want to voice in front of me.

Riven shook his head. "The pain is manageable."

If Feron was surprised Riven had told me about the pain his magic caused, he didn't show it. He only nodded and stared at the shadows with open curiosity.

"If anything changes," he said with an odd edge to his voice, "come to me immediately."

CHAPTER TWENTY-FOUR

I RETURNED TO MY BURL ON MY OWN. Tarvelle had caught Riven on our way to the faelights, and I didn't feel the need to stay to be sneered at. Or entirely ignored, which seemed to be what Tarvelle had decided to do anytime I was in his presence.

I flopped onto my bed and opened the journal Dynara had given me. My pulse raced as I saw that there was a message left on the front page written in an elegant, thin script.

Arrived and welcomed. Curringham is setting sail tomorrow for the Fractured Isles and will journey to Koratha from there. His Lady wife will join him later for an event the Crowned Prince is throwing. I am well. Talk soon.

I scribbled my own reply and pulled a matchstick out of my vest pocket. I ripped the page from the journal and held the flame to one corner. It caught the parchment, and within a blink the entire sheet had turned to smoke and ash.

I chewed my cheek. Thirty years I had worked as a spy for the king, never once had I taken a partner. The feeling was foreign to me. The worry wrapped around my limbs, pinning me to my own bed, before wrapping around my neck too. I'd be useless to Dynara if something went awry. She was risking her life for the Halflings, yes, but I also knew she was doing it for me. I didn't know if I'd survive the guilt if she died on this mission.

My burl felt too tight with all the worry. I tucked the journal behind the far pillow on my bed and left my room behind. The feeling of the wind whipping through my hair as I fell to the grove below calmed my nerves. But they returned the moment I touched the ground.

In the middle of the grove was Riven. His arms were gesturing wildly at his sides and his chest heaved as if he had run for miles. Collin stood in front of him with his arms crossed, refusing to bend to Riven's anger.

"We're not the only ones who feel this way, Riven," Collin seethed. He hadn't heard me land behind him. "Do you think I'm the only Halfling here with family she's killed? How many people in this city had their children snatched away by her or someone at her command?"

Riven's shadows thrashed dangerously against the ground. His violet eyes glowed as he glared at Collin. "We are done discussing this." Riven looked over Collin's shoulder and gave me a sympathetic nod.

Collin turned around and the anger in his face transformed to pure hatred. "Spying again, are you?" He shot Riven a nasty look before tramping to the edge of the grove.

I held out my arm as he passed me. "Collin, wait!"

He turned slowly, like a sword being drawn, sharp and rigid. "As I told Riven. I have no interest in entertaining the killer of my own kin for a moment longer than I have to, Blade." His eyes narrowed before he started walking toward the Myram tree once more.

I took a deep breath and trusted that Feron's suggestion was right. "Your parents and sister were dead well before they were hung in the square."

Collin halted, but he didn't turn around. I glanced at Riven, whose eyes were wide with worry and confusion. I turned away so I didn't have to see that turn to pity.

"I told you I didn't remember their deaths," I continued, unsure if Collin could hear me over the sound of my heart pounding against my sternum. "But that was a lie."

Collin's hands were hard fists at his sides, his bulging knuckles pure white, but he didn't tell me to stop.

"I thought it was kinder to pretend I didn't remember that day, but I was wrong." I swallowed down the tightness in my throat and ignored the tears stinging my eyes. "The tapestries Aemon purchased from your father were grand and lush. The king boasted about them for three days at one of his tourneys. A drunkard at court made a joke about some rumor of your father having a Halfling for a wife."

Collin flinched at my words, but still he said nothing.

"The king became so angry that he pulled out his sword and cut that man down right through his middle." I twisted my fingers as I spoke, remembering the blood of that day.

"For everyone else the joke was forgotten within the week, but Aemon was angry. He felt he'd been made a fool, so he ordered the Shades to confirm your mother's lineage. Within a fortnight he knew that the rumor was true." I gasped for air. The weight of the truth pressed against my lungs and it was hard to draw enough breath to speak.

"What happened after that?" Collin's voice was shaky but he turned to face me. His cheeks red and hot with tears.

"Aemon held a trial without your father's knowledge. He sentenced your family to death. The Shades never included a son in their report, so the king didn't know to include your name alongside your sister's."

Collin choked on a sob. "I'd taken a job with a merchant. I hadn't been home in almost a year."

I nodded, but I knew that truth didn't make it any easier for Collin. "The king sent those Shades back to Cereliath to carry out the sentence. He ordered a cruel and painful death for them all." I took a deep breath and glanced at Riven. There was no hiding the truth now. "The Shades were only girls. The king didn't care what an act like that would do to them, but I did. I rode to Cereliath as soon as I found out so *I* could be the one to carry out the order. I killed them." My hand lifted to the rib where their names were written on my skin. Riven's shadows wrapped around my legs in gentle strokes.

"Toman Franshire, Mariellen Franshire, and their daughter Briar were killed by my hand."

Collin wiped his eyes. "I never told you Momma's or Ri's names."

"I never forgot them." My breath hitched, setting a fire alight in my chest. "Just as I never forgot that I didn't let them die in public disgrace. I fed your mother and sister a sleeping draught. I would've given it to your father too, had I had enough, and they were killed with one quick draw of my blade. It was as painless a death as I could give them."

A feral sound erupted from Collin. "But they were hanging in the square when I returned. No blood stained their clothes."

"A farce I committed to protect the Shades. They were dead before we hung their bodies in the square." I bowed my head. "I'm sorry we couldn't give them the grace in death that they deserved. And I'm sorry if telling you only brought more pain."

Collin flexed his hand several times before wiping his eyes. He looked at me with the same hatred and distaste as before, but also a newfound understanding, like he was seeing some aspect to me he had never noticed before.

"I'm glad I know," he said before leaving me standing in the grove.

CHAPTER TWENTY-FIVE

EVEN AFTER A SHOWER my nerves had not calmed. I paced the width of my burl until my hair dried, wondering if I'd made the right decision in telling Collin. I didn't want to be his friend—I could barely stand being in his presence—but I didn't take joy in reawakening his pain.

My throat ached for the taste of wine, so I could numb the guilt and my own pain that came with it. I rubbed my neck, and for the first time in a long while looked at the pouch holding the elixir Hildegard had given me. I swallowed the pain down. If Collin had to make it through the night with freshly opened wounds, then I could manage my craving on my own.

I sat down on the bed and knew that only another restless sleep would greet me there. The memories that I was trying to forget would chase me into my dreams and turn them into nightmares.

I slid open the bark door, letting in the cool night breeze. The city was already asleep under the sliver of the moon. I swallowed as I looked at the silver slice, knowing as it grew so did the threat to the Shades and Gwyn.

I ran my hand through my hair but there was nothing more I could do for them tonight. All I could do was distract myself for a few hours until I could try to unlock some lost memory again with Feron. Dynara needed time, and I had to be patient.

The fires surrounding the Myram burned low and every burl was dark except for the one directly across from me.

I closed the door behind me and dashed across the bridge. I wore nothing but a sunburnt nightgown. Every inch of my scarred skin was exposed. I wore no glamour ring this time, and even though the city was asleep, feeling the cool air on my scars was thrilling.

I grabbed a thick vine and lowered myself onto the branch outside of Riven's burl. Three soft balls of light floated through the room, yet Riven was asleep in his bed. I paused outside the window. I'd assumed Riven was awake. I didn't want to trouble him; there was no reason both our nights should be restless.

I watched the rise and fall of his chest. He slept so peacefully; the hard lines of his face softened in a way they never did while he was awake. Perhaps the pain of his magic was numbed by slumber, or better yet, it didn't exist there at all.

I knew that feeling. Had it only been weeks ago that Riven had wrapped me in his arms and chased my own pain away? Brenna's face had haunted my sleep for weeks, but one night sharing his bed and the nightmares had gone.

Maybe he could do that again.

I pulled myself through the window before I had the chance to change my mind. I crept over to the bed, careful not to wake him, and slipped onto the mattress next to him. Riven's shadows sensed me first. They spooled from his loose hair and wrapped around me like a blanket. I relaxed into them, into that heavy scent of birch-wood and dew that was Riven's power.

Riven turned toward me, still asleep. His arm fell onto my waist and his eyes fluttered open. He smiled lazily before his hand gripped my hip and his eyes widened. "I thought I was dreaming," he whispered, trailing his hand along my back to make sure I was truly in his bed.

"I couldn't sleep," I whispered back. "And your burl was lit."

Riven pulled me into his chest and tucked his chin against my hair. "I didn't want you to think you couldn't come here if you wanted to." His voice was still thick with sleep.

I pulled back to see his face. His brows were heavy and his pupils were dilated so wide there was only a ring of violet. "How many nights have you slept with faelights flooding your room?"

Riven ran his fingertips up and down my skin. I shivered at the touch. He grinned and pressed a biting kiss against my ear. "Every night since you told me about your fear of the dark."

My chest fluttered as he scratched a nail down my arm. I laid my hand on his chest and realized Riven was completely naked.

That fact seemed to dawn on Riven too. He cleared his throat, but his voice was hoarse and heavy when he spoke. "Why did you come, *diizra*?"

I held my breath, unsure I even had an answer to that question. I knew Riven would give me whatever I needed, whatever I wanted, but I had no idea what that was.

I tilted my head upward. Our faces were so close my lips brushed against his chin. "I can sleep when I'm with you."

Riven's jaw hardened. "Then we'll sleep."

I turned around and let Riven pull me into him. We breathed as one, his chest expanding into my back and then releasing together. I relaxed into the rhythm of it, but the darkness his shadows cast did not lull me to sleep. Riven's touch was like a fire, heating my skin with a warmth it hadn't had in weeks.

My thighs pressed together as I tried to ignore the need growing between them. I slipped backward and pressed against something hard and long. I froze. My heart thrashed against my chest as I leaned my head back against Riven, trying to get some relief.

Riven's hand gripped my thigh.

I placed my hand over his and moved them both to the hem of my nightgown. Riven's breath stopped on my back. I laced the fabric between our fingers and pulled our hands up higher.

Riven cursed and swept his hand up to my hip and pressed me against his hardness. I lifted my hand to his hair and shifted my hips back and forth. His fingers dug into my skin as his teeth scraped along my neck.

A soft moan escaped my lips and everything stopped.

Riven pushed me away from him on the mattress, gentle but quick. "I can't," he breathed, pinching his nose. Shadow covered the entire room and swirls of darkness thrashed at each other along the ceiling and bed.

I raised a brow.

"Your powers don't scare me." I pressed a kiss against Riven's cheek.

He exhaled in one hard breath. "They should, *diizra*." Riven looked down to where his shadows pooled on the bed, circling us both. To him, his shadows were a slither of snakes, dangerous and out of his control. But to me, they were an extension of Riven himself, and for that, they would never scare me.

I reached out to one of the ribbons of shadow and let it curl around my arm. It felt as warm and gentle as Riven's touch. "See? You won't hurt me."

Riven's eyes narrowed. His violet irises flashed bright and the warmth along my arm turned so cold I thought my skin was burning. A moment later and the shadow had detangled itself from me and receded back into the wall. A faint impression was left along my forearm like a rope tied across it too long.

"That was only a taste of what could happen if I lose complete control," Riven whispered, trailing his lips along my arm to soothe the pain but the mark had already disappeared.

I raised a brow and pulled myself closer to him once more. "You made that happen on purpose. It's never happened before."

Riven grabbed both my arms and lowered his face so we were eye to eye. "Because I have *always* been in control. At least enough to ensure your safety. But until I can get ahold of my powers again, I don't trust myself to touch you like that."

A deep line formed between his brows, layers of worry settling onto his face. Worry that he would hurt me, worry that his powers would only continue to spiral out of control until they consumed him, and worry that I would reject him because of it.

I had to make my choice. Despite all my fury and distance, Riven had never wavered. He took it all without protest and made good on his promises to me. Even now, with only a thin piece of fabric separating our bodies, Riven's thoughts were with me: my safety over his desire even though the heat between us threatened to set the world aflame.

I could leave now. Pull myself out of the bed and climb my way back to my burl. Riven wouldn't stop me and he wouldn't think any less of me for it. Or I could stay with the Fae who slept in the light just in case I found the darkness too lonely.

I bit the tip of Riven's thumb. "What if *I* touch *you*?" I wrapped my leg around his hip and lifted my body onto his, pinning him underneath me.

"Keera." My name was more a grunt than a word.

Riven's hands spanned the width of my thighs, leaving indents along my skin. He could easily lift me off him, but he didn't. I grinned and pushed his arms above his head.

I bit my lip. He looked beautiful positioned like that. I couldn't tell where his black mane met his shadows, creating a backdrop of darkness beneath him. He moved his hand to grasp my neck, but I shoved it back above his head.

"You can't touch me," I reminded him. I pressed a kiss to his wrist and trusted him to leave his hands where they were. I shifted back, straddling Riven's hips as I looked down at him. "Is this okay?"

Riven clenched his jaw and nodded.

I bunched the hem of my nightgown in my hands as I rocked along Riven's hips. I could feel his hardness against my thigh but I didn't fully lower myself quite yet. I lifted my nightgown even higher and heard Riven's sharp inhale as he glimpsed how wet I was for him.

"Keera." The tendons in his neck flexed so hard I thought they might burst. "I don't want to be inside you and not be able to touch you."

"Understood," I said, hearing his boundary loud and clear. It felt too fast to have Riven like that just yet. But it didn't mean we couldn't meet our needs in other ways. "Can I keep touching you like this?"

Riven looked like the idea of me getting off him would cause a fatal wound. His voice was barely more than a hoarse grunt. "Yes."

I leaned forward and pressed a kiss against Riven's neck. His hands tangled themselves in my hair, but I grabbed his wrists and pushed them back above his head once more. "You're the one who said no touching."

I pulled the thin fabric of my nightgown over my head. Riven's eyes were sinful as he devoured every inch of my body. He bit his lip as he finally found his way back to my face. "I'm a fool. You should never listen to me."

He took his time admiring me, never shying away from the scars I'd carved into my arms and torso or the ones I didn't along my hip and back. When Riven looked at me, he didn't see a list of names in his bed. He only saw me for who I was—scarred and pained, but whole and beautiful.

I grinned wickedly and licked the hard skin along the middle of his chest. Riven twitched beneath me and I scraped his collarbone with my teeth. His power exploded, covering every inch of the burl in a blanket of shadow so Riven and I were the only things that existed in the darkness lit by a single faelight above my head.

I nipped Riven's bottom lip and pulled his jaw open just enough to scratch the edge of my nightgown with his fang. Riven's brow furrowed as I ripped the piece almost in two.

He frowned. "A shame I'll never be able to rip that off you."

"I have others." I twisted the silk in my hands.

I leaned forward and Riven's tongue grazed across my breast. I lowered myself just enough that he could catch my nipple between his teeth as I looped the silk around each of his wrists. Riven's violet eyes turned dark as I secured the silk to the wooden headboard, locking his arms into place.

I laid my hands flat on his chest. "So you stick to your rule."

Riven groaned as I lowered myself completely for the first time, pinning his length between our bodies. I pressed my weight down on his shoulders and glided my hips. I angled my body so Riven's cock rubbed against me exactly where I needed it.

"Keera," Riven hissed, pulling at the silk.

"Do you want me to stop?" I leaned back so Riven could see every inch of me.

He shook his head and groaned. "I take it back. I want to touch you."

I ignored his plea and moved my hands to his thigh. Watching Riven watch me was dizzying. I could see his hunger as he followed the curves of my body rolling against him in slow, tantalizing strokes.

Riven's gaze burned me. It lingered on the spot where our bodies were so close to joining, yet so separate. Then it traced the stretch of my stomach as I moved my hips forward and then back again. It felt so good, I didn't know if I would survive the day Riven finally entered me.

I placed my hands on his shoulders and dragged myself across him until he moaned. I let my body hang low enough that it was in reach of Riven's mouth once more. He licked my skin where the scars turned smooth just under the curve of my breast. I gasped, and Riven twitched beneath me. He was as close to the edge as I was.

Shadows wrapped around his wrists and spiraled down his arms until I could no longer see the nightgown that held him there. Riven didn't seem to notice, his eyes locked on the movement of my body.

The feeling between my thighs grew, threatening to burst, a few more glides of my hips and it would explode, leaving me to waste away into nothing. I leaned forward, finally kissing Riven's lips for the first time.

We were past the ability to linger, for slow, teasing tastes. Riven's kiss was claiming. He devoured me until I could no longer breathe. My movements quickened and my lip caught on Riven's fang. His tongue licked away the drop of blood, the cut already healed, unable to spare a moment without his lips on mine.

Riven was harder than stone beneath me. I pressed along that hardness and thrashed against him, unable to control myself any longer. Riven groaned my name, taking me over the edge with him as he fell. My body arched and my head fell back with his name on my lips.

When the waves of pleasure mellowed, I looked down to see Riven watching my body pulse on top of him.

He snapped his wrists apart, shredding the fabric in two. The shadows had receded back into the floor but deep cuts marked Riven's arms. I gasped when I saw the red blood dripping down his skin.

I grabbed a damp cloth from the bathroom to clean the wounds. "You should have told me," I said, unable to keep the harshness out of my voice.

Riven flinched as I pressed the towel to his wrist. "Then you would've stopped." He lifted his hand to my jaw and rubbed his thumb across my cheek. "I'm fine and it was well worth it. Believe me."

I rolled my eyes but pressed a kiss to Riven's palm.

Riven's brow furrowed and then his eyes went wide. "Keera," he said in amazement for the second time that night. He pulled his hand back and held up his wrists. We watched as the skin stitched itself back together, transforming into soft pink lines from where the shadows had left deep cuts only a moment before.

"I didn't know you had a healing gift." I was glad at least some of Riven's power didn't cause him pain.

Riven shook his head in disbelief. "I don't. I think you did this."

CHAPTER TWENTY-SIX

RIVEN WAS WAITING FOR ME when my shift in the kitchens ended. We walked in silence through the network of tunnels along the north section of the lower city before coming to a large circular door made of stone. The other doors I'd seen in Myrelinth had grooves along the bottom to glide the door backward, but this door was wrapped in a web of thin roots like the black earth of the wall was embracing it in its arm.

Riven knocked on the stone three times. There was only silence until the roots began to move and slither along the rock, reaching for the edge of the stone in every direction before pulling it back to reveal the room behind the door.

Feron was sitting on the far side of the room next to a lit hearth. He waved his arm casually and the door crept shut behind us. The braces he wore on his legs were strewn across the table between the chair he was sitting in and the chaise across from him. He smiled at both of us and waved his hand over the empty chairs.

Feron rested his hands on his cane. "You have come to ask me something I presume?" His lilac gaze was curious and welcoming. When I'd first met the Fae, I thought Feron's ability to calm people came from using his mindwalking gift, but after so many hours in his presence, I knew it was just part of who he was. Forever kind and gentle.

Riven cleared his throat. "It's about Keera's magic. Something happened last night and . . ."

I smirked as Riven looked down at his boots, too embarrassed to finish.

Feron's brow raised. "And?"

"Riven got too *overwhelmed* and his power hurt him—it cut his arms. But then the wounds healed." Riven turned to me with strained, wide eyes. I shrugged and threw my hands behind my head, ignoring Riven's embarrassment entirely. "That's exactly what happened."

Riven coughed and his shadows scattered across the floor. "I believe it was Keera's magic that healed me," he said, still unable to meet Feron in the eye.

Feron's smile was knowing as he nodded his head slowly. "I am not surprised."

My chest tightened as I glanced between the two of them. "But I thought *Valitherian* could not wield their magic?"

Feron tilted his head. "They cannot."

"I told you it wasn't me." I slapped Riven's knee, happy to be proven right.

Feron drummed his fingers along the top of his cane. "Do not ignore the truth, Keera, only because it seems impossible."

My chest tightened. I turned back to Feron, whose soft gaze had locked on me. I swallowed under the weight of it and the meaning of his words. "You think *I* healed him?"

"I believe it more likely that a Light Fae has the ability to heal others, as many Light Fae before her, than one *Valitherian* having the ability to wield her gift when none of her predecessors have before." Feron stood and walked over to me in slow, careful steps. He perched himself on the edge of the table in front of me and tucked a finger under my chin, studying my face and my silver eyes.

Riven's shadows curled protectively around my legs. Feron studied them too. "Are you meaning to do that?"

Riven's shoulders fell and he shook his head. "This is even with an elixir. The loss of control is getting worse."

Feron's bottom lip jut forward as he watched the shadows. They flowed from Riven in a swirling path toward me, curving around Feron's feet and cane. "Do they hurt you, child?"

Riven's jaw clenched as I shook my head. "They can, but they never do."

"Curious." Feron sat down on the table slowly. "And you were near each other when Riven's wounds closed?"

We both nodded.

A smile grew on Feron's lips. "*Miiskwithir,*" he whispered. He glanced at Riven with a look of pride I didn't understand.

Riven swallowed thickly, each word landing heavy like a brick on sand. "That is not possible."

"I'm going to need someone to explain what *miiskwithir* means." I anchored my elbows on my knees to keep my arms from shaking. The same anticipation that came before a fight bubbled in my belly. I needed to prepare for Feron's next words whether they be a strike or a blow.

"It is said that when Faelin, the first Fae, entered into her magic sleep and woke with both her daughters, that they shared their mother's powers. One daughter received half of Faelin's gifts and the other daughter received the other half. A perfect complement of their magic. And so the first Light and Dark Fae were born."

I pursed my lips. "So Faelin's daughters are the *miiskwithir*?"

Feron smiled gently and nodded. "The first, yes. All Fae descend from those two daughters. The children of Ara'linthir became the Dark Fae and the children of Kieran'thara became the Light Fae. Where those with violet eyes have the power to make plants and blooms move at their will, those with eyes of silver had the ability to grow new life with the touch of their hand. Light Fae were capable of stitching wounds and Dark Fae can heal ailments and maladies. There is a balance to our magic that is beyond even our understanding. And like the first *miiskwithir*, there were times when two Fae would find their magic called for the other. Their gifts would be the ultimate complement, the perfect example of balance."

"Always one Light Fae and one Dark?" I breathed, looking at Riven's violet eyes.

Feron shifted where he sat and sighed. "Not always, though those pairings were the most powerful and most gifted." He leveled a knowing look at us. It made me uneasy.

I swallowed and looked at my hands. I'd never done anything close to the miracles Feron described. "I can't be a *miiskwithir*."

"*Miiskwithir* is not a single person, but a pair." Feron waved his hand in front of Riven and then at me. "You are bonded by your magic."

Riven took a deep breath, his jaw pulsing again and again as he took in Feron's words. My mind swelled with questions, so many I could hardly breathe.

"Bonded . . . like mates?" I'd only heard of it in stories as a child. That every Fae and Elf had one true mate who they would love more fiercely and loyally than anyone else. It could take millennia to find each other and most would spend the rest of their days at their lover's side. No one had mentioned it since I'd arrived, so I had assumed it had been a falsehood like most of the stories told about the Fae in the kingdom.

Feron tilted his head to the side. "They can be. Many *miiskwithir* have found romantic love bloom from their bond, but not always. Sometimes the pairs are siblings, sometimes they are dear friends, and rarer still, they are enemies and reject the bond entirely."

I rubbed my brow unable to look at either Fae. "What does the bond do?"

"Many things," Feron said darkly. "Some *miiskwithir* are able to share their gifts through the bond, though that is very rare. For most, it strengthens their magic to a level they cannot achieve alone."

I looked at my hands. I had always healed more quickly than others I knew, even as a child. I thought it had been a result of my Elvish lineage since the Elverin heal much quicker than Mortals. But that night in Silstra, I would have died without my magic stitching my body back together. Without Riven holding me, anchoring me to life. Only after spending weeks with him had my healing proven itself to be more than ordinary. "I never noticed my healing gift until Riven and I had met." I glanced at Riven, who was a statue beside me. "That night in Silstra."

Riven somehow hardened even more, as if he had to protect himself from the memory of that night.

"Riven strengthened your gift," Feron said before eyeing the shadows still swirling on the floor at my feet. "Just as you have strengthened his."

"Are there any *miiskwithir* left?" I was desperate to prove Feron wrong.

Riven gripped the hard root frame of his seat. "My mother was part of the last bonded pair. Since her death the Elverin have not seen *miiskwithir* since Aemon set foot upon these shores."

I reached for Riven's hand. "Does the other half of her pair still live?"

Riven gave a solemn look to Feron. The ancient Fae took a deep breath, and I could see tears welling in his eyes. "The death of a *miiskwithir* bond is the most painful sensation any Fae can experience. The day Thellia left this world, she took a piece of me with her."

Riven bowed his head. "If Keera and I were bonded, I would be able to sense the bond."

"You may not sense it, but your magic certainly does." Feron raised a brow at the shadows circling my feet.

I turned to Riven. "I called your shadows to me during that first session. They found me even though you did not mean to release your power."

Feron nodded. "That sense is part of the bond. You may also feel the urge to be close together physically—"

"Or an electric charge like the air just before a lightning strike," I finished for him.

Riven's head snapped to me. Whatever I'd felt, it was clear he had felt it too. I had felt that from the very first moment Riven and I touched. Now it was always there, easily forgotten until the charge built up and threatened to explode.

"Is this why my pain lessens at her touch?" Riven asked Feron through clenched teeth. I froze in my seat. I didn't realize I had such a profound effect on Riven's pain.

Feron assessed his nephew with a mixture of worry and happiness. "Perhaps." He turned to me. "Riven told me he sensed something that night in Cereliath. I thought it was just his magic recognizing something in you that was beyond the average Halfling, but now I realize there was more to that first night."

My lungs felt too small, no matter how much air I drew, I couldn't catch my breath. "But if we're *miiskwithir* that means I would have to be—"

"Fae." Feron nodded over the top of his cane. "Undoubtedly."

I grabbed the bloodstone dagger from my hip and pierced my palm with the tip of the blade. Amber blood began to pool in the crux of my hand. "Amber, not red."

"That I have no answer for. Not until we unlock whatever truths are hidden in your memories." Feron stood once more, his long twists swaying along his back as he walked. He stopped and turned. "I will call for Rheih. The Mages have certain elixirs that may help recover your memories."

I spent the rest of the day trying to distract myself from what Feron had said. The implications of that were too big for me to fathom. If it were true, that meant both of my parents had been Light Fae, which made it even more likely that the Light Fae had survived. That they were out there somewhere, and with a bit more hard work, I would find them.

But it also weighed heavy in my gut. Apart from healing a few scrapes in Riven's skin, I did not have the ability to wield magic at all. If I was a Fae, I was a useless one. My throat was dry and scratchy as I climbed into my burl after a long training session with Vrail. The room seemed smaller than usual and more quiet. I could no longer ignore the truth now that I was alone.

If I was a Light Fae, did that mean I wasn't a Halfling? Everything I'd survived, the amber blood that pulsed under my skin, which parts of me were the real truth? Lineage or history?

I laid back on the bed and felt for Dynara's journal. I opened the cover and was relieved to find another message.

Curringham is gone but I've made friends with his assistant. I may have something soon. The house is quiet apart from all the letters Lady Curringham receives. For a foreign bride, she receives many birds. At least four a day. Bank will have funds ready at the end of the week. Thank you, my friend. Be well.

I stared at the blank page of my journal trying to find words to send back to Dynara. There wasn't much to report apart from Collin's obvious distaste for me and Feron's latest revelation. Neither seemed like information that would help Dynara find the piece of evidence to bury Curringham.

Making progress here too. You're welcome, my friend and hero. Stay safe. And bring as many home as you can.

Despite my exhaustion, sleep couldn't find me. Every time I closed my eyes, my heart would palpitate in my chest so hard I thought my ribs would crack. After three restless hours, I left the sweat-stained sheets behind and jumped into the crisp night air.

The waxing crescent moon was already past its apex in the sky, watching carefully over Myrelinth as it slept. The deadline to help the Shades was approaching quickly and I only had more questions with no answers. Nothing tempting enough for the king to overlook the evasion of the Shadow and no lead on where to find the Light Fae.

My throat burned hot at the thought of what I might need to do to keep the Shades and Gwyn safe.

I walked aimlessly through the paths around the Myram tree. With the sliver of moonlight and the balls of flame that never ceased, it was easy to find my way, to study the city how I never could while the other Elverin watched me so closely.

I came to an empty grove at the edge of the city. As far as I knew, no one slept in the trees above apart from Syrra. My stomach knotted as I realized all the groves along the far edge of the city were vacant. Everywhere in the Faeland was the same. More dwellings than bodies to fill them. A constant reminder of those lost over the Burning Mountains and those who would never come home.

I trailed my finger along the base of one of the trees. I had never noticed before, but there was lettering in the bark. Not cut or marked into the tree, but a part of its growth. Old Elvish letters I couldn't read repeated in the same patterns again and again along the base of the trunk.

I checked a second tree and then another. Each were marked with letters, but their patterns were different. Whatever was inscribed upon them was different for each tree.

I followed the groves along the long stretch of the lake. I had seen this part of Myrelinth only from a distance. A sleepless night seemed as good a reason to explore as any.

I followed a path along the edge of the lake. The water glimmered up at me as I strolled across the clearing, no need for a faelight. I came to a statue sat under a tree only tall enough to shade the stony figures.

I stopped at the base of the statue. The sculpture was crafted from white stone that gleamed like a star in the night. There were two figures towering above me.

Elves.

At first glance, a mother and child, though I wasn't sure. She wore a long dress of soft silks that blew in a wind set in stone. Her round face was encircled by coils that pooled down her back, decorated with fresh blooms. Her full lips were caught mid-laugh as she stared out at someone whose likeness had only been captured by the love of the Elf's eyes.

On her lap sat a small child no older than three. They shared the same black coils that hung at their hips and the same wide smile. His hands reached out and somehow I knew he had been trying to grasp a faelight. I could hear the child's giggle like the moment had been caught in time to replay again and again.

They both had wide eyes that were soft yet sharp. I recognized them. The mother of the statue was not Syrra, but their eyes were identical, just like the little boy on her lap.

"I wish I could remember her." Nikolai appeared beside me. The lacing of his tunic was undone and the shirt inside out. The Elf slept less than I did.

"She was beautiful." I reached out and touched the bottom of toddler Nikolai's foot. "You look happy together."

"It was my third moonday. With Feron's help, Riven's mother was able to share her memory of it with me and gave it to a sculptor when I asked to commission this piece. It's one of my earliest days cast in stone and one of my mother's last."

I gave him a gentle squeeze and rested my head on his shoulder. "You look like her."

Nikolai looked up at his and his mother's likeness with a wistful smile. He held a bouquet of tiny silver flowers in his hand. He took a bouquet of fresh roses from the holder and placed the new one at the bottom of the statue. My throat tightened remembering the flowers I'd caught him with before—this was a daily ritual for him.

"These were her favorite. She must've loved the night as much as I do." He pointed to the silver bulbs. "They only bloom under direct moonlight."

Just above the bouquet was a plaque cast in bronze. Even with my heightened eyesight, I could barely make out the inscription written in Elvish.

Maerahl Nieven
A mother, a sister & a friend
Lost but not forgotten

I ran my hand over the base of the statue. It was smooth and slick like marble, but the stone reminded me of the dwellings in Aralinth. White rock that had been risen from the ground with magic. I turned to Nikolai. "Is there a statue for your father?"

He shook his head. "My father was from the Singing Wood. His body was recovered from one of the battles against Aemon's men so he could be properly put to rest with his kin before the treaty was signed. His tree grows there."

"Tree?"

Nikolai furrowed his brow. "I thought the Halflings kept the practice up in the Stolen Lands. I've seen pyres burning."

"We burn our dead because we are not permitted to bury them." The graveyards the Mortals kept were well decorated with stone crypts and wooden symbols to the gods they no longer prayed to.

Understanding crept across Nikolai's face. "In the *Faelinth* our deaths are marked by flame and our lives are celebrated with new life. When someone dies, their body is set upon a pyre. Their hair is braided with the shorn hair of their loved ones and kin—the only time most of us cut our hair—and then the pyre is set aflame. Once the entire pyre is burned away, the ashes are collected and infused with a seed of their favorite tree, which is planted one year after their death."

"Your mother was never recovered." My stomach was a deep chasm, hollow and empty at the thought of Nikolai's mother being taken from him. Not only in life, but death as well. I knew no matter how deep or hollow I felt, it was not large enough to hold that kind of pain.

Nikolai shook his head. "No." Nikolai cleared his throat. "Her tree should have grown as tall as all the others in our city, housed her children and her children's children, but war takes a heavy toll. One that doesn't end even after the memories of bloodshed fade."

I couldn't help but rub my forearm as Nikolai's words echoed through my mind. War had not even begun, and the kingdom had already taken enough to haunt me well after my body was in the ground. My finger caught on the sleeve of my tunic, lifting it above my wrist. For a moment, I thought about pulling it up farther. To show Nikolai the name I'd carried with me from the moment I left the Order. Perhaps there could be some relief in knowing that while the king had taken his mother from him, he had also taken my Brenna from me.

I shoved the sleeve back down. Showing Nikolai one scar would only lead to me showing them all. I was already restless enough as it was. I turned my attention to the tree that stood behind the statue.

"This tree?" I pointed at the trunk, unsure how to phrase my question.

Nikolai smiled lovingly at the vibrant indigo leaves. "My son," he answered with more warmth in his voice than I'd ever heard.

I stepped back, unable to contain my shock. "You had a son?" Nikolai was many things—an ostentatious flirt, a loyal friend, and a brilliant inventor—but I'd never considered him to be fatherly.

His lips twitched up to one side. "His name was Davan." Nikolai reached for one of the leaves above his head, caressing it like the cheek of a babe. "A few decades after Syrra rescued me, I convinced her to take me to the orphanage in Volcar where she had found me." He paused and played with the loose lace of his collar. "I thought I would find something there. Something to help me remember my mother . . . but instead I found a small Halfling boy, barely able to walk he was so young. I knew I had to help him, so I did. I brought him here, raised him as my own until the day he passed."

"I'm sorry, Nikolai." My heart ached for my friend, but my mind wondered how I'd never realized someone as happy as him carried so much grief.

"He lived a long life and died of old age in the comfort of his bed. We had just over three centuries together, a gift many Halflings don't receive." There was a bittersweetness to Nikolai's voice.

I nodded. Three hundred years was a very long life for a Halfling. I looked up at the tree, trying to picture Nikolai's son growing tall and old while his father aged so slowly it was like he wasn't aging at all. The Fae and Elves had opened their arms to as many Halflings as they could, and if we won the war they'd welcome even more, knowing that all those they came to care for would be here only briefly. There was a strength in love like that I didn't have. I let myself care for so few people and each death had taken a piece of me that would never return. If the war came to take the ones who were left, I knew that one way or another it would take me too.

A strong gust blew across the clearing and knocked the bouquet of flowers to the ground. I knelt to fix them in the holder and noticed a tiny band of leather wrapped along the stems. There was a small bronze tag attached to it with two Elvish words embossed into the metal.

From Miiran

I stilled. It was like time had stopped in that very moment. Even the water of the lake paused its breath along the shore and the wind stopped too. My heartbeat slowed, somehow pounding in my head instead of my chest.

I had heard that name before.

"Miiran?" I choked, breaking out of the stillness.

Nikolai smiled down at me. "My mother's pet name for me. I don't use the name she gave me, but when I think of her, I can't come to call myself Nikolai."

I turned away from him then, pretending I was fixing the flowers again, but in truth I needed a moment to calm my racing heart. My lips trembled holding back the truth, the secret festering in my belly like spoiled food that needed release, but I refused to say anything to him.

The truth would not bring Nikolai any peace. He believed his mother died a swift death during the Blood Wars. He didn't need to know that I sat in a dungeon beside another prisoner. One who hummed to herself every hour she was awake and whispered one word over and over again while she slept.

Miiran.

I bit my knuckle to keep the tears from falling down my cheek. After a moment, I stood and looped my arm around Nikolai's. We walked back to the city, each of us finally ready to sleep, and I vowed to never tell Nikolai the truth.

Sometimes secrets were a necessary thing to protect those we loved.

CHAPTER TWENTY-SEVEN

"I WANT TO TRY A DIFFERENT approach." Riven's hands turned to fists at Feron's words. We were back in the library trying to unlock any memory we could. My body was already coated in sweat, but no matter how determined I was to find answers quickly, the memories would not come.

Feron leaned back in his chair. "You seem to be uncomfortable at reliving any memories from your past. The further back we go, the harder you fight—"

My shoulders sunk into the cushions. "I'm trying not to."

"I know." Feron gave me a kind, wide smile before continuing. "For some, sharing their memories with a wielder is difficult. It can be too intimate, especially if they have spent their lives building walls around themselves and their past."

I flinched at Feron's words. It stung to be read so thoroughly. I gripped the material of the sofa between my fingers and fought the urge to run.

"The further back we try, the more inaccessible your memories become," Feron continued. "I think in order to access the ones you do not remember we need to practice with the ones you do but do not want to relive."

My heart hammered against my chest at the thought of which scenes would play out inside my head. There were so many memories I'd tried to forget, so many that I had only ever faced holding a drink. I thought of Collin's family; Feron had already pulled some of the worst forward. I didn't know if I was strong enough to experience that again without a full wineskin.

But I had to be.

I exhaled slowly, focusing on releasing the tension between the blades of my back. "Okay." It was a whisper, but I was glad that my voice didn't shake.

Feron stood and took his place behind my head. I closed my eyes and felt his hands gently caress my skin. They rubbed light circles across my brow and temples, into my hairline, and back again. Over and over until I was lulled into a peaceful state somewhere between waking and sleep.

The warmth of Feron's magic pulsed through my blood and wrapped itself around my mind. My body tensed. It felt like a snake wrapping around its prey, petrifying me with the threat of its fangs. I focused on the rise and fall of my breath, on the softness of Feron's touch as the blackness enveloped me. The serpentine twisting faded, and I was alone in the dark once more.

My resolve crashed like a cymbal sending my heart wildly racing and bucking. My chest tightened and my hands fisted along the chaise I could no longer see or feel.

The hammering in my chest slowed and I took another deep breath, this one steadier than the last. Something familiar hung in the air. The faint scent of birchwood. My body reacted without conscious thought, the tension in my muscles released slowly and my fingers uncurled. The darkness was still unending, and I was still completely alone within it, but something had changed. All thoughts of that dungeon fled from my mind and I was reminded of Riven and his shadows. Of his magic that would never hurt me.

The moment I completely relaxed into the shadows, they started to take shape around me, an old memory swirling into view. Suddenly, I was back at the Order. A moonless night was made darker by the long string of clouds that covered most stars. The air was cold and damp from the spray of the sea that crashed against the jagged rocks surrounding the island. I could taste the salt against my lips.

I sat along the edge of the island—my feet dangling off the cliff—as I stared into the abyss below, willing myself to jump into the sharp shards of rock that pierced through the violent sea. My chest ached and every rapid beat of my heart singed my raw throat. The emotions of that night rushed through my body, surging all at once and then crashing, leaving me with whiplash.

I didn't move though the waves below beckoned for me. My legs were ore, fused to the ground, to the fresh grave beside me. Hot tears fell from my eyes like a spring after snowmelt. I was a hollow shell, a casing designed to hold only the purest, sharpest pain.

There was a familiar weight in my hand. I looked down and between my fingers was the thin, gold handle of my mage pen. The top laid beside me, discarded, as I pulled my forearm onto my lap. It dropped with a thud, like I was lifeless too. But the pain told me the truth—I was alive and she wasn't.

I pulled back the sleeve of my tunic, and saw the splattering of amber blood along the wrist, and revealed my unmarked forearm. I had forgotten about the trio of freckles that I'd cut away when I carved her name into my skin. Or would carve. That part of the memory had only just begun.

I watched through my eyes as a shaking hand lifted the pen and carved each letter into thick blocks. All at once, I was watching myself, unable to stop, and completely present in the past reliving the aftermath of that night. Cutting again and again as if feeling more pain could bring her back.

Brenna almost glowed from my flesh. Permanent and lasting, unlike the real her that rested in the ground beside me. My arm went limp as I sobbed, and I didn't care about the pool of amber blood forming over the newly disturbed soil. Part of me wanted every drop of blood to fall onto her grave, to have my life end in that very spot, leaning over her once more and forever.

"It should have been me," I chanted over and over again between cries. I didn't stop until my voice broke and the first signs of sunlight painted the sky behind me.

The other version of me closed her eyes so I did too. A cold calm ran down my spine. It spread down my limbs and turned into hardened resolve.

I had a choice. I could jump into the inky waters and never live past this night, or I could turn around, head back to the Order, and seek vengeance on the morrow.

If I didn't avenge her death, no one would.

My eyes flashed open and I stood. I looked down at the grave where Brenna would rest. There would be no headstone, there would be no flowers, but at least I left her along her favorite spot of the small part of the world she'd been allowed to see.

I felt myself saying the same words I had said that night, coated with the same visceral conviction. "I promise."

And then I turned back, this time knowing I would never return to that spot again.

The sea and grounds began to swirl as the memory dissolved. I flinched against the couch, the darkness giving way to the soft material as my mind pulled itself from the trance. I could feel the streams of tears running down my face but focused on my breathing. It had only been one memory. Painful and hard to share knowing Feron had seen every moment, but it was not far back enough.

Feron pressed his hands firmly against my skin, sensing my change in demeanor, and whispered in my ear: "Stay with me, child."

His voice was calm, and I let my consciousness sink into that feeling, allowing the warmth of his magic to overtake me once more. This time the memory came forward without a fight. The blackness whirled around me in streaks of color, building the scene from my memory. It was the same day—earlier this time—and I was lying in bed. Brenna was there beside me, our mattresses pushed together as they always had been during that last year. Her blond curls tickled my neck, coaxing me from sleep, as my eyes fluttered open in the morning sun.

I turned my head and saw she was looking at me. The scars through her brows were barely visible in the morning sun. Her bright green eyes flecked with gold pulled me in as always, my body leaning into hers without a thought beyond wanting to close the small gap between us.

I brushed her hair off her cheeks and pressed a familiar kiss to her lips. "What do you want?" I asked between the kisses I was trailing along her collarbone. I felt her swallow against my cheek.

"Why do you assume I want something?" Her words were playful, but there was an edge to them I didn't understand. Not yet.

I moved my body over hers, placing a hand on either side of her head to hold my weight. She grabbed the end of my braid from where it pooled beside her and kissed the leather tie.

I kissed her again before answering. "You only wake before me when you're plotting something."

She bit her lip in response and raised a brow. The playfulness in her gaze had turned sharp, wanting and determined. Like always, I was eager to give her what she wanted. I would have given her anything she asked for. I would have given her everything.

I scratched a trail between her breasts with my finger. She arched into my touch, and my body flushed with pleasure from pleasing her. I pressed my lips against the same spot before grazing the underside of her breast with my teeth.

Her body flowed like the ocean under me. Her sharp inhale merged with another arch of her back like crashing white caps waiting for the storm. I lifted my head and watched how she moved. How many times had I seen her body curve and squirm under mine, soft and vulnerable, only for me? Her image was etched into my mind and her being stitched into my soul. Her body was more familiar to me than my own, but somehow every moment with her felt like a new discovery.

Brenna groaned in frustration from not being touched. I smirked and made a point of not moving an inch. I'd never known her to be patient in anything she did, let alone making the most of the short time we had before the last of the Trials began.

She lifted her head toward me. "You're mine," she rasped before catching my lip between her teeth and pulling my body against hers. She caught my answer between our desperate kisses. Her hand moved between my thigh and there was no denying I was anything but hers.

We were a tangle of the same person, our breath and bodies fusing together with an ease we'd only just mastered. I knew every sound she made before it left her lips. I knew just where my touch would spark a fire that would burn into her skin, pushing us both over the edge.

Rushed for time, we called out each other's names in a rasp of shared air. I kissed her, tasting the salt of her tears on my lips. We were the most prepared of the initiates, but neither of us could deny the risk that lay ahead. Not every initiate passed their Trials. Some perished never having earned their hoods.

My chest broke open, hollowed from the pain that was echoing through me from decades before. I'd never considered that Brenna would have been one of those lost that day. I swallowed the guilt that came every time I thought of my Trial and had no choice but to watch the memory continue.

The younger version of myself wiped her tears away with my thumb and kissed her again, a gentle whisper of a kiss, the one I knew she needed.

A small smile flickered along her lips. "You promise?" The words were so quiet I could barely hear them.

I stared at her with unearned resolve. "I promise," I whispered back, sealing it with a kiss. The confidence I'd felt that morning swelled inside me as if I existed only in that moment, forever locked in the past. As if I didn't know that she would be dead by midday.

As if that promise hadn't been goodbye.

A sob burst from my chest and the memory of Brenna shattered like glass, plunging me into darkness once more. I flung off the chaise unable to breathe. My tears fell to the floor in thick drops. Riven rushed to my side, wrapping his arms around me, but I pushed him away. It felt wrong to be close to him when moments before I had been with her.

I brought my fingers to my mouth. The ghost of that last kiss felt more real and haunting than it ever had before. I could still smell the sea breeze wafting from her hair. I could still taste the honey balm on her lips.

The pain rocked through me like a battering ram. I could barely catch my breath before the next blow shook me to my core. My legs trembled under the weight of that pain as I stood. I closed my eyes and there she was—the face I'd spent decades pushing into the furthest reaches of myself was imprinted on the back of my eyelids in full color.

I took a deep breath and focused on the good inside that memory. The feel of her skin on mine, the way her nails scratched my unscarred back. I let those fleeting moments wash over me like the crashing wave she'd been, forcing the pain back inside myself until I could breathe.

"That was excellent progress, Keera." Feron placed a light hand on my shoulder. I felt the rush of warmth along my skin, his magic working to soothe me. I didn't fight it. I let it pulse through me until my heartbeat slowed and my limbs stopped shaking. Until I wasn't exhausted by the embarrassment of him having watched those last moments.

I couldn't meet his gaze so I nodded instead.

Riven's shadows swirled around my feet. When he spoke, his voice was dark and dangerous. "That's enough for today."

I glanced at him, the shadows along the wall behind him lashed and bent without reason. I nodded again but I didn't approach him. I wanted the feeling of Brenna to last on my skin. I needed to dwell in the essence of her, regardless of the pain.

"I need to leave."

Riven reached for me but I shook my head. Feron grabbed his nephew's arm gently and let me go. I was too much of a coward to look at the hurt that I knew hung on Riven's face. I left him alone, the memory of Brenna trailing behind me.

CHAPTER TWENTY-EIGHT

I RAN TO MY BURL without turning back. I thought I would find comfort in the room that had become something like a home, but even its comforts were not a strong enough refuge from the memories that Feron had called forward. They were still with me, thrashing at my heels with every step, the swipes of familiar monsters who haunted the shadows of my life. My throat burned like a wound that refused to heal, opened once more.

I fetched the small pouch from the back of the chair. I tucked it into my belt and pulled my feet onto the bark-covered edge of the window. A small ball of golden faelight nudged my shoulder, as if calling me off the ledge, but I sent it swirling back over the bed with a sharp breath and leaped onto the branch hanging above my room.

I liked the roughness of the wood on my hands. The scratching distracted from the heat in my throat as I reached for the next branch and then the next. I climbed until the branches became too small to bear my weight. A tangle of vines hung between two boughs and I nestled myself into their hold, wrapped in thick, green rope like the Myram tree was an old friend.

I stared down at where the vial of elixir lay across my palm, but I didn't unstopper the top. Instead I swirled the liquid along the glass, seeing the shades of nightshade and navy blended into the black. The craving flared like flames poked with a fire iron. It hurt to breathe, to swallow, but I didn't place a drop of the elixir on my tongue.

I knew it would help the pain but it would also dull the sense of *her*.

Feron's magic had been more than reminiscing on a memory, it had been reliving it. My mind knew that those events had happened decades ago, but for my body it had been minutes since I'd seen her. I wanted to hold on to the last of that feeling before it too faded away.

Before Brenna was nothing but a ghost again.

A twig broke beneath me and I closed my fingers around the vial.

I peered through a gap in the vines. An unmistakeable mane of black hair was climbing up the tree. Syrra pulled herself beside me without a word, her legs crossed in front of her as she watched me.

"I thought you were Riven." I pulled a loose leaf from the woven hammock and dropped it into the abyss below.

Syrra smiled, nudging my knee with her knuckle. "Riven knew it was not his comfort you needed. He asked me to come."

I pressed my thumb into the top of the vial, refusing to ease up when it felt like the glass would pierce through bone. "Why you?" I winced at the words, hoping Syrra did not sense any meanness in them.

She glanced at the vial before meeting my gaze. "Riven has never known the pain of losing a lover." Syrra tucked a loose strand of hair behind her ear. The tremor in her hand shook and then stopped when she snapped her fingers back into a fist. "He thought it best if you were comforted by someone who had."

I sat up among the vines and squared my shoulders with hers. "He told you?"

Syrra shook her head. "He did not need to." She clasped my hand, her thumb gently gliding back and forth along my skin. "I recognized the pain the night I found you in Caerth. It marks you in a way you cannot shed, a way you might mistake for guilt."

I flinched at the last word. It caught on my breath and dragged a sharp blade down my already burning throat. I wasn't sure I wanted to know how much Syrra had guessed. There were some truths you could not come back from.

Syrra took a deep breath as if preparing for a fight. "I knew when you asked Feron to help retrieve your memories that it would also bring back memories of your love—"

"Brenna." Her name fell out of my lips like a sudden hail. Dangerous and wondrous all at once. It felt wrong to have Syrra know so much about the pain I carried without knowing her name. "Her name was Brenna." My chest loosened, and I could draw more air in the next breath.

Syrra smiled, tasting the name for herself. "Beautiful," she whispered. She stared at something underneath us, far down in the grove. Her dark eyes transformed from a hawklike sharpness to hazy and unfocused. Watching her then, I realized what she'd meant when she said she recognized the pain like a scar both she and I shared. Behind those eyes, she was reliving her own memories, her own pain, with her own Brenna.

I let the silence wrap around us as the blanket of night settled across the sky. As the first stars shone, Syrra's chest rose. Having pulled herself through her reveries, she was present once more.

"When you started your work with Feron, I knew those memories would be the hardest to relive." Syrra let out a hitched breath like her words had cut her as she said them. I felt the weight of her stare flash across my face before she fixed her gaze on the spool of my braid. Her voice had turned to the softest of whispers, as if speaking louder would bring her own painful history swirling back up inside her. "It takes strength to do so. Do not forget that."

I brought my chin to my knees. "Have you ever . . ." I brought my finger to my temple, not knowing a word that described what Feron did inside my mind.

"No." Syrra's answer echoed resolutely against the trees. "By the time I had the strength to try, those memories were at peace. Centuries had passed since my family was killed. It felt wrong to disturb them."

I pressed my cheek to the hard point of my knee cap. I watched the wind blow through Syrra's hair, streaking her face with wavy strands that she did not try to push away. I could see her throat bob as she swallowed her pain away.

"This grove was our home." She pointed to the empty tree to the south. "I lived in the topmost burl. Sylnar lived along the bottom and Favrel lived between us." Syrra chuckled at some joke I didn't understand.

"That second burl would have been Aydar's had she grown old enough." Syrra pulled something small from her pocket. "She never spent a night there though. She was always with one of us, if not us all." I turned to Syrra as a single tear rolled down her cheek. It struck me hard in the gut, like a boulder rolling down a mountain. Even mountains wept; it shouldn't have surprised me to see Syrra teary.

Syrra didn't wipe the tear away, but opened her palm to reveal a tiny portrait. I recognized Syrra immediately even though the painted version of her smiled more freely than I'd ever seen in real life.

On the other side of the portrait stood a tall Elf. He had bronzed skin, a few shades lighter than Syrra's and just as warm. His green eyes seemed to glow despite the battered lines folded into the parchment. Between him and Syrra was a beautiful Fae with piercing eyes of violet that complemented the rich umber of her skin. She had long black curls that were tightly wound just like the lovely babe held between the three of them. She couldn't have been more than two. The perfect blend of the Elf and Fae behind her, yet her soft curls were the same dark shade as Syrra's.

Syrra pointed to the child. "This is Aydar. Our daughter." Pride radiated from Syrra as she stared at the toddler with a solemn reverence.

"Favrel"—she pointed to the Fae in the middle—"she came to train her powers with the warriors of *Niikir'na* and we became inseparable. I thought it would be awkward when I returned with her to Myrelinth. She had already fallen for Sylnar the century before and I had never cared for *niinwir* in that way." Syrra's fingers grazed over the tall Elf with his proud face and long black braid. "But somehow when we met, it was obvious what we all were to each other."

Syrra sucked in a rough breath as her fingers caressed each one of their faces. "They were my family."

Another tear fell down Syrra's cheek, and I looped my arm around her shoulders. She rested her head on mine and settled into the silence before speaking again. "I was wounded during the first of the Blood Purges and could no longer fight. Instead, I was taken to Volcar to see the healers while Favrel and Sylnar took our daughter to a small village near Silstra . . ." Syrra's voice was coated in guilt, catching along her tongue as the words struggled to come. "I told them they would be safe there."

Her voice cracked and she finally wiped the tears away.

"By the time the news reached Volcar, it was too late. The raid had been swift and bloody. I arrived only to find what was left of the village in flames." She folded the picture back and took a shaky breath. "There were no survivors."

My lip trembled but I refused to let Syrra carry my sadness for her in addition to her own pain. "It wasn't your fault."

Syrra sighed. "I know that." She pressed her head farther into my shoulder. "But at the time it did not feel that way. It never has."

I nodded, understanding what she meant. Syrra was a warrior, a protector of her people, and when those she loved needed her most, she wasn't there. I thought of Gwyn alone in the capital and those same fears roared inside me.

Syrra leaned back so she could look at me as she told the rest of her story. "In those first months, the pain only subsided when I slept. It was an *escape* and I needed it more than air. I would beg the healers to give me something, anything, to lull me into a dreamless sleep so I could have a reprieve for a few short hours." She gave me a knowing look. She knew I'd been looking for the same escape that night in Caerth and that I'd found it many times before. My body loosened beside her—somehow it was comforting to know that she understood that feeling. That she understood sometimes the pain was so bad that chasing an escape was worth everything, even our life.

Syrra nodded, agreeing with the thoughts I didn't have to say aloud. "It worked until my injuries were healed. Then I had to go looking for my own reprieves." She pulled the vial from my hand and swished the inky blackness.

"This elixir is infused with magic and brewed from a millennia of healing knowledge. It uses the tiniest bit of *winvra* to do its healing. It can numb pain, quell anxieties, and even lull the most haunted person to sleep."

"You became addicted to it?"

Syrra scoffed. "No, much worse. This elixir is made by healers. It cannot stir an addiction, only help one overcome it. It helps bring your body and spirit into balance by giving you time to heal enough to face what haunts you on your own. If you work hard enough, eventually you will not need it." She handed back the vial. "I did not want something to help me live with the pain; I wanted something to erase it completely. You chose the drink, I chose *winvra* itself."

I couldn't contain the gasp that leaped from my throat. Ingesting *winvra* was said to be complete ecstasy, and for that reason many people had sought out the taste of its black berries. But they were toxic and addictive. After a single taste, most were consumed entirely. Cursed to spend the next weeks searching for berries to eat only to find that the fruit was leeching their life with each taste, within weeks, one's body would be frail and sickly. Most addicts ended up alone and dead within a few short months.

"I started eating just a single drupelet." Syrra pinched her fingers to the rise of a grain of wild rice. "After a month I needed a bud. Then half a berry a day. Then one. Then more." Syrra's throat tightened and her hands turned to fists beside her. I could almost see the memory of that craving burning her throat. I lifted my hand to her shoulder and squeezed.

Syrra's brow creased and her head bowed. "I never fought another day against Aemon and his men. I was consumed by my need to forget." Her shame dripped from her words and flooded the space between us. I knew there was nothing I could say that would lessen the heat of it.

"How did you stop?"

"Feron." Her lips twitched upward. "He saw me wasting away and finally forced me to stop. He had heard that a child might have survived an attack near Volcar. The attack that had killed my sister. I had been too far gone to help fight in that raid and I was certainly too far gone to care once I knew she had died. For years, we thought Nikolai had died too, but then Feron found hope. He helped me get past the worst of it. Two years it took before I was able to make the journey to Volcar and find him."

"Two years?"

Syrra nodded and raised her hand. I watched as it started to shake and the tremor continued up her limb. "*Winvra* has a powerful magic that must be fed. It provides the sweetest euphoria for those who eat it, but it takes its toll. One berry and you may never notice what it took from you, but years of eating it and you will realize it was eating you all along. By the time Feron helped me, I could barely walk. I was on the edge of death with only the thought of my next berry keeping me alive. Even centuries later, I still have tremors. Spasms too. They will never go away."

I blinked. "But you still fight so well."

Syrra gave a solemn nod. "Some days are worse than others, especially if I train too hard or too long. With the help of Feron and the healers, I have regained more than I ever thought possible. The *winvra* killed some nerves, but I am grateful every day that it did not kill me too."

I squeezed Syrra tightly in my arms, grateful she was there beside me. I watched as her hand continued to shake before settling against her knee. "Is that why you refuse to train others?" I nodded to her hand. "Your spasms won't keep you from being a great teacher. It hasn't with me and it wouldn't with others."

Syrra sighed and laid back on the hammock of vines. "The Elverin regard teaching as sacred. Passing knowledge onward is only to be done by those who understand it and are worthy of the task."

I didn't hide my frown. "You don't believe yourself to be worthy?"

Syrra swallowed painfully. "I trained for millennia. I earned these markings knowing that if conflict came, it was my responsibility to protect my people. Yet when they needed me, I failed them. And every day after until the war was done."

Syrra's words struck something deep inside of me. A feeling I couldn't name but knew we both shared. "Failures cannot be undone, but they can be learned from. Another war is at our feet. What will you do to protect the Elverin this time?"

For the first time since I'd known her, Syrra didn't have an answer.

CHAPTER TWENTY-NINE

TRAINING WITH VRAIL didn't clear my head. I'd dreamed of Brenna all night long. I woke in my burl, alone, grateful that Riven understood I needed distance though his burl was still lit when I jumped down into the grove for kitchen duty.

There weren't enough potatoes or punches to wipe my mind of her. Now I was walking through the groves sweaty but not relaxed at all.

Something hit me in the head.

I grabbed for my dagger, crouching on the ground to see who had hit me, but no one was standing there. Instead a hard green ball lay at my feet. It was wrapped in fabric that hung loose from one side like a tail.

"Throw it!" a child's voice sounded from above.

I looked up and saw the trees were filled with the children of Myrelinth, all hanging from branches and vines. Their gazes were locked on the ball at my feet.

"Throw it!" the little boy said again. His laugh fell to a look of pure concentration as I picked up the ball and pelted it to the skies. The air cut through its split tail and it spiraled in a random direction.

One child swung from a vine, just missing it, before it was caught by a girl hanging on the branch below.

"Do you want to play with us?" the little boy asked. His coarse hair was tied in three knots down his head, each decorated with braided vines painted gold and green that matched his robe.

I recoiled in surprise at the question. Four other children looked down at me with wide smiles on their faces. One girl waved her hand, beckoning me to grab a vine. I dropped my weapons belt without another thought and ran toward the lowest branch I could find.

The children shrieked with laughter, swinging higher and higher as I tried to catch them but couldn't. They were young, but they'd spent their entire lives hanging from the tops of the city. My arms burned as I leaped from vine to vine behind them.

The little boy from before snatched the ball from the air and let his body fall beside his vine until he was well underneath me.

"My name is Uldrath." He tossed me the ball.

I caught its tail with one hand. "I'm Keera," I replied in Elvish before letting go of my own grip. I let my body spin around the thick vine, turning three times before using the momentum to launch the ball farther than any other toss.

Uldrath's eyes went wide. "Can you teach me to do that?"

I grinned and nodded.

I dropped once more, spinning slowly so Uldrath could watch. A dozen other children spotted us and came to do the same. Spinning like winged seeds of a sycamore tree, spiraling toward the ground on their vines.

I laughed with the children until my body ached. Only when I dropped to the ground, too exhausted to swing any longer, did I notice Tarvelle standing at the edge of the grove. His arms were crossed and his expression teetered on murderous. He held my gaze for a moment longer than he needed to and left without saying a word.

A chill traveled down my spine. There was something about the way he'd been standing there, watching me in silence. It felt like a threat.

Riven found me in my burl after dinner. I had washed the sweat of training and play off my skin and out of my hair. I was dressed in a long nightgown I'd found in the closet. It's open back and thin straps left my scars bare and comfortable.

Riven stilled when he saw me. His eyes taking their time to enjoy every curve of my body before they settled on my face. "I haven't seen the children so excited in a long time." He nodded out the doorway before he shut it. "They're still spinning down those vines."

I laughed and stretched the tightness at my neck. "It was nice to have a distraction."

"Pirmiith's son even had him up in the vines." Riven chuckled and closed the distance between us. He tucked a damp strand of hair behind the point of my ear. "He's teaching everyone in the city what you taught him."

"I didn't realize Uldrath was his son." It warmed my heart to know that the Elf I'd saved in the Singing Wood was still around to love his son. I grabbed my hairbrush from the table beside the bed.

Riven opened his palm. "May I?"

A rush of heat flashed through my chest and I nodded, passing him the brush. He patted the side of the bed and I climbed up, sitting cross-legged with a perfect view of the window outside. Riven gathered all my hair in his hands and let it fall down the center of my back. He leaned down and pressed a gentle kiss to my neck.

"I love the smell of your hair." Riven's hot rasp warmed my ear.

I leaned into his cheek. "Do you?"

Riven hummed his agreement, nipping my ear before running the brush along the ends of my strands. I raised my brow at him over my shoulder. "Good to know. It's the same hair oil Nik uses."

Riven didn't take the bait. He only grinned wickedly down at me. "I knew there was a reason I liked it so much." He gave my hair a playful tug.

I picked at a loose thread on one of the pillows. "Nikolai told me about his son and his mother. I saw the statue of them together." I closed my mouth before the rest of what I knew spilled out. It wasn't fair to burden Riven with the knowledge I had of Maerhal's death only to assuage my guilt of knowing the truth.

The brush paused against my skull for a moment. "My mother commissioned that statue for him. She and Maerhal were the best of friends. She helped raise Nikolai when Syrra finally found him." There was an edge to Riven's words.

"Is it difficult to have spent so little time with your mother while your best friend got so much with her?" Riven had never told me how old he'd been when his mother married Aemon, but I'd suspected he was young. He only ever spoke of her from the things others had told him.

Riven began parting my hair to braid it instead of answering the question, but I stopped him. I turned around on the bed so I could face him as he spoke. His jaw had hardened, trapping the words inside. But when I grabbed his hand, Riven's entire body relaxed. I didn't know if it was the physical pain of his magic I was easing or the pain of losing his mother, but I was glad to give him some comfort in a world that offered us so little.

I pulled him onto the bed and laid my head against his chest. He stroked my hair with his hand and finally found the words to answer my question. "The jealousy flares at times, I can't deny it. But I'm glad to be surrounded by people who knew her so well, by people she loved like a son. The love I know she would have had for me lives on in their memories of her." He pressed a kiss to my head. "Feron told me that my mother would've loved you. *Adored* was the word he used."

Something sharp and warm crept up my chest. That was a pain Riven and I both shared, the loss of our mothers. Never knowing what they would think of us or the decisions we made. I squeezed Riven's other hand, happy he had people to tell him such things.

I tilted my chin to look at him. "And your father?"

Riven hardened underneath me. He cleared his throat and stared up at the ceiling. "I consider Feron to be my father, even though I call him uncle. He was one of the only Elverin I knew before I gained control of my powers."

My brows stitched together. "You were not raised here like Nikolai?"

Riven shook his head and bit his lip in thought. "It was years before I could be trusted to be around anyone without hurting them or myself. Feron trained me in Vellinth until I was ready."

"Vellinth?"

Riven pressed a kiss to the top of my head. "It's a vacant city in the Singing Wood. Nikolai and Syrra would come and visit me there."

I frowned and placed my hand against Riven's cheek. "That must've been a difficult childhood."

Riven's jaw hardened under my touch. His shadows stirred along the floor of my burl, but I didn't need his answer to know the truth. In some ways, both of us had been robbed of our childhoods.

"It's in the past, Keera." Riven pulled me into a kiss. It was not gentle or soft, but the hurried kind that betrayed his yearning for distraction. I wished I could give him what he needed in that moment, but when I closed my eyes, the image of Brenna was still fresh in my mind. It was unfair to them both to go any further.

I matched Riven's hunger with a soft bite of my own and pulled away. Riven saw the reservation in my face immediately and pulled me into his chest. "Too soon?" he whispered. I knew Feron wouldn't have told him the details of the memory, but Riven knew me too well not to have realized who had haunted me in the library the day before.

I nodded against him and a tear rolled down my face. Riven wiped it away and pressed a kiss between my brows. "Is this okay?" he asked in the gentlest voice. "I can go, if it's not. Or stay, but sit in the chair."

My heart filled with a warmth more powerful than the magic current that hummed between us. I could see the worry in Riven's eyes, felt the care in the way he placed his hands on my waist and arm, holding me and shielding me all at once.

I balled his tunic in my fist and shook my head. "Stay."

CHAPTER THIRTY

RIVEN WAS ALREADY SEATED with Feron and Rheih when I arrived in the library. The Mage sat on a chair next to Feron; her unkempt gray curls had leaves stuck between the strands. Something told me they weren't decoration. From the mud stains on Rheih's boots, she'd been deep in the woods when Feron called her here.

Riven rose from the chaise as I walked in. I grabbed his hand and pretended not to notice the yellow eyes that tracked me across the floor, watching my arms and torso as if she could see the scars through my clothes instead of just knowing they were there.

Rheih pursed her wrinkled mouth. "We meet again, *Valitherian*."

"Nice to see you," I said as I sat next to Riven.

"Is it?" Rheih's pupils narrowed. "Your entire body tensed when you looked at me."

I froze with my mouth hanging open.

She raised one untrimmed brow. "See?"

Riven's shadows swirled protectively around my feet and curved up my calves. The Mage's gaze fell to the floor with wild curiosity. She poked at a tendril of shadow and it recoiled from her finger. "Is this what I think it is?" she asked Feron over her shoulder.

He nodded.

A dubious grin stretched across Rheih's face. "Not so *Valitherian* after all," she murmured. "I see why you need my help."

Riven's grip on my hand tightened. He hated these sessions more than I did. I cleared my throat. "Should we get on with it?"

Feron chuckled, and Rheih cracked her neck. "I need to know what the problem is before I know what paste to make." She eyed the basket of supplies next to her chair. It was filled with glass vials and jars, some contained herbs and flowers while others held liquids I didn't wish to know the name of.

Feron and I explained the trouble we had been having with accessing my memories. "It is beyond any blocks I have ever encountered," Feron said, looking at me with a curious expression. "When I try to pull those memories forward I cannot access anything. It is as if there is a wall between me and them. A cold barrier that feels like nothing else in Keera's mind."

"Perhaps it was put there," Rheih said, digging in her basket for a vial of dark green liquid. Something round and eyelike bobbed inside it.

Feron held his cane with both hands. "Do you have anything that may help?"

Rheih clucked her tongue angrily at the Fae and began mixing ingredients into a small bowl carved from stone. She unlatched a small dagger from her belt and pricked me with it. I recoiled as the blood pooled along my fingertip. Riven stood and put his arm in front of my shoulder.

Rheih ignored him entirely, swatting one of the shadows as it crept up her leg to the bowl on her lap. She rubbed my finger against a small leaf to collect the blood and noticed the cut was already healed.

She glanced at me and then back to the finger before pursing her lips again. "Your healing powers are growing."

I nodded.

"To be expected with a *miiskwithir* bond," Feron said as casually as if he were remarking on what he'd had for dinner.

Rheih's eyes narrowed. "Have you healed anyone beside yourself?"

I leaned back against Riven. "Yes." I placed my hands on Riven's thigh. "Him. Once."

Rheih pocketed her tongue in her cheek and gave Riven a slow assessment. She stared at him like she didn't notice how much stronger and larger he was than her or the rest of us. She gestured for Riven's hand with her dagger.

Riven glanced at me. I nodded and he held his palm out to her. She pricked him and enough red blood pooled in his palm to coat the blade. Rheih flicked it over the bowl and let three drops fall onto the ingredients. She pummeled them and added some of the green liquid, turning it into a foul-smelling paste.

"Give me your sword arm," she commanded, holding the bowl in one hand.

Panic swelled in my chest but I swallowed it down. I lifted my right hand toward her and pulled up the sleeve. Feron's eyes fell on the name he'd watched me carve into myself. I looked at him, expecting to see pity or sadness in his eyes, but Feron's soft eyes burned with something that reminded me more of pride.

He smiled softly and let his gaze fall back to where Rheih was coating the top of my forearm in green paste. She made a circle with it and then she pulled out a horse mane brush and painted a design within the circle. It had jagged lines that formed a square on one leg. Inside the box, she painted a character I'd never seen before.

"What kind of magic is this?" I asked. The circle and symbol were familiar. The Order had been full of designs that followed the same concept. Damien had used one of them to create the jagged scars on my back.

"Runes," Rheih answered without looking up from the paste. "They're not as powerful as a Fae's gifts, but they may help weaken whatever is blocking your memories."

When she was done, she laid me back on the chaise in the same position I always took. She looked to Feron, who placed his hands on either side of my head, waiting for something.

Rheih grabbed a flint from the pocket of the tattered linen trousers that stretched over her shoulders in two thick straps. In her other hand she held her dagger.

A flash of nervousness crashed through me like nausea. "Will it hurt?"

"Not if you lie still," Rheih deadpanned without the hint of a smile.

I gulped and nodded. Riven gave me a final glance, reminding me that I didn't have to do this. I let his shadows lace themselves between my fingers and nodded. I had fewer than ten days to meet the king's deadline. However worried Riven was, he was wrong. I *did* need to do this.

I closed my eyes and listened as Rheih struck her flint. I didn't hear the paste ignite because the black abyss swallowed me whole.

I crashed into something hard. The air flew from my lungs, and I felt something cold and solid beneath me in the darkness. I'd never felt any other presence in the nothingness before. I slammed my hand against it and smelled something burning in the air.

The scent of bark and earth swirled around me in a cloud of smoke. It was dark gray, but against the pitch-black of the in-between, it almost glowed. It swirled around my arm like the golden light that protected me under the lake as I'd walked through the portal. I lifted my arm and pounded the hard ground with my fist once more.

This time it cracked.

The nothingness started to take shape around me. Tall trees of every color sprouted beside me, bright and filled with forest life. The scene was different from any memory I'd had before. The colors were muted like the paint of an aging portrait. That wasn't the only strange thing about this memory. Everywhere I looked, the scene flickered like something was trying to blow out a candlelight and cast me in darkness once more.

Whatever magic Rheih had used, it was working, but it wouldn't last long.

A familiar sweetness hung in the air. It was a light aroma that my nose knew but my mind couldn't place. I heard laughter behind me and I spun my head. A crowd of people was standing in the clearing, tall as giants with the palace of Koratha flickering behind them.

I recognized the trees from when Feron had shown me his memories. I was in the Dead Wood before it was dead.

I reached out in the direction of the palace and noticed the stubby roundness of my arm and fingers. I closed and opened them. The sensation felt fresh and took all the concentration I had. Something moved behind me, launching me into the air so quickly I screamed.

A beautiful sound filled the clearing around me. Laughter so pure it had to have been the sound of Elvish bells and flutes. My hands gripped something hard and I looked down. Giant arms were wrapped around me, big enough to hold me in the single crux of an elbow.

Or I was just that small.

I watched as the arm flickered, darkening and reappearing in front of my eyes. I tilted my head up, and that too took more concentration than it should have. A beautiful woman with long waves of brown hair and petaled lips smiled down at me.

Not a woman, a Fae.

In any other memory, in any other reality, I would have shouted with excitement to meet this Fae, but all I noticed was the silver color of her irises and the way the lines in them look like slashes left by a blade.

They were exactly the same as mine.

She carried me through the clearing and sat in a chair made from the roots in the ground like the rest of the Elverin that laughed beside us. They were all dressed in robes of the purest white. Some were Elves but the overwhelming majority were Fae with silver eyes.

Whenever this memory had taken place, it was well before the Light Fae had disappeared from Elverath.

The scene darkened and for a moment I thought the memory was gone. The smoky scent filled the clearing and the Elverin came back into view.

Drums shook the earth followed by a chorus of flutes and ethereal song. The rest of the Elverin sat, and the Fae holding me placed me upright on her knee. I watched as a beautiful Fae with olive skin and silver eyes that burned like flames walked through the center of the grove. She was dressed in layers of gold that shimmered in the clear day, accented by the gold jewelry cast around her neck and wrists. Her hair was thick and the color of a fallen acorn, cascading in soft waves down her back and decorated with fresh blooms.

She took her place at the center of the seated crowd and looked down the aisle where a Mortal man now walked toward her. He too was dressed in gold, a long robe cut in the same fashion as the ones Feron always wore. His hair was a tangle of curls atop his head and his pale skin flushed with excitement as he beheld the Fae in front of him. They joined hands and an explosion of flowers appeared at their feet, shooting from the ground and blooming in an instant.

The crowd erupted into a chorus of cheers and laughter while the couple sealed their vows with a kiss. The man smiled at the Fae who held me in her arms. There was something off about his smile, a hollowness that did not reach his jade eyes tinged around the pupil with amber.

I flinched, feeling another piercing cut to my hip. I closed my eyes and focused on my breaths once more, forcing myself to stay grounded in the memory but it was already fading away. The blackness took hold of it, devouring every last glimpse of light.

I could feel a pressure building in my chest, pushing me back toward the black abyss somehow, but I fought it. Who knew if Rheih's paste would work a second time? I needed answers.

As if feeling me fight, the nothingness didn't settle; it swirled once more and soon the shadows were taking form again.

This time they transformed into an ancient ruin. A crisp wind blew through the broken pieces of stone that remained, their jagged edges softened by rain and time. The scene flickered, more severe than before. I gripped the ground, anchoring myself to the memory as best I could.

I lay on my belly, hiding between the long shoots of wild grass and watching a crowd of Light Fae whisper among themselves. They stood upon a wide circular slab of stone etched with markings I didn't recognize but reminded me of the training grounds at the Order. And the design Rheih had painted onto my skin.

This was an ancient place, old even in the tongue of the Fae. A tall woman with a long thick braid and silk robe glanced in my direction. I ducked my head but caught a glimpse of those familiar silver eyes. She was the same Fae who held me in the memory before.

The scene flickered again, momentarily fading to black. When it reappeared, the sky was filled with smoke. I didn't think it was part of the memory but an effect of Rheih's paste burning through it.

I became aware of my body then. I was no longer a babe small enough to be held in someone's arm but a child. My hands were small and there was a scab over my right knuckles as if I had taken a fall. My legs were short as they kicked the grass behind me, but I could feel the strength of them. I was old enough to walk alone, to run. From the size of myself, I was seven, maybe eight.

The same age I'd been when I was found in the Rift.

I pulled myself higher on the hill and watched as the Light Fae hugged each other in tight embraces. Each one shared the same resolute yet sad expression. They divided themselves into five groups, with thirty or so in each one. The groups stood equidistant from the others along the edge of the stone circle with the one Fae I recognized in the middle of it all.

She began dancing, her feet pounding into the ground as her arms swayed above her head as if caught in a breeze. The air grew thick, and the braids of the Fae began to raise like they were submerged in water. The group to the northeast began to chant, their voices melding into each other as they wrapped their arms around one another.

The Fae at the center paused her dance just as their chanting reached its peak. There was a bolt of lightning in the cloudless sky and the Light Fae disappeared. Where their bodies had just stood was now a pool of water suspended in the air and taking the form of a symbol I didn't recognize.

The center Fae raised her arms and a harsh wind blew against the water, heading northeast. It dispersed into droplets of rain that never touched the ground and left a trail of blackened grass behind the curve of the horizon.

I was paralyzed by awe and watched as the Fae danced four more times, pausing between each segment as another group turned to liquid. Each time the cloud of water took the shape of a symbol I didn't know but seared into my memory. Then it was blown away, leaving no trace of them behind.

She ended her dance and a final crack sounded across the ruin. It was not the sound of thunder, but the thick stone beneath her feet breaking. The Fae looked down at where a single sapling had sprouted from the large crack.

It had one branch that grew from its green trunk. Along that branch was a single golden leaf and a small, puffy pod hanging from its stem. The memory flickered again just as the Fae knelt down and tugged the pod loose.

I hissed a breath, feeling the sting of fire against my skin. I clenched my jaw and focused on my breathing. I didn't care if the paste branded my skin, I would let it burn as long as the memories kept coming.

I looked down at the Fae, but she had grayed against the grass. I watched as the memory stilled and drained of color. The darkness flashed across the grass and I shouted, to the Fae or to myself, I wasn't sure.

"No!"

The shadows came swirling with the grayed scene before transforming into a different memory. This one was almost drained of all its color. I stuck my fingers in my ears, searching for what was muffling the sound but nothing was there, yet I felt like my head had been plunged underwater.

The darkness flashed once more and I was lying on something hard. For a moment, I thought I was back in that black abyss but above me was the thinnest sliver of pale blue.

Two voices sounded from the shadows at my sides. I stilled, trying to parse the words of their whispers, but they spoke too fast and I could barely hear my own breath.

Something moved above me and I saw those same silver eyes looking down at me. The Fae's lip trembled as she placed a soft kiss to my forehead and stroked my hair.

"*Daanith ikwenirathir ghi Kier'anthar,*" she whispered directly in my ear over and over again. A tear rolled down her cheek and fell on mine. My heart raced, not from fear of what was to happen, but fear of seeing this Fae cry. It unsettled me even though I didn't understand why.

An old woman stepped toward me. She stared down at me, holding a golden handle tipped with a tiny blade I recognized. Her yellow eyes bore into me, pinning me against the stone slab. The Mage glanced to the Fae, who still stroked my hair.

"It's time," she said in Elvish.

The Light Fae nodded, another tear falling onto the stone beside me. The Mage lifted the front layer of my skirt to reveal my bare hip. She spoke in a language I didn't understand so I was unprepared for the first cut.

I screamed as she sliced through my skin but then a hand gripped mine.

I looked up at the silver eyes that stared down at me. She didn't scare me. Neither did the Mage. The version of me that lived through this moment had known what was happening, had expected the pain and pushed herself through it. She trusted this Fae even though I could no longer remember who she was.

The Fae bent down and pressed another kiss to my forehead.

"*Daanith ikwenirathir ghi Kier'anthar.*"

My lips parted and I chanted the words back up to her again and again.

Daughter of the Kier'anthar bloodline.

A searing pain scorched through my body. My blood boiled and I thought the pressure would burst through my bones and flesh. My scream echoed up the long walls of the crevice we were in and then everything went black.

"Keera!" Riven shouted, crossing the room in three strides to get to me. I only noticed I was shaking when he wrapped his arms around me.

I turned to Feron. My head collapsed against Riven's shoulder as I caught my breath. "Did you see that?"

Tears pooled along his eyes. He nodded slowly and one fell down his smooth, black cheek.

"You saw what happened to them?" I asked between wheezes. "Did you recognize that place?"

Feron stood slowly. His left hand shook against the handle of his cane. "I have never seen such magic," he said, sounding like a ghost more than a Fae. "But that proves that Aemon did not kill them."

Riven's hands clenched against my arms as he pulled back from his embrace to look at me. "You saw them?" He whispered in disbelief. "The Light Fae."

"Yes." I nodded, ignoring the searing headache in my skull. "I think they used their magic to hide. I think the Light Fae truly are alive."

CHAPTER THIRTY-ONE

I DIDN'T HAVE TIME TO PROCESS what I'd just learned. As soon as I walked out of the library, Pirmiith was there waiting for me with a wide smile on his face. "Everything is ready," he said in Elvish. "Though I'm not sure how long Uldrath will be able to hold on to the secret."

His eyes warmed at the mention of his son. I placed a hand on Pirmiith's shoulder. "Thank you for agreeing to this."

He shrugged. "You did save my life."

I grinned. "Where is she?"

"Waiting for you." Pirmiith pointed up to the ceiling of the tunnel.

I nodded and led us both to the stairs encased by one of the Myram branches.

Vrail stood at the center of the grove with her eyes covered with a thick ribbon of fabric. She wore the trousers and training vest I'd asked Nikolai to commission for her. The outfit fit snugly over her round hips and belly but was loose enough along her joints and chest. The perfect combination of protection and flexibility.

Nikolai waved at the edge of the field. His eyes were just as bright as the children's who grinned from the vines of the Myram tree above. Though Nikolai's gaze was locked on Vrail. I made a note to tease him about his lopsided grin.

I tugged on Vrail's long braid, which trailed down her back and tickled the ground. "You can take the blindfold off."

Vrail's leg shook in anticipation as she untied the fabric and slid it down her neck. She puffed her cheeks and blew a stray strand of hair out of her face. "The Myram?" she asked, unable to hide her disappointment.

I nodded, biting my lips to hide my grin. "Are you doubting my training method already?"

Vrail's eyes went wide and she shook her head in rapid bursts. "No. I would never. I didn't mean anything by—"

I held up my hand to silence her. The children would be hanging in the trees all day if I let Vrail keep apologizing.

I took her blindfold from around her neck and tucked it into the waist of my trousers. I gripped my wrist behind my back and nodded once. "Take it."

Vrail's eyes narrowed. "You want me to take the linen."

"If you can."

The challenge flared across Vrail's face and she lunged for the ribbon. I sidestepped out of her path, dodging her attack without even moving my hands.

"Take it," I said again, enjoying the way Vrail's brow twitched in irritation.

She circled around me, her footwork the perfect example of all I had taught her. She feigned an attack to the right, but I stepped back out of her way.

She lunged again, this time committing to the right. Her fingers grazed the linen but weren't quick enough to grasp it.

She took a long, slow breath and tried again. This time she spun, forcing me to dodge her kick by ducking underneath her leg. But Vrail had expected it. She abandoned her spinning kick mid-strike and dropped into a roll.

When she stood she held the ribbon in her hand.

I beamed with pride. "Good. Now you understand the rules of the game."

I took the flag from her hands and tucked it into my waistband once more. Vrail looked puzzled. "How many times are we going to do this?"

I smirked at her then. "It's not my flag you will be chasing." I pointed to the children who clung to the vines above our heads. Each one with a ribbon hanging from their waists. "It's theirs."

A chorus of giggles broke out as the children leaped from vine to vine. Some spun down theirs like Uldrath had taught them, their linen flags flattening in the air, teasing Vrail below.

Her mouth fell open. "How many do you want me to catch?"

"All of them."

Vrail smiled like she was up to the challenge. She lifted her arms and waited for my signal. I grabbed the linen from my belt and waved it once. Vrail exploded into a run and started climbing one of the spiraled branches of the Myram tree.

Chaos exploded. The children moved with lightning speed, shaking the trees like a flock of songbirds taking flight all at once. Pale flags and tiny limbs flew in every direction, mocking Vrail with their high-pitched shrills of laughter as they soared above her head.

She ran along the branch searching for her first target. He was a small Halfling but moved with the speed of someone twice his height as he slid down the slick branches to the nearby grove. Vrail stopped her run mid-stride and decided to swing instead.

She clasped a vine and the weight of her body propelled her onward to the next. She eyed her target, a thin vine that was longer than the others.

Her hands opened and she was weightless for a moment, legs spinning toward the thick green rope. She latched onto it and let the momentum carry her to a wide bridge of twisted branches.

The boy had nowhere to go but jump to a vine beside him. She anticipated the move, already launching off the branch herself. Vrail didn't grab for the vine; instead she let her body drop right beside him, plucking the flag from his waistband before landing on the solid bridge of the grove below.

He grinned at her, still hanging from the vine. "Go! Go!" he cheered through his laughter. His giggles echoed through the tree until Vrail had caught each flag.

She landed on the ground with an exhausted thud. The children followed behind her, their chests moving raggedly as they all tried to catch their breath. Vrail slapped the last flag into my hand and fell to her knees. A group of Halflings giggled and dropped in the same way.

Syrra appeared beside me, soundlessly as she always did. "Clever training method," she said to me before looking down at Vrail. "You will train with me every morning while Keera is in the kitchens. Do not be late."

Vrail blinked twice before Syrra's words registered in her mind. She fell back onto the ground with her limbs splayed out and twisted her body in an exhausted dance. I laughed with her as the children dropped around her and did the same.

A chorus of deep laughter echoed from one edge of the grove and I realized the parents had been crowding around the Myram tree to watch the spectacle. Uldrath ran over and wrapped his arms around my waist in a tight embrace in front of everyone.

My heart melted and I squeezed my arm around his small frame.

"Get away from her!" Tarvelle shouted in sharp Elvish. Uldrath's eyes were wide and he searched the crowd for his father, who came to stand beside us with Riven.

Tarvelle marched through the crowd and to the center of the grove. His lips curled back to expose his fangs. Riven's shadows sharpened on the ground, circling me like sharks waiting to feed. Vrail pulled herself from the ground and stood slightly in front of me.

Tarvelle huffed a laugh. His outburst had drawn the attention of the other Elverin. The crowd swelled and those in their burls looked down from above. "I will not stand for this," Tarvelle seethed as loudly as he could. "This killer must stay away from our children."

He looked over my shoulder to someone behind me. Feron stood, walking in slow, uneven steps until he too stood in the middle of the grove. "What are you trying to accomplish, Tarvelle?"

Tarvelle sneered. "It's time the Elverin knew," he shouted in the King's Tongue so even the newest of arrivals would understand him, "that there is a traitor in our midst."

A gasp broke through the crowd and reverberated up to the burls above. The crowd turned to their neighbor in a frenzy of worried glances. A few parents called their children back and clutched their shoulders.

A barrage of emotions pelted me like I had fallen down a waterfall. How was it possible to turn such a perfect moment into one of fear so quickly?

"Someone has been passing information to the kingdom." Tarvelle lifted his arm and pointed. His hair was loose for once and framed the sinister glare he shot at me. "The Blade has been working to steal Halflings for the Crown. She set the Unnamed Ones on us on purpose, hoping to defeat the rebellion in a single night."

The whispers in the crowd grew to angry murmurs.

Tarvelle's lip twitched upward at the sound. "She conspired to learn of the locations of our safe houses only so she could plunder them and set them ablaze."

My mouth went dry. "That is not true—"

"And now she works to gain the favor of your children so she can slip them through the portal and bring them to her king to train as killers too."

Mothers shrieked in horror, grasping their children even tighter. The other Elverin bickered and swore. Tarvelle had taken a ripple of a rumor and blown on it until it'd grown into a wave I had no hope of surviving.

Collin stood at the edge of the grove with a smug look on his face. "She admitted to killing my family."

"Under Aemon's orders!" Riven shouted. He barred his fangs and blanketed the ground in shadow under Collin's feet.

The Halfling didn't balk from the threat. "A killer is a killer. Our people have no hope of surviving, let alone freeing our kin across the Burning Mountains while *Aemon's Blade* sleeps in your bed."

Riven unsheathed his sword. I held my arm out to keep him from bringing me Collin's head. The crowd stepped back as one, their eyes locked on the glint of Riven's blade. The city did not often entertain threats of steel.

It was Feron's voice that quelled the murmurs. "What are you asking for?"

Collin stood beside Tarvelle. They glanced at each other before answering in unison.

"Banishment."

Nikolai and Syrra gasped. A chorus of bickering broke out behind me as the Elverin cheered their support and others shouted their refusal. Vrail flinched from her disappointment in Collin, but he stood tall.

"Only the Elders can decide on banishment," Syrra said with a cold look at Tarvelle.

He lifted his chin at her. "Then proceed with the vote."

I looked to Riven. I didn't understand completely what Collin and Tarvelle were asking for but I didn't need to see the fear in Riven's face to know it was bad. His shoulders drooped and his knees shook with rage while trying to keep his shadows at bay. I grabbed his hand to help calm them but even my touch was not enough.

Feron took a step forward and raised his hand. Two large faelights fell from the branches above. One glowed with the warmth of the suns and the other shone with the silver of the moon. Feron tapped each one and they shattered into hundreds of tiny orbs. He waved his hand once more and they flew through the air, one gold light and one silver hovering above every full-grown Elverin.

Feron raised his arms and the ground beneath him shook. The earth he was standing on split from the grass of the grove and rose on a thick root of the Myram tree. Only when Feron had reached the lowest burls did he drop his hands and the earthy platform stopped growing.

"Tarvelle and Collin have called for an Elders' assembly," Feron said loudly in Elvish. "They ask to consider the banishment of Keera Kingsown."

I flinched at the use of my last name. Riven gripped my hand so tight I could no longer feel the tips of my fingers.

"Each of you must cast your vote. Sunlight for Keera to remain in the *Faelinth* or moonlight for Elders to decide if she must leave." Feron took his time glancing down at the crowd of Elverin below and the ones that stood outside their burls.

I watched as the crowd let each tiny orb of faelight hover over their palms. Tarvelle held out his hand and slowly pinched the golden orb until it was extinguished. I turned around the grove as the rest of the Elverin did the same. Some smothering their silver light and others the gold. It was too close and there were too many for me to tell what my fate would be.

After a long moment, Feron raised his arms and all of the remaining faelights floated in front him. He joined his hands and the golden faelights fused together into one. The result was an orb about half the size of the one Feron had initially dispersed.

I held my breath as Feron clasped his hands once more and the silver faelights fused together. The orb hung over my head like the top of a gallows. The final orb was also half the size of the first silver faelight, but next to the golden orb the result was clear.

The Elders would be called, and unless they decided to go against the vote of their own people, I would be banished.

CHAPTER THIRTY-TWO

RIVEN DROPPED MY HAND the moment Feron confirmed the decision. "I'm sorry" was all he said before he disappeared into the crowd toward the Dark Wood. I watched, helpless and frozen to the spot, unsure of what I should do.

Unsure of what I was even *allowed* to do.

Tarvelle shot one last sneer my way before he and Collin returned to the crowd. Nikolai appeared in front of me, grasping my elbows as he led me down to the stairs of the Myram away from the tense looks of the Elverin.

Vrail and Syrra were right behind him. We stopped at the library, and I sat down in the chaise. "I don't want to talk about it," I snapped when Nikolai opened his mouth.

"I will kill Col—"

"I'm serious, Nik. What happened cannot be undone."

"I can't believe I ever fucked such a prick," he mumbled before throwing himself into the chair.

I turned to Syrra. "How much time do I have until the council reaches a decision?"

She frowned and crossed her arms. "The discussion must last three days at least but I can try to stall the assembly as long as I can."

I nodded. I didn't have time to think about myself. Dynara and the Shades were counting on me to help them. I needed to focus on that until the Elverin stopped me.

"Just before . . . *that*," I started, "Feron and Rheih helped me unlock a memory. It confirmed the Light Fae were not killed, but hid themselves with some kind of magic Feron didn't recognize."

Vrail scurried to stand in front of me. "What kind of magic? Incantations? Fae gifts? Elixirs? Dancing?"

I raised my brows. "There was dancing and chanting though the words were older than the Elvish I know." I explained the memory I had witnessed with the Light Fae disappearing in clouds of water.

Vrail paced back and forth down the stacks of the library. "What did these symbols look like?"

"They reminded me of the pattern Rheih painted on my skin." I swallowed, thinking of the other cut into my back. "Also the symbols that decorate the courtyard at the Order."

"Runes," Vrail and Syrra said at the same time. Vrail did an excited dance and disappeared into one of the aisles filled with books. She reemerged with a brown tome and blew the dust off the cover to reveal a circle with three lines across it embossed into the leather.

Vrail opened the book and started turning the pages in quick succession until she found what she was looking for. "Did they look like these?" she asked, showing me a page full of symbols with tiny explanations under each one.

I studied the pictures carefully. "The one Rheih used looked like these, but the ones from the memory were a bit different. The circle was the same but the lines were more jagged and there were no Elvish scripts used within the circle at all."

Vrail snapped the book shut. "This can't help you, then," she said in an uncharacteristically defeated tone. "I'll need some time to locate the other books that might have the symbols we're looking for."

She turned to Nikolai. "You should go check on Riven." I glanced at her then, but Vrail was making a point of not looking at me.

If Syrra noticed Vrail's odd demeanor she didn't mention it. "I will join you," she told Nikolai, and they both disappeared out the door.

I waited until I could hear their whispers fade down the tunnel. "Why did you send them away?" I whispered.

Vrail glanced uneasily at the door. "Because they will not like what I'm going to suggest."

I raised a brow.

"The symbols you saw, they're runes. I'm certain of it. But they're not the kind of runes we will find in this library or even Volcar." Vrail's leg shook uncontrollably as she spoke.

I leaned on the armrest of the chaise. "What kinds of runes are they, then?"

"Ancient ones," Vrail answered, unable to contain her excitement for the history. "Before the time of Fae, Elves used powerful runes as a form of magic. Over time, the practice changed and became less powerful because the Fae could wield such power at their fingertips rather than carve a rune into the earth."

"Vrail, I need you to get to the point," I said as kindly as I could manage.

She nodded seven times. "If those records still survive, they will be in the library at Koratha."

I shook my head. "The king destroyed all the Elvish books. Ask Killian."

"No, Aemon only *thinks* he did." Vrail took a deep breath. "The Elverin were very good at protecting their sacred knowledge. They had many ways of concealing their books and scrolls. Some of that knowledge was only passed on to the knowledge keepers like me."

Understanding dawned on me all at once. "You want to go to Koratha."

"Yes." Vrail nodded.

"And sneak into the library."

She nodded again.

"For a *book*."

She grinned. "*Niikenth daasowin quil apiithir.*"

Knowledge is the most important of all.

I shook my head in disbelief. "This is not the time for family adages, Vrail."

Vrail crossed her arms and her eyes narrowed until they disappeared behind her round cheeks. "This is the time for action, Keera. If you can find the Light Fae, then nothing Tarvelle and Collin have said or could ever say will matter."

I rubbed my temples. My skull ached like I'd been thrashed about by everything that had happened in the last four hours. "Syrra said the Elders will take three days to decide. If I'm banished anyway, we can search for your book then."

Vrail's black eyes lingered on my face. "Keera, if the Elders decide to banish you, you won't remember the book. You won't remember any of us."

Riven stepped into my burl just as I placed my black cloak into the traveling bag. I turned slowly and crossed my arms, pushing the bag under the bed with my foot. Riven's head hung too low for him to notice.

"I'm sorry I left you there." His voice was nothing more than a rasp, like he had screamed until it had given out. "It took everything I had to contain my powers long enough to watch the vote. I needed to let it out before I did something I would regret."

I took a deep breath. I had felt alone and forgotten when Riven walked away, but I'd known what he was doing. I closed the distance between us and grasped his hand. "Vrail told me what a banishment would mean."

Riven shook his head. His violet eyes were rimmed in red as he looked down at me with a wild gaze. "I won't let it happen. Feron would never do that to you. To me."

I squeezed his hand. "Feron is a wonderful leader, Riv. We both know he will do whatever the Elders decide. It is his burden to bear, but he will bear it."

Riven choked on his own breath and wrapped his arms around me. "I will not leave you," he whispered. "If the Elders are foolish enough to erase your memory, I will go with you."

Hot tears pricked my eyes. "Riven, I wouldn't remember you." Vrail had explained how Feron would use his magic to complete the banishment. My mind would be cleared of all the memories I had about the *Faelinth* and everyone who lived there. Riven would be a part of that. I would only know him as the Shadow, as my enemy.

Riven cupped my face in his hands and pressed a trembling kiss to my lips. "Then we will make new memories."

I shook my head. I couldn't tell Riven what I had planned, I needed him to keep as much good will as he could in case my plan with Vrail failed and my memories were taken from me. "Riven, *if* that were to happen, I need you to promise you will stay here."

His eyes widened with horror. "How could you ask me that?"

My heart ached as I gave him a soft smile. "Because you are the only one I trust to fight for the Halflings *and* the Shades. If I'm not here to defend them, you need to make sure they do not end up being a casualty of this war."

Riven froze. He didn't blink or breathe but just stared at me as the words melted into his mind.

I shook his arms. "I need you to *promise* me." I swallowed the guilt at using that word, but I needed to hear it. I needed to know he would put the Shades above our own interest. No matter how much it hurt.

His jaw clamped shut but he nodded.

I stood on the tips of my toes and pressed a kiss against the lines of worry on his forehead. "I need you to do one more thing," I whispered.

Riven took a deep breath like he was preparing himself for battle.

I caressed his cheek with my hand, inking the image to the pages of my memory. "Trust me."

CHAPTER THIRTY-THREE

I LEFT FOR THE PORTAL just as the moon began to sink below the Dark Wood. It had reached its last quarter, which meant I only had a week before the king would make good on his threat.

And Damien would too.

I threw my bag over my shoulder and pushed those thoughts from my mind. Dynara would find something useful on Curringham to distract Aemon, I was sure of it. And until then I had more than enough to manage on my own.

I stepped inside the thick trail along the Dark Wood, but Vrail was nowhere to be found. My stomach twisted into a knot wondering if someone had taken her. I took a deep breath and pushed those worries aside too.

I was the one the Elverin hated. They had no reason to bother Vrail.

I leaned against one of the thick trees beside the portal. The curved trunks no longer showed Aralinth on the other side, but a moonlit village between Caerth and Cereliath. From there we would journey to another nearby portal, wait for the break of day, and find ourselves in the capital.

I heard steps approaching up the trail. They were heavier than Vrail's, slow and wide whereas hers were quick and short. I crouched down and drew my dagger. If someone was going to try to stop me, then they would need to prepare for a fight. All the better if it was Tarvelle.

A figure stepped into the clearing and I moved without hesitation, grabbing black sleeves and twisting the arm behind his back. I pressed the red dagger into the trespasser's neck before I even realized who it was.

"Killing me definitely won't help your cause," Killian chided.

"You didn't seem to care about my cause earlier," I snapped. "I didn't even see you at the vote."

Killian stilled, his jade eyes narrowing by a fraction. "Had I known there was going to be one, I would have made sure I was back in time to cast my vote."

"In my favor?" I regretted the words as soon as I said them.

Killian didn't dignify my chide with a response.

I let go of his wrist and saw my hand was covered in black ink. I sighed and grabbed the handkerchief from my pocket. It was a habit Nikolai had slowly been installing in me.

Killian shook out his wrist. "Apologies. I spilled ink on myself in my hurry to pack my bag." He tapped the small satchel hanging from his shoulders underneath his jacket.

I raised a brow. "And what made you pack a bag?"

"I saw Vrail lingering around the stables earlier. And Nikolai told me what you saw in your memories. I deduced what you wanted to do from there so it was only a matter of waiting for you to leave your burl." Killian fixed his black collar, looking rather pleased with himself.

"Do you make it a habit to keep an eye on my room?"

I meant it as a jest, but Killian paled and cleared his throat. "Happy coincidence, that is all."

I was about to push the subject further when Vrail appeared in the clearing with two horses in tow. She spotted Killian right away.

"I didn't know you were coming," she whispered harshly. She eyed the suit jacket and fancy trousers of the prince. He was dressed for court rather than travel. "I barely got these horses saddled and through the trail without anyone seeing. We can't risk returning for a third."

She passed me my usual mount. I took the reins and crossed my arms. "Killian isn't coming."

Vrail and Killian spoke at the same time:

"Great, no problem to resolve."

"Of course I'm coming."

I pulled the weather guard over my bag and turned on the prince. "Tarvelle is already going to promote the idea that I kidnapped Vrail. You want him to say that I kidnapped the prince too?"

Killian tucked his arms behind his back and shrugged. "I've already taken care of that problem."

I folded my arms and leaned against my horse. She playfully nipped my shoulder looking for a snack. "And how did you do that in all your hurrying?"

He bit back a coy smile and lifted the sleeve that was coated in ink, though it was hard to tell against the black fabric. "I left word with Nikolai. As far as anyone will know, Vrail and I left to attend to some business in Volcar and will be back before the assembly is concluded. Nikolai will also make it known that he has taken you out of the city to await the Elders' call for your testimony."

"And Riven?" My stomach was twisted into knots knowing that I'd left without telling him. But I knew that Riven would have never let me go alone. Someone needed to stay in Myrelinth to ensure Tarvelle and Collin couldn't wreak any more havoc.

Killian and Vrail exchanged a look.

"It's up to you," Vrail said. "But Killian's sway in the capital could help us get out of there with everything we need. He is the prince after all."

I sighed and shook my head. "Fine." I grabbed the horn of my saddle and pulled myself onto my horse.

Killian's gaze flicked between me and Vrail on our mounts.

Vrail's horse was much smaller than mine, better suited to her short legs, but my mare was tall and powerful enough to ride two for a short time. I chewed my cheek and tapped the back of my saddle. "If you don't find your own mount for the return journey, then you'll be walking back to Myrelinth."

Killian pulled himself up behind me, his thighs squeezing my hips as he steadied himself. "Understood," he whispered in my ear.

His breath smelled of mint and warmed the skin along my neck. It sent unwanted shivers down my spine as his chest pressed into my back. Suddenly, I was reminded of that night in Cereliath when Killian had pressed his lips to my neck knowing I was a Halfling and the act alone could get us both killed. I'd hated the way my body responded to that touch just as I disliked the way my body wanted to lean into him now.

Suddenly, a few hours to cross Elverath felt like too long indeed.

"Here." I handed Vrail a black hood of the Shades. I had stashed it in a tree root outside of Koratha ages ago. Sometimes being a Shade was easier than wearing the black cloak and silver blade. Vrail wiped a cobweb from the hood and sniffed it.

I rolled my eyes. "You only need to wear it to get into the palace. Once we're there, we can find you some servants' clothes to change into."

"I still think we should try the safe house in the city." Killian kicked a pebble toward one of the bent trunks of the Dead Wood. "There might be a glamoured pendant Vrail could use."

Vrail pulled the hood onto her head and sneezed. On close inspection, any Shade would notice that her black garb was too long and too tight in places, but the objective was to move swiftly and hope all eyes stayed on me. "How many Mortals do you see in the royal library when you visit?" Vrail said.

I tilted my head at the prince. Vrail had a point—I'd never seen any of the lords or ladies of court entertain themselves in the library. Not unless Damien was using it for one of his many escapades.

Killian sighed. "I know I'm outvoted, but I wanted to say it again."

"You don't like this plan," Vrail and I started together. She smirked at me before mounting her horse once more.

I did the same and looked down at Killian. "You're sure the guards won't question you?" His plan was to walk along the beach to the palace corridor. If he was questioned by any of the guards he would act as if he had arrived the night before and was taking a mid-morning stroll.

Killian nodded. "I'll swing by your rooms later to pick up my things." He tapped his bag hanging from my horse before walking toward the rolling sea.

I turned to Vrail. "This is your last chance to turn back. I won't hold it against you if you do."

"It's not my first time sneaking around a royal library." Vrail raised her brow. That had been her job in Volcar for decades.

I twisted the reins in my hands and my horse picked up her front hoof. "You didn't have the king, his guards, or his Shades breathing down your neck in Volcar."

Vrail tapped her horse with her heel and started down the path. "No I didn't, but I also didn't have you. You've trained me well, Keera. If you can't trust me, at least trust yourself."

My stomach churned with such intensity I thought I might be sick. I swallowed it down as I took the lead along the King's Road to the outer wall. Vrail had too much faith in me. I trusted her much more than I ever could trust myself.

CHAPTER THIRTY-FOUR

"GOOD LUCK," I WHISPERED to Vrail from under my hood as I left her in the hall outside of the library. She nodded once before entering the room with a duster in hand. She had until dusk to find anything she could about those symbols.

I shook off the tension pulling my shoulders together. Vrail had been hiding among the Mortals in Volcar for years. She could handle a few hours. Besides, from the flyers posted all over the halls, it seemed like the rest of the servants would be preparing for Damien's ball. I grabbed one of the posters and read the fancy scroll along the bottom.

A Party for Prisoners of the Crown

I rolled my eyes. Only Damien could see staying at the luxurious palace for his own safety as imprisonment.

I crumpled the paper and tossed it onto the floor. It was a unique skill of Damien's to turn his father's worry into a farce and manage to insult all the Halflings who were forced to clean these halls at the same time. I huffed a breath, grateful that I would not be at court two days from now to watch the debauchery in person.

I found my way onto the lower terrace of the east tower. I watched through a spyglass as the initiates across the channel trained with the Shades. I spotted Rohan, the Arrow, pacing along the field as she observed their progress. Behind her were Hildegard and Myrrah, watching from the upper landing of the Order.

I watched Hildegard put her hand on Myrrah's shoulder and dropped the spyglass from my eye. A sharp pinch of worry crept up my spine. I had one week to bring the Shadow's head to court or any one of them would be killed.

"Hard to believe the Shadow is lurking on my father's terrace." Damien slithered onto the sunlit tile like a snake. His limbs swayed as he walked with a pretty maiden wrapped under one arm. She gave me a nervous smile and hid behind her black curls and parasol.

"Leave us," Damien commanded without even looking at her. All I saw were wide blue eyes over the fan and then she was gone.

I bowed my head. "Your Highness."

Damien circled me in slow, taunting steps. I felt like I was being stalked by an opponent with no weapon and my arms tied behind my back. The odds were still in my favor but it annoyed me nonetheless.

"You dare return to the capital without the Shadow's head?" Damien's words were as sharp as any blade.

I closed my eyes, hoping I looked frightened enough to appease him. "I'm waiting on word about a possible attack. In case the Shadow decides to attack His Majesty more directly, I've made sure I'm within the city until the threat is cleared."

Damien stopped his march. He turned on his heel to face me and snapped his legs together. "You think the Shadow would attack the palace?" There was a hint of curiosity under his concern. "I'm throwing a party in two days' time. I won't be kind if it is interrupted."

"If I make contact, I will ask the Shadow to reschedule his plans." The words were out of my mouth before I could help myself. All the heat drained from my body and I braced for whatever punishment Damien was about to throw at me.

His jade eyes narrowed to thick slits. "Careful, Keera. You may come and go as you wish, but there will always be at least one fiery little redhead I can take your insolence out on."

I gritted my teeth. If Vrail wasn't in the castle as we spoke, I would've unsheathed my dagger and stuck it into Damien's belly. My time as Blade was swiftly coming to an end. If I couldn't take the king down before it happened, I was damn sure going to take the prince out so he couldn't make good on his threat.

But Vrail was counting on me, so I bowed my head as deeply as I could. "Apologies, Your Highness. I've not been sleeping. I meant no offense."

Damien lifted his chin; the shadows along his face became more pronounced. I could see the resemblance to Killian, but only because I'd come to know the younger so well. Any sculptor would find Damien the more handsome of the two, with his sharp features and strong jaw, but I doubted any painter would prefer Damien's pallid skin and hollow cheeks over Killian's dancing eyes and warm complexion.

Damien pursed his lip, making a point to trail his hand down my back. I gripped my own wrist behind my back to keep from reaching for the hilt of my blade. "I will not punish your insolence this time," he snarled against my ear, never touching my skin but close enough to burn it with his breath. "But if anything goes awry with this party,

I *will* find you personally responsible. My friends and I have been cooped up long enough. We need a night of freedom."

He gave me a devilish grin and then he was gone.

Three hours later, it was dusk and Vrail had still not made it to my chambers. I had been pacing across the window for almost an hour, the glass magnifying the waves so it seemed like I was walking into the tide.

How long did it take to search a library for hidden books?

The second sun sunk further into the horizon, turning the sea red before finally disappearing and casting the waters into shadow once more. Vrail was officially late.

I whipped open the door and started down the staircase. I hoped I would find her on her way to me, but with each turn of the landings, my heart sunk lower into my gut. I had reached the first floor and there was no Vrail in sight. I turned west toward the library and ran into Gwyn.

"Keera," she exclaimed in a hushed voice, wrapping her arms around me. "You didn't tell me you were coming. Again." She stuck out her bottom lip as she looked up at me.

"It was unexpected," I whispered back, looking down the hall. "Again."

I heard shouting and saw two guards running in the direction of the library. Gwyn shivered in my arms. "Are you okay?" I asked her.

She nodded, her green eyes watching the guards disappear down the hall. "I just came from there. The Dagger discovered an intruder in the library. I thought it best not to linger."

The air wheezed out of my chest, taking all my energy and hope with it. Gerarda's ruthless reputation was not for nothing. There was a good chance when I rounded that corner that Vrail would already be dead.

I dropped my arms to my sides and took a breath to steady myself. "Wait in my chambers," I whispered to Gwyn, pulling my hood forward. Any trace of recognition on my face and Gerarda would know there was something between Vrail and me.

I counted my steps to keep me from running down the hall. I tucked my hands behind me, channeling Hildegard's calm essence as I walked toward the library entrance. There were eight guards huddled around the door, trying to grab hold of a flailing Halfling.

My heart skipped. Vrail was alive. Currently captured by the king's guard and the only Shade with a reputation for being as brutal as me, but she was alive.

"What is the meaning of this?" I called down the hall. All movement came to a stop.

Gerarda turned so quickly only her short hair seemed to move at all. "What are you doing here?" she asked in an exasperated tone.

"Is that how you speak to your superiors, Mistress Vallaqar?" I froze at the commanding tone Killian used as he stepped around the corner at the other end of the hall.

Gerarda turned and bowed until Killian was only a few steps from us both. "You have yet to answer the Blade's question." I barely recognized Killian as he addressed Gerarda. He stood tall, almost menacing over her, the gold circlet on his head adding to the threat in his words.

Gerarda bowed her head once more and pointed to Vrail, who was gagged and lifted high enough off the floor the tips of her toes dragged against the tile. Apart from a split lip and a torn head scarf, she appeared to be uninjured. I let my shoulders relax slightly.

"This Halfling was discovered in the library," Gerarda said in a quick, even tone. She stared directly between me and the prince.

"She is not a servant of the palace and she holds no papers. I believe she is a spy." Gerarda added the last part as a whisper.

Vrail thrashed against her hold. I gave her a bored look and snapped my finger at the guards holding her. "If you can't handle a measly Halfling, I will report your names to your captain. And you"—I grabbed Vrail's cheeks hard enough that my nails drew blood—"stop trying to break free unless you want me to break your bones."

I could see in Vrail's eyes that she understood the part I was playing, but it didn't make me feel any less monstrous.

"Who reported the Halfling?" Killian asked, not even looking at Vrail as he spoke.

Gerarda turned to the guard standing closest to us. He removed his helmet before he spoke. "A lord's assistant, Your Highness."

Killian waved down the hall. "Which lord did this man serve?"

"One of the Lords of Harvest. I don't know which one." The guard looked down at his boots.

Killian glanced at me with a creased brow. Vrail being discovered was already suspicious enough, but the poor excuse and the connection to Curringham's house? The mole was behind this.

My jaw pulsed as I stole a look at Killian. How could the mole have predicted where we were going? Only the three of us had even known about the plan.

Vrail thrashed against her hold hard enough to elbow the helmetless guard in the face.

"We will deal with her, Your Highness," Gerarda said, her head still down. "She will be interrogated and then hung along the outer walls of the city like the others who dare defy His Majesty."

Her speech was nothing but cold disdain. As if she didn't realize that nothing separated her and Vrail except the luck of their circumstances. My hand balled into a fist.

Killian glanced at Gerarda and then the guards. "I want to interrogate her myself."

"As you wish." Gerarda nodded at the guards, who lifted Vrail clear off the floor. "Bring the Halfling to the dungeon."

"The gray cells would allow you to interrogate the prisoner in private, Your Highness," I added before the guards could take Vrail away.

Gerarda's black eyes narrowed. "There are many vacant cells among the higher levels. The gray cells would only be an added nuisance."

"If you believe keeping the prince away from other violent prisoners a nuisance," I replied coldly.

Killian glanced at me. All I could do was nod and hope he trusted me enough to agree with me. He turned to the guards. "Do as the Blade suggests."

"She's to be fed and watered once a day," I added to them. "Nothing more." I hoped that order would keep Vrail from being the victim of any unnecessary beatings until I found a way to get her out.

The guards bowed their heads and my stomach dropped to the floor as I watched them carry Vrail down the hall. She looked back at me, her eyes filled with nothing but terror. I didn't move. I didn't give her a smile or even a nod to stoke her hopes. If Vrail died, the cruel face of the Blade would be all she remembered of me.

"I will send word when I wish to see the captive, Mistress Vallaqar. Though I think it best if I wait until after my brother's festivities." Killian eyed a large poster left discarded on the floor.

Gerarda bowed her head once more. "Of course, Your Highness. She shall be interrogated at your convenience."

"Perfect. I will leave you both to your duties." He stepped back and gave me a strained look. There was nothing we could discuss with Gerarda and the guards breathing down our necks. It would have to wait until the palace went to sleep and we could meet at the safe house.

Gerarda rounded on me the moment Killian stepped around the corner. She grabbed my arm and forced me to face her. "What are you doing here?"

"In the city or this particular hallway?" I replied, feigning boredom.

Gerarda sneered. "Why do you insist on treating the king's threats as a joke? Or is it only your own life you care for?"

I slapped her across the face hard enough that the crack echoed down the hall. Gerarda's jaw hung open. "Do not feign a concern for the Shades to cover your own ambition, Gerarda." I pulled out my bloodstone dagger and flipped the handle toward her chest. "If it is my position you want so badly, take it. Why wait until the deadline? You're obviously capable of catching the Shadow before then."

Gerarda took a step closer to me. I could hear the rise in her heartbeat as she stretched onto the tips of her toes to address me. "Your predilection for bending the king's command may serve you well enough, but don't take the rest of us with you because you've finally trapped yourself in a corner." She leaned in close enough that her chest pressed against the handle, pushing the blade into my sternum. "You consider the rules to be beneath you, Keera, but following them saves the Shades. I will not apologize for surviving the king's rage and teaching the rest of them to survive it with me."

I stepped back from the blade and sheathed it once more. I didn't have the energy to fight Gerarda, especially when she was right. "My time as Blade will be done by week's end. Feel free to follow as many rules as you like when you take up my stead."

I grabbed the silver blade that fastened my cloak and wrenched it free from my throat. I tossed it at her feet and didn't stay to see if she picked it up.

CHAPTER THIRTY-FIVE

GWYN WAS WAITING FOR ME when I got to my rooms. Usually she'd be sprawled across the mattress, but this time she was sat on the bench at the end of my bed with her arms folded over her chest. She didn't move to greet me, not even when I tossed my black cloak onto the bench beside her.

She watched me unpack my belt, her wide smile nowhere to be seen. Her lips were a straight line across her face, turning downward at the ends. The usual softness in her gaze was replaced with the aversion I saw on most Halflings' faces but had never seen on Gwyn. It tore at me.

"You saw what happened downstairs." It wasn't a question. The truth was written all over Gwyn's face.

She cocked her jaw to the side and nodded.

"I told you to wait here." My jaw pulsed. What if a fight had broken out and Gwyn had been caught in the chaos?

"You hurt that Halfling." Gwyn's voice was pure ice. For the first time she didn't look at me as Keera her gift-bringing friend, but as Keera the Blade.

I took a deep breath and kneeled in front of her. "Yes, I did. And I have done much worse to Halflings just as innocent as her." My throat ached, shredding against the sharp edge of that truth.

"Why?" I hated the way Gwyn's voice cracked. "No one ordered you to be cruel while you captured her."

I stilled. Gwyn had a habit of pushing my boundaries between what was *right* and what was *smart*. There were so many reasons I could give her, but all of them would involve her in at least some of my secret treachery to the crown. I didn't know if that was a burden I was willing to place on the shoulders of a sixteen-year-old girl.

Gwyn jutted her chin as if hearing my thoughts. "Don't lie to me, Keera. I'm old enough to know the truth."

I opened my mouth as I tried to find the words. "Sometimes, I have to be cruel in small ways so no one notices when I am merciful in big ones."

Gwyn leaned back. Her eyes narrowed over her freckled nose. "She is already set to hang, now she must be cut and hungry too?"

A battle raged inside me, churning my guts until my belly ached. There could only be one victor: the truth or reason. Gwyn glared down at me with a hatred that scarred my soul. I pressed my forehead against her knee and my resolve crumbled. "She is not hung yet. Better cut and hungry than dead."

I pulled the sleeve of my tunic up my arm to flash my scars. "The names are not a record of every Halfling the king has ordered me to kill, Gwyn. Just the ones I couldn't save."

Gwyn blinked. "How many names have you kept off your list?"

"More than I could ever carve into my flesh." I pulled the sleeve back down. "And I will do everything in my power to make sure that Halfling's name isn't carved alongside these."

Gwyn studied my arm and then my face. The aversion was gone and instead she looked at me like she was finally seeing me for who I was. Keera *and* the Blade, all at once.

"I never thought about the toll it must take. Making a shield out of a cruel reputation and then having to decide who is worth the risk to shield with it." Gwyn pressed her forehead against mine. "I'm sorry for judging you. It was just a shock to see the person who fills her own room with sand acting like . . . *him*."

I pressed both my hands to her face. "I could never be like Damien, Gwyn. He brandishes his cruelty so often he knows nothing else. To him, it's a game. Mine is just a mask I have to wear sometimes; you *never* have to fear me."

"I know." Her lips turned upward in a soft smile.

I stood and kissed her forehead. "Have you had any trouble since I was last here?"

Gwyn shook her head. "Damien has been using me as his assistant for this party. He is too busy with that to do anything more than tease or taunt."

I breathed a sigh of relief. "Hopefully that doesn't change."

Gwyn smiled briefly, braiding her red curls down her waist. "How long are you here this time?"

I shrugged. "Only a few days."

Only until I figure out a way to break Vrail out of the dungeons.

The lanterns along the beach had begun to burn low. Soon I would be able to meet Killian. I turned to the bed and clapped my hands together. "I think it's time for presents."

"But you were just here." Gwyn's green eyes swirled with delight.

"And yet I feel like I've traveled across the kingdom and back in that time." I pulled out the small pouch from my bag. "Though if you think another gift is too much, I could return it."

I dangled the pouch above Gwyn's head. "If you insist." She giggled before standing on the bench to grab her gift. She untied the closure and dumped the contents into her palm. Three tiny beads rolled into her hand, each glowing with the silver light of the moon. "What are these?"

"Faebeads," I whispered back. "In the Faeland, orbs as small as these beads and as big as the colored gems atop the palace towers float around the cities, casting the people in the warm light of the sun or the cool glow of the moon." I had pulled them loose from a dress that I'd found in my closet. I preferred giving Gwyn a tiny taste of magic rather than wearing it anyway.

Gwyn's eyes were bigger and rounder than I had ever seen them. "Like magical stars?"

"Exactly like that." I nodded. "These beads do not glow nearly as bright, but I thought they would be easier to hide than a faelight."

"Faelight," Gwyn echoed, trying the word for herself. "If the beads are this pretty, the Faeland must be a beautiful place, if still a scary one."

I leaned in, pressing my shoulder against hers. "It's not as scary as the stories say."

"There are no Dark Fae with the power to take hold of a mind or trees so poisonous they'll kill you with a single prick of their needle? Or what about the creatures that lurk in the Dark Wood, able to shift their skin to lure travelers to their bloody end?" Gwyn gripped her chest dramatically and collapsed onto the bed.

I laughed. "All true I'm afraid."

"Would you go back?" Gwyn opened one eye.

"In a heartbeat."

"Then I will dream of it and hope that my dreams do it justice." There was an edge to the joy of her words.

I glanced at her ankle and saw the magical line of her tether wrapped around it like a shackle. "I have another gift for you," I said, reaching into the bag once more. I pulled out a small black case and handed it to her.

Gwyn's brows creased as she opened it to reveal the three tiny vials of red liquid that sat inside. They were the size of dewdrops clinging to a blade of grass and came to a small sharp point that was capped with hardened sap. "These contain concentrated doses of sleeping draught," I whispered. "I want you to keep one on you at all times." I didn't think Syrra would mind I'd taken them from the training room.

Gwyn's freckled nose wrinkled. "Why? What for?"

I took a breath. I needed to be careful not to say too much. "There may come a time when the king is dead—"

"What do you know?" Gwyn whispered, snapping the case shut and stuffing it into her pocket. "What are you planning?"

I shook my head and raised a finger to my lips. It was too dangerous to tell Gwyn anything more; the less she knew, the safer she was. "There have been reports of the Shadow making another move against the king . . . *If* his attack were to be successful, the king may not survive it."

Gwyn held my stare. My chest lurched at the hope I saw softening her eyes. "These are for Damien," she said plainly. "You think he'll come for me when his father dies?"

"If."

A feline smile crept along Gwyn's lips. It looked unnatural on her round, buoyant face. "I hope he does."

A cool shiver ran down my spine as I saw the hopeful malice spread across Gwyn's young face. I didn't know if she meant the king or his son. I was too much of a coward to ask.

"*If* that happens"—I grabbed both of her arms, squeezing them in the urgency of what I had to say—"then I will come for you, Gwyn. Use my other gift to call me here and I will come as quick as I can. If Damien tries to find you, leave. And if you can't, hide. These vials are only a last resort. I should find you before you ever need one."

Gwyn stood and patted the pocket with the case in it with her hand that wore the gold ring I'd given her months before. "I will keep them on me always like you said. But if you truly think the Shadow has a chance to end the king, I think you should let him."

"Gwyn, you cannot say such things," I hissed.

She headed to the door, turning back to me before she opened it. "I won't say it again, but I will not stop hoping for it."

CHAPTER THIRTY-SIX

KILLIAN WAS ALREADY AT THE safe house when I arrived. A dingy, old shop with boards on the windows and door. For anyone who peered inside the dusty glass it would seem to have already been ransacked and emptied of any goods worth stealing. Though that was only the front room.

I entered from the side alley and found the secret latch along the inside wall. The panel opened to reveal a long thin room with three bunks at the end and a stack of books along a small desk. Comfortable enough for anyone needing to hide out for a few days.

Killian was lying across the bottom bed in his sleek tunic and ebony jacket he only wore at court. Its cuffs and collar were embroidered with tiny red gemstones set in the same pattern as Aemon's crown.

Killian sat up and gestured for me to take the only chair in the room. "That could have gone better."

"The only saving grace is that I arrived before Gerarda had time to slit her throat." I leaned back into the chair and buried my face in my hands. "Just like I will do to the mole when I find them." I felt no guilt issuing the threat.

"I share your anger, but I don't understand how this helps Curringham other than that it distracts the Crown from his own plot." Killian stood and paced the length of the room. "If that is his motive, then you cannot return to court. If Curringham knows about Vrail then he knows about you too. He'd turn you in the moment he thought someone was close to discovering his treason."

I rubbed my brow. I felt like I was stuck between two swirling storm fronts; the more I tried to take control, the harder the winds blew, and the pressure was giving me a headache. "If you're trying to convince me to leave Vrail in that dungeon, you should save your breath."

"I can use my influence to keep her alive until the war is won," Killian said, still pacing up and down the room.

I leaned my neck back and stared up at the dirty ceiling. "I've found you clever, Killian. Don't disappoint me now."

The prince rolled his eyes and picked at the skin around his thumb. "We don't have time for jests, Keera."

I raised my brow at him. "And we don't have time for stupid ideas. You know as well as I do we're already taking our chances that Vrail survives the night. I will not abandon her only to hope to claim her as a prize if we're victorious. She deserves better than that."

Killian halted and bowed his head. "That's not what I meant—"

"I know." I leaned forward and ran my hands through my hair. "You always want to make the clever move, but there are none, Killian. If the choice is between leaving to tell the Elverin that, on top of everything else, I've lost Vrail, or risking discovery while I try to save her, then I know which one I'm choosing. It might not be the clever play, but it is the *right* one."

Killian sat down on the bed. He bit the inside of his lip. "How long will it take to plan a rescue?"

"We have two days." I pulled a poster from the pocket of my vest.

Killian took it from my hand to read it. His jaw flexed. "My brother's party?"

"It will provide the distraction we need to get Vrail out without notice. The Shades and guards will be occupied."

Killian rubbed the back of his neck. I could smell the parchment and ink wafting from his skin. "If the mole was willing to tell Curringham about you, we have to anticipate that Curringham knows about me too."

I exhaled slowly. "Knowing of the treason and accusing the prince of it are wildly different things."

"Enough to bet that Curringham won't expose us the moment he sees us at that party?" Killian's jade eyes bore into mine. The amber rings within his irises were more vibrant than before, or perhaps I had just taken the time to notice.

"For Vrail's life?" I asked. "Yes, I would make that bet—with or without you." I hunched over the chair and let my head hang loosely between my shoulder blades. "I don't think Curringham will reveal us until he's ready to move his *winvra* across the sea. Syrra's spies haven't even confirmed the harvest yet. It's not my place to gamble with your life, but I would take the chance that Curringham is not ready to reveal our secrets so quickly."

Killian's brow creased as he assessed me. "I will take the gamble with you. And I'll send word to the others so they may decide on their own bet."

My mouth went dry. "Not Syrra."

"Why not?" Killian raised a bronzed brow.

"Even if we can keep Vrail's capture a secret, the Elverin will not be happy that I've disappeared. Someone needs to be there so Tarvelle can't feed us to the wolves." My lip curled as I said his name. "Syrra has the most pull with the Elders. She should be the one to stay."

"She won't like that," Killian mumbled.

I shrugged. "Just as I'm sure Vrail doesn't like being locked in the gray cells."

Killian's eyes narrowed with a flash of curiosity. "Why did you have the guards keep Vrail on the lowest level?"

"*Second* lowest level," I corrected, unwilling to meet his eyes.

Killian shot me a sideways grin. "If we have no time for jests, I doubt we have time for semantics. Why so far away?"

My stomach clenched. I didn't want to keep any more truth from Killian, but he needed to focus on Vrail. There was no reason two of us should be distracted by fruitless hopes. I cleared my throat and looked at the lacing on my boot. "The sixth-level dungeons are not guarded. It will make for an easy extraction with less opportunity for things to go awry. Again."

Killian's gaze lingered on me. From the sideline of my vision, I could see his lips pinch as he studied my face but he didn't push the issue further. Instead, he pulled out a piece of parchment from his pocket and a small vial of ink with a crystal quill for a stopper. The ink was red in the bottle, but as Killian wrote the letter, it dried black on the page and on his skin.

"I'm surprised your father's tutors never beat that habit out of you." I pointed to the stain along the base of his left hand from sliding it over the wet ink.

Killian scoffed, flexing his fingers before dipping the quill into the bottle once more. "The day I was born was the day my father stopped caring for me."

"I'm sure Aemon's cold heart warms for his own son." I meant it as a joke, but the hardness in Killian's expression stopped my laugh in the middle of my throat.

"Perhaps if I'd been born as the heir he wanted, my father would have warmed to me, but alas I was born Mortal." Killian signed his name at the bottom of the letter. He held the parchment up to the lit candle and set it aflame. It disintegrated in front of our eyes, not a piece of ash left behind.

"But Aemon is Mortal." I tilted my head at Killian. "I thought he would have been happy that you were born Mortal too and not—"

"A Halfling?" Killian finished.

My cheeks flushed with heat. "I didn't mean to imply you're not one."

Killian sat back down on the bed and gave me a soft smile. "I know you didn't." He shifted his head on the worn pillow. "Feron told you of the lengths my father went to gain his powers. He revered the Fae. Respected their magic and technology—it's why he hoped to rule over a society of Mortals *and* Fae."

"But there's so much the Mortals have wrong about the Elverin. Their stories are falsehoods wrapped around a single grain of truth."

Killian exhaled deeply as he thought. "I suspect my father crafted those stories himself, or at least, the first versions of them. You can learn a lot about a king by taking notice of the texts he keeps and the texts he burns. My father only allows books that can be used to support his version of history to be read. I'm guessing he destroyed the rest long before I was born."

I thought of how ruthless Aemon could be about the royal libraries. Halflings were not even allowed inside them. "His distaste for the Fae is born from their refusal to share their knowledge with him?"

Killian nodded solemnly. "A large part of it, I suspect."

"Then why take a Fae wife?" I sat straight in my chair, ignoring the way my heart raced from asking the question I'd been pondering for decades. "And why did she agree to take him as a husband?"

"Those are two complicated questions," Killian said darkly.

I dropped my head. "We don't need to talk about it if you don't want to."

"I never *want* to, but I think you should know." Killian's stare was full of emotion I couldn't read. I leaned back in the chair and waited for him to continue. "My mother's motives are clearer to me. The gifts of the Dark Fae were receding rapidly when she decided to accept my father's proposal. I think she hoped that by marrying him, she would be able to discover if Aemon's powers had been failing too. She believed there was some secret my father was hiding, something that would be the Elverin's salvation." Killian cleared his throat and looked at his hands. "It is why she was willing to leave her babe at barely a year. She spent the year she was married to my father smuggling as much information as she could back to the Faeland."

My throat tightened. There was no way Laethellia had thought her plan would have had a happy ending. "Very brave of her."

Killian's lip twitched upward. He stared at the bunk above him with his hands folded behind his head. When he spoke, I wondered if he remembered I was there at all. "My father's motivations for the match are more muddled. He ignored me too often as a child for me to ever believe he would answer that question. And by the time I was brave enough to ask it, I had already sworn myself to the Elverin. Drawing suspicion was not worth the risk."

My heart sank for the little boy who spent so much time alone, wondering about a mother he couldn't remember and a father who chose to forget him. "Then what do you think his motivation was?"

Killian puffed his cheeks and let out the air slowly. "I think my father wanted an heir with the gifts of the Fae. By the time I was conceived, he had accepted that his life would be long but not immortal. I think he wanted to leave the throne to someone who could do what he could not—rule as sovereign over Fae and man."

I tucked a loose strand of hair behind my ear. "He thought the magic he had stolen would allow him to sire a Fae?"

Killian stilled on the mattress. His words caught in his throat and he rubbed his face, trying to decide which ones to free.

"My father is many things, but humble isn't one of them." Killian turned to face me. "Perhaps it was hubris and he thought himself beyond the average man. Perhaps he knew something that made him think it was possible. Either way, when I was born Mortal, he had no use for me."

My throat burned with all the words of comfort I wished to say. But I knew there was nothing I could say that would heal the scars of being a lonely child. "Damien would be irate if he knew." I couldn't help the grin tugging at my lips.

"I think he does." Killian huffed a laugh. "Why do you think my brother detests my lineage so much? He's always seen it as a threat. Which is ridiculous considering he would rather spend his days bedding nobility and throwing parties than spend one *hour* performing duties of the court."

"The Bastard Prince," I mumbled under my breath. It was the name Damien always used to refer to Killian when he was away from court.

"A Halfling with red blood." Killian ran a hand through his soft curls. "A Halfling that doesn't belong. In the kingdom or in the Faeland."

I raised a brow. "How can you say that the Elverin do not accept you as you lead them into open rebellion?"

Killian's lips pouted and he refused to look at me. He folded into himself like a wounded animal. I recognized that pain, the kind that raged inside your chest and scraped the deepest parts of you. The kind you carried with you always, bleeding into yourself, while no one around you ever knew. My heart ached for Killian. We both knew what it was to have a heart that beat for our people and bled with every pulse.

"I think that doubt is part of being a Halfling. At least in a world where your father reigns." I swallowed, my throat suddenly dry. "No matter where we are, we never feel like *enough*. Too Elvish to live freely in the kingdom, too Mortal to live happily in the Faeland. Generations of being told to loathe our amber blood—to loathe each other—but they are all lies meant to serve a vile king. Lies I hope one day all Halflings have the chance to overcome, including me and you."

Killian sat up and faced me. His brow was heavy over his eyes and his finger still picked absentmindedly at his thumb. "I've never told anyone this, but when I was a boy, I used to prick my fingers with a hunting knife. Each time I would close my eyes and wish that my hand would bleed amber instead of red." Killian shook his head with a look of disgust on his face. "Do you realize how sick that is? To wish for the same marker that keeps Halflings chained to my father's command?" His eyes were rimmed with tears as he looked at me. "I was a child, but I knew what happened to Halflings at court, and I'd heard whispers of how much worse it could be, yet I wanted to be one of them. All that privilege and I would have thrown it away to sever the tie between me and my father for good." Killian's chest rose and fell with rapid breath.

I reached for his hand. "That is nothing to be ashamed of, Killian. You are one of us. The color of your blood doesn't change that." I was speaking to myself as much as I was to him. Had I not just been questioning my own claim of being a Halfling? Aemon liked to cut us into his mold, but for Killian and me, the mold didn't fit. Yet in the Faeland it didn't matter. Fae, Elf, Halfling—we were all the same. Elverin.

"Doesn't it?" Killian asked. I could see the loathing he held for himself settling along the lines of his forehead. I hated it. I hated the way Aemon made every Halfling feel unworthy and alone. It was exactly what he wanted, to make all of us feel too small to matter so we could never fathom how much power we had as one.

"If blood matters that much, then what about the blood on my hands?" I retorted, heat building in my chest. "I have killed more Halflings than any Mortal ever has, yet you have welcomed me with open arms."

Killian frowned. "It's not the same. You were forced—"

"And you were born. I doubt you had a say in the matter either." I squeezed his hand and rubbed my thumb across his inky palm. "You could have spent your days in luxury without ever having a thought for the Halflings—or ever seeing them as your kin—but you didn't. You've worked to learn as much as you can about the Elverin while you use your rank to *save* your people. If you're going to stack the weight of your father's blood against you, then you must consider the weight of your actions too."

Killian exhaled a long breath toward the ceiling. He shot me a shy smirk. "It takes me hours to come up with a speech half as rousing, and you deliver that on the spot."

I dropped his hand to cover my laugh. "Imagine what I could accomplish if Nikolai were here to practice with me."

Killian chucked a pillow at my head. I dodged it and climbed onto the top bunk with the hope of a few hours of sleep.

CHAPTER THIRTY-SEVEN

My hopes for sleep were pointless. Every time I closed my eyes, flashes of those uncovered memories played across my mind. The Mortal marrying the Light Fae. It had been nothing more than a glance at his face, but now I was sure I recognized his thick hair and strong, square jaw. And those eyes.

The color of sunlit jade ringed in amber. The same ones his son had in the bunk below me.

The memory had been of Aemon, I was sure of it. But who was that Fae he was marrying, and why did none of the Elverin alive seem to know about the union? I had no answer to those questions so they bounced around my skull, keeping any chance of sleep away.

I slid out of the safe house at dawn and scurried down the alley with my hood covering my face. There was nothing I could do for

Vrail until the party the next night, but I could at least try to find some of the answers she'd been willing to get captured for.

My legs carried me to the half-built bridge. The morning glow of the first sun shimmered off the turquoise sea glass, casting rays of blue light on the white sand. I ran across it and launched myself through the series of posts, leaping from one to the next until I reached the other side.

The grounds of the Order were quiet. There was still a half hour until the Shades would be expected in the great hall to break their fasts. I passed the large wooden doors even though my stomach grumbled loudly, echoing off the wide stone staircase.

Hildegard's door was open. I peered in and saw Myrrah and her at the window, each with a cup of tea in their hands. Hildegard was perched on Myrrah's lap, stroking the back of her head as they watched the sunrise.

I cleared my throat to announce myself. Neither of them turned. Myrrah took another sip from her mug.

"The palace better be in flames if you expect me to do anything before finishing my tea," Hildegard said calmly, still not looking at me.

I leaned against the door. "If that were the case, I'd be across the channel fanning them."

Myrrah chuckled into her mug.

Hildegard took a long sip before finally meeting my gaze. "Is this going to ruin my day?"

"Lesser Shades would take offense at that." I walked over to the chair behind her desk and sat down. I made a point of throwing my legs over the armrest.

Hildegard rose from her wife's lap and raised a single brow. Myrrah turned her wheelchair and gave a low whistle. "Disrespect before her tea is done. You have a death wish, Keera." She stretched her neck upward and Hildegard leaned down so Myrrah could kiss her cheek. Then Myrrah tucked her mug between her thighs and headed toward the door.

I winked at her as she left the room. "If I had a death wish, I would've put my boots on the desk."

Hildegard flinched. "What brings you back to the Order so soon? Have you apprehended the Shadow?"

I sighed. "No. But I'm getting closer. It's like I can sense him." I smirked at my own joke.

Hildegard was not amused. She waved me out of her chair and sat down herself, back perfectly straight and hands folded neatly on the desk in front of her. "Yet you're here bothering me?"

"Because I missed you so." I grinned and placed my hands on either end of her desk. "Do you remember much of those years before I came to the Order?"

Hildegard's brows shot into her gray hair. "I have not thought about that in a long time."

"I don't make a habit of it either." I perched on the edge of the desk and watched the tendons in Hildegard's neck flex. "But some questions have been on my mind lately."

Her stare narrowed. "What questions would those be?"

"I remember when those villagers pulled me out of the Rift. They called for the Shades immediately. Most of the people were scared to touch me, they were so convinced I was an Elf. But then Mistress Carston came and cut my palm. Even she couldn't deny the amber blood."

Hildegard nodded slowly.

I cleared my throat and continued. "What I don't understand is why Carston was so set on continuing to prove I was a Halfling? Why spend years testing me only to send me to the Order anyway?"

Hildegard tilted her head to the side. "You've thought that was Carston's doing all this time?" She broke her perfect posture and leaned back in her chair.

Confusion ripped through me. "She hated me—of course it was her." The only time I'd seen Carston smile was when she had reason to beat me.

Hildegard rubbed her brow. I noticed how thin and translucent her skin looked on the back of her hand. My throat tightened. It was unfair how some Halflings aged like Mortals while others kept their youth. "I won't deny Carston was not fond of you."

I huffed a laugh.

"But," Hildegard continued with a pointed look. "She wasn't the one who wanted to run those tests or keep you locked in those damned cells."

"Then who?" I asked, growing impatient at Hildegard's slow pace.

She glanced to the open door of her office. "The king."

I shut it, leaning against the back of it as I shrugged. "I shouldn't be surprised his distaste for me started as a child." I swallowed the bitterness in my mouth.

Hildegard leaned forward on her desk, her voice no more than a whisper. "He didn't hate you, Keera. When you were found in that rift, he was ecstatic. I've never seen him more excited than the day he first laid eyes on you."

I grabbed the back of her guest chair. "That doesn't make any sense," I whispered to myself. "He never involves himself in training Halflings."

Hildegard grabbed her mug and took a long sip. "He didn't want to train you. You would still be locked in those cells if I hadn't made them cave in and used it as an opportunity to canvass for you to be allowed to stay at the Order."

My mouth fell. "That was you?"

Hildegard nodded with a hint of pride. "You were a child. It was a fate worse than death to keep you locked in your entire life."

I exhaled a slow breath. I had come here for answers, but now I only had more questions.

Hildegard walked over to me and placed her hands on my arms. "I'm sorry I can't give you the answers you seek, Keera. But they won't do you any good if you're dead." She tightened her grip on me. "Find the Shadow. The king only grows more reckless in his worry. End it for him before he decides it best to end you."

I grasped her forearms. "You have to stop worrying about me like I'm still one of your girls. Trust that I know what I'm doing."

Hildegard looked up at me with a sad smile on her face. "I will always trust you, Keera, just as I will always worry for you. Try your best not to die."

When I returned to the safe house at midday, Riven and Nikolai were already there. Nikolai was strewn across the middle bunk while Riven paced the room. As soon as I opened the door he was at my side; relief washed over his face as his shadows swirled along the wall.

I raised my brow at them. "You need to keep those under control or you'll be in the dungeons too."

Riven ran his hand down my arm and looped his fingers around my wrist. "No one will see them outside of this room. It gives me a break from holding it all in." He smiled down at me, but I could see the pain behind his grin. The pain that was always with him except when he was touching me.

I glanced down at his thumb. It caressed the skin along my inner wrist while the words Riven had said to me the last time I saw him echoed through my mind, carving at me until my insides felt hollow.

His touch provided me with the same pleasant warmth it always did, a tingle that made me want to lean into him, but I knew that didn't compare to what Riven felt. To how I numbed his pain. I chewed the inside of my cheek, wondering if that was why Riven had come to care for me, why he had been so eager to leave his people behind for me.

For us, there was no greater pleasure than the absence of pain.

I broke out of Riven's grasp and sat in chair across from Nikolai. "Do the Elverin know about Vrail?"

Riven shook his head while Nikolai pulled at his hair. "They know you aren't in Myrelinth, but Vrail's absence hasn't been noticed yet. Though there are some who are whispering your name alongside Dynara's." Nikolai leveled me with a hard look.

I flexed my jaw and stared back without saying a word until Nikolai's gaze fell to his lap.

"There's nothing we can do about that," I said, sidestepping the need to answer what I knew about Dynara. "Our focus needs to be getting Vrail out of those dungeons." I leaned back in the chair, glancing between the two of them.

Nikolai's eyes narrowed. "You have a plan, I can see it twirling around that gorgeous head of yours."

I glanced at Riven, who leaned against the bunks and casually crossed his arms. "If you have a plan, we'd love to hear it," he said. "It was you who planned out the attack in Silstra—"

"Not true," Nikolai said under a cough.

Riven rolled his eyes. "You were the one who perfected the plan in Silstra." He raised a brow at Nikolai. "Better?"

Nikolai wore a bored grin on his face. "Marginally."

They both turned to me with expectant eyes and closed mouths.

"It's simple enough," I said, leaning forward on my elbows. "Killian and Nikolai attend the party—Nik will be disguised, of course—and use the opportunity to learn as much as they can from Curringham. We decide on a time that would allow most of the guests to be in the throne room for the event and cause a disturbance." I looked to Nikolai. "I trust you have an idea on what that could be?"

His answering grin was boyish and gleeful. "I have many ideas, Keera dear."

"Good." I nodded and turned to Riven. "When the court is distracted, I will meet you at the entrance of the dungeons. We'll get Vrail while the others get themselves out of the palace and hide in the chaos."

Riven's bottom lip protruded as he mulled over the plan. "It's simple."

"Simple is good. Less opportunity for the plan to go awry." I rubbed my knees with the palm of my hand and leaned back. Waiting another night to rescue Vrail felt too long.

Riven bit the inside of his cheek. "And what if Curringham decides to make the plan go awry?"

I let out a slow breath. I hoped it wouldn't come to that. I hoped Curringham would be too nervous to make a move against the king in his own throne room. But it was something we had to be prepared for. "The first sign that something is wrong, the plan is off. We can't risk having anyone near the palace if Curringham decides to expose Killian or me. The first hint of something wrong, we leave the palace and meet at the portal."

Nikolai and Riven gave each other a sullen look.

I stood, facing them both. "I need you to swear it. I won't lose anyone else because of my foolishness. One head is already too high a price to pay." My chest squeezed painfully, like my guilt had wrapped itself around my lungs and begun to apply pressure. I drew a wheezy breath but didn't fight the pain. I needed to feel it. It was the least I could do for Vrail, who was locked in a dungeon because of me. Even though my throat seared with the need for a drink, I wouldn't do anything to alleviate the pain. Not a sip of wine or even a drop of my elixir on my tongue. Numbing my pain had made me blunt for years, and my edges needed to be honed and sharp to rescue Vrail and face the wrath of the Elders when we returned to Myrelinth.

I didn't blink as I held their gaze. Finally, Riven and Nikolai nodded. "First sign of trouble, we get ourselves out," Nikolai agreed.

Riven's brow creased as he looked at me with heavy, worried eyes. "We all get out."

I grabbed his hand and nodded, but I didn't speak. Riven should have known better by then.

I didn't make promises.

"Mephitic gas," Nikolai said with a jump. We had spent the rest of the afternoon deliberating over the best choice to distract the party while Riven and I rescued Vrail. Riven had only lasted fifteen minutes of Nikolai flinging wild ideas at us before he left to go check on the other safe house in the city. It was in the east bank and often used by Tarvelle and his team to rescue Halflings.

Three hours later and I wished I had joined him.

"It's perfect. A vial would be enough to cause quite a stir in the throne room. Small enough I could carry it in my pocket and pour out the contents without being seen." Nikolai clapped his hands together like a child who had just beaten their parent at cards.

I pursed my lips to the side. "You think that will distract them long enough? You essentially want to make the throne room smell bad."

Nikolai's eyes were wide and dazed, barely focused on me and the conversation we were having. "Not bad. Very bad. So disgusting that everyone will run out into the garden for fresh air and won't be willing to enter the palace again until the stench clears." He pulled on his hair absentmindedly. "The last time I experimented with the recipe, the smell was so rotten that some nearby Elverin fainted. I'm sure there will be more than a few lords that succumb to it."

"It won't hurt them?" I asked. "We don't need to give Curringham more of a reason to expose us."

Nikolai shook his head. "I'll have to get the ingredients tomorrow, but it won't take long to brew."

He climbed into the middle bunk and lay down, tugging at his hair while he wrote a list in his notebook. I watched him pull that one coil tight, letting it spring back slightly before tugging at it again. Stretched, it only reached his jaw, much shorter than how any of the other Elverin kept their hair.

Nikolai's didn't look away from his notebook. "Just say whatever it is you're thinking about."

"How do you know I wanted to say anything?"

Nikolai used his glass quill to point at my knee. It was bouncing up and down with ferocity. I placed my hand on my leg and stopped it. Nikolai finally looked at me. "What is it, Keera dear?"

My palms were sweaty as I rubbed them down my thighs. "Davan's tree in Myrelinth is tall enough to shade your mother's statue. How many years has it been since he passed?"

Nikolai closed his notebook and took a deep breath. "Next year will be the hundred and fiftieth year since his tree was planted."

My chest tightened. "Yet you still wear your hair short?"

Nikolai smiled, twisting the longer strand between his fingers. "It has been longer than most Elverin would, but not so long to be strange. Feron kept his hair short for a half a century after Thellia died."

I dropped my head. "I'm sorry if the question stirred old wounds."

Nikolai's lips twitched to the side. "Never be sorry for asking about the dead, Keera. Our thoughts are what keep them with us, keep them alive."

I nodded, suddenly finding it harder to draw a breath. My fingers toyed with the end of my right sleeve. "I lost someone," I whispered, so quietly I could almost convince myself it wasn't my voice at all. "Her name was Brenna."

"A beautiful name." He lifted his chin upward on the pillow. "I can see you loved her dearly."

I nodded my head and rubbed at my stinging eyes. "Very much." I took a shaky breath and met Nikolai's gaze, not caring that tears lined my eyes. "I . . . She died because of me. She was the person I loved most in the world and she died because I didn't protect her. And now I've made that same mistake with Vrail."

I didn't sob. I just let the tears roll down my cheek like rain on stone. The truth was calcifying; it hardened around me, turning my body into a shell until I felt like a statue of myself.

Nikolai slipped off the bed and kneeled beside me. He pulled out his white handkerchief and gently dabbed the tears from my cheeks. "Vrail is not dead, Keera, and you are doing everything in your power to bring her home." He grasped my hand, shaking me so hard it cracked through the stone.

"The ghosts of your past are not omens to predict your future," he said, sweeping the hair from my face. "Do you know why the Elverin mourn their dead with trees?"

I huffed a breath. "To keep their memory alive?"

"That"—Nikolai smiled softly—"and because trees, like grief, go through seasons. Their leaves change colors just as our feelings continue to churn and change. Sometimes the leaves fall to the ground entirely, leaving us cold and bare, draining us of hope that the warmth of summer will ever come. But it will." Nikolai gripped my hands even more tightly. "Don't let a moment of fear and grief convince you that's all your life is made for. Vrail came here with you because she believed in you, as I do. But you need to be able to hold some faith for yourself. If not for you, then for her."

I wiped my eyes and nodded. Nikolai grabbed a strand of hair near my brow and gave it a playful tug. "I know it's hard having people to fear for, Keera, but I promise you it's worth it."

I chuckled into the handkerchief. "Perhaps you're right. Though I need to be careful not to care about anyone else. Riven, Vrail, and Syrra are already a lot to worry about."

Nikolai's voice was as deadpanned as his face. "I think you're forgetting a name or two."

"Am I?" I stuck out my bottom lip. "I can't think of any."

The door opened and Killian stepped through. He glanced between me and Nikolai three times before deciding it was best not to ask.

"Killian! You're right—I did forget a name."

Nikolai rolled his eyes.

"Has something happened?" Killian pulled off his black jacket.

Nikolai stood and wiped his hands. "Only that Keera is not nearly as amusing as she finds herself to be."

I turned to Killian. "Nikolai is pretending that he doesn't know he's my favorite."

Nikolai tried to hide the wide grin that broke across his face. He pulled out an apple from his pocket and tossed it to me before biting into another one for himself.

I stood. "I need to return to the palace and make sure no one gets any ideas about Vrail." I turned to Killian. "Nikolai will catch you up on the details of the plan and I will meet you both tomorrow at the party."

Nikolai waved his hand frantically as he ran across the room and pulled a box from his saddlebag. It was wrapped in black velvet and tied together with a red ribbon that I recognized from Wilden's shop. I pulled the ribbon loose and opened the package.

It was a black dress.

"No need to worry about tomorrow night," Nikolai said, folding the muslin fabric back over the dress to protect it. "I have it taken care of and it is going to look *fabulous.*"

"Actually as Blade—" But Nikolai had slipped out the door with his notebook and without another word.

Killian chuckled behind me. "I don't think he cares much for protocol."

"Easy position to have when he'll be wearing someone else's face." I tongued my cheek and looked down at the box in my hands. Wilden's designs were beautiful, but we were meant to be drawing attention *away* from me.

Killian laughed softly and started organizing the pile of books on the table. I wrapped my cloak around my neck and pulled on my boots.

"Keera," Killian said as I reached for the door. I turned and saw his green eyes tracking my braid up my back and along my neck. "Wear Nikolai's dress. If anyone says anything, tell them *I* requested it."

CHAPTER THIRTY-EIGHT

The throne room was packed with guests though the throne remained empty. Ladies spiraled over the dance floor in long, lavish gowns of every color. Their backs were bare and adorned with jewels.

The men were more plain in their attire, wearing muted ascots that matched their dates' gowns. Most of their outfits were indistinguishable from the next, except for the gray-haired man in a vibrant clementine jacket with burgundy embroidery across the hem standing beside Killian. The orange almost glowed next to Killian's layers of black. I glanced at the ring on the man's hand and wondered if it was projecting a disguise on Killian's companion.

Just like that the glamour shattered. The gray-haired man was gone, and Nikolai stood in his stead evidently delighted by his ridiculous attire.

My breath hitched as both their gazes fell on me. My torso was wrapped in tight layers of black silk that squeezed my ribs. The fabric looped under my breasts and crossed up my neck, leaving the smallest slice of unmarked skin exposed above my navel. My sleeves were long and covered my arms as my fingers brushed the swath of silks that hung loosely down my legs.

It was a simple dress. Clean and solid black almost as if it had been designed for me to wear as Blade. The outline of a silver sword embroidered along my spine seemed like a detail only Nikolai would add.

I had added some weapons of my own. Concealed under my skirts were four thin blades strapped to my thighs. Two more daggers were set in the pile of braids that Gwyn had crafted on the top of my head. They looked decorative enough but would be deadly to anyone who got in my way.

I bowed to them both, playing the part of faithful servant conversing with her prince. Killian swallowed, though his jade eyes lingered on the small triangle of skin under my breast. He caught me noticing him and bowed his head to break our gaze.

"Mistress Keera," he said, gesturing to Nikolai, who was still disguised for everyone else, "may I introduce you to—"

"Stewarth Campbell." Nikolai bowed with a wicked grin.

I bit my lips behind my water glass. "Campbell?"

Nikolai stood proudly and adjusted his collar. "I needed something that suited a Mortal in his mid years of life. I have no children apart from my esteemed collection of antique books that I travel with all over the continent as His Royal Highness commands."

Killian rolled his eyes. "I best introduce my *bookbinder*"—he grabbed Nikolai's shoulders—"to Lord Curringham and his new bride." Killian's gaze was locked on something across the room. I glanced over my shoulder and saw Curringham harassing a pretty server for another glass of wine.

"Your Highness," I said with a bow.

Killian stepped beside me as Nikolai grabbed for a drink from a passing tray. He leaned toward me, pretending to adjust his lace collar. "You look radiant, Keera," he whispered.

I froze, thankful Killian walked away so I needn't respond to the compliment. My heart raced. Partly because those words were very dangerous when said in public to a Halfling. And partly because it was Killian who said them.

I parked myself next to a pillar and observed the room. There was not one unfamiliar face in the room. I'd crossed paths with most of the lords in attendance at some point during my tenure as Blade. Most had their wives on their arms, whose faces I knew from countless events just like this one, and some danced with their mistresses, who I recognized because it was my job to know where every person's weakness was.

Mistresses were a common sore point for the men at court.

"It's inappropriate for the Blade to wear a dress to a ball." Damien's cool, slick voice sent a shiver down my skin. Every one of the scars on my back itched like they could sense his presence as he stepped in front of me.

"I wore it at the request of the prince," I answered coldly.

Damien scoffed, his eyes trailing along my body, pausing too long at the patch of skin under my breast. "If I had requested for you to wear a dress, it would have been *much* more revealing." His hand grazed down my back, feeling the ridges of his handiwork along my skin. His resulting smirk made me want to vomit.

"The request was made by Prince Killian." I took the smallest step backward, shielding my scars from Damien by pressing them into the pillar.

Damien planted an arm beside my head. The heavy scent of wine and ale hit my senses like a crashing wave. The stench was enough to know Damien had been drinking for hours already. The mixture made my head spin and set my throat on fire.

"Careful, Keera." Damien's brows creased. "Vexing me with such a heinous lie is a daring game to play . . . especially when I am stuck inside this castle with your sweet Gwyn."

I stopped breathing. I felt like I had been plunged into a frozen lake. My skin stung, raw from the cold shiver that jolted through my spine. "It's true," I whispered on trembling lips. I closed my eyes and hoped Damien was too drunk to remember this come morning.

"My brother." He snarled at the word. He was so close I could feel the heat of his breath along my neck. I leaned back, unable to make a move with so many surrounding us. "He may be a bastard and a Halfling by birth, but my father has made him a prince by right. If you think that he would stoop low enough to *fuck* some dirty Halfling whore—"

A large hand landed on Damien's shoulder and peeled him off me in one, quick tug. I could see Killian's fingers digging into his brother's skin through his shirt. "Brother," he said in an icy cool voice, "these lovely ladies were hoping to get a chance to speak to you." A gaggle of four giggling ladies-in-waiting stood behind the princes, breaking into a fit of laughter and curtsies as Damien stumbled to find his footing.

His green eyes lingered on the large bust of the first girl. "Hello, my dears," he slurred, throwing his arms around two blondes. They carried him away to the lounge at the other end of the hall.

I let my head fall back against the pillar. I was aware of the way my chest heaved as I caught my breath and how Killian's discerning gaze noticed it too. My cheeks flushed with heat. "Thank you," I said with a nod.

Killian cocked his jaw to the side. "He should've never said such vile things to you." His hands flexed his fingers like he was stopping himself from punching the wall.

I stood straight and fixed my skirts. "I didn't realize you overheard that."

Killian made a sound that reminded me of a growl. "I heard every disgraceful word and I will address it with Damien later."

"No!" Panic pulsed through me. Killian's brow furrowed. I scanned the room to make sure Damien was far away and distracted before nodding toward the terrace. Killian followed, and I was glad to find the landing quiet and empty.

"Please don't say anything to your brother." I spoke softly without moving my lips. I planted myself at the edge of the stone terrace, pretending to admire the moonlight glinting off the rolling sea.

"Why not?" he asked in a matching whisper. He gripped the railing with both hands.

"There is a chambermaid who serves this palace." I leaned my head back and looked at the stars; the fear from Damien's threat still lingered on my skin. "Her name is Gwyn. She cannot leave, she cannot hide, and Damien likes to punish me through her."

I could hear Killian's jaw clamp shut. "What do you mean?"

"He knows I care for her." I took a deep breath, trying to find the words that did Gwyn justice. "He knows I love her—like a sister." Killian's brow relaxed. "She never tells me much but I know he hurts her. Threatens her. Keeps her from eating. Sometimes he does it only because he knows it bothers me and sometimes just because he can."

Killian turned to face me. I glanced around the balcony. A drunk couple had entered on the far side and were embracing each other in the dark. Killian didn't seem to care if they saw the prince alone with the Blade. "Where is she? We can take her with us. Take her away from him."

"We can't." I bowed my head. "She's tethered to your father by an old magic. Her mother and her mother's mother, and all their mothers before them. They aren't able to leave the grounds of the palace. Gwyn is stuck here as long as Aemon lives."

A flash of recognition crossed Killian's face. He didn't know Gwyn by name, but he had heard his father boast about the tether that tied her to the palace grounds. Killian stepped toward me. His lips were nothing but a thin line across his face. Even in the dim moonlight I could see his cheeks were flushed with rage. "Gwyn," he whispered, trying the name for himself. "She is the Halfling that was in your room that day. You gave her your mask."

I nodded.

"She can't be more than twenty," Killian rasped.

I shared his disgust. "She's almost seventeen."

Killian grabbed my hand. His grip was tight like he didn't notice how the rage added to his strength. My heartbeat quickened. I should have told him to let me go—it was too dangerous to be so close in public—but I didn't. I was always the one taking risks; I liked knowing that Killian was willing to take a risk for my comfort, even if it was wrong.

"I've survived many things." I bit my cheek. "But I don't know if I could survive losing her. Out of everything I've done, everything we face, the thought of what Damien might do to her if I'm not here when that tether breaks . . ." My voice cracked and a tear pushed through the dam I kept them behind. Killian lifted his hand to my cheek and brushed it away with his thumb.

My heart fluttered at his touch. "Killian, someone might see—"

He ignored me, pulling me closer to him. "We will win this fight, Keera. And when we do, I'll do everything in my power to get her away from him. The end of her curse will not be met by her death."

My chest cracked open at his words. It felt like I had dropped a weight I didn't know I was carrying. Someone else knew to come for her. Someone else would have Gwyn in their thoughts if Aemon died and I wasn't there to save her.

The green of Killian's irises were flecked with tiny spots of amber and gold. It reminded me of sand on the beach. Killian took a breath and his chest grazed mine. It was warm and comforting against the cool breeze wafting from the sea. His jaw flexed and he leaned toward me. He was going to kiss me. I knew I should stop him—I was with Riven and—but I was frozen in place from surprise.

He leaned closer and I tasted the sweetness of his breath on my tongue. His lips opened, and all thoughts drained out of me as I closed my eyes. Killian's hand found my waist and squeezed.

And then he stopped.

I blinked as his face came back into focus. Killian had leaned back, still closer than he should be, but I knew the moment was gone. "Apologies, I should never have done that. It wasn't fair." He dropped my hand and walked back into the throne room.

I lifted my hand to my lips and stood there in the moonlight wondering if Killian had meant it wasn't fair to me or to Riven.

Killian had rejoined Nikolai and Curringham when I walked back into the hall. The Harvest Lord seemed to be in high spirits. His cheeks were flushed from the wine and his hearty laugh echoed over the music. He showed none of the usual signs of deceit, and I still wondered how the oaf had managed to undermine our plans so easily.

Part of me wanted to pull out one of the blades strapped around my thigh and push it against his throat until I had the answers we wanted, but I had to stand guard and trust that Killian and Nikolai would uncover what I could not.

I noticed his new bride was no longer at his side. I paced along the outer rim of the hall looking for her thick curls or pointed, pretty face. She was nowhere to be found.

My stomach clenched as I was suddenly reminded of Dynara's assessment of Curringham. Maybe he wasn't the one pulling the strings after all. Maybe his foreign wife had convinced her husband to move their fortunes to her realm instead of this one. I had watched how determined she had been in courting a rich husband for herself. It took a clever and determined woman to land the richest lord of all.

I continued my slow walk around the room before slipping out of the throne room altogether. At first glance, the corridor was empty. No one stood beside the flickering torches that lit the hallway, but I could hear whispers echoing in the dark. I crept down the hall, grateful for my long skirt to mask the sound of my footsteps.

Gerarda's black cloak and hood blended into a shadowed corner so well I wouldn't have noticed her without the emerald gown being worn by Lady Darolyn—now Lady Curringham—peeking out from the sides. Gerarda stood so close to her, I thought for a moment they were mid-embrace. But I saw they were talking back and forth, obviously not wanting to be overheard.

"You haven't sent a report in three days," Gerarda snapped in a hushed tone.

Lady Curringham did not back down from the Dagger. "You need to practice your patience, Gerarda."

"How am I supposed to help, Elaran, if you don't tell me what's going on?" Gerarda peered over her shoulder, and I pressed every inch of myself against the wall. Since when were Gerarda and the Lady of the Harvest on a first-name basis?

"You aren't." Lady Curringham squeezed Gerarda's hand. "Patience," she whispered once more before disappearing back down the hall toward the visitor wing.

Gerarda turned back toward the party. Once she rounded the corner, there was no chance she wouldn't spot me. I stepped in front of her—I would rather be on the offensive anyway.

"I never realized you knew Lady Curringham, Gerarda." I made a point to stand at my full height.

The Dagger's eyes turned to daggers of their own. "I didn't realize you had the time to spy on your subordinates, Keera." She took a step toward me.

I took a step too. "Subordinate?" I grinned down at her. "Glad to know you've finally accepted your station. Say it again."

A group of drunkards stumbled out of the throne room, filling the corridor with laughter. Gerarda grabbed my elbow and pulled me into the shadows against the wall. "I don't begrudge you your secrets. Why do you insist on involving yourself in mine?"

My eyes narrowed. "I have reason to believe that Curringham is working with the Shadow. That makes whatever conversation I just overhead my business."

Gerarda snorted. "I can appease that worry for you. Curringham is *definitely not* aligned with the Shadow."

I stepped in front of her and flattened my hand just above her shoulder, pinning her to the wall without touching her at all. "Tell me why you know so much about the lord's affairs."

"No." Gerarda's nostrils flared.

I shook my head slowly. "Don't make me ask twice. The Blade commands the Dagger."

"Respectfully," Gerarda whispered, pressing a dagger I hadn't seen to my belly, "I have a blade of my own."

The point of the dagger cut through the silk of my dress and pricked my skin, but I didn't move. "I'm trying to help the Shades, Gerarda." I looked down at the dagger she held. "This only helps you."

The sharp metal dropped by a fraction of an inch. "Glad to know you hold such a lousy opinion of me."

My temper flared and my lips pulled back from my fangs. "Don't act so self-righteous. You've been vying for my position ever since I was named Blade instead of you." I gripped her hand holding the dagger and pressed it harder against me. "Here's your chance. Claim it."

Gerarda shook her head in disbelief. I thought she was about to lash me with her words but instead she laughed. "If I wanted you dead, I would have poisoned your wine or pushed you from a rooftop and pretended you fell. There's not a soul in Elverath who would've doubted me."

My mouth went dry. There were no words to defend myself from that claim. I dropped my hand from hers.

"You're not the only one who struggles with the position they're put in, Keera." Gerarda's words were sharp and harsh. I had to stop myself from recoiling as she spoke. "And to think I bought you time when the king wanted you dead."

My breath stopped. "What are you talking about?"

Gerarda's grin was feline and smug. "I wondered if you would ever bother to figure it out."

My mind raced through all the times the king had threatened my life. He'd alluded to it, hung the threat over my head to keep me in line many times over my tenure as Blade, but he had never said it until I had failed to best the Shadow. Understanding washed over me like I was plunged into an icy pool. "That's why you followed me into the *Faelinth*? To kill me?"

Gerarda had told me entering the Faeland would be a death sentence, yet she had traveled to Aralinth to find me. I thought she had risked her life to find the Shadow first and claim herself victor over me, but she had really been there for my head?

"I may serve under you," Gerarda said darkly, "but I am beholden to the king's command."

I dropped my hand from the wall. Serving Aemon had always been straightforward—cruel, yes, but easily understood. Now the more I learned about the king, the more he seemed to be a riddle. "Why send me to hunt the Shadow at all? If Aemon wanted me dead, he could have killed me in his own court."

Gerarda stepped out from under me, forcing me to press into the wall. "Aemon didn't order me to kill you the day you left for Aralinth. He gave the order the night you became Blade."

I snorted. "Does it often take you thirty years to fulfill a command?"

Gerarda's sneer was deadly. She flipped the dagger in her hand and for a moment I thought she might strike me with it. "His command was clear. If I ever learned you had traveled into the *Faelinth*, you were not allowed to come out alive."

I raised a brow and crossed my arms. "And yet here I stand."

"For now." Gerarda sheathed her dagger without breaking her stare.

"The king reneged his command?"

Gerarda's black eyes narrowed. She lifted her chin as she studied me, like she was trying to read the thoughts spiraling behind my eyes. "I suspect your life was spared because of Silstra. The king needs to keep as many loyal swords as he can." Her lips twitched upward.

"How can I trust you're loyal to the Crown while you sneak into corridors for secret meetings, the purpose of which you refuse to divulge?"

Gerarda stepped back. The torch lit the right half of her face in flaming red as she smirked. "Keera, if we have one thing in common, it is that our actions reveal where our loyalties lie." She fanned her cloak as she walked down the hall and disappeared back into the throne room.

I followed, but when I heard the buzz of the party inside, I continued down the corridor to the small garden under the terrace. I needed a moment to think. Why would Aemon be so protective of me as a child only to order my death as his Blade? My stomach twisted. There was some piece of information that we were missing. One that would solve the puzzle of Aemon's choices and ultimately spell his downfall.

I rested under the shadow of the terrace. The string band still played their music and I could hear the shuffle of drunken dancing. The moon had not reached full height yet. One more hour and Nikolai would release his noxious potion. We just needed to make it until then.

I took a deep breath of the cool night air and someone covered my mouth. I dropped into a crouch, but the attacker expected the move and kept their hold on me. Their finger slipped between my teeth and I bit as hard as I could.

"Let go or I will bite *your* finger off," the voice hissed.

I stopped immediately and turned to face Syrra. When she was confident I would not make a sound, she released me. "Why are you here?"

Syrra shook her hand and pulled off the leather glove. Her finger was bleeding. "When you did not show for your testimony, Tarvelle deduced where you were. He and Collin left Myrelinth and came here to find you. I followed so I could warn you in case their presence upset your plan."

I clenched my teeth. "I doubt they would be brazen enough to storm the palace. Only you would be that foolish."

Syrra shrugged. "If I can beat Aemon's Blade in battle, then there is not a sword here that would challenge me."

I was about to tell her that the king would sacrifice all his swords if he knew an Elven warrior had snuck onto the grounds, but a thunderous boom sounded through the city. The plants growing up the garden walls shook and were illuminated by violet flames that filled the sky. It was the same magical fire that had destroyed the safe house outside Silstra.

Curringham had done this.

Syrra crouched under the balcony without hesitation and silently moved to the garden wall. She pulled herself to the top of it before using the vines growing along the palace to climb to the fourth-floor terrace. She moved like a spider climbing up a trunk; her hands and feet seemed to stick to the stone without need for holds. She assessed the flames from her vantage point and climbed down the far side of the garden wall.

"It comes from the same area as the safe house," Syrra whispered loud enough for me to hear but not to be heard by the party guests who now filled the terrace followed by a foul odor. Nikolai must have released his vial before he'd noticed the violet flames burning through the city.

I closed my eyes and sighed. "There was nothing there of any value."

I could sense the dread in Syrra's voice before she spoke. "Not that safe house. The one Tarvelle uses to harbor refugees."

My body turned cold. "Are there any there now?"

"At least four."

My body was overwhelmed with dread. I looked up at the terrace. Curringham was nowhere in sight. We needed to leave. If he was willing to blow up part of the capital, he wouldn't hesitate to leave us with the blame.

"Go there now. Try to save as many as you can without being seen." I pulled a blade from my thigh and slid it up my sleeve.

Syrra's voice was hard and blunt. "We cannot risk a rescue if Curringham is openly attacking the city. It could be a trap."

I sighed, knowing she was right. It was too dangerous for anyone else to take that risk. "I will get Killian and Nikolai out of here, but don't wait for us. No one else is getting captured."

There was a long silence.

"Syrra, I need to know you'll do as I say." My body tensed. There was no way I could do what needed to be done if I was worried about Syrra and those Halflings dying in another blast.

"I will do it." There was an anger in Syrra's voice I had never heard before. "Keera. Do what needs to be done, but do not die for it."

I breathed a sigh of relief and ran back inside the palace. People flooded the corridor, their screams and chatter boomed off the walls as they ran in all directions. I saw four Shades running down the hall and waved them over. "Assist the guard in getting the guests to their rooms. No one is to leave this castle until the Arsenal gives the clear. Understood?"

Four black hoods nodded and dispersed into the crowd. I craned my neck as I walked, looking for any sign of Killian or Nikolai.

A black jacket slipped through the crowd by the throne room doors. I dodged the bodies and pulled Killian to the side. "Get Nikolai and yourself out."

Killian grabbed my arm. "It's the same flames as before."

I nodded.

"Syrra is here." I tried to keep my voice calm as I scanned the crowd for Curringham or his wife. "The fire was set in the same neighborhood as the Halfling safe house Tarvelle runs."

Killian paled.

"Syrra left to go check for survivors. She'll need help getting them out." A crowd of teary-eyed, puffy-faced lords pushed me into

Killian's chest. His hands wrapped around my waist as he turned to shield me from them.

I froze and Killian's hands dropped. "I'll find Nik and we'll leave together."

My lips formed a straight line.

"Keera, you can't stay." Killian grabbed my arms. "It's too dangerous now, too unpredictable. We will find another way to save Vrail."

I shook myself out of his grip. "I will never forgive myself if I don't try."

"You expect me to just let you go?" Killian's entire body drooped.

"Yes!"

His brow trembled. "If you're discovered, even my crown can't save you."

"Let me go anyway. If I abandon my friend, the guilt would be worse than any loneliness we've ever faced." The words landed like a net, wrapping around Killian and keeping him from moving against me. He was the only one who fully understood the meaning of those words, who knew what it meant to be a Halfling born apart from your kin.

Neither of us would wish that pain on anyone.

Killian wrapped his arms around me, pulling me into a tight embrace. "Come back with both of you alive," he whispered in my ear.

I nodded and he let me go. "Get those Halflings to safety before the city closes. Don't wait for me."

CHAPTER THIRTY-NINE

THE CHAOS FROM THE BOMBING and the stench made it easy to cross the palace without notice. The entrance to the dungeons was on the north side of the palace grounds next to the stables. I slipped into the garden.

I fished out the bag I'd stashed in the bushes on feel alone and peeled off the dress right there. Within a minute I was dressed in plain travelers clothes with my belt of weapons around my waist and my bow and quiver stored on my back. I wrapped my cloak around my shoulders. It felt heavy, but it would give the guards pause.

I climbed up the garden wall and delicately landed on the other side. I followed the stone, using its shadow to my advantage, until I reached the stables. I listened but didn't hear any heartbeats apart from the horses'.

I climbed onto the roof and took note of the guards standing at the entrance of the tunnel. There were two, one on either side.

Long swords sat sheathed at their hips and they held no weapon in their hands.

Easy prey for a Shade.

I crawled along the stable roof, curving around the guards from the southeast. I pulled two throwing knives from my belt and started to run. I threw the first before either of the guards noticed. It sliced through the air and embedded itself in the man's throat.

The other turned to face me, hand reaching for his sword, but my knife was already plunged into his eye. They dropped to the ground, and I pulled their bodies into the tunnel to hide them from the patrol.

I patted their bodies until I felt the hardness of metal. I reached into the blond one's pocket and pulled out a ring of wrought iron keys. I clasped them in my palm and ventured further into the dark.

Each level of the dungeon was marked by a pair of torches. If I passed through them I would find a row of cells, or I could keep going down the slanted tunnel to the cells below. I passed five pairs of torches before coming to a set that barely burned at all. I pulled a small bead from my leathers and held it against the smoking embers of the torch.

The heat ignited the bead, transforming it into a small ball of faelight. I let go of it and it hovered by my shoulder as I stalked down the endless row of cells.

"Vrail," I whispered into the shadows.

No one answered my call. Somewhere I could hear the drip of water against the stone. The wind whistled down the tunnel behind me like a warning, but I kept moving.

Something shifted in the darkness. I paused and waited for the echo of my steps to quiet. "Vrail," I whispered again. It was answered with the soft clang of metal.

It came from the cell in front of me. I ran the next few strides, peering into the cells with the faelight, but I didn't see a body. The clank sounded again, louder this time. I ran to the next batch of cells. The third one had a shadowed lump in the corner.

I started trying keys in the lock. My palms were sweaty and my hand shook more vigorously with each one that didn't work. Finally, a small bronze key clicked in the bolt and turned. I whipped open the iron gate and ran over to Vrail.

"Vrail, it's Keera." My voice was no more than a rasp as I pulled her onto my lap. Vrail only grunted in response. Her eye was black, and I could tell from the way she winced as I grabbed her that more than one rib was broken.

Chained shackles wrapped around her wrist and were anchored to the wall. I could tell from the tiny lock that none of the keys I had could fit. I checked the metal ring bolted into the stone. It was old and rusted. I kicked it with all my might and it bent. I kicked it again and the bolt crumbled from the wall.

Vrail would have to make do with her hands bound in front of her. I pulled the gag out of her mouth and she gasped for air. "Where are you hurt?" I whispered, stroking the hair from her face.

Vrail groaned. "Head. Ribs. Ankle." She wheezed between each word and blood gathered at the side of her lip.

"They weren't supposed to interrogate you," I mumbled to myself.

Vrail choked on her laugh. "I wouldn't call it an interrogation. They didn't ask many questions."

Only Vrail could joke in her own prison cell. I moved down to her ankle and felt for a break. She moaned in pain as I pushed into the swelling. "I know it hurts," I said, pressing down on the other side. "I think it's a sprain."

I looked at the state of her. Vrail was in immense pain, though she hid it well. Her breathing was shallow, and I knew she wouldn't be able to put any weight on that ankle, let alone walk on it. She needed a healer.

"Vrail, I want to try something, but I have no idea if it will work."

She lifted her head an inch to look at me. "Will it make it worse?"

"Possibly."

Vrailed coughed. "You should've lied to me."

"I want to try to heal you." My heart slammed against my chest.

Vrail's brow raised. "Can you do that?"

"I did it once." I shrugged. "With Riven." Though his wounds had not been nearly as severe.

Vrail blinked at me. I could see all the questions she wanted to rattle off, but the pain was too much to let her. "Okay." She nodded.

I gritted my teeth. Vrail's ankle was the biggest concern so I started there. I placed my hands on her skin just like Feron did with me during our sessions. I closed my eyes and pictured the swelling receding and Vrail being able to stand on it just as before. I kept that picture in my mind and breathed slowly.

"Is something supposed to be happening?" Vrail asked, fidgeting on the ground.

"It won't if you keep asking questions," I replied through clenched teeth. I tried to breathe deeply again; Feron was always calm when he used his gifts.

"Maybe don't think of what you want to do, but think of how you felt the first time it happened. What were you doing?"

"I was with Riven," I said with a deadpan stare.

"Oh." Vrail's brow creased. "Ohhh," she said again, realizing what I meant. She made a terrified face. "Perhaps there's another way."

"Wait." I grabbed her ankle once more. "I want to try focusing on the feeling of it instead." I closed my eyes and reimagined that night with Riven. My body was loose with a happy warmth spread over my skin. That warmth had extended out of me, grasping for Riven, to pull him into its hold. As I remembered, the same warmth crept up my spine and flowed down through my fingers.

I didn't dare open my eyes, but I could feel that warmth flow out of me and pour onto Vrail like water down a cliff's edge. It wrapped around her just like Riven's shadows, connecting us in a way I'd never felt before.

Then something cold snapped, and it was gone.

"Did it work?" I looked down at her ankle.

The swelling wasn't gone but it was lessened. Vrail pointed her toes and smiled. "It's still tender but I think I can walk on it."

I slumped against the floor, my energy almost completely drained. "I don't think I can heal your ribs and get us out of here."

Vrail lifted herself up onto two legs. She took a slow step, leaning to one side. "I can make it." She placed her fists on either hip and looked down at me with complete determination. My chest twinged with pride.

"Let's get out of here." I wrapped her arm around me and helped her walk down the row of empty cells. Vrail was wheezing by the time we made it to the torches. I sat her down on a fallen rock and fanned the faelight over the collapsed tunnel.

It was filled with jagged rocks and crushed support beams, but there was enough room between the crevices for a body to slip through. Guards could find us at any moment, but I couldn't leave without checking. No matter how unlikely it was.

I turned to Vrail, who was bent over the rock still trying to catch her breath. "I need you to wait here." I pulled a long dagger from my belt and handed it to her. "Just in case."

"Where are you going?" Vrail wheezed between breaths.

"We don't have time for an explanation." I passed her one of the almost finished torches and climbed over the boulder at the mouth of the tunnel. The faelight followed, floating behind me as I twisted and curved through the rubble. The collapse had formed a winding trail through the debris. I followed it further down until the ground of the tunnel leveled under my feet.

The room was narrow and long. There were no cell doors along the walls and no cracks in the ceiling to let in light or wind. Without the faelight, I would have been consumed by the darkness entirely. Even shadows ceased to exist down here.

Along the floor were six circles made of wood. Each one was as wide as my wingspan with a metal circle for a handle. My pulse raced as I knelt beside the first door and lifted it open. Stale, damp air washed over my face. I coaxed the faelight into the void and saw the gravel and earth-packed bottom twenty feet below.

The pit was empty except for an older rope that hung down the side of the wall. My heart sank into my stomach as I looked at the other doors. The second and third were completely covered in debris. I rushed past them and flung the fourth door open. It was as empty as the first. I opened the fifth door and gasped when I saw the loose brick at the bottom of the trench.

It was the one I pulled from the wall as a child. This had been my cell. I swallowed the taste of vomit on my tongue as I peered at the scratches in the stone. I had scratched at the walls, feeling for a path to climb until my fingers bled more times than I cared to remember. I stood and dropped the door back over the hole. The heavy clunk reverberated in my bones.

I held my breath as I turned to the other door. If the fifth had been my cell, that meant that the Elf who had been held beside me was kept in number six. I kneeled in front of the door and lifted it up with shaking hands.

The stench of sweat and stale breath hit me so hard I fell back onto the ground. I held my sleeve up to my nose and peered over the edge of the hole. The faelight floated a few feet below the door revealing the lifeless body covered in a ratty cloak. My heart dropped, but as the faelight drifted closer to the bottom of the trench I saw that her brown skin was ashen but intact. Somehow she was alive, just unconscious.

I ran to the other side of the room and grabbed the rope from the first cell. It was thinner than I hoped and fraying in some places, but it was all I had. I tied it to the anchor at the top of the pit and slowly rappelled into the tight chasm.

She didn't wake when my feet hit the floor. I knelt beside her and placed a gentle hand on her shoulder. It was warm. My chest heaved in relief. I held my hand to her neck. Her pulse was faint but there. My fingers caught on one of her long, thick chunks of matted hair. I detangled my hand as gently as I could, my stomach wrenching as I saw the dirt and debris caught in the Elf's coils. I pushed the matting from her face and confirmed what I already knew.

Her face was gaunt, but I could still see the resemblance between her and the statue her son made in Myrelinth. The Elf who had been my only companion, the Elf who had spent centuries in this cell, was Maerhal Nieven.

Nikolai's mother.

Syrra's sister.

She had been alive the entire time.

I pulled the dagger from my hip and cut a line across the bottom of my cloak. I tore a large piece from the cutting and used it to wrap her hair as best as I could. With the collapse, it would be a tight squeeze. I didn't want the mats to snag on any of the debris.

I ripped the remaining fabric in half and wrapped it around my face, covering my nose. I could smell the sores on her skin, but my healing powers were already spent. The best I could do was get her and Vrail to Myrelinth as quickly as possible.

Maerhal didn't wake as I lifted her onto my back, underneath my cloak. I wrapped the frayed bottom of the cloth under her legs and tied it as tight as I could around my waist. It formed a makeshift holster, only strong enough because Maerhal weighed so little.

I tugged on the rope. It pulled taut even as I pushed against the wall with my foot and it held the weight of two people. I climbed slowly, making sure the cloak did not slip. One foot over the other, I climbed the wall.

As the faelight floated to the top I saw the problem. A foot below the anchor a fray in the rope had begun twisting free. I picked up my pace. We were no longer being held by a thin, old rope. We were being held by one strand of the braid.

I took two more steps up the wall and some fibers in the rope split. My heart pounded so hard it was all I could hear.

Three more steps.

More fibers snapped.

I abandoned my slow pace entirely and started racing up the wall. The rope thrashed against my wild climb, tugging it in all directions. Finally, the rope snapped, and I pushed off the brick wall and reached for the ledge.

I missed but grabbed a thick root protruding from the wall instead. I mustered all the strength I had to pull us up with one arm while reaching for the flat ground of the room. I groaned loudly as I pulled myself over the top, kicking my leg over, and rolled onto my side. Maerhal was still nestled along my back, unconscious. My chest tightened with worry as I tried to catch my breath.

At least she was alive. The rest could be sorted out once we got her to a healer.

I forced myself to my knees as I heaved another breath. Using my magic had drained me to the point that even my bones ached. All I wanted was to lie down on the ground and sleep for a month, but I couldn't. I needed to keep going. I needed to get back to Vrail.

The journey back through the collapse was even slower than before. Moving uphill was harder on my legs, and I had to bend my body unnaturally to make me and my passenger fit through the small crevices between the fallen rocks.

Finally, I climbed over the large rock where I had left Vrail. I slid down and Vrail woke with a start when my feet hit the ground.

"Who is that?" Vrail asked, holding her hand to her nose. "Are they dead?"

"No." I passed her the other piece of ripped cloak and helped her tie it around her nose. "Though I have no idea why she's not."

I slipped the weapons belt around my waist once more. "Can you walk on your own?" I asked Vrail.

She nodded and started up the tunnel. I held my bow and quiver in my hands. By the time we reached the first level, Vrail and I were breathing so hard I thought our lungs would burst. I peered around the edge of the tunnel and saw the guards lying exactly where I'd left them.

"No one has discovered them." I nodded to the dead soldiers. "Perhaps our luck has turned."

Vrail looked doubtful.

"There's a stable just outside the tunnel." I pulled Maerhal higher up on my back and nocked an arrow in my bow. "If we can steal two horses, we can ride north along the beach."

Vrail moved a strand of hair from her face with her shackled hands. "Aren't there guards along the beach to keep intruders out of the palace?"

"Let me worry about the guards." I looked down at her wrists. "Can you ride with your hands bound?"

Vrail pulled the chain taut. She had over a foot of distance between each hand. "I will manage," she said with a nod.

"Then follow my lead."

I crept out of the tunnel glancing up at the rooftop and garden wall. No sign of guards or Shades. I crouched as I walked and glanced into the stables. There were two guards readying their rides. One was tightening his saddle strap while the other was putting the reins on his horse.

"What a lovely evening, gentlemen," I called, standing to my full height.

They stepped out with their swords drawn but paused when they saw my black hood covering my face. That was all I needed. I shot my arrow through the heart of the closest guard. The other charged at me with his sword. I charged back, pulling the dagger from my hip and lodging it into his gut with one heavy thrust.

His last breath oozed out of his mouth as blood oozed from his belly. I pulled my blade free and he was dead by the time he hit the floor. I turned and saw Vrail staring at the dead soldier. She looked up at me and blinked twice. I pulled down the hood and tucked it out of sight.

I helped Vrail onto the saddled horse. She was a chestnut mare with white socks. I patted her neck and saw her ears flick backward. I turned and saw a group of Shades scaling the garden wall.

"We need to go." I grabbed the other horse and swore. It had no saddle. I grabbed the reins and tied them around the horn of Vrail's saddle. "Whatever you do, keep riding."

I pulled myself onto the bare back of my horse and told Vrail to go. She bolted from the stable doors and thankfully my horse followed. "Left!" I shouted, and Vrail steered both mounts in the direction of the beach.

The Shades were on us in an instant. I aimed my bow, obscuring my face, and shot the first one in the foot. I hoped it was a clean enough shot to heal quickly. I didn't need to kill them—I only had to make sure they couldn't follow us. One Shade knelt beside her injured partner and I aimed my arrow for her hood. It skimmed over her head and anchored her to the garden wall. Not enough to hold her for long, but the added time would help us escape.

Vrail banked left hard when our horses hit the sand. Their gallops slowed and we still had two Shades chasing us. I spun around on the back of my horse, shielding Maerhal from the arrows flying at our heads. "Duck!"

The arrow missed Vrail's neck by a thread.

I loaded my bow once more and took a shot at the faster Shade. She dodged the dart and launched one of her own. Vrail swerved to the right and the arrow missed us by a healthy margin. I only had three arrows left.

I nocked another and took a deep breath as I aimed. I released it and it felt like time slowed. I watched its arc through the air heading straight for the second Shade's chest. *Please not another one*, I thought. She twisted at the last second and the arrow sliced through her shoulder.

My stomach hurled as I heard her scream in pain. I loaded another arrow, but the last Shade had stopped her chase. She turned back to her partner to help her with her wounds.

"Guards!" Vrail yelled. I turned back, facing forward this time and saw four guards charging down the beach.

"Move right on my mark," I shouted to Vrail. She nodded as I aimed my arrow. "Now!"

Vrail turned and my horse followed, giving me a clear shot of the soliders. I launched my arrow, not waiting to see if it hit its mark before I launched the other. The two guards dropped onto the sand, dyeing it red with their blood.

The other two raised their swords, readying to strike our horses' legs as we passed. "Bank right again." I grabbed two thin throwing blades from my leathers. My timing had to be perfect.

"Right!"

Vrail turned so far right we were running toward the walled-off rings of the capital. I held a knife in each hand and threw them at the same time. Each found their home buried in the chest of a guard.

"Left!"

Vrail corrected our path. "Can you teach me how to do that?" she yelled as Koratha shrunk behind us.

I laughed and untied the cloak at my waist. I pulled Maerhal into my arms, holding her as gently as I could while she slept. "Get us home and I'll consider it."

Vrail's smile was all I needed to know that, no matter the consequences that waited for us in Myrelinth, the risk had been worth it.

CHAPTER FORTY

Riven was standing at the portal when we arrived in Aralinth. We had already traveled through one in the Dead Wood and another along the shores of the Pool of Elvera only to arrive in the midst of the Dark Wood and spend the entire day trekking through the forest.

My entire body ached. I was holding myself and Maerhal up on the horse by will alone. I couldn't feel the tips of my fingers and the rest of my hand throbbed from fatigue. That was nothing compared to Vrail, who was slumped so far forward on her horse I thought she would impale herself on the horn. Her breath wheezed from the broken ribs and the endless travel. We hadn't had time to forage for food or even rest.

"Grab her," I rasped to Riven. He ran over to Vrail, his shadows trailing behind him and curving around my limbs. His brow furrowed as he noticed her blackened eye and cut lip. "Careful of her ribs," I said as he pulled Vrail down from her saddle and held her in his arms.

Riven gathered the reins of her horse, stopping mine too. I pulled Maerhal higher up on my chest and slowly lifted one leg over our horse's back. Riven ran toward me and looped one arm around my waist. He carried all three of us for a moment as he let my body drift toward solid ground.

His hand found my cheek and slid down to the side of my neck as his assessed the rest of my body for injuries. I looked up at him, warmth returning to my extremities with the surge of electricity from his touch. His lips were a hard, straight line that matched the deep crease between his brow. A stranger would think he looked violent, readying to kill, but I knew that wasn't true. He was almost feral with worry.

"You're not hurt?" His voice cracked at the end as he finally exhaled.

"Apart from the desperate need of a shower, I'm fine." I tucked Maerhal closer against my chest.

Riven's gaze finally locked on something other than me. He raised a brow. "Who is that?" he asked, unable to see Maerhal's face against my body.

Vrail opened one eye and looked up at Riven through her thick lashes. "She won't say. Asked so many times." Her head lolled back against his arm and she fell asleep.

I gave Riven the same answer I'd given Vrail the three hundred times she'd asked. "You can't be the first to know."

I expected Riven to resist, to ask again in some other way, but he only nodded. The look on his face was gentle and understanding. Complete trust. My chest fluttered at that silence. All Myrelinth believed I was a liar and a threat, but Riven's faith gave me enough strength to do what needed to be done.

I nodded down the path to where the twinned trees stood. "We need to go; it's almost sundown." Riven nodded and pulled out a handful of pressed flowers, passing two to me. We stepped through the portal and landed in the Dark Wood side by side.

Two balls of faelight hovered in the clearing. Riven flicked them down the trail with a wave of his hand. "Feron sensed you nearing Sil'abar. It's how I knew to be there waiting."

I swallowed. "To walk me to an uproar or a welcoming?"

Riven let out a slow deep breath. Some of Vrail's long hair blew out away from her round cheek. "The Elders are not happy that you left. They took it as a sign of disrespect."

I knew they would have but it didn't make the blow any easier to take. If the Elders thought I was a traitor to the Elverin, the truth no longer mattered. "I expect Tarvelle and Collin will throw a celebration in my honor when the Elders throw me out and take my memories." I swallowed. "Or worse."

Riven's shadows splintered across the forest floor like jagged pieces of glass before curving against the roots and trees, slithering like snakes. His voice was hard and vicious. "If they do, they both will answer to me." Riven's hands turned to fists against Vrail's legs and back.

"Doesn't surprise me that they want to stay away from you." I pointed to the shadows that had begun to thrash and nip at each other.

Riven only grunted in reply.

We reached the end of the trail. I could see the Myram tree, lit in the warm glow from the setting suns. Riven stopped beside me as I readied myself.

I turned to him. "You go ahead. Let them see Vrail and you first and call the healers."

"I stand with you, Keera." The words were commanding and forceful, like thunder booming through a stormy sky. But thunder could only sound after lightning was brave enough to crack on its own.

"I need to stand alone." I turned to Riven, hoping his trust wouldn't waver.

His nostrils flared as he let out a deep breath. "You expect me to abandon you? I don't care what the Elverin think—I allied with you, as I ally with you now."

I gave him a soft smile. "We both know they don't see two allies when they look at us. They see a huntress and her prey caught in a trap. Riven, *please*, give me this."

Usually Riven's eyes burned like the violet flames that had flared in the capital, but now they were hard like ice. There was no hope left to warm them. "So we're at an impasse. If I ignore your wishes, I lose you. If I do as you wish, I'm sending you to the wolves." His entire body wilted like a brown flower finally giving in to winter.

"I am the Blade," I said, trying to sound lighter than either of us felt. "I may survive the wolves yet."

Riven didn't laugh. He didn't even breathe.

"After the Elders make their decision, I'm yours." I pressed a kiss against his shoulder. "For as long as we have." My heart ached knowing that if they decided on banishment, it might only be minutes.

Something in Riven snapped and his shadows exploded. They blanketed the entire clearing, reaching up to the burls above and covering the faelights glowing from the Myram tree. If the Elverin hadn't known we were here before, they did then.

Riven gave me one last look. His long black hair covered half his face, but I could still see the forlorn mask he wore beneath it. It reminded me of the sailor wives in Mortal's Landing, standing along the port with their arms raised in a hesitant wave as they burned that memory into their minds, not knowing if it would be the last they ever shared with their sailor.

Riven's shadows faded as he walked away. I could see a crowd beginning to form around the Myram tree as three loud booms from a drum thundered through the grove. A tiny ball of faelight swirled around my head, getting closer to Maerhal with each pass. I looked down at her and saw her eyelids open slightly, only to close again.

"You're safe," I whispered in her ear in Elvish. "You've been in the dark a long time. Keep your eyes closed until the healers can help you."

She coughed against my chest. It was weak and feeble just as she had become in seven centuries of captivity. She inhaled deeply and a soft smile pulled at her full, chapped lips. "*Giiabitha*," she whispered. Her voice sounded like the wind blowing through shattered, dusty glass.

"Yes." My throat burned as I took my first step toward the Myram tree. "You are home."

Maerhal's smile grew and then her head pressed against me once more, falling back into that deep sleep. I walked with her slowly. Each step felt like I was wading through feet of billowing snow, but it was only the harsh stares of the Elverin. They split in front of me as I walked, only creating enough room for me to step through the crowd toward the Myram where the Elders were waiting.

Some snarled as I walked by. Parents gripped their children as if I would rip them from their arms. Most held up their hands to protect their noses as I passed. I couldn't even smell the soil and decay from Maerhal anymore. The odor had singed my nostrils hours ago.

I looked up and saw Feron and Syrra standing with the four Elders who held my fate in their hands. In the center was Darythir, who stared me down with a curious glint in her heavy-lidded gaze.

Each one wore an expression of steep disappointment as I walked to the center of the city.

Collin stood to the east of the Myram. His face was almost gleeful as he grinned at me.

Feron stepped forward. I thought he was about to speak but instead he turned to Darythir, who began to sign. He interpreted for her.

"You have openly shown your contempt for this assembly and our people by fleeing our judgment." Feron said the words in his usual calm manner, but I could tell from the heated expression on Darythir's face and the way her ancient hands signed with hard, emphatic movements that she was far from calm.

I bowed my head. "I always planned to return to testify, but a matter of greater importance kept me away." I braced myself for the sharp sting of Darythir's words.

"More important than the will of the Elverin?" She peered down at me and it felt as if the air itself was pressing onto my shoulders, pushing me into the ground. I stepped forward with my foot.

I nodded. "And more important than my life."

Darythir did not raise her hands again; she only lifted her chin and narrowed her eyes at me. Feron nodded for me to continue.

"I believe the Light Fae still exist, and I will be the one to find them," I spoke loudly so the entire city could hear my words echo off the trunk of the Myram tree. A gasp broke through the crowd but Darythir only had to raise one hand to silence it.

"Vrail and I left for Koratha in search of an answer that would help us find them. We expected to return before the assembly was called, but Vrail was captured. I couldn't leave her to be another Halfling who died in Aemon's clutches." I pointed to where Vrail lay on the ground surrounded by Elvish healers. Nikolai stroked her hair and held her head in his lap.

"I do not leave friends behind." I gritted my teeth as I stared at Collin's shaking head. I turned around and addressed the crowd. "I realize now I could have been more open about why I allied with Riven. Why I have been working for *decades* to save as many Halflings as I could. But my words didn't mean much to Riven when we struck our deal, so I assume they have little value to you now."

I turned to Darythir. "I was found in Calen's Rift. A fissure so wide and deep only the most ancient of magic could make it." I nodded to Nikolai. "I earned his trust, and the trust of Syrra and Riven, when I swore a blood oath that I would never cause Nikolai any harm."

Darythir's eyes fluttered as Feron finished signing what I'd said. She turned to Nikolai. "Is this true?"

He nodded and replied by both tongue and hand. "Riven and Syrra witnessed it as well."

Darythir turned to the Elders behind her. Syrra stood among them and nodded once too.

"I bound myself to the safety of one Elverin that day, but now I'll bind myself to you all." I grabbed the bloodstone dagger with one hand and carefully tucked the hilt between Maerhal and the hand holding her. I skimmed my free palm across the blade until it was thick with blood.

I marched toward the Myram tree and swiped my hand across it. "I swear to you that I will never betray the Elverin. I want to end Aemon and his crown as much as you do."

Hushed whispers echoed through the grove. Everyone's eyes were on Darythir as she studied the bloodied mark I left on the tree. "You cannot undo the oath. Any betrayal would mean the death of you."

"My life will end in service to the Halflings and the Elverin." I lifted my chin higher as I trapped Darythir in my gaze. "I promise you."

Darythir did not speak for a long silence. I could hear my heart throbbing in my skull but I didn't balk from her stare. She nodded once. "You have made your vow. If you decide to break it, may the magic of Elverath claim you." She eyed Maerhal's crumpled body. "You seem to have another surprise."

I cleared my throat and nodded. "There were *two* Elverin locked in Aemon's dungeons. I could not leave either behind."

Darythir's thin, white brows lifted. "*Two?*" Her gaze locked on the Elf in my arms.

I nodded, swallowing so hard it felt like my throat would tear. I glanced to Syrra and Nikolai, now only speaking to them. "When I was a child, I was kept in the deepest cells of Koratha. Lost in the darkness for years before the king decided to send me to the Order. They were five long years, years I only survived because someone else was locked in the cell next to mine. An Elf, who until recently I had every reason to think was dead."

Syrra took a small step forward. The thick muscles along her neck were flexed, in fear or hope, I didn't know. Nikolai only blinked, looking back and forth between the thin bundle in my arms and my face as he stood.

I cleared my throat before speaking as loud as I could. "I've returned to bring Maerhal Nieven home."

Nikolai froze. His mouth was open and his eyes were wide circles that refused to blink. Syrra's brow creased with a deep line as she ran toward me. She gently lifted her sister from my arms, turning her face to see her for the first time in centuries. Syrra's brown eyes darted across her features, matching them against the memory of Maerhal in her mind. Recognition bloomed in her face as tears welled in her eyes. She dropped to her knees like a fallen feather, making sure Maerhal was safe in her arms, before crumpling over and releasing a sob so loud it shook the trees.

Three healers who were circled around Vrail ran over to Syrra and Maerhal. They started examining her limbs, uncovering the sores along her skin that were so deep they exposed her bone. They whispered among each other.

"Elvish sleep."

"Ulcers along every pressure point on her right side."

"We need to bathe her immediately."

"Start the baths."

"Get Rheih too."

One of the smaller healers, an Elf with a round face and soft hands, grabbed Syrra's shoulder. "We need to take her now."

Syrra shook her head, tightening her grip on Maerhal. "I will bring her to the healers' quarters." She stood with Maerhal in her arms, passing by Nikolai who was still as a statue.

Nikolai's eyes fell on Maerhal's gaunt face. The recognition was not a slow settle, but punched Nikolai in the gut so hard he lost his breath and fell to his knees. He glanced at me as if in a daze, unsure if what he was seeing was truth or dream.

"Mother?" he whispered.

And then he fainted.

CHAPTER FORTY-ONE

I WOKE IN MY BED, alone, with a view of the first rays of sunlight gleaming off the gold peaks of the Burning Mountains. I dressed in my training leathers without thinking, only to realize that Vrail wouldn't be meeting me to train.

I left my weapons belt behind and jumped down to the ground below, grateful that none of the Elverin filled the grove so early in the morning. The Elders' decision to accept my blood oath had not been a popular one.

I found the nearest spiraling branch of the Myram and climbed down the staircase hidden in its root. Vrail and Maerhal were staying in the infirmary, and I wanted to see them both before the crowds of Elverin arrived during the day. I cut across the wide hall of the undercity and took the maze of tunnels to the southeast side of the city that Riven had showed me the night before.

I stepped into the room, blinking at the brightness. The infirmary was not lit by masses of faelight floating from the ceiling; instead, where packed roots and earth should have formed a roof there was glass. The morning dawn filtered through the few feet of water and into the room, casting shifts of turquoise across the crisp linens of the dozen beds.

Vrail was in the first. I stood over her bed, happy to see that her ribs were bandaged and her black eye had almost completely faded. Her eyes fluttered open, sensing my shadow over her face, and she smiled softly.

"I'm sorry I missed training," she said in a pained whisper.

I folded my arms and shook my head. "I think I can make an exception for your absence. This time." I sat down on the stool beside her bed and grabbed Vrail's hand. It was soft but cold. "I'm sorry you went through all of that for nothing."

Vrail winced as she grinned. "It wasn't for nothing. I got the book."

I squeezed her hand. "Vrail, there was no book with you in the cells."

"My bag has a glamour on it." She reached for the table beside the bed, holding her stomach as she winced. As soon as her fingers touched the wooden tabletop I was able to see that it wasn't empty at all. A wide leather bag sat on top, holding something thick and flat.

I grabbed the bag and pulled out a white leather book with a golden symbol embossed into the front. It was in the same rigid style as the symbols from that memory. I opened the book and saw that each page held one symbol at the top with details on its function written in Old Elvish along the bottom.

I turned through the pages, looking for one of the symbols I'd seen in the memory. On the tenth, my breath hitched.

"You found one of the symbols the Fae had used?" Vrail asked shakily.

I shook my head. "No. But it's one I recognize."

I turned the book around and laid it gently on Vrail's lap. She studied the Old Elvish slowly, trying to decipher the meaning of the ancient script. "It's a kind of magical seal," she said, dragging her finger across the pages. "It's used to lock magic away in a container or—"

"A person?" I finished dryly.

Vrail stuck out her bottom lip in thought before referencing the page again. "It doesn't say it *can't* be used in that way. But I doubt the Fae would have sealed someone's magic away."

I swallowed once. "But they did."

"To who?"

"Me." I stood and undid the laces on my trousers. Vrail's eyes widened as I pulled them down low enough for her to see the only scar I'd always carried. "I saw the memory of that Fae and a Mage cutting this into me." My throat tightened until it hurt to speak. "Feron was right. I'm a Light Fae."

Vrail blinked in disbelief. "But why lock your powers away? And why are they breaking through the seal now and not before?"

I took a deep breath. I'd thought finding answers to the questions I'd been chasing would have felt like a victory, but the truth only filled me with acute sadness. "Perhaps they knew it would be safer for a child to have no magic in case she was found." I looked down at my hands. "I didn't want to believe Feron's theory, but it seems he's right. About everything."

"Everything?" Vrail echoed.

I met her gaze; it was open with curiosity and worry. "Riven and I are *miiskwithir.* Our magic is bonded together."

Vrail raised her brow. "The seal can't contain the increase the bond gives your gifts."

"They're sealed either way." I shrugged.

Vrail jabbed the book with her finger. "Keera," she said softly. "We have the answer to unlock it right here."

My head snapped to her. "What do we need to break the seal?"

"According to this"—Vrail scanned the text once more with her finger—"you need to return to the place where the seal was set. The magic should've left a mark behind."

I shook my head. "I've been to the Rift many times. There's nothing but shadows there." Vrail opened her mouth, but I continued. "And it was searched the day they found me. Thoroughly."

Vrail lifted her hands. "I was not there that day, but our records have never steered me wrong before. I would wager every book in Volcar that if you journey to the Rift, you will find a way to break that seal." She eyed my trousers where it covered the scar.

I huffed a laugh. "That's a strong wager coming from you."

Vrail nodded. "That's why you should listen to me. I was right about going to Koratha, and I'm right about this."

I raised a brow at her. "You were captured and almost died."

"It all worked out for the best." Vrail shrugged and winced. She lifted her arm to her ribs.

I gave her a half-hearted smile. Part of me wanted to run out of the room and journey to the Rift immediately, but I couldn't. I only had three days until the king's deadline. I needed to be here in case Dynara was able to find something I could use to take Curringham down instead.

I watched Vrail's eyelids flutter shut and her fall back into a peaceful sleep. Curringham deserved the worst for what he'd caused her. And if Dynara couldn't find the proof I needed, I would still return to the capital with a blade ready for the lord, the prince, and the king. Seal broken or not. I had to be ready.

I glanced down the room where Maerhal slept too. Her hair was still matted, though not as badly as the day before. Her skin had been cleaned and bandaged and a warmth had returned to her brown skin.

Vrail woke when I stood from her bed. Her gaze landed on the Elf and then back on me. "She's through the worst of it now. Though how she survived as long as she did is a miracle."

"Did the healers say how long it will take for her to recover?"

She shook her head. "There's no way to tell. They believe she only survived by going in and out of an Elvish sleep. The trance keeps the body alive but it can have devastating consequences on the mind."

I bit my cheek. Maerhal had already been erratic and spoke in riddles when I was kept in the cell next to her. I could only imagine that another sixty years in the cell had pushed her mind to the limit. "What about the ulcers? Were they able to heal them?"

"They cleaned and drained the wounds, but it'll take time for her body to heal." Vrail grabbed my hand. "Don't feel guilty, Keera. You saved her. A fighting chance at life is more than she or her family had until you brought her home."

I stood and walked over to Maerhal's bedside. Her face was still hollow and her body gaunt, but there was a vitality to her skin that I hadn't noticed the day before. I grabbed her hand and concentrated on that warmth inside myself. Somehow knowing that I had the ability this time made it easier.

"Keera, don't!" Vrail shouted, reaching out for me. "You already exhausted your magic with me. With the seal constricting your power, this will be too much."

I ignored her and closed my eyes. I thought of that moment between Riven and I—created a world where I was that peaceful, that content once more, and imagined that warmth pooling out of me. At first, it was nothing more than a daydream, but then I felt the shift. The warmth pressed against my skin and finally released, swirling around Maerhal's arm and then her torso.

Her body was like a hole at the bottom of a lake, shifting the flow of my magic downward like a drain. I didn't fight the current. I let her take all that she needed, felt the pain leaving her body as I was pulled deeper and deeper, until I couldn't breathe at all.

My eyes opened and I saw the blackness around her bandages fading, the necrotic tissue healing itself with my magic. I smiled and then the room went black. For a moment I thought I'd been plunged into the lake, too deep to see the light of the suns, but no shocking cold followed me.

This darkness was warm, wrapping around me like a blanket. I could feel the shadows taking shape underneath me, catching me as I fell back into the black.

"Why did you let her try this?" Riven's voice was a roar that echoed in every direction.

My eyes fluttered open. The shadows had almost receded, leaving the room and Vrail visible once more. Vrail crossed her arms and raised her chin. "I warned her, but we both know there was no stopping her."

Riven's grip tightened underneath me. "I'm okay," I whispered against his chest. "I think it worked. Unwrap one of her bandages."

Riven clenched his jaw but slowly moved to the stool next to Maerhal so he could sit me on his lap. With one hand, he untucked the end of the bandage from her arm and unwrapped it. He pulled it free as gently as possible in case the skin was still loose underneath.

I gasped when I saw smooth, flat skin. Riven grazed his finger over it. There was barely a scar left behind. "How did you do this?"

Vrail blinked and leaned back against her bed. "If you're able to do *that* with the seal still intact, then I can only conclude your gifts will be devastating when you break it."

Riven didn't ask Vrail what she meant. He only stared down at me and gently caressed my cheek. "How did you do this?" he asked again.

"I don't know." I collapsed into him. "I'm so tired I can barely breathe."

The last thing I remember before passing out was Riven's violet eyes and the feeling of his hands on my face.

I wasn't in my burl when I woke. I wasn't anywhere I recognized. I was lying on a plush blanket thrown over a bed of faelight. I stretched my limbs; they felt heavy and stiff like I had been riding on horseback for a fortnight with no rest.

I pulled myself up and realized my boots has been removed as my bare feet touched the rocky floor. It was damp and gritty like someone had topped the rock with a layer of sand. The same rock continued up the wall and formed the ceiling.

The air smelled fresh, laced with the scent of pine and rose. The lines of the rock glowed with golden light that reminded me of a portal. They stretched through the cave in every direction like veins on a leaf, soaking me in their auric warmth.

Riven appeared at the entrance of the room. He wore a long robe of teal that tied at his waist. I could see his bare chest framed by his long hair, which he wore loose. He smiled at me. It was wide and radiant, one he never let anyone else see, probably because the moment he did it his shadows filled the room like a fog rising from the floor, covering my legs in darkness as they swirled around me like a quiet storm.

"You slept all morning and most of the afternoon too." Riven walked toward me, each step heating my skin as I watched him watch me. His gaze was heavy, tangible, as it swept over my body in slow waves.

He held out his hand. "Can you stand?"

"The better question is do I want to." I tugged on his arm.

Riven laid a teasing kiss to my lips. "Trust me, you will want to." He pulled me onto my two feet and reached for the robe that was hanging from a hooked edge along the wall of rock. It was made of the same turquoise silk Riven wore. Tied by only a small sash along the waist.

I glanced at Riven's open chest. The robe would not cover all my scars if it was just as open. Riven's hand found my chin and he pressed his lips to my ear. "We're alone." A warm shiver tumbled down my spine and ended between my thighs.

I pulled the laces of my trousers loose, but Riven grabbed my wrists and lifted them to his mouth. "Let me" was all he said before he kneeled in front of me. He took his time pulling the laces free and lowering the pant over the curve of my backside. He left a trail of kisses down both thighs as he lowered the trousers with tantalizing slowness.

He cupped one leg under the knee and lifted it out of the trousers, trailing down my calf with his mouth until I thought I might fall back onto the bed of faelight. He did the same on the other side, scraping his fangs against my knee and sending a rush of goosebumps up my thighs.

I looked down at him and my breath hitched at the sight of his angular face and violet eyes staring up at me like I was the only thing in the world, the only thing that could satisfy his need for me. It was hunger, thirst, and longing all in one. I knew because I could feel the same look settling onto my face as Riven's hands fisted the end of my tunic and pulled it over my head.

I was completely bare except for the bead wrapped in leather around my neck. Riven's hands fell to my shoulders and then my back before settling behind my neck. His finger tugged at the knot, but I reached for his hand. "The necklace stays on," I whispered, kissing the palm of his hand.

Riven nodded and wrapped the robe around my shoulders. He kneeled in front of me once more and placed a hard kiss just underneath the glass bead of my necklace, between my breasts. My fingers entangled in his hair as he scored the fabric with a loose tie that barely covered anything but my arms.

"Can you walk?" Riven asked as he stood. "It's not far."

I grabbed his hand and nodded. Riven took two careful steps, watching my feet to make sure I was steady before leading me out of the small room of the cave and farther into the tunnel. The entire tunnel glowed, blanketing Riven in gold rays that made his light brown skin almost glimmer against his dark features.

The ground was slanted, guiding us deeper and lower into the cave with every step down the path. Just as my breath began to rasp, the ground leveled out and we stepped into a wide opening. The room was shaped like a dome with golden cracks glowing along the ceiling reflecting across the shimmering pool below.

The water swirled with ribbons of gold just like a portal but there was no destination on the other side of the water. Instead, steam whirled through the air, keeping the room damp and hot. Riven stood behind me and grabbed my braid. He smiled when he pulled the leather hair tie loose from my hair and detangled the strands from each other until my hair hung in a shower of thick waves down my back.

Riven pressed a kiss to my shoulder and then he stood by the edge of the pool. Without breaking our gaze, he untied his robe and let it hang from a boulder of rock next to the water. I bit my lip, unabashedly staring at Riven's nakedness for the first time. That spot between my thighs burned and scorched up my belly.

There was something achingly beautiful about knowing that he was the only one to see me entirely, my scars, my past, my names, while I was the only one who had seen him. We were both people who had receded into our pain, hiding ourselves away, only to find a refuge in each other.

How could I ever want anyone else but him?

Riven stepped into the pool and I watched his hips disappear into the water. "The water is healing, Keera. It will restore your strength more quickly than sleep could on its own."

I dropped my robe onto the same rock and lost my breath when I turned and saw Riven looking at me. His entire body was submerged up to his violet eyes, which skimmed the surface. He wasn't close enough to touch me, but his gaze devoured me so completely my legs shook as I took those first few steps into the pool.

The water rippled away from me with golden crests. The heat from the water warmed the outside of my body, but there was a different kind of warmth stoking beneath my skin. It reminded me of the touch of Feron's magic or the electric pull between me and Riven. At first it was nothing more than an ember, warm and smoking in my belly, but as I walked far enough into the pool that my shoulders were underwater the ember had grown to a flame.

"I feel better already," I said in disbelief. My whispers echoed off the ceiling and back at me. I reached out for Riven but he swam backward to the edge of the pool.

"First, we eat." He pointed to a small island of rock at the far edge of the lagoon. It was covered with berries, nuts, and cheese. Suddenly I forgot all about my hunger for Riven and could only focus on the grumbling coming from my stomach.

I swam to the edge of the floating table and plucked an almond, tossing it into my mouth. It was soft from the hot air, almost melting on my tongue as I bit into the hard meat. Riven loaded up a leaf with some of everything and placed it on the open area in front of me. I smiled gratefully at him before I gave in to my grumbling stomach.

I finished the first plate and then a second. Riven loaded up another and I blinked. "I've never been this hungry."

"An effect of using your magic to the brink of burnout." Riven's jaw was hard. "That is dangerous for any magic wielder, but for one whose magic is still sealed? Keera, you could have died."

I shrugged and caught a purple berry between my teeth. "It was worth it."

Riven froze. "How can you be so cavalier about your own life?"

I stopped eating and levied Riven with the gentlest look I could manage. "I'm not. Maerhal has spent *centuries* locked in those cells. I spent five years down there and I cannot imagine how she survived it. If I had died taking away her pain, I would have died knowing I was doing the right thing."

"So her life is worth more than your own?" Riven's shadows crept over the water, long strands of darkness rippling from the cloud like steam from the pool.

"Yes."

Riven shook his head in disbelief. "I hope when the seal is broken I don't have to worry about you healing people at the cost of your life."

I sunk lower in the water. "Is that the only reason you wish my magic released?"

Riven tilted his head to the side, his long arms stretched out over the water, blending with his shadows. "What other reason would there be?"

I swallowed a mouthful of air. The question had been lurking in the background of my mind, but now that the moment was here, I didn't know if I wanted it answered. I braced myself and asked it anyway. "If my magic is unsealed, the *miiskwithir* bond will grow stronger."

Riven nodded slowly, his dark brows hanging low over his eyes.

"I'm glad that this bond or whatever it is gives you any kind of relief, but some days I think it would be easier to do this"—I waved my hand between us—"if the bond did not exist."

Riven stroked my arms. "How so?"

I sighed. "I've fought so hard to have control over my life, over myself. Now, just as I'm finally steering my life, rather than having it determined for me, it feels that our bond is steering the ship instead." I bit my lip, unsure if I should continue, but there was no judgment in Riven's eyes, no hurt from my words. All he wanted was the truth, to peel it back and look at it together. "When I lay awake at night, I can't help thinking about how much this bond is directing me. It makes me wonder if you and I would have come to appreciate each other at all without it. It makes me wonder what would have happened if . . . if history had played out differently."

"If Brenna had survived, you mean?" There was no malice in Riven's voice.

I turned my face away from him but nodded. "Sometimes this bond feels like fate and sometimes I can't help but wonder if it is a trap."

Riven nodded his head slowly. He stepped close enough that I could feel the heat of his body warming the water around us. He kissed my forehead and my shoulders relaxed into his touch. "If Brenna had survived, then we would have been great friends, I think. You, me, and her."

My face crumpled into his chest, and Riven stroked my hair. "If we are *miiskwithir*, then the bond between us only brings us together in life. The choice to be lovers, friends, or enemies has always been up to us." Riven cupped my face in his hands. "Even now, if anything about the bond makes you feel uneasy, we do not need to continue . . . with this. Whatever time or distance you need, Keera, I am more than willing to abide by your choice."

Guilt pulled at my throat. I had been keeping my anxiety hidden from Riven out of fear that he would reject it or reject me. Yet he stood in front of me with nothing but concern and comfort. I looked down at my arm; Brenna's name was distorted by the water.

Choosing Riven now did not taint the love I had for her, and his acknowledgment of that lessened the guilt strangling my heart. Like Riven had said, the choice was mine. I could choose to see the bond as an extension of my guilt or a lifeline pulling me out of it.

I looked up at Riven and pressed my hand to his sharp cheek. "I choose you, Riven."

He closed his eyes and leaned into my touch. I wrapped my hand around his neck and pulled him to me, sealing my choice. The first touch of our lips was soft and tender. Riven wrapped himself around me, melding our bodies together. His hand found my jaw. The hold pinned us in place, keeping the kiss soft, but I wanted more.

I nipped his bottom lip and grinned at the soft grunt Riven made. When I kissed him again, it wasn't a soft, chaste touch of the lips but a needy bite. Riven's hands dropped to my waist, pressing into my skin but going no further.

"I'm not made of glass," I whispered in his ear. I could see the shiver that trailed down Riven's neck and set his violet eyes ablaze. His hands reached to my thighs, lifting me out of the water in one quick move. Riven pressed his forehead against mine, breaking our kiss. His chest heaved as he tried to catch his breath. I scratched my finger down his neck and watched his throat bob. "I want this," I whispered, thinking Riven's sudden lull was a crisis of conscience.

He closed his eyes like he was in pain. "We can't. You were just on the brink of burnout. You should be resting and nothing more."

I raised a brow. "You don't want me, then?"

Riven lowered me until I felt his hardness pressing against my thigh. "I do. Though I might be the only one in this pool who cares about your well-being."

"Will it kill me?"

Riven flexed his jaw. "It could."

I rolled my eyes. Riven gave me a smug grin and stepped toward the edge of the pool. As soon as my body was lifted out of the water, the fatigue settled into my bones like a battering ram. I collapsed against his chest.

Riven chuckled and lowered me back into the pool. He found an edge to perch on, and we sat with me wrapped around him, happily submerged in the water. "It's the restorative benefits of the pool. You feel more refreshed than you really are, sometimes to the point of euphoria." He pressed a gentle kiss to my neck. "I will not have you here, especially after what you just told me. If you still want me when your magic has returned and we are far from this pool, then I will be at your mercy."

I laid my cheek against his shoulder and felt the tug of sleep pulling at me once more. That electric current knitted us together until our hearts beat as one. When that time came, I would be at Riven's mercy just as much as he would be at mine.

CHAPTER FORTY-TWO

RIVEN HAD A GOWN WAITING FOR ME when I woke. It hung from the rocky wall beside the bed of faelight Riven must have laid me on to rest some more. It was made of layers of white silk and tiny fae-beads that sparkled with the light of the sun. The layers of fabric were so thin I could see my hand through them, but the dress was lined with an opaque white fabric along the body and the sleeves. It was not the usual style of the Elverin. My heart twinged as I realized Riven had had that element of the dress added in.

My hair smelled of cedarwood and had dried in soft waves. I was still tired, but the fatigue no longer ached. I felt as if I had had a restless night, doomed to spend the day slow and weary but capable. My legs didn't shake and my fingers were no longer numb. That pool had worked its magic and then some.

Riven was waiting for me at the entrance of the cave. He was dressed in a long black robe that trailed to the floor and was stitched with silver stars along the hem. The robe had no sleeves, leaving Riven's strong arms to be dyed gold by the setting suns. His mane was loose instead of its usual half braid, perfectly straight and black as night.

His violet eyes swirled with desire as I stepped out of the cave. We were somewhere in the Dead Wood, though not on a path I recognized. "Beautiful," Riven whispered as he pressed a kiss to my cheek.

He placed a *winvra* berry in my hand. "We need to hurry. Nikolai won't be happy if we're late."

"Late for what?" I asked, but Riven had already grabbed hold of my other hand and was tugging me down a small trail to a beryl pond with water so thick we couldn't see the bottom. Riven tossed his berry into the pond and I did the same. The two *winvra* sat on the surface of the water, held up by the thick coat of green algae, before an orb of gold light appeared below them and began to swirl through the surface.

Riven tightened his grip on my hand and we stepped into the pond. Even though I had traveled through several portals, I still felt uneasy walking through the thick scum along the water in my white gown, but the water never touched me. I could feel the pressure of the water, the weight of it, but I was not wet nor my robe dirty.

Riven took another step and I followed. This time we appeared at a small pond with a stream that opened up into the lake at Myrelinth. I could see the highest branches of the Myram tree and stopped walking. "Maybe we should have Nikolai meet us here."

Riven shook his head. "He's planned a feast to celebrate the return of his mother. If anyone should be there, it's you."

I nodded my head, tightening my grip on Riven's hand. Everyone who lived in the outer groves was nowhere to be found. I swallowed. That meant they were all headed to the Myram too.

As we got closer to the Myram, I could see that the entire grove was decorated in yellow. Strands of honey-colored fabric hung from each twisted branch. The sunset turned the bolts of fabric over the root-bound tables gold, while only sunny faelights floated above our heads. Riven leaned against my ear. "Her favorite color was always yellow."

My chest ripped open at the sight of the celebration. The thought of Maerhal being kept in that prison for so long, where her favorite color didn't exist and the light of the suns couldn't touch her, pierced through me.

I grabbed Riven's arm as we stepped into the circular grove. I could feel the stares of everyone locked onto us with enough force to lose my breath, but I could only see the miracle in front of me.

Maerhal was seated at the first table by the Myram tree. She was slumped back in her chair, tired and healing, but her eyes were alert as they flitted across the grove, taking in the sights she never thought she'd see again.

Tears lined my eyes as I ran toward her. She startled before breaking into a wide smile when I kneeled in front of her. Her hair had been shorn, not to the skin, but only a small halo of tight curls were left. I lifted my hands to her ear. My mouth went dry; it was unfair that Maerhal had to lose anything more to the darkness.

"Birds cannot cry," she whispered in Elvish. The tears that lined my eyes fell at the sound of her voice. "And feathers grow quicker under the sun than in the shadows." My stomach fell as I realized Maerhal still spoke in riddle. She wiped away a tear from my cheek with a shaking hand. Her fingers were thin and bony, knuckles grayed and split. It seemed impossible, but her cheeks were rounder now, still too thin, but brushed with the hope of recovery.

I looked down at her arms. The bandages were gone and only small scars remained from where the ulcers had eaten away at her. I let out a slow breath and nodded. I had no words; they caught in my throat, piling up until it hurt to swallow. I had spent my life trying to save as many lives as I took, balancing the spill of blood by bringing forth a future where Aemon no longer reigned and Halflings no longer died at his hand or mine. That goal had kept me alive when all I wanted was to succumb to the darkness and end my life by the same blade that had ended so many.

I had always been a blade, with only a choice of who I cut. But looking at Maerhal's closed, smooth skin, that view of myself shattered like a glamour. I could be a sharp edge, a weapon wielded against the Crown, but I could be more than that too. I had healed others, taken away their pain with only a touch.

I had spent my life searching for that kind of healing, chasing the bottom of every bottle and barrel thinking oblivion was the only remedy that existed, but all the while I had held the power underneath my skin. Not just to heal myself, but heal the pain around me.

I didn't have a chance to process the emotions churning through my chest because Nikolai appeared behind me. He wrapped his arms around my waist and lifted me in the air, spinning us around and around as the grove was filled with his laughter and then his mother's and then mine too.

"Keera, you marvelous, brave, wondrous creature," he yelled, emphasizing each word with a turn. "There is not enough food or jewels or words that could repay you for what you've given me."

He put me down and I finally saw the joy strung along his face. Both dimples proudly on display, wet from the tears that flowed unabashedly down his cheeks as he glanced from me to his mother. He pulled me in for a tight embrace until I couldn't breathe. "Thank you, my dearest friend," he whispered to me in Elvish.

He finally let go of me and I noticed his long black robe. It was solemn and dark against the background of yellow he had constructed around us. All the other Elverin wore bright shades of blue, yellow, and white, creating a tableau of a sunny sky even though the second sun was almost set.

Drums sounded and the entire grove fell into silence. "That's my cue," Nikolai said, turning in the direction of the large drum beside the Myram tree. He turned back to me and kissed both my cheeks and then my forehead. "I hope you know that I will never be able to repay you for the happiness you have given me."

I squeezed his hand. "There are no debts between friends, Nikolai."

He shook his head. "No, Keera, there are no debts between *family*." He walked away, commanding the attention of the entire crowd in the way only Nikolai could.

Nikolai held a wooden contraption up to his face when he spoke. It was shaped like a cone with a handle on the bottom that he used to hold it up. "I am so happy that so many of our kin could gather for such a delightful homecoming," Nikolai said in Elvish.

I glanced around the crowd and saw some Elverin whispering translations in the King's Tongue into the ears of Halflings who were not yet fluent, and behind Nikolai, Lash was interpreting for Darythir.

"My mother, Maerhal Nieven, has made it home at last, and that would have never happened if it weren't for Keera's selfless act and willingness to risk herself to save not one of us, but two." A tense murmur moved through the crowd like a rising tide. It turned into a long moment of silence. No one dared to breathe as Darythir stared unblinkingly at Nikolai. Nik didn't back down from her gaze, he held it, smiling proudly until finally the old Elf nodded her head once.

Nikolai clapped his hands together and spun back to the crowd. "Now on to more amusing affairs," he shouted just as the last rays of sun settled behind the Burning Mountains. Nikolai pulled something from his pocket. It was a glass vial a little larger than his hand. Nikolai grasped the neck of it and threw it to the ground.

The glass exploded on impact and a large cloud of golden light billowed through the air. It shimmered and glowed like faelight but was so fine the only word to describe it was *dust*. Nikolai stepped through the cloud and the crowd gasped.

His outfit of nightshade had transformed into a long robe of auric silks that trailed behind him. Strands of shimmering gold and beads were laced in his short curls and his face was painted with gold ink along his eyes and brow. Nikolai had transformed himself into sunshine, and the result was breathtaking.

"It's time to dance," he yelled, raising his glass, and the band began to play as the crowd cheered.

Riven grabbed my hand and pulled me onto the dance floor. I shook my head. "I don't think now is a good time."

"This is your home as much as theirs, Keera," Riven said with an edge of determination in his voice. "Let yourself enjoy it."

Riven's hand settled on my waist, waiting for me to choose. I nodded my head and he whisked me away onto the dance floor with the others. Nikolai and Syrra joined us, and we danced as a foursome, trading partners and spinning across the grove in every combination.

"I have not seen my home this happy in a long time, child," Syrra whispered as she lifted me into the air and spun. "You have brought me and our people great joy." Her face broke into a smile wider than I believed possible and she laughed. It was like the deep rumble of a storm coming to a head, cracking as it continued, until the entire grove boomed with her laughter.

I joined her and we laughed and danced until we could no longer breathe.

An hour later the tables were stacked with hot food and drinks of every color. The music stopped as the drums sounded once again, and this time it was Darythir who stood at the front. Feron stood beside her and gave me a knowing smile from across the grove.

A group of Elverin moved around the crowd, passing them cups of the same tea that they had drunk the night of the new moon. I didn't take one. Darythir may have chosen to allow me to stay in the city, but that didn't mean that the Elverin considered me one of their own.

Darythir raised her glass and the crowd fell to silence once more. Lash waved his hands and a root sprung from the ground beside her, acting as a tray for her to place her cup. She set it down and Feron began to interpret her words for me and the other Halflings who were not fluent in her language yet.

"This tea is brewed with the magic that flows through the Myram, just as it flows in all of us. We drink it as one, as a way to bind the Elverin together as one people, connected to each other and the land always."

Darythir picked up her cup but she did not drink it. Instead she took slow, uneven steps toward me. I couldn't move, trapped in her heavy gaze until she placed the cup in my hand. "You may drink this with us, child, for you are one of us. Today and forever more."

A sampling of cheers broke through the crowd. I turned to see Uldrath and Pirmiith in the middle of a group of Elverin from the kitchens. They beamed at me and cheered once more.

Darythir noticed their waves and raised her hands to silence them. She glanced back at where Maerhal and Nikolai sat together holding hands. "You, like many Halflings who have made their way out of the Stolen Lands, have lost the name of your foremothers. Tonight, we give you your own. Drink, Keera Waateyith'thir."

Savior from the shadows.

CHAPTER FORTY-THREE

THE REST OF THE NIGHT WENT by in a blur of laughter and fun. Collin made a show of leaving the feast in a foul mood and Tarvelle was nowhere to be seen. The children circled around me, dancing as one big group, and none of their parents came to snatch them away from the Blade. In fact, many of them had come to make formal introductions of their families for the first time.

It had been hard to sneak away when the party became too much. I'd finally found my place among the Elverin, among my people, but it could very well be short lived. I climbed up to my burl and grabbed the journal from under the pillow.

I sat with it on my lap for a long moment before I cracked open the cover. I sighed in relief when I saw the message. Dynara was alive and she'd done it.

Sending the deed to Curringham's new house in his wife's homeland and the purchase order for five dozen ships. They will arrive by dawn. I'm staying here for now. I'll return when my plans are complete. Make sure he gets everything he deserves. Always yours, D.

My tears fell onto the parchment and I had to wait to calm myself before I could even hold a plume long enough to respond to her.

This is more than enough. You make almost as good of a spy as you do a friend. The Shades and I will never be able to thank you. Send word if you need help with your plans. Yours as well, K.

I laid back on the bed and could feel the stress leaving my body. For the first time since the king had made his threat, I felt like I was in control. Curringham and his mole had been setting the pace for far too long, but come dawn, I would overtake them.

I closed my eyes, and for the first time that I could remember, I slept alone and without nightmares.

"You kept this from us?" Killian didn't hide the hurt in his voice. Riven paced along the back of the meeting room, his shadows scaling the wall behind him. As soon as the papers Dynara had procured had arrived, I'd called a meeting.

Only Vrail was missing. Still healing in the infirmary.

Nikolai's smile was mischievous with no hint of anger that I had kept so much proof from them or Dynara's mission. "You're asking the wrong question." Nikolai raised a brow. "Which one of us did you think was the mole?"

Syrra stopped eating her breakfast and Riven's angry pacing halted too. "I didn't want to think of any of you as the mole."

Nikolai's eyes narrowed. "Yet you felt strongly enough to keep it from us. Bold move, Keera dear."

Killian threw his arms up in exasperation. "The answer is obviously me." He shoved Nikolai at the shoulder and winced when his hand pressed against the Elf's arm. "But that doesn't mean it was a good idea to have us traipsing about the capital without any knowledge of the king's threats or the strength of Keera's suspicions against Curringham."

Nikolai's smile fell. "Are you truly in a position to be angry at Keera for keeping secrets?" He raised a brow and Killian's mouth snapped shut. Riven shot both of them a hard glare, his shadows curled around my legs more tightly.

"I won't begrudge anyone for feeling hurt by what I did, but I stand by the decision." I looked at each one of them. "For the first time, we're ahead in this war. We have what we need to take down Curringham, and if Vrail's right, we may be well on our way to finding the Light Fae. This isn't a time for squabbling. We need to act, *now*."

Syrra stood. "When do we leave?"

My chest swelled with gratitude. If I had her, the others would follow. "In an hour."

CHAPTER FORTY-FOUR

We separated into three groups when we reached Koratha. Killian headed for the castle to ensure that he was there when I called for an audience with the king. Riven and the others went to the safe house that hadn't burned to await our arrival and prepare for the journey into the Rift. I stayed behind to send word to Gerarda on what I needed her to do.

I waited the one hour we'd agreed on and then I rode for the palace gates. The city was even more in shambles now than it had been on my first visit. Beggars lined each ring of the city, most too sick to raise their hands any longer.

My throat tightened and I forced myself to look ahead. The hunger of his people had been easy to ignore when it had only been reports of the poor in other cities, but now they filled the king's own city.

I only hoped our war against him would be swift enough that the hungry didn't perish before it was over.

I passed through the final stone wall around the palace and waited for the guards to open the wrought iron gates to the palace grounds. "Tell the king I have arrived and his enemy is defeated." I patted the largest of my saddlebags and watched the guard visibly green thinking it was the Shadow's head.

He nodded and scurried away in his chainmail to the king. I dismounted my horse and left her with the stable boys to stow. I waited in the garden until the guard returned, out of breath, as if he'd run the entire way there and back.

"The king requests your presence in the throne room immediately," he wheezed.

I nodded and pulled my hood over my face and marched down the corridor to the king. Two guards stood outside the white birch doors that towered over my head. They glanced at my empty hands before pushing the grand doors open.

The king was seated in his throne. His face was paler and thinner than I'd ever seen it. Red eyes were sunk deep into his skull. His hair had grown longer, and the two spots of gray he allowed above his ear had stretched across his entire head. His clothes fit loose around his shrunken belly. Even his crown sat somewhat askew on his head. But there was a wild determination in his eyes as I entered the room. He licked his lips in anticipation as I stepped across the marble floor.

Killian and his brother were already there. The younger sat with a straight back, hands gently resting on the armrests while Damien was slumped over his chair dangling a goblet of wine over one armrest and a leg over the other. He looked as if he'd been up all night.

I kneeled and removed my cloak.

The king grunted and I stood. "I see no head in your hands," he boomed, though his voice didn't echo as deeply as it had before.

"No, Your Majesty." I bowed my head and tucked my arms behind my back. "I do not have the head of the Shadow."

Damien laughed darkly. "Then what have you called us here for? To plead for more time?" He sneered down at me and took a swig of his wine.

"I have come because the task you have set me is not possible." I met the king's jade gaze straight on. "I cannot bring you the head of the Shadow, Your Majesty, because the Shadow does not exist."

Damien scoffed as his father's cheeks turned a violet shade of pink. "What is the meaning of this?" the king demanded, slamming his hand against the throne.

"Father." Damien sat upright in his chair. "She means to distract you so you do not make good on your threat." He turned to me. "Why should we reward your empty hands?"

I bit my cheek to keep from grinning. "Because I have not arrived empty-handed."

Killian feigned a look of shock as I turned around and nodded at the two Shades who stood guard along the inside of the doors. They immediately grabbed the long handles and pulled the doors open to reveal Gerarda behind them with Curringham bound and gagged in her hands.

Damien's lips twitched and he relaxed back into his casual stance in his chair.

The king's graying brows rose. "Why have you fetched me a lord and not a Shadow?"

I took a deep breath. It was time to bury Curringham for good.

"Your Majesty, in my search for the Shadow I discovered a plot to weaken the throne and bankrupt the kingdom." I turned to Curringham as Gerarda flung him to the ground. "Lord Curringham has been hiding the true value of his *winvra* harvest for years. I've checked the books myself and will have the Arsenal write you a full report, but it is true."

Curringham fought against his bindings and his pleas were trapped behind his gag. The king lifted one hand. "Enough," he told the lord before turning back to me.

"He planned for this to be his final harvest. He has acquired enough ships to ferry all the viable *winvra* left in the kingdom to his new home in his wife's realm." I walked the leather folder up to the king and presented him with the deed and purchase order for the ships. "The ships are docked along the Fractured Isles. I will have the Shades procure them so they can be added to your naval forces."

Killian lifted his chin, pretending he was hearing this for the first time. "But what does this scheme have to do with the Shadow?"

I bowed to the prince. "Curringham hired several well-trained fighters from the kingdom and the other realms to masquerade as the Shadow. It was how he appeared to be everywhere all at once, but no one could give a single description of his face. Curringham created the Shadow to keep the Crown's attention off him while he ferried shipments of *winvra* out of the kingdom. Some of them he even reported stolen by the Shadow so you would not grow suspicious." Curringham bucked against his bindings at my lie. "I am only grateful I was able to uncover his plot before he fled, Your Highness."

"Ungag him." The king's words were murderous. "What do you have to say to these accusations?"

Gerarda removed the gag in one swift tug at his chin. Tears rolled down Curringham's face as he pulled himself up onto his bound knees. "It wasn't like that, Your Majesty. I wasn't acting a—"

His words were cut off by Damien's boot in his gut. The crown prince kicked him again. "You dare lie to your king after all the trouble you've caused him and this court?" Curringham's eyes widened as Damien levied another kick. He collapsed onto the ground and whimpered. Damien knelt and pulled the gag back into place before standing before his father.

"You do not need to entertain this oaf's lies. The Blade"—he turned to me with a look of satisfaction—"has done her job well. You have all the proof you need to make an example of Curringham."

The king's brow raised for a moment but then he nodded. "Throw him in a cell until we can gather a crowd to watch his body swing from the city wall."

Damien smiled gleefully and reclaimed his seat.

"What of his lady wife?" Killian asked, ignoring the crumpled pile of Curringham being dragged out of the room by the king's guard.

I turned to Gerarda. She lowered her hood and answered Killian's question with a bowed head. "With such little notice, our focus was on capturing Lord Curringham. Lady Curringham was not in her chambers, but I have sent four squadrons to find her."

The king nodded. "Were any other lords involved in this scheme?"

"Not that I know of, Your Majesty." I glanced at Gerarda. "Though we can have the Shades raid the House of Harvest by tomorrow to find out what else Curringham had been up to in Cereliath."

Gerarda nodded. "I will send word as soon as you give the command, my king."

Aemon's fingers drummed along his armrest before he nodded. "Keep that oaf locked up until the raid is complete. I do not want any of his conspirators to know that the Shades are coming."

Gerarda and I both nodded.

The king stared down at us. "I expect a full report and answers for how such a scheme was able to fester."

"Of course, Your Majesty." I kneeled at the dais and waited for the king to dismiss me.

He stood and so did Killian. Damien stayed slumped over in his chair, his usual boredom returned now that his plaything had been taken out of the room.

The king looked down at me with hard eyes. "I expect my Blade to cut more quickly in the future."

I bowed my head as I stood. "I shall, Your Majesty."

I would cut right through his heart.

CHAPTER FORTY-FIVE

"Please tell me this is the last one," I groaned. We were waiting for the second sun to set behind the horizon before riding our horses through the next portal. Waiting in the Barren Lands, trying to stay warm next to two large stones that towered above our heads. Large spindles covered in fur wrapped around the towers like long-haired snakes. I leaned closer to the fire Syrra had lit and some of their fur fell onto my head.

My body shook so violently, I would have preferred to ride to the Rift directly from Koratha. Saving two days wasn't worth this cold.

"Thankfully, yes," Nikolai answered through chattering teeth. "I hate the cold."

Cold was an understatement. Despite the thick cloaks Killian had made us pack, I was so chilled I couldn't tell if my fingers were still attached. I fought the urge to ask Nikolai and Riven to pull closer together so I could remember what body heat was supposed to feel like.

Syrra chuckled and poked the top log of the fire. She wasn't even wearing her cloak, baring her scarred arms like a sick joke. "It is almost time." Her eyes turned to the space between the stones.

When we had stepped through them an hour earlier, we had been in the Dead Wood. My teeth shook. "We should have taken our chances with the poisoned air." The last portal was in a black swamp that bubbled with the burnt remains of dead trees and who knew what else. Syrra had taken one sniff of the sludge next to matching stones of the portal and motioned us through to the snowy desert before our horses could even rest.

Riven shifted beside me. He didn't lean his body into mine but wrapped his cloak around my shoulders, adding an extra layer. I was partially convinced my bones were ice, so I barely noticed the difference, but I appreciated the gesture.

A strong wind blew across my face and doused the fire in one blow. The thick smell of ash and rotting wood filled the air. I turned to the large stones and watched as swirls of golden light merged with swirls of silver. They dissipated just as the sun sunk under the snowy horizon and night settled over us.

I jumped up and grabbed my horse without hesitation. I snatched a *winvra* berry from Killian and tossed it above my head. The furry vine snapped it out of the air with one of its leaves. I swore it had teeth, but I was too cold to care. I stepped through the rocks and felt the welcome night air of Wendon.

"For someone who took down a brumal bear, you sure do complain about the cold," Nikolai mumbled.

I pulled myself onto my horse's saddle, brushing the snow from her mane. "Harsh words from someone still wrapped in their cloak." I raised a brow at Nikolai, who had his furs wrapped around himself so tightly he could only walk a few inches at a time.

Syrra stepped around him and shoved Nikolai with her hip. He toppled over and then started rolling down the field. Riven laughed in his saddle beside me as Killian chased Nikolai down the gentle slope. Syrra shot me a rare grin and started down the path to the village below.

Wendon was quiet. From the smell that wafted through the street, most of the villagers were inside with a warm supper. The ones who weren't were wrapped in tattered clothes between the houses. I saw Riven flick them spare gold as we rode by.

Syrra stopped outside of a small inn. It was two stories with rooms along the top and a full kitchen on the bottom. I volunteered to bring our horses to the stables while Killian sorted out our rooms. Riven grabbed Nikolai's horse and helped me corral all five mounts toward the sleeping stable boy.

I untied the pack of my horse and felt Riven's strong arm reaching over my shoulder to grab it. I let my hands fall and leaned into the warmth of his chest. I heard Riven's breath stop. "I'm still cold," I whispered before stepping out of his touch and tipping the stable boy who carried the rest of everyone's bags.

The others were sitting along a large table in the corner of the pub. Syrra and Nikolai ordered some wine while the rest of us filled our water glasses and waited for the hot soup and cooked meat to arrive. My stomach growled but I couldn't eat. All my thoughts were at the Rift, wondering what waited for us there on the morrow.

I prodded my plate with my fork, moving the sliced carrots across the ceramic design without care. I didn't even notice when Killian rose from the table and went to bed. Sometime after, Nikolai stretched out his arms and yawned. It was like a signal—suddenly we all stood, ready for bed.

Nikolai spoke to a Mortal with little hair left on his gray head. He passed Nikolai two keys and sauntered back down the hall into his chair where he fell asleep in seconds. Nik dangled the keys in his hand. "Keera's choice." He winked at me. "Are you rooming with Syrra or Riven?" He ran the tip of his tongue across his teeth.

I folded my arms. "But what if I want to choose you?"

Nikolai's jaw dropped for a second before his flirtatious smile returned. "Is that a choice you want on the table?" He bit his lip devilishly, but I caught the glance he gave Riven with cautious eyes. Riven was a hard rock behind me.

"No." I shrugged with a wicked grin. "I've just never known you to take yourself out of the running."

Riven hid his laugh behind a cough.

I grabbed the key hanging from a red ribbon on Nikolai's finger. "I'll room with Riven," I said, tossing the key into the air and catching it again. I could feel Riven's sigh of relief on my back.

Nikolai's gaze flicked between us, his smirk growing. He jutted his chin up at Riven and leaned closer to Syrra. "I told you," he murmured.

Syrra grabbed her key and smacked the back of Nikolai's head.

Riven left me in the room to use the bath in private. I unpacked while I waited for the order of hot water I'd asked for to arrive. A Halfling boy carried burnt metal buckets of steaming water and poured them into the small basin that was meant to be a tub. I dripped in some of the cedar essence Nikolai had given me and took a deep breath as I lowered myself into the water.

It stung, almost verging on painful, but I didn't get out. The heat on my skin focused the thoughts swirling in my mind. I had no idea what we would find in the morning—if we would find anything at all. Part of me was scared that I would fail everyone in some way. That the Rift held no secrets, no key to winning this war. But there was a larger part, a part of myself I was ashamed to admit, that was terrified by whatever waited for me in that rift.

I swept a washcloth over my limbs, reading the names as their corresponding faces flashed through my mind. So many terrible nights, horrific deaths that I had committed, and I remembered every single one. Even when I had spent so long trying to forget them.

I didn't know what could be terrible enough for me to forget my past, but it filled me to the brim with fear. My lungs squeezed against my chest, unable to catch a full breath, as my heart hammered against them.

I dunked my head under the water. The lather in my hair washed away and I grabbed the pitcher the Halfling boy had left to rinse my strands once more. I heard Riven come in, but he didn't call for me. I pulled myself out of the basin and dried my body and hair.

I wore one of my nightgowns. It was a bright silver that made my eyes glow in the looking glass. I stepped out and saw Riven had already changed and slipped between the covers on the far side of the bed. He wore a simple cotton tunic that he left unlaced down the front.

I placed my old clothes back in my saddlebag and turned to face him. His eyes were hungry and a bright violet even in the dark room. His gaze felt heavy, like it was his hands roaming over my body instead, first my arms, then legs, finally lingering on the short hem of the fabric just between my thighs. My body flushed with that familiar warmth, and I instantly relaxed against the dresser. The scent of Riven filled the room and pushed all my fears away.

We existed only in that moment. Me and him, with no thought of tomorrow or the war to come.

I slipped into the bed beside him. Riven didn't move but his chest stilled under the sheet. I knew he was waiting for me. Like the shirt he wore beneath the blankets, he was giving me the choice. Even in this, he deferred to my need. Letting me know that he would have me however I was, in whatever way I wanted.

I pulled my body into his, wrapping my leg between his own and resting my head on his chest. I could feel the weight of him sink into the mattress with relief as he wrapped his arms around me. We laid like that for a long while, watching the single candle burn and drip. I cherished the moment of peace. It was a gift that only Riven seemed to give me.

He dragged his thumb in large strokes across my side, his cheek pressed against my hair. He inhaled deeply. "I will never tire of the scent of you," he murmured.

"What do you think will happen tomorrow?" I pressed a kiss to his chest and traced circles into his bare skin. "What do you think we'll find?"

Riven stilled for a moment. I looked up at him and saw a faint crease form between his brow as he considered my question. "I agree with Feron. I think there is a reason you don't remember your past and that reason likely waits for you in the Rift."

I nodded, wrapping my leg tighter around him. "I think so too," I sighed.

Riven tucked a gentle finger under my chin and lifted my face to his. His kiss was soft and comforting. I melted into that softness and kissed him back.

He smiled against my lips and pressed a peck of a kiss to my nose. "Are you frightened?"

There was no judgment in his question. I could tell by the way Riven's hands gripped me tighter that my fear worried him, that all he wanted to do was help me carry it. "Yes," I admitted. I laced my fingers though his hand. "I've spent most of my life believing that I would never know the truth about my past. I'm scared of knowing what I left behind—of what my life might have been if I was never taken to the Order." I swallowed, turning my face into Riven's chest so I didn't have to look at him. "But mostly, I'm scared of knowing *who* left me behind."

A tear rolled down my cheek and Riven was there. He pulled me up the bed so he could kiss the tears away. My chest broke at his gentleness as he stroked my jaw and neck. He curled me into a ball against him and cradled me like a child.

In that moment, I was one. I was that scared girl who'd been pulled from one dark crevice and thrown into another, wondering why she'd been left behind. Crying out, asking the darkness who would leave a child in a place like that and pleading for whoever had done it to come back and save her.

I cried for her. That girl who had to overcome her fear of the dark all alone. I wished that I could go back and pull her into my arms the way Riven held me now. I would stroke her hair and tell her that one day the darkness wouldn't be a place of pain and fear. One day she would be wrapped in the shadows of someone who knew her deepest fears and her greatest pain and she would welcome the darkness then. I would tell her that one day the darkness would feel like home.

Riven held my face in his hands and pressed his forehead to mine. "Whatever we find down there, I'll be with you. You don't have to face it alone." He kissed me and that electric current pulsed between us. "You never have to face anything alone again."

I grabbed his hand, stretching it out wide and brushing my fingers across his. Every time our skin touched I could feel that electric tingle and knew the call of my blood coursed through Riven at a level I couldn't understand. "Do you think you would still have come to care for me if my touch didn't numb the sting of your power?" My cheeks flushed with heat. That question had sat on my tongue for weeks and now hung in the silence between us.

Riven sat up, lifting me onto his lap. I crossed my legs around his back and held my breath, waiting for his answer. His hand wrapped around the back of my neck and forced me to look at him. His gaze was hard and resolute. He opened his mouth, but no words came. I watched his brow tremble as he tried to find the truth. "I know you think our bond is some sort of miracle that cures my pain, something I can't resist, but you have it wrong, Keera. The miracle is *you*."

My eyelids fluttered against his breath. "But I—"

Riven grabbed my hands and kissed them. "Keera, I was never looking for a way to curb my power or the pain that comes with it. I had accepted that part of me long before I ever met you." He tucked my hair behind my ear and kissed my neck. "To be honest, I liked the pain."

I leaned back and stroked his sharp cheek with my hand. He leaned into my touch. "I spent years hating the way my magic raged inside me," he continued. "I'd convinced myself I had failed somehow. Failed my people for not having enough control, enough power. I would train with Feron and Syrra, safe in the *Faelinth*, but my thoughts would be with all the Halflings trapped under Aemon's rule. Left defenseless. Abandoned. I never felt like I was doing enough."

I frowned. "But you became the Shadow. You've saved hundreds of Halflings."

"After *decades* of having so much power and doing nothing with it." Riven's tongue poked through his cheek. "And then I saw you in Aralinth. You were the Blade, sent there to fetch my head, but all you needed was the smallest hope, the *smallest* chance, and you took it. Knowing you had no refuge—no recourse—if things went wrong. You didn't take decades to decide, you didn't even take hours. You were willing to fight and die for the *possibility* that we could save your kin."

My lips quivered. I opened them to tell Riven he was giving me too much credit, but he silenced me with a kiss. He pulled my arms to his neck and ran his fingers down my scars. My back arched and he kissed a line of names along my bicep. "I know you see these names as a ledger," he whispered against my skin. "To you, they're a record of all the pain you've caused and can never undo."

My chest tightened. Riven had seen my nakedness, his lips brushed over the scars along my skin knowing what they were, but I had never felt as exposed as I did in that moment.

He kissed the inside of my elbow. "But that's not what these names are to me. To me, each one is a choice. You could have succumbed to the pain and let another take your title and the sharp edge that comes with it, but you didn't. You leveraged the little power the king had given you and used it to help when others would not. Even though it hurt, even though each choice cut you worse than the scars they left behind, you made the hard choice *every time*."

Riven lifted his hand to my face and brushed his thumb along my cheek. "That strength is what made me care for you, *diizra*, not the warmth I feel at your touch." He gave me the softest kiss, stealing my breath as he pulled back again. "I would gladly live with the pain of my magic for the rest of my days if it meant I got to share them with you. We may be *miiskwithir*, Keera, but a life of loving you is the only gift I need."

I felt weightless at his words. I tightened my legs around him so I couldn't float away as my heart raced against his chest. I ran my fingers through his hair, memorizing the lines of his face. The face of a Fae who loved me.

"If what Vrail thinks is true"—I paused to take a breath—"then tomorrow my magic will be unleashed and the bond will come into its full power."

Riven nodded. "Most likely."

I gripped the bottom of Riven's tunic in my fists. I took a deep breath and tugged the linen upward until his shirt was a crumpled pile on the floor. The cuts and curves of his chest were only intensified by the dim light. I leaned down and kissed Riven with a hunger that had been growing from the moment I crawled into bed. I moved my hips against him, letting him feel my nakedness under the nightgown.

Riven pulled my hand from his hair. "Keera." His jaw flexed. "I don't want you to regret anything."

"I don't care about what you can't tell me." Riven opened his mouth but I pressed a finger to his lips. "You said you know I can make hard choices. This isn't a hard choice, Riven. Whatever it is, I trust you. I trust you've made a hard choice and chose well."

I pulled my nightgown over my head. We sat there, completely bare and intertwined. I pulled him in for a kiss, tasting his need for me in each bite. My lips trailed down his neck to his ear. "I want you to know that no matter what happens tomorrow, I wanted this." I shifted in his lap and felt his want beneath me. "If Feron is right, I want you to know I loved you before I felt your blood call mine."

Riven's hands tightened on my waist. Violet eyes looked up at me, full of tenderness as a tear fell down his cheek. I kissed it away, just like he had done for me, and then I kissed him. Our patience had burned away in the heat of our bodies. Riven's hand gripped my neck, tugging at my hair as he devoured me with his lips. I felt the sharp graze of his fang on my mouth and it sent shivers down my spine.

Riven's kiss followed them. He leaned me back on the bed, holding his weight above me, as he kissed my neck and then the middle of my chest. His nose grazed over the curve of my breast as his mouth tasted my skin. He flicked his tongue over my nipple and my back arched against him. His arm wrapped under me, pulling me tight against his torso as his fingers scratched along the curve of my back.

He nipped at the bottom of my breast and a soft gasp escaped my lips. Riven rose to catch it, pulling me into a hungry kiss with no end. His fingers scraped the inside of my thigh, getting closer to where I needed him with every kiss. His hand brushed between my thighs and I whimpered, opening my legs, wanting to feel the weight of his touch there again.

Riven smiled against my lips. His fingers brushed against me once more and my breath stopped. He did it again and I squirmed, but his touch was not exactly where I needed it. I opened my mouth to beg, but Riven wouldn't hear it. Instead he captured my lips with his as his hand pressed against that small, throbbing spot.

Riven played with me in small circles that pulled my breath from my body in low moans. When my hips started matching his rhythm, Riven grabbed my nipple between his teeth and plunged a finger inside me. My nails dug into his shoulder but Riven didn't seem to mind. He licked the soft curve under my navel while his finger moved in slow strokes inside me.

He spread my legs wide, placing them on either side of his broad shoulders. He looked up at me, smiling as I watched him, and pressed a gentle kiss to my hip before he devoured me. The first taste was a soft swirl of the tongue, like a first kiss, slow and testing. Then the strokes quickened and he pushed a second finger into me. I grabbed a fistful of his hair. My legs closed around his head, but Riven didn't stop. He teased me until my body tensed and then he kept going. Waves of pleasure pulsed through me as Riven's name fell from my lips. My legs shook along his back and I tried to catch my breath but couldn't.

Riven smiled and licked his lips clean. He crawled up over me. "I will never tire of the taste of you either."

I flashed my fangs as I lifted myself to his mouth. I wrapped my legs around his hip and flipped him on the mattress like we were we sparring. In some ways, we were. I was determined to discover his every desire and every trick, like readying for a fight. I observed how his body responded to my movements, to my touch. My mouth laid a trail of kisses down his body; it looped and turned around his muscles, which gleamed with a thin sheet of sweat.

I grabbed the hard length of him and Riven flinched at my touch. I smirked as I stroked him, watching his brow crease and his lip quiver. I twisted my wrist as I pleasured him and felt his legs shake under mine. He would never tire of the taste of me, but I wanted to taste him. I took him into my mouth and Riven groaned. I moved down, taking as much of him as I could manage. Riven's hand fisted the sheet and the muscles in his neck tensed. I ran my tongue along the underside of him and Riven slammed his arm into the pillow.

His shadows exploded through the room, covering the walls in a thick blackness. They swirled around his arms and mine, but I kept going, even as they coiled around my neck. Tickling my skin. "Keera," Riven gasped. "I need you. Now."

He pulled me on top of him and kissed me with abandon—like he had gone weeks without my lips instead of just minutes. Riven turned me gently on the bed so his chest pressed against my back. He pulled my hair from my neck. His teeth grazed the exposed skin. "Do you want me?" My ear burned against his breath.

I moved my hips back into him, teasing his hardness. "Keera," he groaned, "I need you to answer me." He nipped the flat skin along my shoulder.

"Yes," I breathed. "I want you. I want this."

One of Riven's arms wrapped around me and palmed my breast. The other trailed along my hip and pulled my leg over his. He kissed my neck and I turned to meet his gaze. It was full of wanting and concern.

"I want this," I echoed, kissing his lips.

Riven swallowed. "I'll go very slowly. I don't want to hurt you."

My heart swelled, understanding his hesitation. I had never had to explain to Riven that he was only the second person I'd shared myself with. Physically, and in every other way. From the moment he saw my scars and learned Brenna's name, he knew there had been no one else. He knew this was a first for us, a first for him, and a first for me.

"I know you won't hurt me," I whispered, but the shadows only grew denser with his worry. "But I'll tell you if you do."

Riven nodded and the crease in his brow faded along with the black sheets covering the walls. My leg was still hooked around him. He reached down and caressed that sensitive spot between my thighs. My head fell back against him as he entered me.

That electric surge that had become so familiar between us swelled. My mouth opened but no sound came out. He thrust a little farther, testing my body's ability to take him. I reached up, burying my hands in his long mane and nodded. Riven gave a final thrust and we were one.

"You're mine." The words felt carnal on my tongue, but I didn't take them back.

Riven thrust inside me again and snarled at the sharpness of the pleasure. "I'm yours," he rasped. His hand stroked me in steady circles. I tugged on his hair and moved my hips to meet each one of his thrusts. I could feel the current building in us both and we teetered on the edge of ecstasy.

Riven moaned my name and the electric charge burst through us and the room, ripping Riven's shadows into shreds. I could feel Riven's heart pounding through his chest against my back. I turned slowly, my body melding into his. Somehow our touch felt closer than it had before.

Riven pulled me by the chin and kissed me as the aftershocks of our pleasure pulsed, leaving us breathless. His face broke into a wide smile—the one he saved only for me.

"You love me." It wasn't a question. Riven let the truth of that statement hang in the air.

I kissed the underside of his jaw, laughing as his shadows swirled up my body, tickling the joy out of me. "You love me too." I smiled at him.

Riven pulled me on top of him once more and our need for sleep was forgotten.

CHAPTER FORTY-SIX

WE CONVENED OUTSIDE the inn just after dawn. I yawned, tightening the straps of my saddle, and Nikolai raised a knowing brow at me. He placed his foot in the stirrup. "Long night, Keera?"

I grinned, biting my lip as I glanced at Riven riding down the trail with Killian. "Not long enough, actually."

Wide-eyed, Nikolai launched himself over the saddle with too much vigor and fell over the other side. I barked a laugh so loud my horse jerked. Syrra shook her head and pulled a smiling Nikolai off the ground.

"We must make haste." Syrra mounted her horse in one elegant motion and chuckled as she passed her nephew. I stifled my laugh and followed her out of the small stables, throwing a coin at the stable boy who lay sleeping in the hay.

Nikolai rubbed his hip and sulked behind us until the second sun had completely risen over the horizon and we reached the Rift.

The soft morning breeze turned violent as we approached the chasm. It whistled through the earth like a scream, keeping most travelers at a safe distance along the road. We steered our horses to the ledge, close enough to see the rocky, earth-packed edges disappear into the bottomless darkness below.

The Rift split across the earth so far I could not see the end of it. It would take days riding along the fissure to reach its end and days more to journey up the other side. It was said that deadly creatures lurked in the Rift, trapped and hungering for human flesh. It was why Wenden was one of the only villages close by. Mortals preferred to keep their children far away from the monsters and ghosts that haunted it.

We gathered at the northernmost point—where the earth was flat and then broke into a tiny sliver of darkness before widening toward the south until it spanned the entire horizon, so wide that no bridge could cross it.

"This could take a while," Nikolai mumbled. He took a bite of a muffin from his pocket. It crunched as he bit into it and he spat it on the ground. "I forget most Mortals are terrible cooks."

"I don't see you spending much time in the kitchens either, Nikolai." I gave him a knowing smile.

Killian rolled his eyes and dismounted his white horse. The red tinge of the morning clouds matched the collar of his jacket. He'd left the thick cloak at the inn.

Killian peered over the ledge. A gust of wind scurried up the side strong enough to knock the prince down. Nikolai ran to help him up as the rest of us laughed.

Killian swatted Nik's hand away and glanced at me from the grass. "Where should we start?"

I dismounted my horse too. "Hildegard told me once that I was found along the northwest side. It must have been somewhere close to the road because a traveler heard me crying and found me on a ledge. We only have that to work from—I don't remember that day at all."

Riven wrapped his arm around my shoulder. I leaned into him and felt my chest loosen. Syrra passed Nikolai a bundle of rope and placed another on her shoulder. I pointed along the western side of the Rift. "We're looking for a ledge low enough that a child could not climb free but close enough to the top that she could be hoisted out. It must be close to here—I was found within a day's ride from Wenden."

Syrra split us into teams. Riven and I searched the first segment of ridge and Nikolai and Killian searched the next. Syrra steered her horse in a canter along the edge and claimed her section over the soft hill of the road.

I racked my mind for a hint of a memory, but there was nothing but dark and cold. I had no way to know if those memories were from the Rift or the earliest days of my captivity in the black cells. I didn't remember anything about the ledge, and looking at the rocky walls of the Rift did nothing to stir my memory.

Riven used his power to bend the darkness within the Rift, pushing the shadows down and splitting them in two to search the lower depths as well. But he found nothing but added layers of earth and cracked stone. He halted his power and the blackness of the Rift flooded back together like water.

An eagle cry split through the air. Riven stood immediately and grabbed our horses. "That's Syrra."

He leaped onto his horse and we cantered down the road. He gave me a sly smile before bringing his hand to his mouth and releasing the loud, piercing cry of a barn owl. He had not undersold his talents.

We overtook Nikolai and Killian, who were laughing hysterically as they tried to mount their rides. "She will seek revenge for that, Riven," Nikolai shouted after us between his laughs. Riven's violet eyes were full of boyish mischief. I savored the moment, a glimpse of what our life could be once the fighting was done.

Syrra stood at the edge of the Rift with her arms folded and a heavy brow. Her eyes narrowed as Riven dismounted her horse and sauntered over to her without a hint of a smile. "It is not time for games, Riventh"

He shot her a sly grin, his shadows licking playfully at her feet. "I have no idea what you mean."

I looked down at the spot where Syrra had wedged a stick between a crack in the earth a few feet back from the ridge and tied her horse. I tied my horse's reins with hers and watched as she pulled a large metal stake from her saddlebag. She hammered the sharp pin into the ground and twisted a knob at the top of it. When she tugged the pin, it didn't move an inch.

Nikolai nudged Killian with his elbow. "One of my designs. The twist releases barbs into the ground like roots to anchor it. It's strong enough to lower our horses down there if we needed."

"Hopefully that won't be necessary." Killian's eyes widened as he leaned over the edge of the Rift and saw the small ledge multiple stories below. It was large enough to hold a child though there was nothing discerning about it to my memory. Still, it was the only ridge we'd found that fit.

They tied off their horses, and I helped Syrra secure the rope to the metal loop on the stake. Riven leaned over the edge and tried to push back the darkness that settled within the Rift like an inky fog. It retreated from the ledge but lingered just below it, lurking like a snake in the reeds, watching as each one of us descended into its trap.

I landed first. My boot shifted on a piece of rubble, and the sound of the scratch echoed down the chasm and into the swirling storm of shadows. Syrra dropped soundlessly onto the ledge followed by the heavy mass of Riven's jump off the rope. Nikolai slid down, protecting his hands with handkerchiefs wrapped around the palms. He lurched to a stop, hovering just above the rocky ledge, and pressed a cautious toe to the ground like he was testing the temperature of a pool. Satisfied, he stepped down with his full weight and fixed his hair.

I pulled a faebead from my pocket and smashed it with my foot. A faelight the size of my head erupted from the bead and hovered at my shoulder, casting the Rift in a silvery glow.

"Whoa," Nikolai gasped. He held his arm in front of him, letting Killian use it as he dismounted from the rope, but his gaze was locked on where the ledge met the convex wall of the Rift. The shadows had withdrawn like low tide and revealed haphazard steps leading into the darkness.

Riven grabbed my hand and squeezed it once before taking the lead down the staircase. His jaw was permanently flexed as he took a cautious step on every rocky stair, pushing the shadows back with his power when they reached for us from the abyss.

Killian pulled a glass quill from his pocket and leaned over the first step. He reached out, letting his arm be covered in shadow.

I held my breath, waiting for a scream of pain or the screech of a monster but nothing came.

When he pulled his arm back, his hand was empty. Each of us froze, not daring even to breathe, as we listened for something other than our pounding heartbeats. No clink or shatter echoed up the walls. The quill was still falling or the sound of its landing had been swallowed by the shadows, keeping its secrets in the dark.

Riven's shoulders tensed in front of me as he took another step. We traveled like that, in single disjointed steps, until the air grew cold and damp and my ears ached with pressure. We huddled together as Riven tried to keep the darkness at bay, but it coiled around our legs like snakes, cold and stinging, unlike Riven's power, with an eerie weight that threatened to pull us off the steps altogether.

I jolted against Riven. I had taken a step, expecting to lower even further into the darkness, but we had reached a flat surface. It was softer than the first ledge or the rocky steps, but I had no way to tell if we had found the bottom of the Rift or not. The thick fog covered the sky above our heads and the shadows covered our feet. We could be standing on another ledge with no way of knowing where a step would keep us safe or where we would plummet to our deaths.

I took a small step forward and the shadows rescinded, revealing a large flat ledge covered in moss. I blinked and held up my arm to shield my eyes. A large Elder birch stood in the middle of the ledge, its bark glowing silver against the shadows. Its leaves were not gold or red, but the color of a pearl, glimmering in silver light, like the moon had set just behind the tree and scattered its light into the darkness.

Riven's arm was up too, shielding his eyes, while the others still peered out into the darkness like they could not see the Elder birch at all. He stopped and stared at the tree, but I kept going. Something called me closer. A familiar scent wrapped around me and my head felt light and dizzy. The silver glow that wrapped around the trunk and branches pulsed like a slow heartbeat. I realized mine was hammering inside my chest.

There was a split in the middle of the tree. It reminded me of the great door in Aralinth, but this one was much smaller. I would have to fold my limbs into myself to fit through the crack. Yet something told me I should reach out and grasp the darkness within it.

I heard Riven call my name, and like an echo across water, it rippled through my mind, the syllables slow and stretched. My hand reached for the tree so slowly it felt like time had paused. My fingers brushed against the paper-like bark and the entire Rift was engulfed in silver light.

CHAPTER FORTY-SEVEN

I OPENED MY EYES and all I saw was light. Pure, white light that extended in every direction without a hint of shadow in its midst. I reached out and my hand disappeared into the paleness, like I was walking through a cloud I could not feel but could only watch as it shifted around me.

An eerie feeling crept up my spine, warning me that I was not alone.

"Hello?" I called out in the white abyss.

A silver light reflected against the whiteness, and the cloud began to swirl around me, capturing me in a ball of alabaster smoke. I was lifted into the air, and the white smoke around me transformed into a ball of water.

But I was not wet or unable to breathe.

Strands of golden light appeared in the liquid, swirling around my limbs and torso, just like I was passing through the portal to

Myrelinth. The whiteness took shape around me, shadow and colors appearing against the blank canvas.

It was the same day as that memory of the wedding. I floated above it, watching like a bird. I could even see myself as a babe bouncing on the knee of the Light Fae who held me once again. I called to them, but my voice was silenced by the water. No one could hear me.

But then she did.

The Light Fae looked up, her silver eyes glowing bright, as she stared directly at me. She lifted her finger, and the orb of water drifted closer to her so I floated next to the bride and the groom I believed to be Aemon. I glanced back at the Light Fae who could see me and she nodded once. Then she waved her hand and the memory swirled once more.

It was the same garden, lined with blooms and trees of every color. There was another Light Fae standing at the center of the grove, dressed in a robe of silver that matched his sparkling eyes.

Beside him stood a Mortal. Tall for a human, but much shorter than the Fae that gathered around the couple. Her hair was long and loose around her ears, thick blond waves with hints of gray at the temples. But it was her eyes that made my breath hitch.

Eyes of jade rimmed with amber.

The same as Aemon's.

I glanced around the crowd of witnesses and saw that some of the guests were the same as in the first memory but younger. They smiled happily and cheered with joy as the couples sealed their union with a kiss.

I turned away and saw the same Light Fae as before standing by a small Elder birch. She stared at me with glowing eyes and waved her hand once more.

The memory shifted again, this time taking the form of a pebbled beach. I was floating above the scene and watched as a crowd of

Light Fae and other Elverin embraced the same couple from the wedding. The bride's belly was large and round. Her mate placed a gentle hand on her round belly before walking her to where a small boat was ready to ferry them to the ship anchored out at sea.

"We'll return soon," the woman shouted at the crowd in stilted Elvish.

The Light Fae looked up at me floating overhead and the memory shifted once more.

We were in the Rift, but it was different. There were no shadows between the walls. The clear sky was a blue spot high above our heads. I looked down and saw myself as a child lying on a hard rock while the Light Fae and a Mage embrace.

I slammed my fist against the bubble holding me in the air but the effort was pointless. I could not break myself free and they refused to hear me. I watched helplessly as the Fae turned toward a green patch of moss along the floor of the Rift. She placed her hand over the greenery, and my mouth hung open as the ground bloomed with new life, lush and thick.

She pulled something small from the pocket of her robe. It was the bulb she had plucked from the sapling that sprouted from the earth the day the Light Fae had disappeared into droplets of water. She placed the seed pouch on the grass and covered it with her hand. She closed her eyes and silver light glowed from beneath her fingers.

When she pulled away, a short sprout poked out from the ground. Within seconds, it had grown to her hip. In the next blink, it was as tall as the Fae. A moment longer, and its silver branches stretched deep into the chasm and covered the Fae and Mage in silver light.

There was a split down the middle, just large enough for a child. I pounded the wall of water once more, knowing what the Fae was about to do. She picked up the version of myself that lay asleep on the stone and gently pressed a kiss to my forehead. Little me stirred against her chest as she lifted me into the crevice of the trunk.

I floated so closely to them now that the only thing that stopped me from reaching out and touching them was the barrier of magic water between us. I watched as the eyes of my child self fluttered open and she smiled softly up at the Light Fae. Her eyes were not silver but a light brown.

"Mava," she whispered gently before falling back asleep.

A tear rolled down the Light Fae's cheek as she wrapped her arms around the trunk of the tree and dissipated into water too. A gust of wind blew through the chasm, so strong I was shocked the tree didn't bend. It carried the droplets of water away, out to the sea, and left behind a trail of black fog that only seemed to grow.

I whispered to myself in disbelief, "Mava."

The Elvish word for mother.

I woke laying at the base of the silver Elder birch, though it was not in the Rift. Instead that same circular garden bloomed around us with the tree at its center instead of a couple about to wed. I stood on shaky legs and sighed in relief that I was not bound by a sphere of water.

I walked through the garden, smelling the blooms and watching the songbirds dart from branch to branch. Something shifted behind the tree. I crouched in slow steps until I rounded the trunk to find the Light Fae standing there smiling at me.

"Hello, Keera," she said in a voice that reminded me of a lullaby. "I have been waiting for this for a long time."

I studied her face. Her ears were long like mine, but sharper. The hard line of her nose was familiar as was the shape of her mouth. She had silver eyes, identical to mine.

The truth fell from my lips unceremoniously. "Mother."

She nodded, her wide smile faltering for a moment. "I am, but I know you do not remember. You may call me El'ravaasir if that brings more comfort."

My throat tightened. "You mean my memories won't come back?"

A solemn shadow fell across her face and she shook her head. "It cannot be helped. You spent too long locked in this tree." Her hand pressed against the trunk of the Elder birch. "Memories fade and you were so young to begin with. There is nothing left to recover."

Understanding washed over me like a violent wave at sea. I had been so sure that my existence proved the Light Fae were still alive, a certainty that only grew when Feron's suspicions of my lineage seemed to be confirmed. But if I had been locked in that tree long enough to forget every moment of my childhood, then I was much older than any of us had known. And whoever I had been all those years before was gone forever.

I bit my lip. It shouldn't hurt to lose something I couldn't remember having, but it did. My chest ached, longing to feel that same familiarity I could tell El'ravaasir felt with me.

The tree shook behind us. Its branches thrashed so hard that the ground rumbled beneath our feet. Several leaves fell from their homes and landed on the ground. Their silver glow turning dull the moment they hit the earth.

"We do not have much time, Keera." My mother swallowed, staring at the dead leaves. "There are things you have to know to prepare yourself for the fight ahead."

"Those weddings you showed me." I pulled at the edge of my sleeve. "The Mortals were related."

My mother took a deep breath. "Then you understand that part of the story."

"That woman was Aemon's ancestor, wasn't she?" I could still picture her jade eyes, an exact match for Aemon's and his sons'.

"His great-grandmother." My mother sat on the ground and patted the space beside her.

I remained standing. "But that would make Aemon a Halfling?"

"And it would be the truth." She frowned slightly.

The revelation shook me more than the tree had. My mind clouded over with every memory I had of the king's public distaste for Halflings. Every order I had carried out just because Aemon didn't like the amber color of our blood.

I paused mid-thought. "But Aemon's blood runs red."

My mother nodded. "It always has."

The hypocrisy settled on my mouth like poison. I fought the urge to wretch. "He knows this to be the truth?"

My mother nodded once again.

"But why? Why would he come to these lands only to murder his kin?"

My mother leaned back onto her hands and pursed her lips to the side just like I did. "Aemon's great grandsire was a powerful Light Fae gifted with the ability to bend water to his will. That ship you watched them load onto was sailing to the Mortal realms. They planned to only go for a visit, but the ship was lost at sea. Aemon's great-grandmother only survived because her mate used every last bit of his gift to bring his pregnant partner ashore. But he burned through his magic and drowned at sea."

"And the wife?" I asked, taking a seat on the grass beside her.

"She returned to her family with no husband and a child on the way. Through the generations the story of Elverath and the immortals who lived there was passed on. Most of her descendants believed what all the other Mortals did at that time: that the stories were only fanciful dreams with no truth behind them. Aemon was born a poor boy with a thirst for ambition and power. He came to Elverath under the guise of reconnecting with his kin but what he really wanted we could not give him."

I knew the answer in my gut—it was what Aemon had valued more than anything else. Why he had taken a Fae bride, Killian's mother, in hopes of giving it to his son. "Immortality."

The tree shook violently once more and even more leaves fell dead to the ground.

My mother gripped my hand and I held my breath. There was no warmth to her touch, only a faint pressure. I swallowed and looked up at her. "You're not here, are you. Not really?"

Tears rolled down her cheeks freely as she shook her head. She looked at a dead leaf beside her. "This short amount is all the time we have left, *miraa*."

I wiped the tears from her cheek, but I felt no wetness on my fingers. "Aemon was able to lengthen his life beyond any Mortal or Halfling before him. He almost achieved immortality on his own."

My mother's face turned hard. "What we could not give Aemon, he took." She sighed and looked out at the garden to where it shifted into the white abyss once more. "He did not take it from the Elves as he claims. Aemon was eager to learn as much of our history as he could in those early years. The Fae who took him as her mate was young. She worked in the library of Koratha and showed Aemon everything he asked for. She had no reason to know what he would do with that knowledge. None of us did.

"He experimented, used our methods to collect magic from the earth to take more than he should. Then he moved onto living creatures. When his mate discovered what he was doing, he killed her and used her death to bond himself to the magic of these lands."

"What kind of bond?"

"He took what he knew of the *miiskwithir*, specifically their ability to share and call each other's magic. He was able to create a bond that siphoned the magic from the very land on which he stood. It is what has been keeping him alive. What gave him healing powers so strong his skin was impenetrable. What allowed him to nullify the gifts of the Fae when they came to fight and use their own power against them."

My heart pounded in my chest even though we were sitting in the grass. "But he does none of this now. He has been aging for some time."

My mother smiled. "That was because the Light Fae were able to impede him from siphoning the magic of Elverath. Though it came at great sacrifice."

The memory of my mother dancing while the Light Fae disappeared replayed in my mind. Vrail and I had been too focused on the symbols, thinking there was some connection between their locations, that I had never stopped to wonder why they had all appeared as water.

Understanding washed over me, leaving me cold and shivering. "You are the reason the magic has been fading?"

My mother nodded.

"The symbols—they're places aren't they. All separated from the mainland by water."

My mother smiled proudly. "Aemon's bond doesn't reach those points. Magic cannot be destroyed, but it can be siphoned. We used the last of our powers to form five siphons in the hope that the magic would dwindle to a point that left Aemon vulnerable enough to end his tyranny."

I looked down at my hip to where my bloodstone dagger hung. It was the only weapon that I had carried with me into this dream. Or memory. I wasn't sure what was happening anymore. "This dagger. The Mage had it the night you placed me in that tree."

My mother swallowed hoarsely. "Magic has a way of bringing you the tools you need. This dagger has the power to break the seal and collapse each of the syphons."

I pulled the dagger from its holster. "I've had the power to kill Aemon all this time?" My stomach churned and I thought I was going to be sick.

My mother put her hand on my shoulder. I wished it was warm and full of life. "He has only just become vulnerable enough for the blade to work. You could not have acted sooner."

"I kill him and the magic returns to the realm? The Dark Fae will regain their powers?"

She nodded.

"And what of you and the Light Fae?" I asked, though my chest tightened, steeling myself for the answer I knew was coming.

"We made our choice long ago."

Her words pierced me like arrows, draining me of all my hope. I had been so determined to find the Light Fae, to have their healers join our cause and save as many Shades as we could. But I had misunderstood the letter that Vrail had found. The fruit of the Elder birch hadn't been a referenced to the Light Fae and their magic, it had been a reference to *me*. The girl hidden inside its trunk for centuries.

The tree shook once more. Most of the leaves had fallen and even the trunk had begun to lose its silvery glow. My mother gripped both my hands. "I am so sorry that you spent so much of your life alone. And I'm so sorry that I had to leave you with this task."

Another leaf fell. Time was running out to ask my questions.

"When you placed me in that tree, my eyes were not silver like they are now."

There was a sadness in my mother's smile as she caressed my cheek. "An unexpected side effect of the protection the Light Fae gave you." She looked at the silver Elder birch. "Every Light Fae sacrificed some of their gifts to make this tree. It seems your healing gift from being born *valietherian* allowed you to become a catalyst for that magic. Over the centuries, you absorbed those gifts from the Fae and they became your own."

I pricked my finger on the sharp point of the blade. The amber blood pooled into a small drop before my skin healed itself. "So I am a Halfling?"

My mother smiled. "Yes. You were born of Fae and Halfling. I cannot say why the blood of the Halflings turned amber after the Light Fae were gone, but it seems to mark the descendants of the Light Fae who sacrificed themselves that day. Under Aemon's cruelty that has become every Halfling now."

"Except for him and his sons."

The tree shook one last time. There was only one tiny leaf at the very top left clinging to its branches. My mother cupped my face in her hands and pressed a kiss to my forehead. "Kill Aemon with the blade and all the seals will break. Just as yours has now. You must do it with this blade, Keera. I do not know what would happen if Aemon died by some other way."

The tree shook one last time, splintering along the trunk from the hole in the middle that once held me. A tear rolled down my mother's face as the dream began to swirl around us. I reached out for her, wanting to stay by her side, but when my fingers brushed against her hair, she was gone.

And I was alone once more.

My hip seared with pain so piercing I screamed. I opened my eyes, and I was in the Rift. The Elder birch was standing tall beside me as something lifted me into the air. The skin along my hip ripped open and the entire Rift began to glow.

I could feel the weightlessness of my body. My braid was suspended behind me like I was submerged in water once more. I looked down and saw the shocked faces of my friends.

"Your eyes," Riven rasped in disbelief. "They're glowing."

And then everything went black.

CHAPTER FORTY-EIGHT

I WOKE UP LYING ON THE FLOOR of the Rift. The cloud of darkness had disappeared entirely and instead the walls were full of new blooms and lush greens that continued down the chasm as far as I could see. The Elder birch stood above me, though it no longer glowed silver and its leaves had turned gold just like its cousins that covered the far side of Burning Mountains.

Riven was there, kneeling over me with his hand on my cheek. I reached up and touched my face. Amber blood coated my fingers. I must have cut myself in the fall.

"What just happened?" Nikolai choked.

I looked up at him, too dazed to process his question.

Killian huffed a breath. "We were in the dark. We heard Riven call your name and then the next thing we saw was the tree and you burst into silver light." There was nothing but worry on his face.

"The Light Fae are gone." My voice was a hoarse whisper. "They are not coming back." I watched as four pairs of eyes flashed with defeat.

Killian's shoulders fell and he squeezed my arm. "We will find another way to win this war."

I shook my head, feeling for the bloodstone dagger, which was back in its sheath. "We don't need their magic to win the war. I know how to defeat Aemon."

The crease between Riven's brow deepened and his shadows swirled around me. "What happened when you touched that tree?"

I pulled myself up and told them everything that I had seen since I'd touched the tree. I thought I had been lost in those memories, that dream, for an hour or more, but Nikolai shook his head and said it was only a few seconds.

"If Aemon dies, the magic returns?" The crack in Syrra's voice was so shocking I flinched. "And the Dark Fae gifts will be restored?"

I nodded. "With their powers restored, we no longer need to wait. With the Fae we have at full strength, we can take control of the capital before Damien is even crowned. The guards will lay down their swords the moment they see a sign of magic."

Killian shook his head. "We should wait and devise a plan, Keera."

"There's no time!" I pulled myself up from the ground. "The king has already threatened the Shades. There's nothing stopping him from doing it again, especially if he knows he's vulnerable. I will not stand by with the power to end his reign once and for all and let any more Halflings die while we argue over details."

Killian folded his arms. "I will not let you sacrifice yourself. Take a moment to think, Keera. There must be another way."

"My magic has been unsealed. Aemon's guards will be no match for me."

Killian pinched the bridge of his nose. "And you have no knowledge of how to control it. No training at all. Even with full access to your power, you will burnout quickly without knowing how to use the magic efficiently."

I turned to Riven to see if what Killian said was true. He nodded.

"The last time you used your magic, you almost died," Killian continued. "If we wait to plan an attack, you can train with Feron and the others. You need to learn how to use a weapon before you wield it, Keera."

"I am well aware of that, my prince," I said sarcastically. I clenched my jaw and turned to the others. "Then we put it to a vote. I move to travel to Koratha immediately and kill the king."

Killian shook his head. "And I move for us to travel back to Myrelinth and discuss this with the others. Especially the Fae whose gifts hang in the balance."

I looked to the rest of the group and gave a hard command. "Vote."

Nikolai glanced uneasily between me and Killian. "I told you I stand with you, Keera. I meant it then and I mean it now." He walked over and stood behind me.

Syrra crossed her arms. Her face was calm as it always was. She looked at me and frowned. "You cannot allow one of your Shades to die just as I cannot allow you to make yourself a martyr." She stepped behind Killian and bowed her head.

We both turned to Riven. My stomach twisted into knots. I could see the worry in his face, the urge to grab me and bring me to Myrelinth himself. When he met my gaze, his violet eyes were pools of sadness and worry.

He looked at me like I had ripped his heart from his chest. "There is still the mole to contend with. Going back could jeopardize any plan we devise. I stand with Keera." He stepped behind me, and I reached back to squeeze his hand, unable to breathe.

I lifted my chin to Killian and Syrra. "Your motion has been denied. Can I trust you to stand with us or should we part ways now?"

Syrra pulled her circular blades out from her belt and bowed her head. "My blades are yours."

Killian closed his eyes. His leg bounced as his gaze shifted among each of us. "I stand with you. Let's kill the king."

CHAPTER FORTY-NINE

THE SUNS WERE AT THEIR MIDDAY PEAK when we climbed out of the Rift. Syrra and Nikolai left for the portal immediately, back to Myrelinth to gather the few Fae that remained and bring them to the capital.

Killian and Riven rode with me past Wenden and toward the King's Road. There was another portal only a few hours' ride from the village that would take us to the outskirts of the city. We rode in silence, the tension of what lay ahead growing thicker until it felt like I was trying to breathe water instead of air.

Finally, we came to a small cavern hidden within a grove of trees along the road. Killian pulled out a vial of *winvra* and handed a berry to each of us. I dropped mine into the small pool of water that sat at the top of a flat boulder. Gold light began to swirl around it, and I stepped into the pool.

I dropped through the stone and reappeared standing in its twin. I was in a grove to the south of the city. I stepped out and waited for Riven and Killian to travel through. We had to leave our horses behind, as the portal was too small for them to travel through. They were left to graze in the fields north of the Rift.

"I need to warn the Arsenal that there is about to be a coup," I said, looking at the white miniature palace just coming into view. "I don't want any Shades caught in the confusion. Hildegard needs to know."

Killian nodded his head. "I will return to the palace. I'll try to get as many of the servants out as I can before the Fae arrive."

Riven's jaw flexed. "I will be waiting at the gate ready to lead the Fae when they arrive."

I gripped his arm. "I will join the fight as soon as I can."

Riven pulled me into his arms. The only words he said were the only ones that mattered. "I love you, *diizra*. Come back alive."

I couldn't promise him. But I hoped with every fiber of my being that I would live to see the world the Elverin created once the king was dead. But if I ended up dead to bring that future into existence, I would die happily. My penance finally paid.

"I will try," I whispered back. It was the most I could offer. My heart twinged when Riven's lips twitched to the side; he knew it was the best I could give him and he would take it gladly.

"I hope to see you both in the world to come," I said, and then I ran toward the Order.

My body felt stronger than it ever had before. My lungs filled with more air and my strides were longer somehow. My heart pumped, and with every beat I could feel the strength of the magic churning under my skin. I would save it. Use whatever gifts I had been given to finish Aemon and his court once and for all.

I made it to the shore of Koratha in record time. The tall white stone wall towered above me, six bodies hung along it, all with amber streaks dripping from where they hung. My chest ached for them. The last victims of Aemon's reign. I took solace in knowing there would be no others.

I stepped onto the sandy beach and something hot flared against my chest. I pulled open the lacing at the neck of my tunic. The tiny faebead wrapped in leather was glowing.

"No!" I yelled. Gwyn was calling me to the palace. Something was wrong.

There was a loud boom, and the wave from the explosion was so strong it pushed me over. The air fled my lungs. I took me a few moments for my head to stop spinning and for the ringing in my ears to quiet. I laid flat on my back, staring up at the blue sky beginning to glow with the first streaks of sunset. A cloud of purple smoke appeared in the sky. It grew wide and taller than the palace.

I turned on my side and screamed. The glass bridge was gone. There was nothing left of it but violet flames that devoured it whole. They moved to the stone pillars sprouting from the sea, and I watched in horror as they too crumbled into the waves below.

A wall of soldiers I didn't recognize formed a border around the flames, pushing passersby away from the fire. They were dressed in red, not the black of the Shades or the blue garb of the king's guards.

"Move!" one of them yelled, and I heard the rugged edge of his accent. He was not a citizen of the Crown. I listened more carefully and heard the same accent again and again. They weren't soldiers but sellswords paid to destroy that bridge and who knew what else.

The faebead burned hotter against my chest. I pulled myself off the beach and ran toward the stone wall of the first circle. The beach was too difficult a path now, but I was swifter in a crowd.

I dashed through the merchants and peasants and passed through the first ring. I climbed onto the roof of a merchant house and began to run along the stone tile, jumping from dwelling to dwelling with no care who saw me.

"I think that's the Blade!" someone shouted down below.

"It can't be; she wears no cloak or hood."

"It *is* her!"

I leaped from the roof of one building onto the next circular wall of the city. Somehow I knew my renewed body would be able to make the leap. I ran with every bit of strength I had, only able to think of one thing.

Gwyn.

The tolls of death rang out from the palace temple. The bells only tolled when a royal was born or dead. They had not rung since Killian's birth ninety some years before. There was no royal babe expected so that meant a royal was dead.

The cacophony of brass sounded again, so loud I could feel it in my chest. Gwyn's warning seared my skin. She would not be in danger if it was Damien who was dead. Her tether would still be intact.

Which meant it was the king.

All the hope drained from my body, and I almost collapsed onto the crowded streets below. How was it possible? How could the chance to restore Elverath have slipped through our fingers so quickly?

There were no guards standing at the gate when I ran through the door. I dashed up through the kitchen looking for Gwyn, but she was nowhere to be found. There were no servants anywhere I searched.

I ran up the nearest staircase to the fourth level. When I reached my chambers, the door was already open. Nothing in my room was amiss apart from the pool of amber blood spilling from the other side of the bed.

"No!" The sound that ripped out from my chest was not a noise I knew I could make. It sounded like the shriek of a creature in agony. I fell to my knees.

Gwyn was splayed out on the ground, gripping her stomach where the linen of her maid's dress was ripped as well as her skin. A line of amber blood dripped from her mouth and covered her copper curls.

I pulled her onto my lap, sobs ripping out of my chest until I thought I was bleeding too. "No, no, no," I wheezed. I grabbed Gwyn's cheeks and shook her. Her body was warm but her heartbeat was so faint I could barely feel it.

"Gwyn, I'm here. I'm so sorry, but I'm here now." My mouth trembled as I pressed it against her hair. My body shook violently like it was my blood covering the floor. I could stop this. I had the power to make it all better.

I tapped her cheek. "Gwyn, open your eyes, please." Tears streamed down my face and dropped on hers.

Her eyelids fluttered open and I swore in relief.

"Keera," Gwyn whispered. Her voice barely made a sound. She coughed and blood splattered on my tunic. "It's gone. Keera, it's gone."

Gwyn moved her hand and I saw how badly the slash had cut her. Her entire stomach cavity was exposed to the air, pooling with amber blood. It was a miracle she was still alive. I pulled out a cloak and wrapped it as tightly as I could around her middle.

I needed to try to calm myself so I could use my powers to heal her.

"It's gone, Keera," she whispered again. Her head lolled back like she was about to fall asleep.

"No, no, no!" I cradled her head once more. "You need to stay awake, Gwyn. You hear me? Stay awake! What's gone? What are you talking about?"

"Ankle" was all she had the strength to say. Tears flooded my vision as I glanced down at her bare feet. The ankle where that magical tether had taken hold of her life was gone. It was the only part of her not covered in blood.

"At least I get to die free." She smiled up at me and her teeth were coated in amber.

I shook my head. "You are not dying today. You're not allowed. I haven't given you my present yet."

Her brows twitched but she didn't say anything more. I took a deep breath that burned my lungs and forced myself to calm. I held Gwyn's hand and pictured that warmth flowing to her limbs. Gwyn moaned underneath me just as I felt the magic begin to flow through me to her.

I could feel her pain behind the adrenaline that coursed through her body. She was clinging to life by will alone, fighting to the very end. Her need for my power drained me. I could feel the energy, pulling from me until even my bones ached. My skin pulled taut, fighting against the release of any more of my power, but I gritted my teeth and continued on.

Gwyn needed it more than me. I opened my eyes and the slash around her abdomen was closing slowly. I collapsed on top of her but didn't stop. I laid on her chest, my eyes fighting to stay open until that last bit of skin fused together. It was red and jagged, but it was done.

I finally dropped Gwyn's hand and fell back onto the floor.

When I opened my eyes again, I was lying in a pool of cold amber blood. I groaned as I pulled myself up from the floor. My body felt like it was made of stone rather than skin and bone. Gwyn was lying on the floor beside my feet. Her chest rose softly as she opened her eyes and saw me.

"How did you . . . ?"

I shook my head and lifted her off the ground. In that moment, Gwyn was heavier than anything I had ever lifted. My muscles screamed at me, almost tearing out of exhaustion, but I didn't care. I laid Gwyn on the bed. "Be still. You need to rest; you lost too much blood."

Her eyes widened and sharpened for the first time. "Your eyes are glowing," she whispered.

I laughed and pressed a kiss to her hair. I didn't care about the blood on her face or mine. "They do that now," I whispered back.

I stood but Gwyn reached for my hand. Her fingers brushed my wrist, missing my hand entirely. "I got him. You would be proud."

My blood turned to ice. I had been so consumed by finding Gwyn in such a state I had forgotten to ask who had done this to her. "What do you mean?"

Gwyn hooked her first finger and scratched the air just like she did the day I gave her the ring. "Rawr," she whispered. "I missed the thigh, so I went for his face." A smug grin crept up Gwyn's face. In that moment, she was no longer a girl. If I were honest with myself, she hadn't been from the day that tether took hold around her ankle. The innocence and fun of childhood had been ripped away from her.

Gwyn's eyes closed and she fell asleep. I wanted nothing more than to stay by her side. Grab her in my arms and take her with me to Myrelinth. But if the king was dead, there was no way I could unseal the magic from here—and that left Damien with an empty throne.

I might have missed the chance to kill the king, but before the day was ended, Damien would finally pay his penance in blood.

CHAPTER FIFTY

I GRABBED TWO OF THE SWORDS that hung on the wall of my chambers and left the room. Blood covered half my face, and I left a trail of amber down the hall as it dripped from my braid, but I didn't care. All I could think about was Damien and how ruthless his death would be.

I stalked down the stairs. I passed two chambermaids who stared at me with wide eyes before scurrying into a nearby room. A guard stood at the end of the hall. He paused when he saw me, and I rewarded that pause with his death.

I came to the main corridor of the palace and let my blades drag on the floor as I walked. I needed to conserve the energy I had left, and it served as a warning to the servants to stay out of my way.

A lady-in-waiting walked out of a room with one of the Halfling servants and shrieked with terror at the sight of me. He caught her in his arms as she fainted.

"Drop her there and run," I rasped. He didn't need to be told again.

I turned the corner and stepped into the corridor of the throne room. A group of forty sellswords was waiting for me. They had red armor with an embossed chest piece decorated with a golden letter *D*.

I lifted my blades and readied my stance. "Whose death shall I claim first?"

Two of the men at the front charged me. I cut down the first at the knees and then through the neck for good measure. The second only took a single jab to the eye. His helmet flew off his head and rolled onto the stone corridor. The sound echoed down to the white birch doors. There was a moment of silence before the guards charged as one.

It was a whirl of swords. Steel clashed against steel.

I spun. I swiped. I swung.

All despite the burning ache of my body.

I stabbed one solider through the neck and used him as a shield while six others swung at my head.

I slipped the small knife out of my boot and threw it into the tallest man's eye. He screamed in pain, toppling over like a giant tree and taking three others with him.

They were dead before they had the chance to stand.

Two more men charged at me. I launched one of my blades at the first. It ran through his mouth and he fell dead too.

The other lifted his sword above his head. I threw my second blade, casting it in a spiral that slit the soldier's throat. He fell to his knees and his last words were nothing more than a gurgle of red blood.

I grabbed his sword as it fell to the ground and ran toward the remaining men. I leaped into the air and screamed as loud as I could. A large gust of wind blew through the corridor, carrying me farther-than I could possibly jump on my own.

I landed on the shoulders of one of the men and ran that stolen sword through his heart. He crumpled underneath my feet, and I readied myself for the next blow.

It didn't come. The other men had dropped their weapons, each scratching at their throats while their faces turned red and their lips turned blue. The gust of wind had pulled the air from their lungs and now they could no longer breathe, as if the air around them didn't exist.

They dropped to the ground and I collapsed too, trying to catch my breath. The corridor held no windows nor did it open to a terrace. That wind had not been one of nature but of magic. I looked down at my hands. They were shaking just like my breath.

I pointed the sword into the ground and used it to support myself just as the door opened and another group of soldiers unsheathed their swords. I tried to stand, but my knees buckled under my own weight.

I had no energy left to fight the soldiers off when they grabbed me. I let my body fall lifeless as they bound my hands behind my back and carried me into the throne room where a new king sat on the throne.

Damien.

He sat with one leg flung over the armrest and his father's crown askew on his head. I was dropped onto the floor, my knees cracking on the cold stone tile. In front of me was the dais. It held the large gilded throne and no others. The princes' chairs had been removed, as if they had never existed.

But that was not the most remarkable change.

Damien's handsome face had been slashed from brow to chin. A jagged cut started just along his right brow and spread down his face to above the jaw. He wore a bandage over his eye socket. But from how deep the skin had been cut and the uneven stitches holding the flesh together, I doubted he had an eye left at all.

"Pleasure for you to join us, Keera." A wicked smile stretched across Damien's pale face. His gaze trailed along my tunic that was coated in amber blood. His jade eyes seemed to glint with glee. "I see you received my present."

I spat at his feet. Damien snapped his fingers, and one of the large men kicked me in the gut.

"I suppose I have you to thank for this." He snarled as he lifted his hand to his face. When I didn't say anything, he pulled something from his jacket pocket and threw it on the floor. It bounced once, before rolling in a circle in front of me.

It was the gold ring I'd given Gwyn. The tiny blade that was usually concealed within the gold was jutting out from the ring like a claw.

I didn't hide my grin from Damien. "A pity she got the handsome side of your face, Your Highness. Had it been the other, perhaps you'd still have a chance with the ladies at court."

"It's Your Majesty." Damien snapped his fingers, and I received another kick, this time to the chin.

I refused to groan from the pain and only smiled up at Damien again, tasting my own blood on my lips.

He was a viper curled around the throne. A small smirk crept along his face, showing the threat of his venomous fangs. "Don't look so happy, Keera."

My skin turned to ice as he stepped toward me. There was something vile in his smug expression and the way he tucked his arms behind his back. He waved at the guards to make me stand and leaned in close enough that I could feel his breath like a scalding iron, but he made sure not to touch me. "She might have pricked me with that ring," he hissed like a snake in my ear. "But I was the one who gutted her with it."

He pulled back just enough for me to see his face and tilted my chin up at him with his gloved hand. "If only you could see the masterpiece I made of her. How many generations had that tether claimed? Always ensuring that there was an heir to continue the line. But she was determined to be the one who ended it, wasn't she? Did she tell you the things she would say to me? The dreams she had of killing herself before she could bring another child into this world to inherit her curse?"

My nostrils flared but I refused to let Damien bait me. He thought Gwyn was dead, that I'd come to avenge her death. I had to make sure he had no reason to doubt it. It was Gwyn's only hope for escape now.

"I needed to see that magic for myself. I used that cursed ring you gave her and cut her mound to belly. Her womb was black as night. I doubt any child could have been born from something so sickly. I guess in the end she got her wish. My first act of king's mercy."

I shrieked with rage and thrashed hard enough that one guard let me go. I smacked my forehead against Damien's chin and watched him tumble to the floor. A guard punched me in the jaw and my own blood splattered across the tile.

My body collapsed into itself. My lungs burned, urging me to breathe, but I could not find the will to do so. Tears ran hot down my neck as I closed my eyes and pictured Gwyn's sweet face, heard her giggle like honey in my ears. Damien had beheld that same girl and seen a monster. Filleted her like a fish at market for his amusement, all because she was a Halfling and he could.

Now he stood with the crown on his head.

Damien picked himself up off the floor and narrowed his eyes at me. I thought he was going to order the guard to beat me again, but he only walked back to the throne and fanned his jacket out behind him before he sat.

He raised his hand in the air, signaling the guards stationed at the door. "I think it's time for my first meeting as king."

Rohan walked to the front of the dais with six guards flanking her tall frame. Her legs were bound so tightly that all she could manage were tiny half steps across the marble. She looked at me with narrowed eyes, unable to say anything with the gag stuck in her mouth. They had removed her weapons but the silver arrow was still pressed against her throat.

Hildegard was next. Her steps seemed more frail bound in rope. Her tight bun had come undone, long strands of gray hanging loosely down her back. She didn't glance my way as the guards placed her next to me.

Myrrah was brought in behind her. They had cruelly bound her legs as well, holding her just high enough off the floor that her feet dragged behind her. The guards dropped her beside Hildegard, letting her body fall to the floor. She twisted onto her side using her pinned elbows to push against the floor and propped herself in a half-sitting position against her wife's legs.

My cheeks flushed with rage. Damien had surpassed proving a point; he was making a mockery of the entire Arsenal. I waited for the guards to bring in Gerarda, but no one else came through the door.

"Bring in my bastard brother." Damien snapped his fingers and the doors behind the throne opened. Four guards carried a thrashing Killian between them. His black tunic was ripped and his lip was bloodied. His legs were bound as well though he was not gagged like the rest of them.

"What is the meaning of this, Damien?" Killian kicked the guard to his left and received an elbow to the skull. His head lolled back in a daze.

"Have I not been obvious?" Damien cooed, his wicked grin returning. "As the rightful heir of Elverath, I've claimed my throne." He pointed to the crown slanted across his head. "And you are still the bastard heir of nothing."

"You killed our father." Killian spat at his brother's feet. The guard next to him levied two kicks to the gut. Damien waved his hand, almost bored by the accusation.

"True. Though I would have killed him ages ago had our father not refused to die. Funny, considering it was his hair dye I'd laced with poison. Not that it matters now. No one here writes the history books, brother, and they will say he died by the hands of a poisoner sent by the Dark Fae." Damien studied his nail beds, swinging his leg back over the armrest of the throne.

"And who will believe such a falsehood with no poisoner to blame?" I spat, barely feeling the punch to the jaw that followed my question.

"I'm afraid I'm a few steps ahead of you again, Keera." Damien pointed his hand at the large cathedral windows. The curtains were drawn, hiding the view of the garden and the terrace. Two guards pulled the thick velvety drapes back and revealed what Damien wanted us to see.

Two bodies swung from the upper terrace. Lifeless and bloody.

I recognized Curringham's dark coat immediately. It was the same one he'd worn when the guards had dragged him to his cell. But the other's clothes were too shorn to recognize.

I gasped as the body slowly turned, revealing the face of the long-haired victim.

Tarvelle.

I glanced at Killian, whose face was drained of any color, but I didn't dare to speak.

"He was such a helpful informant," Damien said, gazing up at the hanging bodies with pride, like they were a painting he'd created.

My jaw dropped. "It was unfortunate that their usefulness ran out so quickly, but at least I found a use for them in death. I would never want to be called anything so depraved as wasteful."

I snorted. "Do you plan to kill all your spies?"

Damien looked at me with a serenity that made the hair on my neck stand up. "Tarvelle served his purpose, and that purpose was to be a traitor to his own people. What use do I have for someone whose loyalties are so easily bought?"

"But he was working with Curringham . . ." I blinked. Tarvelle had been the one who pulled the pin free from the carriage in the Singing Wood. He had levied the accusations against me and called for a vote. I thought the mole had been helping Curringham, but Damien had been using Curringham as a scapegoat all along. "How long have you been working with him?"

"There she is." Damien smiled down at me like a father praising a child. "I was worried you had left your sharp mind in a pub somewhere."

Killian thrashed against his bindings. "You chose Curringham as your accomplice to commit treason? The man may be an oaf, but I doubt he would have easily agreed to aid a kingslayer."

Damien shrugged. "He may have thought our treason would strictly be of the *financial* variety, though I doubt he cares much about anything now."

My body throbbed with every heartbeat, but even worse was the rage that boiled inside my belly. I needed a way to release some of the fury. "That gold will not last long now that his *winvra* has failed."

Damien's lips curved into a feline smile. "We have more than enough *winvra* to suit our needs and fill our coffers." He pulled out a black berry from his pocket it and twirled it between his fingers. "My father was not a man of foresight. When the Mortal realms came knocking for their chance at a taste of *winvra,* he sold it to them without much thought of the future. He let his orchards die by overtaxing them, sent the berries overseas to be refined into powder on foreign lands for foreign lords to pocket the money.

"Meanwhile, I played the part of a drunkard and a rake at court, but I was studying the properties of this berry. How it could be used and reshaped into something much more valuable." He looked out the window, past Tarvelle's body, to where the large cloud of smoke from the bridge still billowed into the sky. "There are many things the magic of this land can do. Many weapons our trade network is *very* interested in procuring."

My knees buckled out from underneath me, and I let my body drop to the floor. The guards pulled my torso up so I could face Damien in all his smug glory. "Weapons of unimaginable strength. You've already seen my fire that can only be doused by special elixir. Explosives strong enough to destroy an entire city. This latest one has toxic smoke to those who stand by too long." Damien almost giggled. "Do you know how much the Mortal realms are willing to pay for such things?"

Killian finally stopped his thrashing. "If you've been plotting this for years, why show your hand now?"

"Father finally died." Damien shrugged. "I've been poisoning his hair dye for a decade. I have no idea why it finally started to take hold now."

"You've been waiting in the shadows all this time?" Killian's voice was full of disgust.

Damien blinked. "Brother, we already covered that. Keep up. Besides, you're not in a position to be throwing around vile accusations while you and the Blade have been partnering with the Shadow."

I let out a heavy sigh, ignoring the wide-eyed gazes that the Arsenal were giving me. Killian's brow fell and he leaned back against the guard behind him.

"Yes, I know all about your traitorous plots and alliances." Damien fixed the crown on his head so it sat even more askew. "Do not chastise me for killing our father while it has been your sole objective these recent years. I might be a kingslayer, Killian, but I am no hypocrite."

"Hang us and be done with it," I seethed, pulling at the binds around my wrists to no avail.

Damien drummed his fingers along the arm of the throne. "I can't kill either of you. The death of one king I can convince the public to accept, but the death of a beloved prince on the same day? I don't wish to invite an insurrection. And you, Keera, still have years of service left in you."

I scoffed. "You believe that I will serve you? I have no secrets to keep anymore. I would rather die."

Damien shrugged. "You don't have a choice." He waved his fingers and five of the largest, most brutish men I'd ever seen stepped from behind the throne. They were cloaked in black and each of them had a silver pin along their chest. Damien nodded at them approvingly.

"Your time as Blade has, thankfully, come to an end. You may spend the rest of your days on the Order. I have a new Arsenal now." He raised his hands to the men behind him.

I swallowed a mouthful of my own blood. My powers were so exhausted I couldn't even heal myself. "And what do you expect me to do there?"

"Bleed."

Damien stood from the throne and took a slow step off the dais, so slow he seemed to float rather than walk toward me. "Do you know what has been even more successful than *winvra* in building our weapons?"

Damien knelt and plucked the gold ring off the floor. He popped it on his ring finger and pricked my palm. I closed it into a fist. There was a drop of amber coating the sharp end of the blade.

My mouth turned dry.

"The Shades have served their purpose and now they will serve another." Damien smiled wickedly at me. "Their blood will return this kingdom to its former glory."

"The attacks on Silstra and Volcar. You stole those Halflings for their *blood*?" I thought I was going to vomit on Damien's boots.

He wiped the ring blade clean on the shoulder of one of his sell-swords. "I needed specimens to test my theories on. The ones who survived will join you at the Order."

Rage filled my body, stole my breath as I shook, not from exhaustion but from fury. "You are a vile excuse for a man, let alone a king. I will rip your heart from your chest after I gut you from nether to navel."

Damien ran his hand through his short hair, seeming to revel in my outburst.

"Was your last lesson not enough?" His question slithered along my skin like a snake coiling around my neck. "I could kill you now for your insolence."

"No!" Killian shook his shoulders, straining to escape his bonds, but his attempts were fruitless.

Damien gave a playful look to his brother and grabbed my cheeks between his hand, squeezing them until my lips parted. He pulled a small dagger from his jacket and wielded it with his other hand. Myrrah and Hildegard's screams were muffled by their gags but Killian's echoed throughout the room. I tried to look at him, but Damien was still holding my face.

"Oh brother, don't worry." Damien pushed my face in Killian's direction. His cheeks were wet with tears. "Keera and I both know that killing her would be a kindness, and I do *not* reward Halflings." He let go of my face and my head fell, bobbing against my chest.

The scars along my back and forearm were taut, as if they were trying to pull me away from Damien, sensing what was about to happen. Damien lifted the point of the dagger to his finger, spinning it between his palms until the edge was wet with his red blood.

"Keera is going to play a game." I could hear the wicked pleasure in his voice.

I collapsed against the guards holding me. "No," I whispered, my voice cracking as a hot tear fell to the floor.

Damien ignored me. He paced in front of each of us, twirling the dagger faster and faster. "Keera has threatened her king and the penalty for that is death." He stopped, standing directly in front of me. "So choose."

"No." The guards dropped me to my knees, sensing I was too forsaken to run.

"Come now, Keera." Damien cooed. "You've played this game before."

Killian's gruff voice interrupted his brother. "What is the meaning of this?"

Damien's smile grew. "You don't know? Keera made a choice that impressed our father so much he made her Blade in a matter of months."

Killian went rigid. His eyes found me on the ground, cautious and apologetic.

"The final night of her Trials, Keera was presented with a choice." Damien pointed the dagger at my head. "Her and another initiate . . . what was her name?"

I snapped my head to face him. "You know her name."

"Brenna, was it?" Damien slid a hand across my cheek, coaxing me. I flashed him my fangs and snapped at his hand. "Yes, Brenna." Damien turned back to Killian slowly, enjoying every moment. "Keera was given a choice. A test of her loyalty to the Crown. Only one of them could live: her or her Brenna."

"Don't say her name!" I shrieked, my chest cracking with each sob.

Killian's face shifted with understanding. Damien pressed the flat edge of the dagger against my chin. "The Blade proved her ruthless nature that night. She chose herself without a moment's hesitation."

Killian's face was lined with tears of his own. "Keera," he whispered in a broken breath.

I wanted to reach for him. To tell him the full version of what had happened that day, but I couldn't reveal the truth. Not there. Not with Damien listening with a blade in hand.

"Who will it be, Keera?" Damien leaned into the blade enough that a dot of amber blood pooled along it. "Which one of the captives will you choose this time?"

I glanced around the room. Killian was lost in his thoughts, unable to look at me. Rohan stood strong and glared down at the new king. Hildegard stood in front of Myrrah, guarding her from Damien's blade. They were watching each other, having a wordless conversation the way only lifelong lovers can do. When they turned to me, they both nodded their heads.

I felt the bile push up my throat. They were giving me permission. Permission to choose them. I turned back to Damien and twisted my legs so I could stand once more. "The same choice as last time?"

Damien nodded. The hand holding the dagger shook in excitement. I watched his eyes dart from face to face, anticipating who I would choose.

I stepped forward. The guards reached for me but Damien shook them off. I took another step, forcing the point of his blade into my chest directly above my heart.

I lifted my chin and smiled as I said the word. "Me."

Damien's face crumpled with rage. His bandage shifted as his forehead creased with sharp lines and a snarled lip. "You dare vex me," Damien spat, pushing me backward. The guards caught me, holding me upright between Rohan and Hildegard.

"I choose me," I repeated. My chest rose with a final breath. "I chose wrong once. I will never choose wrong again."

Damien lunged forward, slicing the air with the dagger. I closed my eyes, feeling a sharp sting of the blade on the back of my shoulder. A gasp echoed throughout the room, and I opened my eyes to the horror at my feet.

The blade had cut me at the end of his swipe after Damien had sliced through Hildegard's throat. I fell to the ground beside her, slipping on the large pool of blood that had already spilled out of her neck. My hands were bound. I could not hold her as she stared at me, gasping for air with wide eyes, unable to process the shock.

Myrrah leaned over her dying wife, her last words to her muffled by the gag in her mouth. She wailed in piercing sorrow as Hildegard took a final breath and then her eyes went cold.

I tried to call my magic forward, but there was none left. The effort alone caused my vision to blur and my head to throb. There was nothing I could do for Hildegard. She was gone.

A sob cracked through my chest like thunder through a storm of rage and pain. My pants were covered in hot, amber blood.

I looked up at Damien. He held out his arm to the side, his face the picture of disgust, and dropped the blade. He shook his hand, sprinkling Hildegard with droplets of her own blood. I hissed at him from the ground, throwing my body on hers to protect it from whatever else he wanted to do with her.

"Take the body away," he told the guards. I shrieked as they peeled me off her, leaving me to rest in the pool of her blood.

The guards pulled Hildegard out of the room by the back of her cloak, leaving a thick trail of amber blood along the marble and out the tall, white doors. I stared at the blood without seeing it, too tired and too numb to fight anymore.

Damien snapped his hand. "Lock my brother in his chambers and do not let him out."

Killian thrashed against their hold, hitting one guard in the nose with the back of his head. "Keera!" He yelled over and over until I could no longer hear the echo of his shouts rebounding through the corridor.

Damien lifted his hand in the air. "Blade." Damien turned to the tallest of his new Arsenal. "Bring me the elixir."

The tallest and strongest of the five men dressed in black approached Damien with a tray of vials. Damien pulled a glass contraption off the silver plate. It had a long container and a tiny, pointed tube made of glass. He filled the larger end with a vial of the red liquid.

He jammed the vial into my arm and gave me one last wicked grin. "You'll get to be the first to try out our next round of experiments."

I collapsed at his feet as the throne room spun and everything went black.

CHAPTER FIFTY-ONE

"WAKE UP," A VOICE CALLED out in the silence. "Keera, wake up."

My eyelids open slightly, only to see a torchlight held too close to my face. I pushed the person away from me.

They poured a waterskin on my head and covered my mouth as I shouted. "Make yourself useful," Gerarda said as she shoved the torch into my shackled hands. She took out two long pins from her sleeve and placed them into the lock.

"What are you doing here?" I whispered groggily as the lock clicked open.

Gerarda looped her arm around my shoulders and pulled me to my feet. "Doing what I always do—saving your ass."

I could barely keep my eyes open as Gerarda walked me through the hall of cells where every guard lay on the floor. Dead or unconscious, I didn't know.

A horse waited for us at the entrance of the dungeons, already saddled and ready to flee. Gerarda lifted my leg into the stirrup and pushed to propel me into the seat. "Stay low," she ordered as she loaded a full quiver onto her back.

She led the horse out of the tunnel by the bit, checking the high points of the palace for guards. She shot two arrows into the night and all I heard was the distant thud as the bodies hit the ground. We curved around the stables and onto the beach without being spotted.

Instead of bursting into a full run, Gerarda walked the horse along the walls of the city, using the shadows to keep us hidden from the sentries above and the guards patrolling the beach.

Gerarda took two more guards down with perfect precision, the sand muffling their falls. She silently pulled herself up behind me and made haste for the Dead Wood. Some guards shouted from behind us and Gerarda sighed.

"Can you ride?" she yelled.

I nodded my head and took hold of the reins.

Gerarda stood on the back of the horse, gripping the saddle between her ankles. She aimed her bow four times, and once again we were met with silence.

"Gwyn!" I shouted, finally coming out of that sleepy state. "I can't leave her behind."

Gerarda squeezed my arms so I couldn't throw myself off the horse. "I already grabbed her. Just ride, Keera."

The questions swirling in my mind only made the headache worse. We rode until the twisted, burnt branches of the Dead Wood grew too thick to see. A figure appeared along the road. I pulled back on the reins, reaching for a weapon I did not have.

It was Gwyn.

I slipped off the horse and wrapped her in my arms. She squeezed me back and burst into tears.

"We don't have time for tears or reunions." Gerarda tossed my weapons belt at my feet. My heart twinged at the sight of the bloodstone dagger. I thought I would never see it again after Damien's guards caught me.

"Why are you here?" I asked Gerarda. "Why did you risk your life to save me and Gwyn?"

"Because I promised Hildegard that I would save you no matter what." Gerarda's voice was raw. She wiped her tiny hand across her eyes.

"It was quick." They were the only words of comfort I could give her.

Gerarda nodded and passed me a folded piece of parchment. "She told me to give you this the morning of Aemon's death."

I took it out of Gerarda's shaky hands and took a deep breath. I pushed the image of Hildegard's last moments from my mind and imagined the strong, wise Halfling who watched over her girls like a hawk.

There were only three lines written on the parchment in a quick uneven scrawl that was nothing like Hildegard's usual neat script.

I trust Gerarda with your life and the lives of the Shades.
Listen to her for once in your life. I know I couldn't save your love,
but please do what you can to save mine.—H

I folded the piece of parchment again and tucked it between my tunic and my pants. I wrapped the weapons belt around my waist and placed a firm grip on the bone hilt of my bloodstone dagger.

I lifted my chin to Gerarda. "Hildegard says I can trust you, so I will. We're headed to war. Do you fight for the Crown or the Elverin?"

Gerarda crossed her arms. "I fight for the Halflings."

"That's good enough for me."

Acknowledgments

This book was a trial unlike any other and I am so grateful for everyone who played a part in seeing these words transform again and again. You helped me find Keera's voice through the drafts and for that I appreciate you much more than I ever could accurately describe here.

To Laura, my amazing editor, who read so many versions of this story and was able to find the heart of it every time. Thank you for your keen eye and helpful insight. Not only did you make Keera a better character, but you made me a better writer. Chi-miigwetch.

To my sister, Emma, who read page after page and spent countless hours on the phone talking out ideas and easing my anxieties, please know this book would not exist without you. And thank you for always answering your phone even during my 3 a.m. editing sessions.

To my friend Marissa, for keeping me stable through one of the hardest and most challenging years of my life so far. I am so grateful you exist and if you somehow don't know that, now my words are inked on the pages of this book forever. Chi-miigwetch for all you've done for me and for Keera.

I'd also like to thank my mother, Cheryl, for believing in my wild idea to release the first book in this series and her complete unsurprise at every blessing that has come my way in the past year and a half. Whenever I've thought myself into a corner of self-doubt, you're always there to pull me out, and for that I say chi-miigwetch with all my heart.

Thank you to Jenny and Dan for all your hard work in promoting this book and me. I'm so grateful that Keera's story has found a home with people as kind as both of you, and I can't wait to see all the fun we have with this release.

I would also like to thank the countless readers and supporters of mine who have made my dreams a possibility. To everyone who has found something in Keera's story to love, I will never stop appreciating you, and I hope you only find more as the story continues.

And lastly, I would like to thank the members of Scooby Gang. Not only have you been a vital part of some of my favorite moments as an author, but this series would have never found the audience it did without your enthusiasm or belief in Keera's story. I'm so grateful that we have found our way into each other's lives and for that I say chi-miigwetch to Alex, Amivi, Bri, Cabria, Cait, Deeqy, El, Frances, Gracie, and Tori. And yes, the soup scene was written especially for you.